"A stiff-upper-lip whodunit boasting political intrigue and uncomfortable truths about anti-Semitism."

—*Entertainment Weekly*

"Is there anything Jo Walton can't write? . . . It's a clear-eyed, passionate meditation on universal themes: injustice, civil liberties, the fear of the outsider. No wonder it reads as if it was written just this morning."

—Lisa Goldstein, *Locus*

"A quietly convincing horror, a tale of a world that might have been and that we're damned lucky we never really saw. Read it, think about it, and count your blessings."

—Harry Turtledove, author of
The Guns of the South

"Beneath the facade of a classic English country-house mystery, Jo Walton unfolds a disturbing tale about how easily freedom can be let drift away. . . . This is a thought-provoking story that kept coming back to trouble my thoughts long after I had read the last chapter."

—Jane Lindskold

"A wonderful book, simultaneously a gripping mystery and a harrowing cautionary tale. Walton's credible—and entirely convincing—alternative history becomes a terrifying meditation on class, power, and persecution. I only wish it seemed more like science fiction."

—Susan Palwick

"*Farthing* starts out as a cozy period house-party mystery, becomes a brilliant alternate history yarn, and at last reveals itself to be a chilling cautionary political thriller. It's smart, riveting, and deeply moving. Once you start reading, don't plan to put it down." —Emma Bull

BOOKS BY JO WALTON

HA'PENNY

Jo Walton

A TOM DOHERTY ASSOCIATES BOOK NEW YORK

HA'PENNY

The quotation on page xi from *Gaudy Night* by Dorothy L. Sayers is copyright © 1935 by Dorothy L. Sayers and is used by kind permission of the author's estate and of the publisher, HarperCollins.

Edited by Patrick Nielsen Hayden

A Tor Book
Published by Tom Doherty Associates, LLC
175 Fifth Avenue
New York, NY 10010

www.tor-forge.com

Tor® is a registered trademark of Tom Doherty Associates, LLC.

ISBN-13: 978-0-7653-5808-0
ISBN-10: 0-7653-5808-5

First Edition: October 2007
First Mass Market Edition: July 2008

Printed in the United States of America

0 9 8 7 6 5 4 3 2 1

ACKNOWLEDGMENTS

Sometimes, truth is sufficiently stranger than fiction that it becomes hard to believe. I would like to note that the IRA bombing campaign of 1939 is historical, and so is the case of the German bomb accidentally dropped in Dublin. In some other cases I've started from truth and moved it towards plausibility, because this isn't the real world, thank goodness. Generally I have as far as possible used real names of people who don't have speaking parts in the narrative, like Winston Churchill, but fictionalized names and lives of those who do.

Thanks to my LiveJournal correspondents for coming up with fast answers to odd questions, particularly Tim Illingworth and David Dyer-Bennet, and for cheering me on while I was writing this (papersky.livejournal.com).

Thanks to Lis Riba for asking a useful question, to Emmet O'Brien for diligently checking my Hiberno-English, to Patrick Nielsen Hayden for taking time out on a busy morning to be helpful and for always being a great editor, to Mary Lace for reading this as fast as it was being written and making helpful suggestions, to the production people at Tor for doing a really good job on all my books so far, to Janet Kegg for finding and sending me Anne de Courcy's *1939: The Last Season*, to Sarah Monette for alerting me to the existence of *Five and Eighty Hamlets*, without which I'd probably never have thought of this story, and to Sherwood Smith, Laura Tennenhouse, David Goldfarb, Madeline

x ACKNOWLEDGMENTS

Kelly, David Dyer-Bennet, Jennifer Arnott, and Janet Kegg for beta-reading.

I'd also like to thank the late W. T. Roberts of Ynys-y-Bwl for keeping every program from every performance of every theatrical event he went to throughout his long life, and Mary Lace for giving me access to the ones from the era covered in this novel. They contain marvels nobody could make up and are like a whiff of the real theater world of the time. I'm glad to say they are now collected in the University of Leicester for the benefit of anyone else who wants to use them.

Christmas is coming, the goose is getting fat,
Please put a penny in the old man's hat.
If you haven't got a penny, a ha'penny will do,
If you haven't got a ha'penny, then God bless you!

— Traditional British children's rhyme

"When I was a lad," replied the foreman, "young ladies was young ladies. And young gentlemen was young gentlemen. If you get my meaning."

"What this country wants," said Padgett, "is a 'Itler."

— Dorothy L. Sayers, *Gaudy Night* (1935)

1

They don't hang people like me. They don't want the embarrassment of a trial, and besides, Pappa is who he is. Like it or not, I'm a Larkin. They don't want the headline "Peer's Daughter Hanged." So much easier to shut me away and promise that if I keep very quiet they'll release me as cured into my family's custody in a year or two. Well, I may have been an awful fool, but I've never been saner, and besides, I can't stand most of my family. I've never had the slightest intention of keeping quiet. That's why I'm writing this. I hope someone someday might get the chance to read it. Pay attention. I'm going to tell you the important things, in order.

It started in the most innocuous way, with a job offer.

"You are the only woman I can truly imagine as Hamlet, Viola." Antony gazed into my eyes across the table in a way which someone must have told him was soulful and irresistible, but which actually makes him look like a spaniel that needs worming. He was one of London's best-known actor managers, very distinguished, quite fifty years old, and running a little to fat. It was an honor to be given one of Antony's famous lunches, always tête-à-tête, always at the Venezia in Bedford Street, and always culminating, after the mouthwatering dessert, in the offer of a leading role.

That was the year that everyone was doing theater cross-cast. It was 1949, eight years after the end of the war. London's theaters were brightly lit, and full of the joys and struggles of life. Palmer did it first, the year before, putting on *The Duke of Malfi* at the Aldwych. Everyone said it would be a fizzle at best, but we all went to see how they did it, out of curiosity. Then, with Charlie Brandin getting raves as the Duke, Sir Marmaduke jumped on the bandwagon and did Barrie's old *Quality Street,* with all the men as women and all the women men. It was the success of the winter, so when plays were being picked for the summer season, of course there was hardly a house playing things straight.

I'd scoffed as much as anyone, or more, so much in fact that I'd turned down a couple of parts and thought of leaving town and lying low for a little. But if I left, where could I go? London theater was putting up a brave struggle against the cinema, a struggle already lost elsewhere. Theater in the provinces was at its last death rattle. When I was starting out, a London play would be toured all over the country, not by the London cast but by a second-string company. There might be two or three tours of the same play, the second company doing Brighton and Birmingham and Manchester, and the third doing a circuit of Cardiff and Lancaster and Blackpool. The deadliest tours played at every tiny place, crossing the country by train on a Sunday, staying in the most appalling digs. It was the way you started out, and if you were better known and wanted a rest from London, the second companies were panting to snap you up. But since the war tours were rare, and there was fierce competition for them. There was only London, and the occasional tryout elsewhere. People in the provinces could just whistle for theater. They were starved of it entirely. I can't think how they managed. Amateur productions and coming up to London when they could afford it, I suppose. Either that or they really were quite happy with the cinema instead.

In any case, there was no hope of a tour for me. If I didn't work, I could afford to lie quiet for a season, if I lived carefully. The problem was that I couldn't count on it being only one season. The theater lives from moment to moment, and once your name isn't seen it can easily be forgotten. I didn't want to leave acting, and besides, what was I supposed to do, starve? Well, the choice would be to starve or go back to my family, which would, I felt sure, be much worse than starving. My family are like cannibals, except that they wear pearls and diamonds instead of necklaces of skulls.

I gave Antony one of my best indecisive glances. Indecisive glances would be helpful if I took the part. Hamlet is famously indecisive. Besides, even if my friends did laugh at me for a few days, how often is anyone given the chance to play Hamlet? I'd gone along for lunch with Antony knowing it meant a good meal, almost sure I'd turn down whatever he offered me. Antony was never stingy, and the wine at the Venezia was always good. Hamlet, though. There are so few truly good women's parts in the world, and Hamlet was a dream of a role, as long as the cross-casting didn't make the whole play absurd. I could picture the lights already: VIOLA LARK AS HAMLET.

"Will you reverse everyone?" I asked, moving a little away from Antony and signaling to the waiter that my plate was utterly empty of tiramisu and could be taken away.

Antony took up his wineglass and sipped. "No," he said. "Consider Hamlet, daughter and heir to Denmark. How much more likely that her uncle would usurp? How much more difficult that she assert herself? Hesitation would be much much more natural than for a man. Her relationship with Gertrude, with Claudius, works perfectly. Horatio wishes to be more than a friend. Rosencrantz and Guildenstern can be seen in the light of Penelope's lovers. Laertes, too, Laertes is Hamlet's true love, which makes the end sing. In fact, the whole play makes much more sense this way."

He almost convinced me. "But Ophelia?" I asked, as the waiter glided over and poured more wine. "Surely you're not thinking of making that a sapphic relationship?" It's funny, there are enough women in the theater who wouldn't look at a man, and men who wouldn't look at a woman for that matter, but everyone would have forty fits if you tried to put a storyline explicitly mentioning them into a play.

"There's no real textual evidence it is a physical relationship at all," Antony said, dreamily. "Or one could read whatever one wanted into their earlier relationship, why not, get thee to a nunnery, after all."

"But surely Polonius sets her to entice Hamlet?" I shook my head, realizing that I'd have to look at the text again to make sure exactly what Polonius said. I'd never played Ophelia, all I had was a vague impression of the speech. "I can't see a pompous stick like him encouraging a sapphic enticement, or if he did, I can't see the Lord Chamberlain allowing us to show it."

"The wonderful thing about you, Viola, is that there's something in your head already," Antony said. "So many young actresses have no ideas whatsoever. Hmm. We could reverse Ophelia, and make her another suitor; Hamlet beset by suitors. The two brothers, Laertes and Ophelia. That works, my dear. We'd have to cut the nunnery line. I don't want to change lines, except for the he/she stuff, obviously, but *Hamlet* is always cut, judiciously, but cut. At full length, it would play almost four hours."

I could imagine a female Hamlet beset by suitors, doubts, and ghosts. She'd be virginal, disgusted by her mother's sexuality and unsure of her own. I was feeling my way into the part already. "I'll take it," I said, draining my glass.

"Very good," Antony said, beaming. "And with your well-known family background, I don't need to ask if you're British born."

"I was born in Ireland, actually," I said, resenting the bit about well-known background. The papers had always made such a meal of my family, it had been a real handicap when I was starting off. I hated thinking people came to see me on the dancing bear principle. "Pappa was still Lord Lieutenant there at the time. But I'm a British subject."

Antony frowned. "Do you have a new identity card?" he asked.

"Of course I do." I fished it out of my bag and dropped it on the table, open. My rather wide-eyed snap looked up at both of us. "The Honourable Viola Anne Larkin. Date of Birth: February 4, 1917. Age: 32. Height: 5 feet and 7 inches. Hair: blonde. Eyes: blue. Religion: Church of England. Place of birth: Dublin. Nationality: British. Mother: British. Father: British." I folded it up again. "And you could add to that grandmothers and grandfathers back to when one Lord Carnforth married a French countess in 1802, or back to the Conquest on Mother's side."

"That's all right," he said. "I'm sorry, it's just that with the new regulations we simply can't employ anyone who isn't really British."

"The new regulations are a stupid waste of time," I said, lighting a cigarette.

"I couldn't agree more, my dear, but I have to observe them or I'll be in trouble." Antony sighed. "My own mother was American, and in some eyes that makes me suspect."

"But the Americans are our cousins across the Atlantic, sort of thing, surely?" I said, blowing out smoke.

"Surely," Antony repeated, cynically. "But for some people they'll always be the land of Mrs. Simpson, and President Roosevelt refusing to help us in 1940. I had a certain amount of difficulty with the registration for the new card. It was nonsense, as you say." He drained his glass.

"You shouldn't let it upset you," I said. "Have you cast anyone else?"

The waiter, as smooth as a machine, and to tell the truth, as oily, brought us coffee. Antony stirred sugar into his, being a man and not caring about extra inches. He got his mind back to the play, finally.

"I thought of taking Claudius myself. I imagine Claudius as a man bad enough to commit murder, but with enough conscience to come to feel guilty. Very interesting part. Complex."

I tried my coffee. It was excellent. Italians always know how to make good coffee. "I'm sure you'd be splendid. And how lovely it would be to work with you again." That was only half soft-soap. He really was a very good actor, when he played the right type, and Claudius could very well be the right type for him. I could remember him smoldering embarrassingly in Byronic parts and was terribly glad he was too old for that now.

He smiled, vain like all actors. "I've managed to get Lauria Gilmore for Gertrude. She'll really do justice to her."

Lauria was a theater workhorse; she'd played Gertrude before, along with almost any part you could mention. "I played with Lauria in *The Importance of Being Earnest,*" I said.

"She was a glorious Lady Bracknell," Antony said, gazing into the distance. "And you were a splendid Gwendolen too," he said, loyally.

I'd played Cecily, but I couldn't really expect him to remember. It had been eight years ago, the first season after the war, when everyone had been slightly frantic at the Blitz being over and Hitler stopping at the Channel. Nobody had been really sure if the Farthing Peace would hold, or if we'd all be plunged into war again at any minute. All the theaters had either run daring revues or frothy comedies striving for wit. We needed laughter as we'd come to terms with not being about to be bombed to bits. Wilde's genuine wit had hit just the right note.

"How about the suitors?" I asked.

"I haven't made any approaches, but I thought perhaps Brandin for Laertes, and Douglas James for Horatio. I hadn't thought about Ophelia at all, at least, I was thinking in terms of a woman. There won't be many women. No—I could make the Player King and the whole troupe women, and have the play-within-the-play work something like a ballet." He wasn't seeing me at all.

"That would be glorious," I said. "How about Mark Tillet for Ophelia? I played with him in *Crotchets* two years ago, the play was nothing and it didn't run, but I thought he was jolly good."

"Hmm?" Antony came back from his reverie. "Who?"

"Mark Tillet?"

"Oh no." Antony sighed. "Jewish, my dear, and therefore ruin at the moment. I wouldn't even want the word Jew whispered around a play of mine this season, unless it was *The Merchant of Venice*."

I finished my coffee. "Mark? Really? I had no idea. He doesn't look Jewish."

"You mean he doesn't have a hooked nose and long ringlets and a copy of the *Protocols of the Elders of Zion* under his arm?" Antony laughed without mirth, a stage laugh. "A young lady of your background would probably be surprised how many Jews there are in the theater."

"Leave my bloody background out of it," I snapped. "I've been treading the boards since 1936. That wasn't what I meant at all."

"Sorry," Antony said, insincerely. "Nobody would doubt you know your way around the theater by now." He set down his coffee cup and signaled to the hovering waiter. "Well, since I have secured your services as a

leading lady, I shall leave you, and attempt to secure the
rest of my cast. Rehearsals begin on Monday, ten sharp,
in the theater."

"You haven't told me which theater, yet," I said,
laughing.

"The Siddons," he said. "Appropriate, isn't it?"

"Very appropriate," I agreed. There may have been
women who had played Hamlet between me and Sarah
Siddons, but I couldn't think of any.

"Oh, and one other thing, now you've agreed," he
said, confidentially, leaning towards me. "I've told Lauria, but nobody else at all, so keep it to yourself until it's
announced officially. The first night, which will be Friday, July first, we'll have a very distinguished audience—
the Prime Minister and Herr Hitler."

I wasn't a snob and didn't give two hoots, but it did
mean that the play was likely to get lots of attention
from the papers. "Good," I said. "What a coup for you,
Antony!"

We parted on the pavement outside the Venezia. It was
a typical English June day, drizzling in a fine mist, the
kind of day my Irish nanny used to describe as "soft." I
wanted to go home and read the play, though I couldn't
really start learning my lines until I had a proper acting
copy with Antony's "judicious cuts" and whatever he/she
changes it needed. I started to walk briskly through
Covent Garden towards the tube station. I shared a flat
behind the British Museum with my dear friend Mollie
Gaston and our dresser, Mrs. Tring. Mrs. Tring wasn't
really our dresser. She was a dresser, but she wasn't
picky, she'd dress anyone. She'd been my dresser back
in the summer of 1941 in *The Importance of Being
Earnest* and in the chaos that London was then, just after
the Blitz, had happened to mention that she was looking
for somewhere to live. She'd been making me comfortable ever since, and the flat, chosen because it was so
cheap, had become like a home. Mollie and Mrs. Tring

were like family, only better than my own family because less bloody poisonous.

People always think that because my father is a lord, I must live off the family wealth. This is total rot. I could, of course, or to be more precise, there was a time when it would have been possible. In 1935, when I was eighteen, my mother wanted me to be a debutante and I wanted to act. I'd done her thing for one season, incidentally learning quite a lot in the process, and thereafter I went my own way. She said she'd never speak to me again and the family would cut me off with a shilling, and I walked out. Our relations have been rocky ever since. Swearing you'll never speak to someone again is easy, but of course very hard to keep up. But I've never quite forgotten it, and I never go to Carnforth. My little sister Dodo comes to see me when she's in London, and when she brings her children up we all go to the zoo and I take them out for ices. But when Rosie unexpectedly came to see me in *Crotchets* and sent round flowers, which was sweet of her, I didn't invite her backstage. The theater is a different world. I knew she wouldn't understand.

I ran into Charlie Brandin coming out of the lift at the Underground as I was about to go in. "Viola!" he called. "Have you heard?"

"Heard what?" I asked, stopping and walking back outside with him. Actors love gossip worse than parlor maids. "I heard Antony's going to offer you Laertes in his new Hamlet, so we're to play lovers again, and we can languish madly at each other."

Charlie's a pansy, the theater is full of them as I was saying, so it's quite safe to tease him about this kind of thing. "But Laertes is Ophelia's brother . . ." he said, taking a moment to get it. "No! You're playing Hamlet?"

I grinned. "I couldn't resist."

"My dear, I'm so relieved I'll be able to eat this season without showing my legs in a skirt that I shall endure the torments of being your lover with hardly a pang," he said. Some of the theaters were casting cross-dressed as well as cross-cast. "Shall we go to Mimi's and eat pancakes to celebrate?"

"I've been stuffing myself at the Venezia with Antony. I couldn't eat a thing. But I could drink coffee and watch you eat, if you like."

By common consent, we turned and walked back into Covent Garden. Mimi's is a little café on two stories with rickety stairs between them, catering largely to the theater crowd.

"This cross-casting thing, it's just a fad," Charlie said as we walked. "It'll die out in no time."

"Maybe. Or maybe one day they'll say in theatrical histories that in Elizabethan times men played all the parts, even the women, then they started to allow actresses in the Restoration, and for a while people believed everyone should stick to their own gender, then in the late forties people began to experiment and now anyone can play any part. . . ."

Charlie laughed. "By next year, everyone will be back in their right clothes again. I bet you a fiver."

"No bet, because I think you're right, really," I admitted. He held open the condensation-streaked door of Mimi's for me and I led the way inside.

Mollie was sitting in one of the coveted downstairs booths, eating a curled-edge ham sandwich. She waved at me. "Have you heard?" she asked.

"Heard what?" I asked. "Can we sit with you?"

"I was lunching with Pat, but he's gone, as you can see, and I was just about to go, but I'll have more coffee as you're here."

The waitress came over. She was not, like half the staff at Mimi's, a would-be actress, but a local woman. "What do you want, love?" she asked.

"Three coffees, and one pancake stack," I said. I slid onto the bench beside Mollie, and Charlie folded himself onto the bench opposite.

"Lauria Gilmore is dead. She's got herself blown up," Mollie said.

"I was going to tell you that, but you distracted me with your Hamlet news," Charlie complained.

"Blown up?" I asked. The waitress brought the coffee and set it down on the table, slopping mine into the saucer. "How? Anarchists, like those people who blew up that castle in Wales?"

"Well, it might have been anarchists, but why would they want to?" Charlie asked.

"I suppose they simply go around blowing people up, just for fun," I said.

"She might have Known Something," Mollie said, darkly significant.

"Or she might have been In Their Way," Charlie said in a dreadfully fake Russian accent.

"I don't know, she was always rather left than otherwise," Mollie said in an ordinary voice. "Frightfully keen on women's rights and unions and voting and all that."

"Nonsense," I said. "She was an actress. Actors aren't political. It seems much more likely to me that she was just in the wrong place at the wrong time. Poor Lauria. Now she'll never play my mother."

Charlie laughed immoderately and put his hand to his heart. "Dead, and never called me mother," he said, in tones of deepest melodrama.

I giggled. "Never called me daughter, more like," I said. "But we shouldn't laugh, I mean, whatever happened, it's awful. I liked Lauria, and she was a good solid trouper, one of the best, a real old-school actress."

"You'll have to go to the funeral," Mollie said. "If she was in your play."

"Antony said she'd agreed. But we should all go to the funeral anyway. I haven't acted with her since *Ernest* but it's showing respect."

"I should think the whole theater will go," Charlie said. "What could be more dramatic than being blown to pieces, after all? Nobody will be able to resist. Besides, Lauria was at the top of her career, or she would have been if she'd been a man. There aren't all that many roles for older women, but all the ones there are she's played magnificently. She'd have been wonderful as Gertrude. She was when she played her before."

"Had you ever played with her?" Mollie asked.

Charlie shook his head. "It would have been the first time. And now I never will. The funeral will have to be very splendid to make up."

Mollie laughed. "You are awful, Charlie!"

The waitress brought his pancakes, which really are practically the only edible thing on the Mimi's menu, being made fresh when you order them.

"I can't quite believe she really got blown up," I said. "Who told you?"

"Bunny," Mollie said. "You know he was always chummy with her. It'll be in all the papers tomorrow. It might even be in the late edition of today's *Standard*."

And it was. When Charlie had finished his pancakes and we walked back to the tube station the new hoarding headline for the *Evening Standard* was "Actress Blown to Bits in New Terrorist Atrocity."

2

"Nasty day, sir," Sergeant Royston said as Inspector Carmichael slammed the car door.

Carmichael didn't deign to reply. Royston put the car into gear and eased it out into the traffic of High Holborn. "Supposed to be June, but it doesn't look like June."

Carmichael grunted.

"At least we don't have to go right out into the country, this time, sir," Royston offered.

Carmichael stared straight forward as the police Bentley purred through the gray London streets. The hard edges of the buildings were dampened and softened with rain. Selling out, he thought, should mean selling out body and soul. You were supposed to get Helen of Troy when you sold your soul, you shouldn't have to go on afterwards doing the same things you used to do when your soul was still your own, dealing with reprimands for the car left on the meter and listening to Sergeant Royston talking platitudes.

"I said, at least we don't have to go right out into the country," Royston repeated, looking sideways at Carmichael as they stopped at a red light. "Sir—"

The last thing Carmichael wanted was a conversation with Royston about the state of their souls. "Hampstead," he said, letting his loathing of the place show in his voice. "Hampstead's almost as bad as the country, or worse in some ways. Full of people who have money and pretensions."

"Funny place for an actress to live, come to think," Royston said.

"No doubt," Carmichael agreed. "Where would you expect an actress to live, sergeant?"

"Bloomsbury," Royston said, promptly. "Or Covent Garden, maybe. Somewhere central, anyway, and near the theaters. Hampstead's more stockbroker country, like you said, pretentious."

"One of the villages London swallowed up," Carmichael said, as Royston turned into the Finchley Road. "Once, Hampstead would have been like those awful places we drove through down in Hampshire, deep in the country, miles from London. Children playing on the green. Flowers in the hedgerows. In Dr. Johnson's day, parties of Londoners would ride out to Hampstead Heath for picnics. Now it's been swallowed. It's on the Underground. I don't see why an actress shouldn't live there as well as anywhere else, if she's been doing well for herself."

"And getting herself blown up?" Royston asked, turning into Bedford Drive, a tree-lined avenue of Victorian villas.

"That's another matter," Carmichael said.

Royston slowed to a halt halfway down the street as they came to a police barrier. On one side stood a young bobby in uniform. On the other were the massed ranks of the press, who would have been recognizable even without their notebooks and cameras by the unmistakable predatory cast of their features.

"Scotland Yard," Royston said to the bobby, showing his card through the window. "Inspector Carmichael and Sergeant Royston."

"They're expecting you, sir. Park here and come through, I can't raise the barrier," the bobby said. Royston parked carefully at the side of the street, and as soon as they stepped out the press began to photograph them.

"Was it terrorists?" shouted a man in a beige raincoat, beginning a barrage of questions, impossible to distinguish individually. Carmichael stopped and held his hand up for silence. Royston scuttled through as they closed in on Carmichael.

". . . same as in Wales?" one last journalist trailed off, embarrassed.

"I don't know any more than you do. When I know anything, I'll come out and make a statement," Carmichael said.

"Oh, be a sport and give us a quote," a woman said, smiling at him under a dripping hat.

"You're the same Inspector Carmichael who solved the Thirkie murder, aren't you?" asked a sharp-nosed man half-leaning on a little red Austin.

"Yes," Carmichael said, scowling. Flashbulbs popped. "When I have a statement to make, I'll see you're given it."

"Can you confirm that Miss Gilmore has been killed?" the woman asked.

The rest was lost in the clamor as they all began to shout again. Carmichael ducked around the barrier and joined Royston on the far side.

"It's number thirty-five," the bobby said, indicating a set of steps leading up from the street through a grass bank to a garden gate. "Go around the back."

Carmichael followed Royston up the steps. The shouted questions of the press sounded almost like the baying of hounds. He wondered if he'd get any hunting in this year. A few days in Leicestershire in November, perhaps. There was nothing like the feeling of going hell for leather forward across whatever territory lay before you, following wherever the fox led with no idea of what you might be getting into.

The rain was easing off to a fine mist. Royston opened the gate. It was green ironwork, Victorian like the house. The path forked. One branch led through two flower beds, overflowing with roses and pansies, to a pink front door. The other curved away down the gap between this house and its identical fellow on the left. Carmichael followed Royston down the gap.

"What would you call this gap between houses, sergeant?" he asked.

"Alley, sir," Royston replied. "Though it's small for one."

"They'd call it a ginnel in Lancashire," Carmichael said, as they came out into the back garden.

There had been rosebushes here, too, and a little lawn. The explosion had disturbed the earth and the roses lay uprooted. There was a tremendous quantity of broken glass everywhere, crunching under Royston's boots. There was a gaping hole in the back of the house, through which could be seen the remains of what had probably been a dining room. Torn shreds of wallpaper dangled around the hole, fluttering.

"It's like the Blitz," Royston said, touching a twisted length of dark green metal with his foot.

A tall man in Royal Engineers uniform came striding out of the hole in the house. "Not quite, not quite," he said. "In the Blitz, all the bombs came downwards. This one definitely started off inside."

"Scotland Yard," Carmichael said, and they showed each other identification. The sapper's name was Curry, and he was a captain. The two officers from the Metropolitan Police came out and were introduced as Sergeant Griffith and Inspector Jacobson of the Hampstead office. Everyone dutifully examined everyone else's cards and shook hands.

"I'd suggest we go inside, but there's just a chance the ceiling will come down on us, so we're better off here in the rain," Jacobson said.

"If you call this rain," Griffith said, contemptuously.

"So this definitely wasn't a bomb left over from the Blitz?" Carmichael asked Captain Curry, declining the conversational possibilities of the weather.

"Well, I thought at first it could have been a UXB, an unexploded bomb, you know. There was a greenhouse, you're walking on the remains of it, and it might have been built more recently over a bomb from 1940 that had buried itself and then went off. That does happen sometimes. I've heard of cases in France where a shell from the Great War is sitting underground until a farmer pokes at it and up they both go." Curry poked the ground thoughtfully with his toe. "But it doesn't add up. The center of the blast was inside, not in the greenhouse, and nobody keeps old Jerry bombs sitting around in their dining room. Besides, I won't be quite sure until we've done the analysis, but I'm almost sure that this was a homemade bomb."

"Jewish terrorists," Griffith said, eagerly.

Carmichael turned away to look more carefully at the ruin. Terrorists? Or was it like last time? Did the government have some reason for killing this actress? Was she someone else who knew more than she should? Had Royston and he been sent here because the powers that be knew they would acquiesce in a cover-up if necessary? Bring it on, he thought bitterly. Covering up for bombs, bombing people, throwing children into gas chambers. He knew how he would act if put to the test.

Jacobson also seemed uncomfortable with Griffith's enthusiasm. "Why would anarchists want to blow up Lauria Gilmore?" he asked. "Did you ever see her act, any of you?"

"I saw her as Cleopatra when I was a nipper," Royston said.

"I envy that," Jacobson said. "I'm a bit of a theater buff myself. I saw every show she was in since the war. She was the best of her generation."

"I saw her in *The Importance of Being Ernest,* just after the war," Carmichael admitted. He and Jack had gone along, to support dead buggers, as they'd put it. He remembered laughing and coming out envying the couples he saw who could hold hands. "I thought she was very good."

"But however good, nothing but an actress," Curry said, putting the damper on the theatrical reminiscences. "Not political."

"Two people were killed," Jacobson said, suddenly businesslike. "The bodies have been taken to the police mortuary at Hampstead. One has been definitely identified as Miss Gilmore, the other is most likely her . . . friend, Matthew Kinnerson. Mr. Kinnerson owns this house, and pays the rates."

"Does he live here?" Carmichael asked.

"Officially, he lives with his wife in Amersham, sir. In practice, it seems he lives here," Griffith said. "We were called to a break-in here last year, and I thought they were husband and wife until it came to taking down names. He had his arm around her and she was calling him darling, darling nonstop."

Royston made a note.

"Will Mrs. Kinnerson be able to identify the body?" Carmichael asked.

"There's a chance Kinnerson's dentist will be able to make an identification," Jacobson said. "He isn't a sight I'd want to show a wife, even if they were estranged."

"Who identified Gilmore?" Carmichael asked.

"I did," Jacobson said. "She wasn't quite as badly mutilated as Kinnerson, or whoever. Her face was unmistakable."

"Have her relatives been informed?"

"She doesn't seem to have any," Jacobson said. "She was married for a few minutes just after the first war, I think, then divorced. Her parents are long dead."

"How about servants?" Royston asked. "Do they know anything?"

"She has those all right," Griffith said. "Or she did last year. A cook and a gardener, a married couple, and her own maid. The couple have been with her for years."

"Where are they?" Carmichael asked.

Griffith spread his hands, as if to say they were not visible in the garden. "Maybe it's their day off?" he ventured.

"Maybe, or maybe one of them planted the bomb and told the others to scarper," Royston said, making a note.

"Who called the police?" Carmichael asked.

"Neighbor, name of Slater. Several neighbors called, actually, it was very loud, but Slater was the first." Jacobson looked uneasy. "I've sent a man to speak to all the neighbors and find out what they know. I hope I'm not treading on your toes, Carmichael?"

"Exactly what I'd have asked you to do," Carmichael said. "Let me know the results." He turned to Curry. "Can you make the house safe?"

"I can, but it will probably be more economical to pull it down and build another." Curry looked at it and shook his head.

"We're going to need to go through the house for clues as to where the servants are and why someone would make her a target," Royston said. "Sir," he added belatedly as Curry frowned at him.

"I'll get some more sappers out here and make it safe for an investigation," Curry said.

"Would you be able to commit yourself at this stage as to what kind of bomb it was?" Carmichael asked. "A homemade bomb, you said?"

"Fertilizer and bleach," Curry said. "I can't swear to it, yet, but I'm sure of it. The strange thing is how it got there. It wouldn't be stable enough for a parcel bomb, and while it's killed two people and made a mess of the house, you couldn't count on that if you just planted it, couldn't count on anyone being near it at all. They're terribly unstable. You can't use a proper timer with them. Very often people blow themselves up making them. That might have been what happened in this case."

"But what would an actress and her boyfriend be doing making a bomb?" Carmichael asked.

"It's no more crazy than the other way, sir," Griffith said.

"It's complete nonsense as I said to Captain Curry before," Jacobson said.

"I'll be off and get the shoring-up organized for you, inspector," Curry said to Carmichael, ignoring Jacobson.

Carmichael put out his hand to stop him. "How long will it take you, Captain?"

"I can't say exactly. It'll be done by tomorrow morning for sure, you'll be able to go around it then."

"Thank you," Carmichael said.

Curry nodded generally and stumped off around the house, glass crunching loudly under his feet.

"Well, time for us all to start getting organized," Carmichael said. "I think the first thing would be to get hold of the servants and see what they know. Do you have their names, sergeant?"

Griffith shook his head. "They'll be on file in the station, but not here. The lady's maid was Mercedes, like the car, I do remember that."

"Well, find out their names, and round them up," Carmichael said. "If there's even a slight possibility that one of them planted the bomb, we have every right to take them all into custody if it comes to that. The neighbors' servants may know about days off and so on. If it is their day off, they'll be coming back presently as normal and we can collect them then. Which reminds me—why is the street closed off?"

"We were afraid there might be another bomb," Jacobson said. "Captain Curry has checked thoroughly now, and there's no reason not to reopen it."

"Do that, but bring the bobby to the bottom of the steps, to keep the reporters out," Carmichael said. "They'll be crawling all over otherwise, safe or not, and we don't want that. Better be on the safe side and leave a man on guard here as well, which is going to mean two men on night duty. Damn the press. I'd better go and give them something to keep them quiet."

"Will you need anything on her career?" Jacobson asked, eager.

"They'll have that on file already," Carmichael said, gently discouraging. "I'll go and tell them she's dead, it was a bomb, and it wasn't the same kind of explosive used in the Campion bomb, or anything left from the Blitz. I won't tell them the bomb was definitely inside the house. That ought to keep them going for now."

"They're not ravening beasts, surely?" Jacobson said.

"I think you'll find they are in a case of this nature," Carmichael said. "I think I'd better come to your station, after I've given my statement, to get the names of the servants. Then, unless they've turned up to be questioned, I'll head down to the Yard and get some investigations going there. Tomorrow morning, we should all meet up here to go through the house. Curry should have the results of his tests by then, which will let us know more about the bomb."

3

I suppose it sounds awfully cold-hearted when I'd just been told Lauria Gilmore was lying dead, but I went home and read *Hamlet.* I started learning lines and thinking my way into the part. I'd always done this, ever since I was a child and first started to dream of acting. I read the play all through, then I read my part separately and thought about why I was saying this. By the time I'd been all through *Hamlet,* I'd quite come round to thinking that Antony was right, the whole indecisive thing did make more sense for a girl, who wouldn't expect to inherit automatically. A son and heir being usurped would be a fool to do nothing about it, whether or not his father had been murdered, but a daughter was different. My father had always wanted a son, which is why he had six daughters rather than stopping sensibly after two or three. Hamlet had been to Wittenberg, which was a university. He was there when his father died, and he'd just come back from there with his best friend, Horatio. For a girl to go there must have been rather like when my sister Olivia insisted on going to Oxford. Mamma and Pappa didn't like it, even though we lived close enough that she could drive herself in and out and didn't have to live at college. They'd never have allowed that.

Hamlet's family lived in Elsinore, which must have been like living way up in the north of Scotland. I went there once, Scotland, not Elsinore, to stay with Lord and Lady Ullapool. The journey took forever, and when you were there, nothing but hills and sea and desolation, beautiful in a bleak sort of way. There was nothing to do except stalk deer, ugh, and the rest of the house party were all as dull as ditchwater, and the house big enough I was always afraid of getting lost between my room and the drawing room. No wonder Hamlet took Horatio back with him. I'd been invited because the Ullapools' son Edward wanted a chance to propose, and thought it more likely I'd agree if I had a chance to see his wide acres first. I went because Mamma absolutely forced me. Even that year when I was doing what she told me to I utterly loathed country house parties and wearing tweeds.

I was surprised to find out in the gravedigger scene that Hamlet was thirty. I'd been thinking of her as much younger, twenty-two or -three, the age my sister Rosie was when she wanted to steeplechase. Thirty, only two years younger than I was. She must have got her degree. Not even a Ph.D. would take that long. Maybe she'd stayed on at Wittenberg to teach. Maybe she thought she'd never have to go home to horrible Elsinore. Then her father died. Would I go home if my father died? Would I even know if he died? Well, yes, it would be in the papers. Mrs. Tring would tell me. And even before that one of the others would be sure to phone me, even if Mamma didn't. I suppose if there were a memorial service in London I'd go. But I'd never go to Carnforth. Still, it wasn't the same. Mamma would have the others, or anyway most of the others. I wasn't the heir. Hamlet was an only, which must have made a huge difference. I find it very hard to imagine what it must be like not having sisters.

I was in a kind of dream, thinking about Elsinore and

Ullapool Castle and the fight Hamlet must have had to get away to college and the fights my parents had with us about all the things my sisters and I wanted to do, when Mrs. Tring came in. She knocked first, and then walked straight in and sat down on the end of my bed. I was standing at the window at that moment, looking out at the darkening sky, what I could see of it over the rooftops and chimney pots.

"Sorry to interrupt when I can tell by the muttering you're learning lines," she said. "Mollie tells me you're going to play Hamlet."

"I know you don't approve of the cross-casting, and I don't either, really, but this is different. It isn't silly sex stuff done to get a laugh, it's practically only Hamlet who's reversed, and in a way it makes more sense of the play."

Mrs. Tring laughed. "If it made more sense, you can trust that Shakespeare would have written it that way round first off and saved a lot of trouble. What I wanted to ask you was whether you'd be needing me to dress you."

"I don't know. Antony didn't say. I hope so. It's in the Siddons, you know, and it starts in two weeks. Two weeks' rehearsal, for *Hamlet*!"

"I can do it, if you need me. But I'd like to know. Be nice to have a couple of ha'pennies to rub together."

We'd been living together for eight years. For me they were years in which I'd gone from playing Cecily to playing Hamlet, but for Mrs. Tring nothing had changed; she'd been a theatrical dresser then and was a theatrical dresser now. She was two years younger than I was and looked ten years older.

"I'd love to have you if it works out," I said. "I'll ask Antony on Monday."

Mollie tapped on the door. "These have arrived for you," she said. "Sent round by messenger. I caught him just as I was on my way out."

Antony had sent round the script, which was very

good of him, and a big bunch of roses, which was just
his way of being polite.

"I'll put them into a vase," Mrs. Tring said, getting up
at once.

"Three vases," I called after her. It was a long-standing
rule of the flat that when we got flowers we shared them.
Mrs. Tring, who, naturally enough, never got sent flowers herself, was always inclined to pretend to forget and
give them to the person who had been sent them. Mollie
and I had once discussed, safely away from her, why
she never had boyfriends. "Her hea-aart is in the gra-
aaave with her husband," Mollie had wavered in the
tones of the banshee in *The Curse of the Caledons*.
We'd laughed, but I think on the whole it was true.

"Are you off anywhere special?" I asked Mollie, who
was lingering in the doorway. She was dressed rather
splendidly in a red velvet coat over a long black skirt.

"LDG," she replied, meaning Loathsome Daily Grind,
or in other words, an audition for a part she didn't especially want. "Susan in Marmaduke's revival of that Rat-
tigan thing," she elaborated.

"I can't remember, is Susan the wife or the other
woman?" I asked.

"What does it matter, they're all the same," she said.
I looked at her, surprised.

"It's all very well for you, you have a part and a plum
of a part, but I don't have anything and if I do it'll be in
some dreary nonsense nobody wants to see anyway. I'm
getting old, and there are no parts for old women, and
even if I manage to get the ones there are, people's comic
mothers and Lady Bracknell and Lady Macbeth—put
your mother in there and you'd have the three witches,
rather, wouldn't you—it'll all end up in being blown sky-
high like poor Lauria."

This, without the last comment, wasn't an unfamiliar
chorus from poor Mollie these days. In the last eight
years her stock had definitely fallen. She was thirty-nine
and looked older.

"I can't say that's exactly a common end for actors," I said. "Oh Moll, you'll be all right. Something will turn up. Maybe Antony will want you for his Player King, Queen, and we'll be together."

"Did he mention anything?" she asked, her face brightening.

"He said he wanted a woman, that's all," I said, hating to disillusion her. "I could suggest you."

"He probably has someone by now," she said, sinking down to the bed in the attitude of mourning for Adonis. "I'm sorry to be such a drip."

Mollie was really good to me when I was just starting out and didn't know which end was up in the theater. She could have laughed at me like all the others, that would have been the easy thing, but she helped me when I really needed it. I met her when I was the maid on the tour—the third-rank tour—of *Buttered Toast,* and she was Lucinda. We laughed together on a lot of those ghastly cross-country train trips.

"I'll ring Antony right now and thank him for the flowers and suggest you," I said. "It's nothing, really."

The telephone was in the hall on a little table. It was a perfectly normal phone like everyone else's, but one of Mollie's boyfriends had lacquered it red, which made it seem rather dashing. I dialed Antony's number, and waited. For a wonder, he was in, and for another, he was glad to hear from me.

"Viola! Darling! Did you get the script?" he asked.

"I was just ringing to thank you for it," I said. "And for the lovely flowers too."

"Have you heard about Lauria? Blown to bits, absolutely blown to bits. Nobody's safe in their beds. Thank God for Mr. Normanby and his stern measures or it would all be as bad as the war."

"Do you have any idea why they might have wanted to kill Lauria?" I asked.

"Probably the communists don't want me to be able to do my *Hamlet,*" Antony said.

I laughed, though he sounded absolutely sincere. "I was going to ask you what you thought about Mollie Gaston," I said.

"Is she old enough?" Antony asked, dubiously. "The last time I saw her she was a bright young thing in something or other. Lovely expressive voice, of course, great range. Wonderful sobbing."

"Old enough?" I asked, and then I twigged.

"Yes, Gertrude has to be old enough to be your mother," he went on. "Particularly with you being female, there has to be a real contrast. Lauria would have been simply perfect."

"I think Mollie could look old enough." Mollie, standing in the door to my room, looked absolutely aghast, and in that instant old enough to have played Hecuba. I went on, "Besides, she's got to be young enough to be sexy, young enough that Claudius finds her attractive. It isn't a marriage of convenience. Hamlet's disgusted with how sexual they are. Paddling in her neck." I'd just been reading that, so I could quote it confidently. "And age is largely a matter of body language, and that Mollie can do. The rest can be managed with makeup." I happened to know that Antony was mad keen on body language, because he'd once, in rehearsals for *The Seagull,* told Pat to walk on in such a way that it was clear to the audience that he was thinking about shooting himself. I don't think Pat ever managed it, or that anyone else could either, but the point is that Antony was sure he should have been able to.

"She could sob over Polonius. And then that speech after Ophelia drowns. She has a dark brown voice, which would suit that speech very well. But we shouldn't count chickens. She probably isn't free," Antony said. Mollie was making the most awful faces at me.

"I happen to know she is at the moment, she told me she's been offered a part but she hadn't accepted yet," I said. "I don't want to rush you, but she's here right now, would you like to speak to her?"

Mollie's faces redoubled in urgency; she shook her head violently. "I don't know." It had been the wrong thing to say, now Antony sounded as if he thought I was pushing him into something he didn't want.

"If you decide she's too young for Gertrude you could try her as the Player Queen," I said.

Mollie went quite still and leaned on the door frame. Mrs. Tring came out of the kitchen with a vase of roses in each hand and stood there, looking at us, puzzled. "I suppose I could," Antony said. "Ask her if she can come and see me at the theater in the morning. First thing— ten o'clock."

"I'll do that," I said. "Thank you for listening to me, Antony, I really appreciate that." Mrs. Tring took one of the vases into her own room and came past me with the other towards mine.

"We all want to keep the actors happy," he said. "Good-bye now, Viola, see you on Monday, and make sure you know your lines."

"You know I always do," I said. "Good-bye, Antony."

"What did he say?" Mollie asked.

"He immediately thought I meant you for Gertrude, because his mind's full of Lauria being blown up, and he thought you'd be wonderful at the sobbing. He must have seen you in *Dunkirk,* you cried a lot in that, didn't you? But he was afraid you weren't old enough. I tried to say that Gertrude has to be sexy as well as old enough to be my mother, so he wants to see you tomorrow, even though it's Sunday. He likes your voice. I'd try to look mature but sexy, if I were you."

Mrs. Tring laughed. "Mature and sexy, that's quite a job. I don't know how you dress for that one."

"Like my sister Pip," I said, thinking of a recent photograph I'd seen in the papers. Pip's only two years older than I am, but she's had four children and she's always had a matronly figure.

"Which one is that," Mrs. Tring asked. "The one who's married to Hitler or the one who paints?"

"It isn't Hitler, it's Himmler," I said, humming the "mm" and stretching it out. "And yes, that one. The one who paints is Dodo."

"I don't know how you keep up with your family," Mrs. Tring said. "One married to Himmler and practically queen of the Czechs from what they say, one married to a duke, one a communist, one married to that atom man, and you. Not a normal one among you."

I laughed. "I'm perfectly normal. And Rosie, that's the one married to the Duke of Lancashire, she's perfectly normal, apart from being batty about hunting. She did everything just as Mamma expected. And my oldest sister, Olivia, who was killed in the Blitz, was normal, except for going to Oxford. And come to that Dodo's normal apart from the painting. You can't blame her for being married to a scientist. It's only really Pip and Siddy who are eccentric."

"And the absurd things you call them!" Mrs. Tring said.

"Well, you have to call people something, and with the absurd names Mother gave us, we had to make up something better."

"Your mother liked Shakespeare, I don't see what's wrong with that," Mollie said.

"Olivia, Celia, Viola, Cressida, Miranda, Rosalind," Mrs. Tring said. It had been a kind of catechism in the society papers at about the time when Mamma brought Dodo and Rosie out together.

"Tess, Pip, me, Siddy, Dodo, and Rosie," I countered. "And they used to call me Fatso."

"You could have changed your name," Mollie said. "Though I suppose you did, in one way. Why do you call yourself Lark in the theater instead of Larkin?"

"I didn't want people who read the *Tatler* calling me 'the one who acts,'" I said, looking at Mrs. Tring, because of course it was from her weekly perusal of the *Tatler* that she knew so much about my sisters. "Though they do anyway, of course. Besides, Mamma said they were casting me out of the family. I couldn't keep using their name after that."

"Most of the time, nobody would think you were any different from anyone else," Mrs. Tring said. "But it does show through sometimes."

"I hope not!" I said, horrified. "Point it out to me next time it does so I can change whatever it is."

"You've changed your voice," Mollie said, reassuringly. "It's not that awful bray anymore."

"I didn't mean anything bad, dear," Mrs. Tring said. "It's just strange thinking of you being brought up in a castle and now living in a flat with the rest of us."

"The flat's a great deal more comfortable than the castle ever was," I said, which is nothing but the truth. "Pappa doesn't believe in using more coal than he absolutely has to, so Carnforth Castle is always icy, especially the bedrooms. If anyone dares complain, he tells them they shot people for less in the trenches."

"If I'm playing your mother, maybe I ought to play her like your real mother," Mollie said, smiling to herself. "Would you think Gertrude might have been like your mother?"

I thought about it for a moment. "Not very like. But as nobody ever murdered Pappa, I'm not sure how she'd act in those circumstances," I said.

For some reason they both found this frightfully funny and started to shriek with laughter, so I went into the kitchen and poured myself a glass of wine and took it back into the bedroom with me where the script was waiting.

4

Carmichael and Royston got back into the car outside the Hampstead police station. Carmichael held a piece of paper with the names of the servants, as well as a signed photograph of Lauria Gilmore as Kate in *Happiness,* provided by Inspector Jacobson and showing some signs of having been recently removed from a frame.

"Where next, sir?" Royston asked.

"It's half-past four," Carmichael said, looking at his watch. "We can't expect the servants to be coming back yet, assuming they're going to come back. Let's go out to Amersham and have a word with Mrs. Kinnerson, whose husband seems to be the other victim. We ought to be able to find out something there."

"Break the news as well," Royston said, glumly, putting the car into gear. "Not one of my favorite jobs. And difficult, with a grieving widow, to explain that her old man's been blown up with his fancy piece."

"She may be relieved to be a widow, sergeant," Carmichael said. "A merry widow, perhaps, relieved of a philandering husband."

Royston grunted.

It took them nearly an hour to wind their way out to Amersham. "We'd have been quicker coming on the train," Royston grumbled.

Carmichael didn't like Hampstead, but on the way to Amersham he reflected that Hampstead was at least a part of London. It had the Heath, an open piece of parkland, and the houses had little gardens, but houses and streets were packed closely together in recognition that land was precious. It was outer London, perhaps, but it was the city. Amersham, on the outer edges of the Metropolitan line, was far leafier. Houses stood detached in their own plots of ground. They were laid out along streets, as in town, but stood separately, as in the country. Miss Gilmore's house, before the explosion, could be recognized as kin to Royston's house. Mr. Kinnerson's house in Amersham, with its gravel drive and garage, its shrubs and lawn, looked as if the kinship it wanted to claim, at whatever remove, was rather with Farthing and the other great country houses. If Hampstead had been a village two hundred years ago, Amersham had still been one at the end of the Great War. The coming of the railway had brought speculators here to build houses and season-ticket holders here to live in them. The houses were new, almost painfully so.

"Thirty years ago, this was probably some farmer's field," Carmichael said, as they parked outside one of the identical villas.

"There isn't a shop or a pub for miles," Royston pointed out.

"Probably is in the old village. A shop with a little van that delivers."

"I wouldn't live here for all the tea in China," Royston said. "Neither one thing or the other, is it, sir?"

There was a Morris Traveller parked on the driveway. The garage door behind it gaped open, showing a workbench and a pile of boxes. There would have been plenty of room for the car.

They walked past the car and Royston pressed the bell-push beside the neat front door.

A little maid in a neat cap opened the door, and when they asked for Mrs. Kinnerson disappeared inside. The hall had fitted peach carpet and clean white paintwork. There was a mirror on the wall above a pine telephone table.

The maid came back and showed them into an empty room, furnished with a sofa and two matching arm-chairs, a huge veneered wireless and, on top of it, a television set. The peach carpet extended from wall to wall in here. The curtains matched it, and the walls were painted a pale peach. There were no pictures, or photographs. There was a clock hanging on the wall. The hands pointed to twenty-five to six. The maid left them standing there. Royston raised his eyebrows.

The door opened again to reveal a woman in her mid-twenties, with neatly permed fair hair and an anxious expression. She wasn't at all what Carmichael had expected; much younger and prettier. You wouldn't expect a man to run around with a woman thirty years older than his wife. Still, there was no accounting for taste.

"It's my husband you'll want," she said, without hesitation. "I only drive to the station to meet him, and I've never been over the speed limit. You'll have to talk to him, and he's not here. I'm about to go and pick him up."

"Sit down, Mrs. Kinnerson," Carmichael said. "My name is Inspector Carmichael, of Scotland Yard. I'm not here about the car."

She looked at him anxiously. "I have to go and pick my husband up from the station. I'll be late."

"Sit down, please," Carmichael said. "And might I sit down? And perhaps you could ask the maid to make some tea?"

"There isn't time," she said.

"I think you'll find there is," Carmichael said.

She made a gesture, spreading her fingers. Carmichael found her hard to interpret; was that a shrug, a shudder, acquiescence, negation? She perched on the edge of the sofa, but did not summon the maid. Royston and Carmichael took the chairs. Royston took out his note-book and pencil.

"You are Mrs. Kinnerson?" Carmichael asked.

"Mrs. Matthew Kinnerson," she replied, proudly.

"And your Christian name?"

"Rose," she said, licking her lips nervously. "I don't quite see—"

"And you were expecting your husband, Matthew Kinnerson, home tonight?" Carmichael went on.

"Yes, on the five-forty, and I need to be at the station to meet him or he'll have to walk home and he won't like that." Her fingers played with the fringe on the arm of the sofa.

"And where has he been?"

"To work. He works at Solomon Kahn, the merchant bank."

He must be doing well there, too, to be able to afford to run both these houses. Though perhaps he had private means. "He works Saturdays?"

She looked puzzled. "Yes. Well, not every Saturday, but quite often, yes. He's working today."

"You weren't expecting him to go to the house he owns in Hampstead tonight?"

She looked up, startled. "No. What do you know about that?"

Carmichael felt like a brute. "Mrs. Kinnerson, it seems your husband may have gone to Hampstead this morn-ing, to see Miss Lauria Gilmore."

"No," she said. "No, he was going to work. He wouldn't have gone there. He'd have told me if he was going. Anyway, he wouldn't have gone in the morning, he'd have gone after work."

"Did he spend the night there last night?" Carmichael asked.

"No. Spend the night? I don't know what you're talking

about. He was here last night and he left here on the eight-fifteen, I drove him to the station myself. I don't suppose he's ever spent a night in Hampstead in his life."

Royston and Carmichael exchanged glances. Royston shook his head pityingly at the depth of her denial. "Do you think we might ask for that tea, now?" Carmichael prompted.

Mrs. Kinnerson's eyes went to the clock on the wall, and realized that five-forty had come and gone, and with it the train. She shrugged again, and went to the door. "I don't know what my husband will say," she said. Then she stepped out into the hall. Royston shook his head. They could still hear her. "Hannah! Bring tea."

"But what about—" they heard the maid ask.

"Never mind. I don't have the slightest idea what's going on. Mr. Kinnerson will just have to walk from the station, that's all there is to it. Bring tea, the police gentlemen have asked for it."

She came back into the room and sat down more firmly. "Now, I've ordered tea for you, so could you please tell me what this is all about?"

Carmichael took a deep breath. "There was an explosion this morning in 35 Bedford Drive, Hampstead. Miss Lauria Gilmore was killed in the blast. There was a man with her. He was also killed, killed instantly. We have good reason to believe he was Mr. Kinnerson."

She didn't collapse into hysterics as he had half-expected. She sat silent there for a moment. "No," she said. "He was going to work, he wasn't going to see Lauria today." Then she began to weep, hopelessly. "She was always pestering him when there was trouble. The burglary last year, and when she was ill in the winter, and now this I suppose."

The maid came in with the tea, and left, giving only one look to her weeping mistress. Royston poured a cup for her, adding milk and plenty of sugar. "Drink it," Carmichael said. "It'll do you good."

She took the cup. Her hand was shaking so much that her teeth chattered against the rim and she slopped half of it into the saucer.

"Have you any idea why anyone would want to bomb your husband, or Miss Gilmore?" Carmichael asked, as gently as he could.

She looked at him incredulously. "Reason? What reason could there be? My husband *works* for the Jews, they wouldn't want to murder him. It must have been left over from the war. That would have been just like Lauria. She'd find a bomb left from the war in her garden, and she'd have called Matthew to sort it out for her, called him at work, instead of the police. And he'd have gone round straight away, and, oh God!" She began to cry again.

"Did your husband know about bombs?" Royston asked. "Was he in the sappers in the war? Or the ARP?"

"No, he was in the Navy. He wouldn't have known anything." Mrs. Kinnerson blew her nose, noisily.

Carmichael wanted to know about Kinnerson's relationship with Gilmore, but couldn't think of a way to approach the subject.

"How long has Mr. Kinnerson owned the house in Hampstead?" he asked.

"How long—" She pushed back her hair with both hands. "Years. Years and years. I think he bought it right after the war. Before we were married, anyway."

"So Mr. Kinnerson and Miss Gilmore have been friends a long time?" he asked, gently. Before he married? And had she known about it all the time but continued to deny it?

"Friends?" she asked, and then began to laugh, peal after peal of hysterical laughter. Carmichael considered slapping her face, but settled for offering her more tea. He sat down beside her on the sofa. She drained the cup. "Did you think they were lovers?" she asked, hiccuping. "That's just her theater manner. No, Inspector, though she dressed like lamb and called him darling or sweetheart every few words, Lauria Gilmore was my husband's mother."

"Well, that explains why he bought a house for her," Royston said, calmly.

Carmichael thought that he'd flay Griffith the next time he saw him for so misleading him. How could he have built so much on the impressions of an insensitive Hampstead sergeant? "Who was his father?" he asked.

"Oh, it all was perfectly ordinary," Mrs. Kinnerson said. She wiped her eyes. The clock struck six. "Matthew's father was a naval officer called Harold Kinnerson. He was married to Lauria Gilmore briefly. Matthew was born, and the marriage foundered because she cared more about her career. She went back to the stage, and Matthew was brought up by his father, when he wasn't at sea, and by his Aunt May, who is still alive and the sweetest old lady imaginable. She lives in Leigh-on-Sea, in Essex. This is going to break her heart. I always said Matthew should think of her as his mother, not Lauria. But Lauria had the glamour. She didn't want him as a child, but as an adult he was useful to her, someone at her beck and call. He adored her. His father was killed in the war, sunk with his ship in Norway. Matthew was twenty, twenty-one. He sold his father's house and he used most of the capital to buy that place in Hampstead for Lauria. After that it was a case of her lifting her little finger and getting him to do things for her. They'd have terrific rows sometimes, but she'd always charm him again. She was always asking him around. And now her silliness and her selfishness have killed him."

The door opened. Carmichael looked up, expecting the maid, and saw a self-possessed man in his early thirties, in a pin-striped suit and Marlborough tie.

Mrs. Kinnerson screamed. Royston looked horrified.

"Hello, I'm Matthew Kinnerson," he said, inquiringly. His tone said that he well understood how to use politeness as a weapon.

"They said you were dead!" Mrs. Kinnerson shrieked.

"Well, the reports seem to have been exaggerated, as they say, so do calm down, Rose. Who are these gentlemen?"

Carmichael stood. "I'm Inspector Carmichael, of Scotland Yard, and this is Sergeant Royston. I'm afraid there's been a mistake."

"Ah." Kinnerson looked Carmichael up and down. "Should you perhaps be next door? Might it not be as well to check on such things?"

"Your mother, Lauria Gilmore, is dead," Carmichael said.

"I am aware of that, although your colleagues neglected to inform me and I had to garner the information from the pages of the public press," Kinnerson said, tapping the newspaper under his arm. " 'Actress Blown to Bits.' Poor Lauria. Yet in a way, she would have liked to go with a bang. Am I to believe that you had reason to believe I was blown up with her?"

"Somebody was," Carmichael said. "He was unrecognizable."

"And you jumped to the conclusion that it was me? Why didn't you telephone my office, where I'd have been delighted to speak to you, instead of driving all the way out here and distressing my wife?"

That was a very good question, and one for which Carmichael had no good answer. "The Hampstead police had your home address, but not your work telephone number," Carmichael said. "I'm very sorry for the inconvenience."

Kinnerson raised an eyebrow, and Carmichael squirmed.

"They thought she was your girlfriend," Mrs. Kinnerson said, her voice cracking. "They were taken in by her makeup and her way of talking and thought she was a tart you were keeping in Hampstead. They wanted to know if you were there overnight."

Carmichael felt himself blush under Kinnerson's considering gaze. "Another misapprehension of the Hampstead police," he said.

"Not quite what one expects from Scotland Yard," Mr. Kinnerson said. "Go and tidy yourself up, Rose."

Mrs. Kinnerson, seeming glad to be released, made for the door.

"Well, now that this seems to have been cleared up, can I say good-bye to you two gentlemen?" Kinnerson asked.

"I want to ask you some questions about your mother," Carmichael said.

"You seem to know very little about her if you imagine she would allow herself to be a kept woman," Kinnerson said.

"I know almost nothing about her except her reputation as an actress," Carmichael said. "That's why I want to talk to you. I want to know who her friends were, who she was, who might have been with her this morning, why someone would want to blow her up, or why she might have been making a bomb herself."

Was it his imagination, or did Kinnerson tense a little at that last question?

"I didn't know her very well," he said. "I don't expect I can be much help to you. Does this have to be now? My wife's upset, I'd like to go to her."

His wife was upset, but he wasn't. Cool as a whole plate of cucumber sandwiches, Carmichael thought. "I could talk to you in the Yard, but we're here now, and there isn't all that much to talk about, as you've said," he said, as professionally as he could manage. "Let's get it out of the way now, shall we?"

"Very well, Inspector," Kinnerson said, and sat down on the chair that Carmichael had first taken. "What do you want to know?"

"I suppose you are Lauria Gilmore's next of kin?"

"I suppose I must be. Not that she had anything to leave. The house is mine, as you know."

"The house is probably going to be pulled down," Carmichael said. "It was badly damaged in the blast. And an insurance company will want to know exactly what happened before they agree on compensation."

"No doubt," Kinnerson said. "In any case, it is mine. Beyond that she only had some trinkets. She was never wealthy."

"Your mother's friends?" Carmichael prompted.

"I don't know them. We didn't share social circles at all. She called on me on precisely the occasions when she didn't want her friends involved. She knew everyone in the theater, of course. I don't believe she had lovers, not in recent years at least. She was over fifty, you know. She had a strong sense of independence. The only time I was ever close to her was during and directly after the war, when we saw a lot of each other."

"She never mentioned close friends to you, more recently, I mean?"

"Every time I saw her, but not in a useful way." Kinnerson rolled his eyes. "She'd say she'd been to lunch with Peter, darling boy, and that dear Marmaduke was considering her for a part in his new play, and would you believe that Biff was seeing JuJu now, as if that nonsense with Dandy had been completely forgotten." He stopped. "If you didn't know the people, it wasn't always easy to follow. My wife found her difficult company, so we didn't see much of her."

Carmichael could imagine. "She called on you for support when she wanted someone who wasn't in that world?" he asked.

"That's right, Inspector. I was happy to help her. It wasn't, whatever Rose may have led you to believe, all that often. I don't suppose I've seen her three times in the last twelve months. A burglary last year, which seems to have been what led to this confusion." He smiled, tight-lipped. "Taking her to the doctor when she had the flu last winter. Oh, and we had her here on Boxing

Day for dinner and a little drinks party with some of our friends."

Carmichael couldn't imagine that going down very smoothly. "What were her politics?" he asked.

Kinnerson looked at the clock, and then at Royston. "That surely can't matter now?" he asked.

"On the contrary, it may be highly important when establishing what motive someone may have had for bombing her."

"Well, she was more left than anything else." Kinnerson frowned.

"A communist?" Carmichael tried hard to keep his voice even. All the same, Kinnerson took fright at the word.

"Good God no! What I mean is, she used to vote Labour. She loved Ramsay MacDonald, I remember that, when he was Prime Minister and I was a little boy. She liked Bevan, now, Nye Bevan, she used to say he was the only honest man in Parliament."

"Did she know him personally?" Carmichael asked.

"I don't know. Probably. She was always meeting politicians. She'd met Ramsay MacDonald at a first night, I remember her telling me about it. She knew Churchill too, and was quite friendly with Lord Scott. But her politics, well, it wasn't that sort of thing. She'd started off frightfully poor, and she'd got by on her own talent, and she had a sort of fellow feeling for poor people, thinking they ought to get the dole and compensation and so on. Unions. It was more sentiment than anything. She was very talented, and very beautiful when she was younger, but she wasn't really very bright. But all the same, she's the last person any sane communist would choose to blow up."

"Who do you vote for, sir?" Royston asked. Carmichael frowned at him.

"I don't believe that's any of your business, sergeant," Kinnerson said, closed tightly back into his shell.

"No, sir, sorry, sir," Royston said.

"You don't have any idea who might have been with her this morning?" Carmichael asked.

"I'm afraid not. Now, if that's all, I really must get back to my wife."

Carmichael stood. "If I might have your card, Mr. Kinnerson? It's possible I may think of something else to ask you, and as you said, telephoning you in the office would be more convenient. Someone will no doubt be in touch with you in any case about funeral arrangements for your mother, and about your Hampstead house."

Kinnerson took a card case from the inside pocket of his jacket, drew out a card, and handed it over. "Here you are, Inspector. My home number is here as well."

Carmichael glanced at it. "Solomon Kahn," he said. "I knew David Kahn, you know."

Kinnerson gave him a quick glance, then looked away. "Did you?" he asked, his voice indifferent. "I met him once or twice, but we never worked together. Solomon Kahn is a big bank, employing a great many people, and he had his own division."

"Of course," Carmichael said, and handed Kinnerson his own card, with the Scotland Yard number. "Well, I apologize again for the distress we caused your wife by our confusion, and I'd like to thank you for answering our questions. Do get in touch if you think of anything else."

Kinnerson showed them to the door himself, and stood there until they drove away.

"Why did you ask who he voted for, sergeant?" Carmichael asked. "He was opening up before that."

"Sorry," Royston said, again. "I wanted to see him crack. He was too smooth altogether, I thought."

"Do you think he blew up his mother, or knows who did?"

"I wouldn't be surprised," Royston said. "I have a feeling he was hiding something."

"A hunch?" Carmichael asked, then laughed. "Not a

hunch, because I have exactly the same feeling. The trouble is that what he's hiding may be something totally innocent. But I'm quite sure he knows something he wasn't saying."

5

I kicked off my shoes and flung myself facedown on the bed with the manuscript. I read and memorized and when, every so often, I sat up to take a sip of wine, I saw the roses Antony sent sitting in full bloom next to my mirror. Unfortunately, I didn't have long in this undisturbed bliss before the phone rang. Mrs. Tring answered it, then knocked on my door.

"For you, Vi!" she called.

"How too bloody," I said, getting off the bed. I heard Mrs. Tring laugh in the hall, which was why I'd said it. I'd spent a few years after leaving home trying to teach myself to swear the way people do, but it never came naturally. I decided eventually that if it was always going to sound affected anyway, I might as well cultivate that.

The receiver was lying on its side on the table. I picked it up and spoke in my best telephone drawl. "Hello?"

"Fats? It's Sid."

It was more than a year since I'd spoken to my sister Cressida, and then only casually. I seldom saw the family. I usually kept up with them through Mrs. Tring's reading of the *Tatler* and gossiping with Dodo every few months. But I'd been thinking about them, they seemed somehow caught up with Hamlet, with Elsinore, so it hardly seemed strange at all to hear from her.

"How are you, Siddy?"

"Thriving, as ever. I need to see you." The phone made the bray of her voice seem thin.

"Are you sure you want the hassle with Mamma?" I asked. "You know how she feels." She had once forbidden the younger ones to see me alone because of the supposed immorality of acting, which could rub off on unmarried girls. Even now she would subject Dodo to days of cold-shouldering every time she saw me.

"If you're in the second circle, I'm in the ninth," she said. The ninth circle of Hell was reserved for traitors. "I don't give a damn about Ma. Come and meet me."

"All right, let's have lunch sometime," I said.

There was a pause at the other end. "I thought you theater people lived in a blaze of wild immediacy," she said, and although I'd never heard it before I could tell from her inflections that the phrase was a mocking quote from something. "Come and meet me now, Fatso."

I've always hated that name. "No," I said. "Are you drunk, Siddy?" There was something about the way she was speaking that made me wonder.

"Drunk, that's a good one. Haven't touched a drop."

"Still saving your pennies for the DW?"

She laughed, though it was a very old joke. When she was five or six, and I was about ten, at the time of the General Strike, we'd all been in London so Pappa could drive a bus. Uncle Tom had taken us all to Gunters and offered us cakes, and little Siddy, who had been reading a harrowing account of the miners' conditions in the *Manchester Guardian,* had said she'd rather have the money to give to the dear workers. The dear workers, quickly abbreviated to DW, became a standing joke. "You don't know how true. But come and meet me, Vile, do. Meet me at the Empire, Leicester Square, in an hour."

"No!" I said, horrified. "Look, Sid, I am rather busy, I have a part to learn. You can't just expect—"

"Ginns," she interrupted. "Ginns, Fats."

It's strange how reluctant I am to set down that word and explain my response to it. My family are noted for being eccentric. They're not necessarily people I'd choose to know, if I had a choice. But when you're the third of six sisters born in eleven years, when you all live together for a long time, growing up, there are shared things that just do mean something. There are jokes, like Siddy and the DW, there are names, there are memories, and naturally there are words that have a private meaning. We fought a lot, growing up. We had feuds, we had friendships, we had rivalry. "Ginns," simply enough, is short for "Now begins," which is from a piece of ghastly poetry we all had to learn. What it means though is that something is absolutely urgent, a truce must be declared, ranks closed and help given. None of us ever abused ginns, not even the littlest ones. Although I hadn't so much as heard the word in the twelve years since I'd left home, my response to it was immediate.

"I'll be there," I said, and put the phone down.

Mollie came in from her audition as I was putting my belted beige raincoat on. "How did it go?" I asked.

She groaned and ran her fingers through her hair, pulling off her scarf. "Where are you off to?"

"As a matter of fact, I'm going to have a cup of coffee with my sister Cressida."

Mollie stopped dead, theatrically, and raised her eyebrows. "Are you sure that's wise?"

"No," I said, frankly. "But why do you ask?"

"Your sisters always unsettle you," she said. "I think it has to do with the terrible way you were all brought up with nobody but each other and all the things you had to go through. In a dozen years away from them, you've turned out a lot more like a reasonable person, but where they're concerned it's as if you're instantly ten years old again and they've shut you in the barn overnight."

I shuddered. Mollie was the only person I'd ever told about that. "Whether she unsettles me or not, I think I have to go," I said.

"If you're sure," Mollie said. "There's no obligation. You're grown up now. You could stay at home. I'm going to make some cocoa."

It wasn't "ginns" in itself that made me drag myself away from cocoa and Mollie and our cozy flat and take myself down to the tube. It was the tone I now thought I'd heard in Siddy's voice all through the conversation, the tone that in itself meant ginns. She wasn't getting in touch with me idly, she really needed me. What I should have worked out from that was that the best thing to do would be to disappear, to take the tube the other way, to King's Cross, where I could get a night train to Scotland and never be seen again. Not being gifted with foresight, I went dutifully down to Leicester Square Underground station, and then walked up out into the square itself, towards the huge cinema there that they called the Empire.

The thing everyone knows about the Empire, Leicester Square, was that when the old king was dying, his last words were to ask what was showing there. The people whose duty it is to write down last words of kings then claimed that he'd said, "What about the Empire?", a much more appropriate thought for a king in his dying moments, and I expect it warmed the hearts of people from Calcutta to Calgary, until they heard what he'd really said, which was soon leaked. "What's on at the Empire?" Silly old fool.

I never go to the cinema. Partly this is because I was either working and didn't have time or wasn't working and didn't want to waste the money. But there was also an element of being a stage actor and not wanting to support the thing that was killing theater. I'd often seen the Empire, as I crossed Leicester Square, and marveled at how hugely vulgar it was, but I'd never been inside. Banks of lights on the front proclaimed that they were now showing Humphrey Bogart and Katharine Hepburn in *Travels in Tartary*. It was half-past nine, and a kind of dusky dark; the sun hadn't long set, as it was June, but of course the rain made it darker.

Siddy was standing under the shelter of the awning, lighting a cigarette, her hands cupped around the match and lighting her face from below with odd flickering shadows. She dragged at it impatiently as I walked towards her. She looked up, scanning the crowds, but didn't see me. I thought she looked tired and anxious, and terribly like Mamma.

"Fats," she said in acknowledgment, when I came up close. "Not that you are the slightest bit fat, I don't know why we call you that."

"I had puppy fat for about two weeks when I was fourteen," I said. "It was when Tess was coming out, and we all had dresses made for it."

"White frilly ones with horrid puffed sleeves that made you look a fright," Siddy said, smiling. "I remember."

"I always hated being called Fatso," I said.

"I can't remember, what did we call you before?" she asked.

"Vile, which I suppose is only natural," I said.

"Like me being called Mustard, I suppose," she said, dropping the butt of her cigarette and grinding it out under her heel. "I always hated that, too. Awful the things we did to each other. What do your friends call you now?"

"Viola," I said, dryly. "It doesn't seem too strange to theater people. Or Vi, sometimes."

"You'd think with Ma being nuts about Shakespeare she'd have liked you going on stage, not acted as if it was a den of vice," Siddy said. "Want a fag?" She offered the packet. They were long and tipped, du Mauriers.

I took one, and she lit them both. "Shall we go somewhere and have a coffee?" I asked.

"Yes, let's," she said, but didn't move. "Did you take
a cab?" she asked.

I shook my head. "I came on the Underground."

"Did you? How frightfully clever of you. I don't
think anyone was following me." Siddy started to walk,
and I followed.

"What's this about?" I asked.

"Let's sit down somewhere first. Where?"

"There's a nice little place called Mimi's in Covent
Garden," I suggested.

"Not somewhere they know you, silly!" Siddy looked
at me sideways, moving only her eyes, not her head,
something she'd always done. It made her look rather
like a Siamese cat.

"There's a Joe Lyons Automat on the corner of Charing Cross Road," I said.

"That would be good." We walked in silence through
the rain towards the Lyons. It was packed, as usual, but I
didn't see anyone I knew. Siddy seemed charmed with
the automatic nature of the hatches. "You can get a cold
chicken leg for two shillings! Or chocolate cake for
ninepence!"

"Yes, it's simply lovely for the DW, now can you get
what you want and let us sit down?"

She slid money in and released an anemic slice of apple tart. I settled for coffee. We took our trays over to
an empty table Siddy had spotted on the second level.
"This has a good view of the door," she said, as she sat
down.

The place was overlit, as such places always are, and
it made the gloom outside seem like black night and the
interior almost as bright as a stage. Siddy stubbed out
her cigarette in the cherry-red ashtray.

"You're looking good, Vi," she said.

"You too," I said, but it wasn't the truth. The bright

light showed lines in her face, and her ash-blonde hair was a little shaggy and needed cutting. "Sid—" I was going to ask her why she'd called me, but she held up a hand.

"The trouble is," she said, pulling out another cigarette, "that we hardly know each other. I didn't realize until I saw you. I thought, well, I suppose I thought, 'She's my sister, who is closer than your sister,' but the truth is that almost anyone is closer when there's been such a gap. I should have thought. You haven't really known me since I've grown up. I've seen you act, but I don't really know who you are, now. The last time we really talked I was in my nonsensical 'in love with Comrade Stalin, what can we do to help the Dear Workers' phase. How can you even take me seriously?"

"Are you in trouble?" I asked.

"I'm in trouble, you're in trouble, the whole country is in trouble or haven't you noticed?" Her match flared briefly, then she shook it out and dropped it into the ashtray.

"You're right that we don't really know each other beyond a shared past that seems a long time ago to me, but if you're in trouble I'll try to help," I said.

She drew deeply on the cigarette, and put her head back, exhaling, showing her long throat like a sacrificial animal. Then she leaned forward and put her hand on mine. "Promise you won't tell anyone what I asked, whether you agree to help or not?"

I nodded. "Nope to die," I said, in our childhood formula.

Siddy smiled. "Good old Fatso, Viola I mean." She looked at me for a moment. "Where do you stand politically?"

"Oh come on, Siddy!" I said, drawing back.

"By which you mean you're an actress, politics is boring, let the Bolshies and the Nazis bash the hell out of each other, it's what they both deserve, thank God for the Farthing Peace?"

I tried my coffee. It was dishwater, which was what I'd expected. "Something not very different from that," I said, noncommittally.

"And this latest nasty business, with that bloody worm Mark Normanby rewriting the unwritten constitution and sliding us close to outright fascism here, that doesn't alarm you at all?" She tapped ash off her cigarette impatiently and drew on it again at once.

"Actually I think it's a lot of silly hysteria, but if there are Jewish and communist terrorists going around blowing people up, then I suppose the innocent Jews and communists must expect a certain amount of trouble. Is that what this is? Are they after you for being a communist? Don't they know who Pappa is?"

"Don't you see how terrible it is that it makes a difference who Pappa is?" she asked, passionately. "Everyone should be equal before the law."

"Well if you want to be equally going off to some camp," I said. "But surely they can't imagine you'd blow people up?"

She leaned forward to me across the table. "Oh yes I would. I've visited Pip in Prague. I know what really goes on in those camps. They aren't prisons. They work people to death, on starvation rations. They are slaves, and when they get too weak to work they kill them with poison gas. They keep records, endless efficient relentless Germanic records."

"You can't really believe all that guff," I said. "Isn't it all like the stories about the Germans spitting Belgian babies on their bayonets in Pappa's war? Just propaganda? They make them work in the camps, yes, but all those stories about the showers with stone soap and poison gas are just to make you shudder."

"They're not." Siddy drew hard on her cigarette, and her face was set. "I don't suppose there's any way of making you believe, but I've seen them filing through the streets from the camp to the factory, like walking skeletons, and the guards . . ." She trailed off. "I'm a communist, but that doesn't matter anything like as much as being opposed to all of that. The worst of it is that the Left don't understand people like Pa any more than Pa understands what it's like to be a miner. I don't care about the economic side of things, except that it obviously isn't fair that Rosie should spend on one dress what would keep a family of eight in Bolton for a year."

"It wouldn't matter if they all had enough," I said. "If the family in Bolton had enough to keep them as well as Rosie having the dress."

"Maybe in theory, but it never works out that way," Siddy said. "In reality there are always more needy people than spare money for Dior dresses."

"Why did you call me?" I asked.

She blew out smoke. "I saw you on stage," she said.

"What was it?" I asked.

"I think it was called *Creatures of the Summer Heat*."

"Oh, that silly thing." I was embarrassed. "I don't know why you hit on that one. It hardly ran."

"I thought you were jolly good." She stubbed out her cigarette and reached for the packet.

"No, have one of mine," I said, and offered my case.

She took one and turned it in her fingers a moment. "Players. I have the theater cigarettes and you have the workers."

"Siddy, will you for God's sake tell me what this is about, or I swear I'll walk out of here and never see you again."

She looked at me a moment. "I can't. I can't trust you that much, and I can't trust myself to explain it to you so it makes sense. I thought I'd be able to talk to you but I can't. It ought to be Uncle Phil."

"Uncle Phil?" I echoed, idiotically. Uncle Phil, better known to the wider world as crazy old Scotty, was my godfather. He'd been in Parliament, in Government even, in the Churchill period, and now he sat sulking in the House of Lords, or at home in Coltham Court, pon-

tificating loudly about how terribly the current generation were messing things up. "What does this have to do
with him?"

Siddy shrugged, and lit the cigarette. "Everything.
Nothing. Look, I don't think I can possibly explain. Come
down to Coltham for lunch tomorrow."

"I have to learn a part," I said, automatically. "I have
to know it by Monday." Then it hit me. "You have inviting privileges at Coltham?"

"Not usually." Siddy smiled. "But just at the moment
I do."

"You're seeing Boo?" It was the only explanation.
Siddy had been married twice, to Tommy Bailey and
then to Geoff Russell, and was presently divorced. It
was no secret that Uncle Phil's son Benjamin had once
been in love with our oldest sister, Olivia, and devas-
tated when she'd married James Thirkie. He had cried at
her wedding. Mamma had thought it terribly bad form.
Siddy looked quite a bit like Olivia, though without her
poise. Olivia always had poise, whereas Siddy replaced
it with intensity. I wasn't sure where Boo was in the
marriage stakes at the moment, and while he was quite a
lot older than Siddy it would actually have been a better
match than most of her romances.

Siddy shook her head, laid down her cigarette, and took
a forkful of her pie. "Horrid," she said, setting the fork
down again. "Will you come to Coltham for lunch?"

"I can't possibly, not tomorrow. In any case, how
would I get there? I don't have a car." I don't know why
I relented even that much.

"There's a good train, from Charing Cross. Someone
could meet you at the station. There are *frequent* trains.
You could be back in London for dinner. Uncle Phil will
explain everything, or if he can't, I promise I will."

"Then why not explain now?"

"I can't here," she said, gesturing around the restaurant. "I don't know how to start. Take the eleven-eighteen
train, and someone will meet you at the station." She stood

up, leaving her pie almost untouched. "Please, Fats, Viola I mean."

She had never been my favorite sister. It wasn't because I liked her. I didn't like her or even trust her. It was true what she said, I hardly knew her. But she looked desperate and weary and she was my sister and I believed she was in trouble. Or maybe she just infuriated me so much that she drove me crazy with curiosity. Anyway, I must have been absolutely mad to agree.

6

On Sunday morning, Hampstead looked asleep in the sun at nine o'clock. Curtains were drawn and milk bottles stood neglected on doorsteps. The policeman at the gate of 35 Bedford Drive seemed by contrast almost unnaturally alert.

"Even the press are still in bed," Carmichael said, as he shut the door of the Bentley and surveyed the street, empty but for a scattering of parked cars.

"Not their work, though," Royston said, indicating the papers sticking from the letterboxes of many of the doors around them. "They keep late hours. I expect we'll have them shouting round again later."

"No doubt," Carmichael said, then turned to the bobby at the gate. "Good morning. Has the house been secured?"

"May I see your identification, sir?" the bobby asked.

Carmichael and Royston both fished out their papers and handed them over. The bobby scrutinized them carefully and handed them back. "Well?" Carmichael asked impatiently.

"Only following orders, sir," the bobby said. "And yes,

the house is secured, least, that's what the man I was re-
placing told me."

"We'll go in then," Carmichael said. "If Inspector
Jacobson arrives, please ask him to join us."

"That bloody yid," the bobby muttered.

"I beg your pardon, constable?" Carmichael asked,
silkily.

"Jacobson, sir. He's a Jewboy. Didn't you know?"

"I didn't," Carmichael said.

"Shouldn't allow them in the police," the bobby said.

"I'm surprised they do," Royston put in.

"Oh, they allow it," Carmichael said, weary of the
whole conversation. "They think if they can stand the
constant pinpricks of dealing with people who hate them,
they'll make good police officers. Not Scotland Yard, of
course, but in the Met and the provincial forces. Come
on, Royston, let's see the house before it falls down."

The bobby at the back had seen them the day before.
He saluted. "The sappers said to say, sir, that fortunately
there isn't any gas, and the water main was secured
right away, so the damage is mostly to the kitchen and
the back of the house."

"Thank you, constable," Royston said. Carmichael
nodded at the bobby and they made their way carefully in.

The house had been shored up with timber and tar-
paulins. The dining room, the site of the explosion, was
a shattered ruin. The kitchen, next to it, was also badly
damaged and showed signs of water damage. "Not
much point looking around in here, sir," Royston said.
"This is probably a job for the forensic boys."

"They'll be around," Carmichael said, stepping over
the remains of a table. "Let's look at the rest of the
house."

There was a little sitting room at the front. The windows had been boarded up. Royston took out his torch
and played it around. It was a conventional enough
room, with sprigged wallpaper and a three-piece suite.
A large looking glass hung cracked and crooked over

the mantelpiece, reflecting the torchlight and the room crazily.

"Blast," Royston said, using the word accurately. "Reminds me of the Blitz. Not much to see in here, sir."

The room across the passage from it was more informative, and lighter, as the windows had survived intact. It was a small study, almost filled by a large untidy desk. The walls were covered with photographs, posters, and framed press cuttings, some faded and others quite new.

"Some of these go right back to the twenties," Royston said, examining one of the posters.

"Even before that, sergeant," Carmichael said, looking at a cutting. "This review of *Mary Rose* is dated 1917. She was a great hit in it, apparently."

"Strange, in a way, isn't it, sir?"

"What's strange?" Carmichael turned to look at Royston, who was examining a photograph of a young Lauria Gilmore as Desdemona, looking as if she was about to dance the Charleston, complete with feathers and shingled hair.

"There's nothing more dead than an old play." Royston gestured to the picture. "There must be people alive who saw that thing, and other people who acted in it, and at the time it must have seemed exciting and important, maybe people queued for seats, but now it looks silly and dated and it's gone completely leaving nothing behind, except for what people remember. Strange, and a bit sad, when you come to think of it."

Carmichael sighed. "That isn't getting us anywhere, sergeant. Let's search the desk."

"Yes, sir," Royston said, immediately, but before he moved to the desk he straightened the Desdemona picture.

Carmichael hit pay dirt almost at once. Under a note from someone signing himself Antony inviting her to lunch at the Venezia in Covent Garden on the previous Friday, he found a small floral appointment diary. He turned to June and found each page bordered in climbing roses.

Her handwriting was small and precise, not at all like the extravagant signature on the photograph Inspector Jacobson had given him. Carmichael read it aloud to Royston. "Friday June sixteenth, AB, Venezia 1 P.M. Dinner, 7 P.M. Dinner is underlined. Saturday June seventeenth, PM 10 A.M., GM 8 P.M."

"PM," Royston repeated. "Someone must have reported a PM as missing."

Carmichael flipped through the book. He looked ahead first, at the appointments she had made and would not keep. The rehearsals and first night of *Hamlet* were marked off decisively, on pages bordered with sunflowers. The first night, Friday, July 1, was underlined twice, as was the time, 8:30 P.M. Apart from that she had one more meeting with PM, on June 30, again at 10 A.M., the day of the final dress rehearsal. There were other dinner appointments, and a few lunch appointments, decisively crossed out. The *Hamlet* dates, the crossings out, the emphatic dinner, and the PM appointment were in blue ink. The others were in black.

Looking backwards, he saw evidence of a busy social life, with many friends, all initialized. PM cropped up irregularly, generally for lunch or dinner. Carmichael flipped back further. May was daisies, and April daffodils. The only appointments she had other than for lunch and dinner were theatrical. This early morning appointment had been unusual. He read back. February was snowdrops and January winter jasmine. The ink colors changed regularly, between blue and black. It probably didn't mean much. He turned back to June. "Lunch AB" was in black. He picked up the letter from Antony and noted the address. He would have to find out who this Antony B. was, as well as PM. Judging by the infrequent appearances of "MK," Kinnerson had probably been telling the truth about how often he saw his mother.

"Bingo," Royston said suddenly. Carmichael looked up. Royston had been going through the other things on the desk. "Address book." The cover showed a languishing Pre-Raphaelite maiden with too much hair. Royston flicked through it. "Sadie Moorhead, Peter Marshall, Mary Marsden, Daniel Miniver, Pat McKnight, Frank Moston, C. Mitchell, Margaret MacDonald."

"Pat McKnight or Peter Marshall," Carmichael said. "Good work, sergeant."

"Unless one of the others is nicknamed P," Royston warned. "Margaret MacDonald could be Peggy."

"Even so, it'll be much faster to contact them all than to check every missing person in the country," Carmichael said, taking the book from Royston. He picked up the phone on the desk and listened for a moment. He had half-expected it to be dead, but it hummed happily, so he began to dial. There were two numbers for Peter Marshall, one a London exchange and the other Portsmouth, both neatly inked in black. The London number rang for a long time without response. Carmichael tried the other, waiting while the operator put him through.

That phone was answered quickly and breezily. "HMS *Valiant*."

Carmichael was made wary by his experience with Kinnerson. "Is Peter Marshall there?"

"I'm afraid he's not." The breezy voice at the other end made nothing of it.

"Can you tell me when he will be?"

There was a slight pause. The line crackled. "Well, to tell you the truth he should be here by now," the voice went on, a little less cheerfully. "Lieutenant Marshall was due back from leave this morning, which means by eight, but he had a forty-eight in London and he's late reporting in. Can I take a message, old boy?"

Carmichael looked at his watch. It was nearly ten. "Can I speak to Lieutenant Marshall's commanding officer?" he asked.

"Who is this?" The voice sounded wary.

"This is Inspector Carmichael of Scotland Yard," Carmichael said, with a great deal of satisfaction.

"Oh don't tell me Peter's busted up his car again?"

"I certainly shan't tell *you* anything of the sort," Carmichael said, silkily. Royston, who was still sorting through the piles on the desk, looked up and grinned at his tone. "Could you please let me speak to Lieutenant Marshall's commanding officer?"

"Yes, sir."

The line crackled again, as Carmichael was transferred. He put his hand over the mouthpiece. "Seems like Marshall is a possibility," he said. "Naval man. Due back from leave today and not shown up."

The phone sputtered back to life. "Captain Beddow speaking," it barked.

"Good morning, sir. I'm inquiring about one of your officers, a Lieutenant Peter Marshall."

"Seems the fellow's late back from leave, hey?"

"Yes, sir. I—"

Captain Beddow clearly wasn't prepared to wait for Carmichael's explanation. "What's your problem, Inspector?"

"Did Marshall say anything to you about an intention to see Lauria Gilmore while he was in London, sir?"

"Didn't say anything to me that I recall," Beddow said. "Lauria—what, that actress woman who was blown up?"

"Marshall knew her," Carmichael said.

"He might be intimately acquainted with the whole chorus line of the Gaiety for all I care," Beddow said. "I'm a busy man, Inspector."

"There's a possibility that Marshall was the man killed with Miss Gilmore yesterday. The body is very difficult to identify. Is Marshall habitually late back from leave, sir?"

"I—what? No, no he isn't. Some of the others—well. I was expecting you to tell me he'd piled up his silly car."

"No, sir. What kind of car did Marshall drive?" Carmichael wondered what Captain Beddow regarded as silly.

"Little red Austin. But you really think he's dead?"

"There's a distinct possibility, sir. At present making an identification of Miss Gilmore's companion would be most useful to us. What I'd like to ask would be for you to wait until mid-day for Marshall to report in. If he does report in, please call me at the Yard and I'll continue to pursue other possibilities. If not, then I'd like you to send an officer who knew Marshall well to London to attempt identification."

"Yes. Yes, I'll do that, Inspector. Terrible business. Terrible. Getting himself blown up having lunch with an actress. Not safe in our beds. The Prime Minister's quite right."

"Yes, sir," Carmichael said, though he wondered again whether Mark Normanby might have had rather more to do with setting the bomb than trying to prevent it. Though why would an aging actress and a naval lieutenant have become a danger?

"Just like that bomb in Wales," Beddow went on, underlining Carmichael's thoughts.

"Can you tell me anything about Marshall?" Carmichael asked.

Beddow spluttered for a moment. "Good man. Good sailor. Came into the service in the war and stayed in. Patriotic. He was due for promotion, overdue really, but with the naval cuts nobody's been moving on as fast as they could. The sort of man the country really can't spare."

"How old is Marshall?"

Beddow seemed a little taken aback. "I'd have to look it up. Within a year or two of thirty, I'd say. Shall I have his records sent to you?"

Young for Gilmore, even if she had a thing for sailors, Carmichael thought, then immediately reproached himself for jumping to conclusions again. Though surely he couldn't be another son? "That would be very useful, sir," he said. They rang off in an exchange of platitudes. Carmichael repeated the gist of the conversation to Royston.

"A red Austin?" Royston asked.

"They both seemed to think he'd crashed it. He must have been a terrible driver. Or maybe he drank. The Austin's not a dangerous car."

"It's not that, sir," Royston said. He went to the window. "There's a red Austin right outside the house. And it was there yesterday too, I remember noticing it while you were talking to the reporters in the rain."

"Yes, one of them was leaning on it," Carmichael said. "It could be a coincidence. They're not that rare. All the same, I have a strong feeling Marshall never reports back to his ship and we don't need to ring the rest of these names."

"A hunch, sir?" Royston asked.

Carmichael rolled his eyes wearily. "Have you found anything else?"

"Lots of rubbish mostly, bills for dresses and letters arranging parties. More cuttings. But there's this." He handed Carmichael a thick sheaf of stained and yellowing papers, stapled in the corner with a rusty staple. Carmichael looked through them at first casually, and then again with interest.

"These look like instructions for building a bomb," he said.

"That's what I reckoned," Royston said. "And they were close to the top of one of the piles."

"It seems ridiculous, but maybe she really was making a bomb herself." Carmichael felt his spirits lift at the thought.

"Kinnerson said she was a red," Royston pointed out.

"So he did," Carmichael said, looking down at the yellowed pages, so different from the elaborately floral diary. "Where I really do have a hunch, sergeant, is that we're going to be finding out an awful lot more than we want to about Lauria Gilmore in the near future."

"And I remember you said that you always followed up hunches that mean extra work," Royston sighed. "I can't imagine why she'd have wanted to make a bomb."

"When we know that, we'll know everything about the case," Carmichael said. "Let's get on with that desk. Jacobson will be here any minute, and I want to check the other rooms, just in case."

7

The station for Coltham is Eskridge. It was a perfect June Sunday, and of course there was nobody there to meet me. As I stood there fuming and cursing Siddy, I couldn't imagine why I'd ever thought for a minute that there would be. In all my childhood memories of her she was unreliable and sometimes actively treacherous. I stood there fuming at myself.

It's a boring little nowhere place, Eskridge, not really even a village, just a slew of ugly little houses that look as if they've washed up around the railway station. Nobody else had left the train. I was alone on the platform but for a few iron benches painted green and a hanging basket of geraniums. I went out through the station. A ticket collector nodded to me. I walked out onto the forecourt impatiently. There was absolutely no sign of anyone. I might as well have stayed in bed. Just as I was turning to look at the timetable to see when there would be a train back to London, a little open-topped sports car drew up with a squeal of brakes and a total stranger got out.

The car was smart as paint, and the stranger was smarter. He was tall and dark and, yes, handsome, in a devil-may-care way. You stop taking much notice of looks in the theater; you see so many pretty faces and lots of them belong to people who don't deserve them, or who think that owning that face means it will be their fortune. They have to learn that no face is anyone's fortune without an awful lot of hard work going with it. Still, this man had such perfect features, such artfully cut hair, such an air of arrogant charm, that I kept looking at him to see if he could keep on carrying it off.

"Viola Larkin, I presume?" he asked. His voice was educated, impeccably top-drawer, and had just the faintest touch of Irish.

"Lark," I corrected him automatically. "But yes, I am."

He smiled, consciously turning on the charm. "I'm Loy Farrell," he said, offering his hand. "They sent me to get you. I'm sorry I'm late."

There are people you can trust as soon as you meet them. Loy wasn't one of them. No, more than that, Loy was the opposite. I had a strong feeling I couldn't trust him. I shook hands with him warily.

He opened the car door for me. I took a scarf out of my bag and tied it over my hair while he came around the car again and got in at the driver's side.

"What a pity," he said.

"What?" I asked, frostily.

"That you're covering up your pretty hair."

I looked at him incredulously. He must have seen that his roll-on charm and shallow compliments weren't getting anywhere with me, because he laughed.

"Well, it was worth a try," he said, as if I couldn't possibly hold it against him. He started the car, and drove off, looking at the road and smiling to himself.

"So, are you staying at Coltham, Mr. Farrell?" I asked, after he'd swung the car around a few corners in silence.

"It's Sir Aloysius, actually, but please call me Loy, everyone does. And no, I'm just like you, come down for lunch with the old man."

What I'd hoped for was an explanation of who he was, how he knew Uncle Phil, why he was there. What I'd been given satisfied none of this curiosity but opened up more. He was awfully young to be a knight—was he a baronet? He seemed awfully young for that too. He had only a few wrinkles in the tan around his eyes. I doubted he was even my age. Sir Aloysius Farrell. I'd certainly never heard of him. I'd have to ask Mrs. Tring.

"I hope you've been enjoying your stay, Loy," I said, blandly.

"You're even prettier in person than on stage," Loy replied.

At that moment the road turned a corner and came onto a straight stretch and he put his foot down. Trees passed by in a green blur. I ignored the flattery. "Oh, have you seen me act?"

"I saw you in *Creatures of the Summer Heat*," he said.

"With Siddy?" I asked.

He glanced at me for an instant as if I'd scored a point. "You're not at all like her, you know," he said, as if it must be news to me. "Were there ever sisters so different?"

"Siddy and Dodo look like Mamma," I said. "Pip and Rosie and I look like Pappa." Poor dead Olivia had looked like Mamma too, but I wasn't going to bring her up to Loy.

Loy didn't say anything for a moment, he was overtaking a station wagon. "You're not *very* like Lord Carnforth either," he said, consideringly.

I laughed. "How do you know Pappa?"

"I know everyone," Loy said.

That was no sort of answer, because Pappa didn't know anyone. The only conclusion was that Siddy must have introduced them. But she wouldn't have done that unless she was very serious about him, and not even then perhaps, if Mamma really had cast her into the ninth circle of Hell. If she was involved with Loy, that contradicted my theory about her and Boo and why she had the right to invite to Coltham. But then if they'd gone to the theater together a year before, they must have been seeing each other then. What I really wanted to ask him was whether Siddy was all right and what all this was about, but I couldn't because I didn't know who he was and where he fit in, and I didn't want to air my sister's mysterious private business in front of someone I didn't trust.

We turned into the gates of Coltham then. I hadn't been there since the year I came out. It's a pretty Queen Anne manor house built of soft golden stone that has weathered well. It looked glorious in the sunshine. The garden seemed very green after the rain the day before. Loy parked on the circle of the drive, next to two or three other cars.

"Thank you for coming to fetch me," I said, very formally. He came around and opened the door for me, that sardonic look on his face. It occurred to me that he was exactly the sort of man I most disliked and, if he was rich as well as titled, which he gave every sign of being, exactly the kind of man my mother had most wanted me to marry. In my ordinary life, I met rather fewer men like Loy. There are men in the theater who think themselves God's gift to women, but few of them have the instinctive arrogance of those who have been born to privilege.

I got out and pulled off my scarf, shaking my hair as I did, so that it would fall together, which would have to do until I could get a comb to it. I wasn't about to comb my hair on the front drive in front of Loy. Then I heard a voice, much more distinctly Irish than Loy's, though I absolutely refuse to spell out the accent.

"Well, it's the luck of the Irish you have after all, Loy." Coming around the side of the house was a man, as ugly as Loy was beautiful, as rough as Loy was smooth, as genuine as Loy was false. "Getting the chore of driving to the station and fishing out such a very pretty one."

"Miss Larkin, Devlin Connelly. Devlin, Miss Larkin."
Loy's introduction was as smooth and untrustworthy as
the rest of him.

"It's Viola," I said, taking Devlin's large hand. "And
Lark, not Larkin."

He smiled.

His eyes were blue, his hands were strong, his smile
was kind and interested and there's no kind of descrip-
tion that's going to do justice to him. You'd think you
could find fifty just like him digging up the streets of
London, yet you can't, because Devlin was unique. I
can't explain why it is that while Loy's flattery irritated
me, Devlin's charmed me. It may be because it was plain
that Devlin was saying it because he felt like saying it,
not because he expected to achieve anything from it.

"You'll be the actress, now," he said. "I loved you as
Saint Joan year before last."

"Oh, did you?" I was absurdly gratified.

The front door opened and Uncle Phil came out. "Viola, my dear child!" he called. "How lovely to see you.
Come in, come in."

Devlin let go of my hand. Uncle Phil and I embraced.
We went through the house and out to the terrace at the
back, where Siddy and a young man were sitting on
lawn chairs. Malcolm, Uncle Phil's secretary, was sitting
on the grass.

"Here's Malcolm, and I don't suppose you've met Bob
Nash?" Uncle Phil asked.

The young man rose and Uncle Phil introduced me
and we shook hands. I resigned myself to being Larkin
again for the afternoon. Malcolm came and hugged me.
I had seen him and Uncle Phil only a year or two before,
when we'd had supper together after they'd seen me in
Much Ado.

Siddy was looking much prettier than the day before in
a full flowered skirt and a white blouse. I felt grimy next
to her after the railway carriage and the open-topped car.

She put her cigarette down in an ashtray and hugged me.
She seemed terribly thin.

"So, the inner circle," Loy said as he took a chair.

Siddy shot him a quick glance. He smiled back,
smooth as a Jameson whiskey and twice as expensive.

Devlin sat down next to me. Uncle Phil rang a little
bell and summoned a servant, who brought a drinks
tray. The whole thing was absurd, like something in a
farce. The inner circle of what? I asked for a martini
and excused myself to powder my nose.

I did powder it, reapplied lipstick and combed my
hair, which desperately needed it even after the scarf.
My hair is fair and horribly fine, and despite having the
best cuts I can afford, it likes to fly all over the place
given any chance at all. When I came out again, Loy was
sipping a scotch and giving Siddy one of his sardonic
looks. Uncle Phil was saying emphatically, "Absolutely
sure we can trust Viola!" and I wondered whether the
words before were that he was or he wasn't.

Lunch was awkward. We ate all the things people like
Uncle Phil always eat in June, salmon and watercress
and strawberries and cream. Oddly, I almost never ate
things like that anymore, but the first taste took me back
to Pip saying it was the most boring menu in England
and the sign of a terribly unimaginative hostess, and
Olivia bursting into tears. That was the year after she
was married, it must have been June of 1933, immediately before Pip went to Germany. She was supposed to
go for a year to be finished and improve her German,
but instead she fell in love with Himmler and never really came back.

I was seated between Uncle Phil and young Nash,
who was bland and English and who, it seemed, was in
the Navy and had recently lost a good friend, who
everyone else had also known, whose name was Pete.
Nobody seemed about to explain anything to me. People kept starting to say things and then stopping. The

situation would have been completely dire if not for Devlin, who started talking to me about Shaw and the way
Saint Joan had been directed at the Aldwych when I was
in it compared to the way he had seen it done in Dublin
years ago. He was interesting, and he took the trouble to
talk about something of interest to me. I found myself
liking him more and more. Siddy sat at the end of the
table and acted as hostess. Uncle Phil had never considered remarriage after Auntie Pam had died. They'd
never got on very well together. She was killed in the
Blitz, very early on, by the same bomb that killed my
sister Olivia. They were in the same shelter, one for
government wives, while the government members
themselves were, typically, in a much better shelter
somewhere else, and survived. I think on the whole Uncle Phil was happier with Malcolm looking after him.

After lunch, Uncle Phil took me into his study as if it
were the most natural thing in the world. I had always
loved his study. When we were children staying at
Coltham, Pip and I would sometimes dare each other to
creep in when Uncle Phil was at the House. The whole
room was wood paneled, and there were carvings of
roses in the center of the panels. We never found the secret passage Boo had told us about, though we tried tapping often enough. The room had an extremely
masculine smell of leather and pipe tobacco, which
hadn't changed at all. The chairs were upholstered in red
leather and squashed satisfyingly when you sat in them.
There were two narrow windows, one on each side of
the desk, which looked out over the back lawn down to
the lake. There was a folly at the lake's edge, looking
like a ruined Grecian temple. One of the windows
framed it exactly. I sat where I could see it.

Uncle Phil sat by his desk, piled with papers as always. He lit his pipe. "Siddy tells me she didn't tell you
anything," he began.

"Not a thing, and I'm frightfully curious," I said. "Is
she in some kind of trouble?"

"No more than we all are," he said. He looked at me for a long moment. "Viola, before I go any further, I want your solemn word that nothing I tell you must go beyond this room, whether or not you agree to help us."

"Uncle Phil—I'll promise, of course I will, I won't give you away, but what are you involved in that could possibly need this level of secrecy?" There wasn't all that much it could be, and my mind leapt to the possibilities at once. The thought of Uncle Phil of all people brewing revolution was quite incredible.

"The country has been taken over in a bloodless coup, and the saddest thing is that nobody seems to care at all."

"You said that in the House of Lords, and I read it in *The Times*," I said, calling his bluff. *The Times* had called him "Crazy Lord Scott" and the *Daily Herald* had called him "Crazy Old Scotty." He was quite right that practically nobody seemed to care.

"It's true, though, Viola, however many times I've said it. Things have gone too far and they have to be stopped. This is not what we expect of England." He looked at me seriously. I didn't say anything. "I know you're a woman, and an actress, and I know you haven't thought very seriously about politics. But you were brought up the right way, and I know when it comes to the crunch a Larkin's heart will be in the right place."

With Siddy a communist and Pip a fascist? But I didn't say it. I really wanted to know what this was about.

"What do you mean, stopped?" I asked.

"I have tried to do everything I can through legitimate channels," he said. "There only remain to us desperate measures."

"Desperate measures?" I echoed.

"You see here at Coltham this weekend a very strange alliance." He hesitated, put down his pipe. "Lieutenant Nash, like his friend Lieutenant Marshall, represents the fraction of the armed forces who agree with me.

Malcolm and I, necessarily, represent legitimate government. Your sister represents the working classes. Sir Aloysius and Mr. Connelly . . ." He hesitated, and I waited for him to say they represented the Empire or something. "They agree with me, and they have the practical knowledge we need."

"What are you intending to do?"

"Miss Gilmore was one of us."

"Lauria Gilmore?" I couldn't believe it.

"There are true patriots in unexpected places."

"I suppose there must be," I said, doubtfully.

Uncle Phil hesitated. "I know I can trust you, Viola, whether you help us or not?" He looked at me sternly.

"Of course, Uncle Phil," I said. It was true too, I would never have gone to the police to denounce him.

"Miss Gilmore had read my speeches and realized that I was a lonely voice speaking out against the government. She wanted to help. She and Peter Marshall were building a bomb, which she was going to place in a box in the theater on the opening night when Mark Normanby and Herr Hitler will be attending the play. Removing them will cause a power vacuum both here and in Germany, and I will be standing by to step into that vacuum here and turn back what the Farthing Set have done. I won't seize power myself, of course. I shall attempt to persuade Mr. Churchill to come back and form a government."

He was living in a dream of 1940, when this had actually worked. Mr. Churchill was even older than Uncle Phil, he must have been nearly seventy.

"If he won't come back, I shall attempt to persuade Mr. Attlee to form a government. He is the leader of His Majesty's Opposition, after all." He sighed. "Whoever does it must be better for the country than Normanby. We will remove an incipient dictator, for the general good."

"But Lauria and Mr. Marshall blew themselves up," I pointed out.

He looked at me, and frowned.

"Are you asking me to plant a bomb for you?"

"Security at the theater will be very tight, with the Fuhrer and the Prime Minister attending the performance," Uncle Phil said. "You will have the perfect reason for going in and out, as Miss Gilmore would have."

"But even granting what you say about England and incipient dictatorship, aren't you asking me to take a tremendous risk?" I asked. "Lauria blew herself up and didn't even take Hitler and Normanby with her."

"That's why I asked Sir Aloysius to bring in an expert this time," Uncle Phil said. "Mr. Connelly will do all the difficult and dangerous work with the bomb. He knows about these things. I wish I'd consulted him before this tragic accident. All you'll have to do is get the device into the theater. You'll have to work quite closely with Mr. Connelly, of course."

And then what happened? I could imagine the theater, the first night, smuggling in the bomb and putting it in the box, inside a box of chocolates perhaps. I could imagine the explosion, the disruption of the performance. Uncle Phil's mind then leapt to the political vacuum he would fill. Mine saw the bleeding bodies of the innocents who had come to see *Hamlet*—and my body. That's the way the script had to go. If I survived the blast, I'd be hanged, perhaps with an affecting speech about some vague freedom that had never been real anyway. It wasn't me they wanted, it was Saint Joan. The brave heroine part they were expecting me to play would inevitably end with me dead. I hadn't come here to audition for that. Ginns, Siddy had said. Well, that wasn't enough.

"No," I said. "I'm sorry, Uncle Phil. Of course I won't tell anyone what you're doing, and I wish you all the best of luck with it, but I really don't care enough about all this to take that sort of risk."

"You're afraid because of what happened to Lauria?" Uncle Phil asked, quite gently.

It wasn't fear, or not the way he thought. "Not only that," I said. "You say Normanby had a bloodless coup. What's the difference between that and the bloody coup you're suggesting? I think you're exaggerating how awful they are and how much difference you could make. Nobody cares. You're a good man, but politics is politics. Mr. Churchill, or Mr. Attlee, wouldn't really do anything differently from the way Mr. Normanby's doing it. As for Hitler, what happens in the Reich isn't any of our business. Why is any of this something that I should be prepared to die for?"

Uncle Phil looked tired and old and didn't say anything for a moment after I said this. It must have hurt him to see that I was in accord with the papers and everyone else in thinking him crazy. "Even if you don't see it as your patriotic duty, will you talk to Malcolm?" he asked.

"Of course I'll talk to Malcolm," I said. "But I can't see how he could change my mind. I'm decided."

Uncle Phil got up, patted my shoulder, and left the room. I looked out at the view, not really seeing it. They couldn't do it without me, so I didn't need to let anyone know, which I had in any case promised not to. Poor Uncle Phil. Poor Siddy. They must have been desperate. What a feeble alliance. I really didn't understand how they could imagine it would make a difference.

8

Jacobson interrupted them as they were coming back downstairs. He didn't look Jewish, Carmichael thought, with that sandy hair and handlebar mustache.

"Any news?" Carmichael asked.

"I've found the servants," Jacobson said. "They came here last night and seeing as they had nowhere to go and we knew you'd want to speak to them, we put them into a hotel in Belsize Park overnight."

"All three of them?" Royston asked.

"Yes, all of them. They said they'd been given the day off. The Spanish girl knew about the bomb, she'd seen the papers, but it was quite a surprise for Mr. and Mrs. Green."

"Did you question them?"

"Not really. I didn't want to tread on your toes. We looked at their papers, asked what time they'd gone out and how long they'd been employed here, that's all."

"Good," Carmichael said, pleased. It would be much better to talk to them himself, and have their first reactions. "Did you ever meet Miss Gilmore, Inspector?"

Jacobson colored. "I saw her act as often as I could, but I was never introduced to her."

Carmichael decided not to break the news about his idol's bomb-making activities just yet. He very much wanted to talk to someone who could shed some light on precisely why a successful actress might decide to make a bomb.

"Let's get on and see the servants," he said.

"They were asking about their belongings," Jacobson said.

Royston glanced at Carmichael, who nodded. "Their rooms, at the top of the house, aren't much damaged. There's no reason they can't have their things, once we've gone through them a bit more."

"Anything we might want to look at would be papers, not clothes or anything like that," Carmichael added. "Do you have a discriminating constable who could do that?"

"Not here," Jacobson said, blandly. Carmichael belatedly remembered the anti-Semitism of the constable on guard. "I can send someone round to do it."

Carmichael nodded. "Tell them not to touch Miss Gilmore's room. For one thing, it's not really safe."

Jacobson came with them to Belsize Park in the Bentley. It made sense because he knew the way, but Carmichael found his presence surprisingly inhibiting. He was used to using their interludes in the car as times to talk to Royston uninterruptedly, to toss ideas at him.

The hotel looked grim enough in the sunshine that Carmichael was glad not to have seen it the day before. There was a neatly lettered sign proclaiming it the Hampstead Gardens Temperance Hotel, prop. S. Channing.

"Give me a nice pub any day, sir," Royston said, echoing his own thoughts.

"Do you often use this place, Inspector?" Carmichael asked Jacobson.

"Often enough," Jacobson replied. "If we have a witness come up from the country, maybe, or if there's someone, like now, we want to hang on to without putting them in a cell. It's respectable and quiet, and not too dear."

It was respectable enough, in fact painfully, excruciatingly respectable. The spikes of the iron railings repelled, the narrow windows seemed to frown, and the window boxes were all bare.

Jacobson knocked at the front door, which opened to emit a faint smell of much-boiled cabbage, mixed with the kind of starch used to stiffen tablecloths. The maid who opened it shrank back a little at the sight of the men. "Mrs. Channing's ever so cross," she confided to Jacobson.

"We want to see the people Sergeant Griffith brought here yesterday, please," Jacobson replied.

The maid retreated inside, and the policemen followed her into the front hall of the hotel. It was painted dark brown and held a little desk, like a lectern, bearing a diary and a telephone. There were flights of stairs leading both up and down, and a number of closed doors. One of them opened with a bang, increasing the smell of cabbage considerably.

The figure who opened it was clearly by her bearing and ample proportions not a maid, but the landlady herself. She was frowning. "Mr. Jacobson, I am disappointed in you," she declared.

"Mrs. Channing?" Jacobson replied in an inquiring tone. The maid who had opened the front door took the opportunity to escape down the stairs.

"Two of the persons Sergeant Griffith brought here last night proved to be Jews, once I had the chance to inspect their papers."

"Mr. and Mrs. Green, yes," Jacobson said, patiently. His face was wooden.

She drew herself up. "You were aware of this?"

"We'd seen their papers, naturally. Mrs. Channing—"

Carmichael decided to interrupt with a little charm.

"Sometimes duty compels us to unpleasant tasks," he said.

Unmollified, Mrs. Channing turned her frown on Carmichael. "And who are you?"

"Inspector Carmichael, Scotland Yard," he said, taking out his police identification.

"Well, your duties might, mine do not extend that far," she said, raising her chin.

"We would like to speak to all three of the people who were brought here yesterday," Carmichael said.

"You can see the Spanish girl in the lounge if you want to, but I sent the others off," Mrs. Channing said.

"Do I understand that you refused to house Mr. and Mrs. Green?" Carmichael asked.

"They were Jews! This is a respectable house! I am a respectable widow, and this hotel is how I make ends meet. I'm under no obligation to have Jews here. The police pay, but I have my other customers to think about. They come here because it's respectable. What would they think about sitting down next to dirty Jews?"

"Where are Mr. and Mrs. Green now?" Carmichael asked, as calmly as he could.

"How would I know?" she asked, sullenly.

"They didn't say where they intended to go, having been cast into the night?"

"I certainly didn't inquire." She sniffed.

"You just let them go?" Jacobson asked.

"This is not a prison," she said. "This is a hotel. The police can tell people to stay here if they want to, but I'm not responsible for keeping them here. And I will not have Jews sleeping in my beds. I'd have had to burn the sheets. Never send any here again, do you hear me, Inspector Jacobson?"

"I think you've made your feelings perfectly clear. It remains to be seen whether we send you anyone again. For now, then, I think we'll talk to Miss Carl," Jacobson said.

"Wait in the lounge," she said, opening a door.

The lounge was a cheerless room with mismatched chairs placed at geometric angles to each other on a square of carpet. A fire was laid but not lit. There was a large wireless set on a table under the window. The three men looked at each other for a moment, then Jacobson laughed, and the others joined him.

"What an outburst!" Carmichael said.

"It'll make it twice as hard, needing to find them again," Royston said.

"Doesn't she know you're Jewish?" Carmichael asked.

Jacobson stopped laughing. "Of course she does. Her husband was Jewish!"

"So she's the respectable widow of a dead Jew?" Royston said, and guffawed again. "She'll have to burn every sheet in the place."

Carmichael ignored him and turned to Jacobson. "She let them go?"

"Looks like it. Though that was a hell of a performance. What beats me is why they needed to be let go. We didn't have anything against them. What could they have known? Unless they were the bombers?"

Carmichael thought of the faded notes on bomb-making on Lauria Gilmore's desk. But she could have been in a conspiracy with her servants, as well as PM. "They've just risen very high on my list of suspects," he said.

The door opened and a girl came in. She had heaps of dark hair, done up on top of her head, and she was dressed quite smartly in a pale pink dress trimmed with lace. Carmichael realized as he saw her that he had been subconsciously expecting her to be like poor Agnes Timms, who had been a lady's maid before she became a hairdresser and was shot for knowing more than she should have. One look at Mercedes Carl was enough to dispel the thought. She had a pretty, lively face, big dark eyes, and nothing of Agnes's air of taking careful thought for the future. She looked apprehensive now, but despite that her face looked as if she liked to laugh.

"Miss Carl, thank you for coming," Jacobson said. "Please sit down. Inspector Carmichael has a few questions for you."

Mercedes took a frayed red velvet chair in front of the door.

Carmichael had been standing by the wireless. He hastily sat down himself, next to Royston, on a spindly legged chair. Jacobson remained standing, by the fireplace. Royston took out his notebook and pen.

"Your name is Mercedes Carl?"

"Carlos," the girl corrected. "I call myself Carl here, to be easier, but properly it is Carlos. But please call me Mercedes." She had a noticeable Spanish accent, but that wasn't what disconcerted Carmichael. She didn't speak like a servant, but as if she considered herself his equal.

"And how old are you?"

"I am twenty-five."

"And how long have you been working for Miss Gilmore?"

"Three years now," Mercedes replied.

"Your English is very good," Carmichael said.

She smiled. "When I came it was very bad."

"Why did you come here from Spain?"

"Lauria was playing in Barthelona, and she stayed in the house where I was then working. My mistress lent me to her, to help her dress, and we liked each other. When she left she asked me to come with her, so I came."

"Do you like England?"

"London, I like. I like the cinemas and the shops and the Tube. Other parts of England I have seen when Lauria is on tour, I do not like so much." She gave a little shudder.

Carmichael noticed that Royston nodded approvingly and Jacobson went so far as to give a sympathetic shudder. Lancastrian that he was, Carmichael still had sufficient sympathy to smile at the girl. "Now, tell me what you did for Miss Gilmore."

"I looked after her clothes and her hair and helped her dress. She was beautiful, but she was getting older, and when you get older beauty takes more effort and time. I used to read the papers for her, *Vogue* and the papers from Paris, and if there was anything that would do for her I would show her. Making her look good was our shared project." She smiled, then stopped smiling abruptly. "I can't believe she is dead. She was very good to me. She helped me so much. I had plenty of time to myself, not like in Spain. When I first came she had one of her friends act as tutor to help me learn English. And she always took an interest in my affairs. She was a friend as well as an employer. She helped me get papers."

"I suppose I should look at your papers," Carmichael said, and extended a hand. She produced them from her bag. Carmichael had expected to see a work permit, and was surprised to see that they were British identity papers, proclaiming her place of birth as Barcelona, her parents as Spanish, and her religion as Roman Catholic, but nevertheless recorded her as a naturalized British citizen. Lauria Gilmore had certainly not stinted her help with papers.

"Will you go back to Spain now?" Carmichael asked, looking up again.

"I? Spain?" For a moment she looked almost afraid, perhaps realizing how empty her future was without Lauria Gilmore. Then she smiled. "No. I will look for work here. I like London too much."

"Do you have any idea why Miss Gilmore might have been killed?"

She shook her head. "None. I was shocked when I saw it in the *Standard*. Why would anyone bomb Lauria? She was kind and good."

"Did she ever talk to you about bombs?" Carmichael asked, though it was a long shot.

Mercedes looked puzzled. "You mean the Blitz? Yes, sometimes, stories about the war. She worked in a canteen."

"What were her political views?"

"She hated Mr. Normanby." Mercedes smiled again. "How she would go on about how she hated him. She hated Hitler in Germany too, and Franco in Spain, Stalin in Russia, and all the others. She liked democracy, voting, that's why she got me my papers, so I could vote. She liked little people, underdogs she called them. She liked Mr. Bevan, very much, and Mr. Atterly."

"Atterly?" Carmichael asked.

"Attlee, she means, sir," Royston said, looking up from his notebook. "I've written down Attlee." Attlee, the leader of the Labour Party, the Official Opposition, a colorless man who Churchill had once described as "a sheep in sheep's clothing."

"Atterly, yes," Mercedes confirmed, smiling at Royston.

"Did she know them personally?"

"She had met, yes, at parties, you know how it is, theater people, political people meet sometimes. She had to sit at dinner once next to the one who was killed, Thirkie, she told me about it after. She said he was the best of a bad lot." Carmichael could hear the echo of the mistress saying it in her maid's voice.

"So, yesterday," Carmichael said. "Was Saturday usually your day off?"

"Not usually, but if I want a day, Lauria usually lets me change, unless she needs me particularly."

"And did you especially want to be off yesterday?" Carmichael asked.

"Yesterday, yes, because I was meeting someone." She looked down coquettishly. "My friend was free Friday and Saturday, and I asked Lauria if I could change and have one of those days, and she said yes, she didn't need me after Friday morning. She had an appointment for lunch on Friday, with Antony at the Venezia, which meant a part."

"Antony who?" Carmichael asked.

Mercedes opened her big eyes wide. "Antony Bannon, the famous director," she said.

Jacobson sighed, clearly recognizing the name. "Did he offer her a part?" he asked.

Mercedes looked over at him. "I don't know. I didn't see her afterwards. She said after I dressed her for lunch on Friday, she didn't need me until Saturday evening. She had tickets for Glenn Miller at the Albert Hall."

GM, 8 P.M., Carmichael thought. "So you dressed her for her lunch, and then went off, and came back last night in time to dress her for Glenn Miller?"

"Yes, but by then she was dead and wouldn't need dressing again," Mercedes said.

"So you didn't see her yesterday at all?"

"No. The last time I saw her was on Friday morning. She got a taxi to Covent Garden, and I said, 'Break a leg,' meaning to wish her luck getting the part, you know. And she said, 'Give my love to Gregory.' Gregory being my friend I was seeing. And that's the last time I ever saw her alive." Mercedes wiped a tear from her eye with a little lace handkerchief.

"Did you know the Greens had yesterday off?" Carmichael asked.

"Yes, they always had Saturday. In the winter, Friday evening to Saturday, in the summer, all day Saturday. The Sabbath, you know? Mrs. Green always left cold food for me and Lauria, if she was eating in."

"Do you know what they do?"

"They go to the synagogue, which is like church for them, and then they go to the house of a friend and do nothing. They really do nothing, they are obliged to, Mrs. Green told me. They can read, or talk, but they can do no work. Isn't that amazing?" Mercedes's expression showed that she clearly thought it little short of miraculous.

"How long had they been with Miss Gilmore?" Carmichael asked.

"Years and years. Since just after the war, I think. Mrs. Green was English; Jewish, but English. Mr. Green came from Holland when they threw away their Jews."

"Threw out, not threw away," Carmichael corrected her gently. "Were they and Miss Gilmore close?"

Mercedes stopped to consider. "In some ways close, in others not. She and I were more like friends, where with them they were always servants. But she treated me like a child to be indulged, whereas she took them much more seriously. She had been good to them too. She had helped Mr. Green with papers, as she did with me. Mrs. Green always says she didn't know where she'd be without Lauria, and that she'd do anything for her. So I suppose they were close, yes."

"Do you know where they might be now? Mrs. Channing wouldn't let them stay here, you know."

"That was very strange. At first, she didn't mind, then afterwards she made a great fuss, shouting and raving."

Carmichael could imagine. And all faked. "Did they say where they were going?"

"Not to me. But I suppose they would stay with friends," Mercedes said. "Probably their friends from the synagogue."

"Do you know their name?"

"I know some of their names. It wasn't always the same family they visited. They had a lot of friends."

Royston took down the names, while Carmichael drew Jacobson over to the window. "Can you find out where these people live from the synagogue?" he asked. "Or from the station?"

"It shouldn't be a problem," Jacobson said. "But if the Greens have anything to hide, they won't be there."

Carmichael looked at Jacobson, wondering if he could be trusted. "Does Mrs. Channing know you know her husband was a Jew?" he asked.

"If there's an International Jewish Conspiracy, they

threw me out years ago for not paying dues," Jacobson said. "She knows. And she must therefore have expected me to back her up. I'd never do such a thing. I'm Jewish, certainly, but I never let that get in the way of doing my job."

9

Malcolm kept piling me up with information about the terrible conditions in the Reich and I kept saying it was none of our business. If there was one thing the Farthing Peace had settled once and for all it was that the Continent was its own lookout. Why should I care what Hitler—or Pip for that matter—was doing to the Jews of Europe, even if I believed it? In fact, as I'd said to Siddy, I knew it was vastly exaggerated.

At last he shook his head and looked at me. "Your upbringing was eccentric, to say the least, and I always felt sorry for you Larkin girls."

I drew myself up, not about to take that kind of thing.

"No, listen," he said, and because he was Malcolm and Uncle Phil's companion and I'd always known him, I did listen. "If you'd been an ordinary family your parents would have been up in court for neglect, the way they let you grow wild. You've tried hard since to be something real, in the theater, I respect that. But your roots are in shallow soil, like all of your sisters. There's no use saying you'll always be a Larkin, as Phil does. I'm asking you not to be a Larkin but for once to be a decent human being and do the decent thing. We're on a slippery slope. We're well on down it. This could be the last chance for democracy, for liberty."

"You're asking me to destroy the only thing that really matters to me, for something that isn't even real," I said. "I have my life, and my life has nothing to do with my duty to the country, to the Larkins, and certainly not to Humanity. My life is about theater. It always has been. What you want me to do, I see quite clearly now, is wreck a play, one of Shakespeare's greatest plays, to kill two politicians, who are probably only the tips of icebergs and can easily be replaced by others just as bad."

Seen in this light, the light of ages, the light of Art, I felt my position was unassailable. Malcolm's arguments certainly couldn't touch me.

He sighed, and gave me his hand to help me up.

When we came back out into the garden, everyone was sitting on the terrace as they had been before lunch. Malcolm looked over at Uncle Phil and gave a little shake of his head. Uncle Phil stared out over the roses. Siddy was gulping a cocktail, and smoking. She ignored me. She didn't even look up. I suppressed the feeling that she was in trouble and needed me. I was furious with her. Ginns, indeed. What she needed me for, after all these years, was to die for her, putting a bomb in a box in the theater. There wouldn't have been a dry eye in the house when they hanged me.

"I think I'll head back to London now," I said, as brightly as I could manage.

Loy began to rise from his chair. Devlin, beside him, put a hand on his leg, stopping him. "I'll do it," he said.

"Are you sure?" Loy asked, raising his eyebrows. "I thought—"

"You had the privilege of driving Miss Lark from the station this morning. Let me take care of this," Devlin said. He smiled at me. I smiled back. I liked the fact that he called me Lark, instead of Larkin. Loy tossed him the keys.

Uncle Phil and Malcolm shook my hand formally, a change from the hugs of this morning. Lieutenant Nash shook my hand too, but didn't meet my eyes. Loy bowed over my hand, sardonic as ever. Siddy didn't get up, she kept drawing on her cigarette and staring out over the ha-ha. "Good-bye then, Sid," I said, as I went around the side of the house with Uncle Phil and Devlin.

"She's taking it hard," Devlin said.

"Go carefully," Uncle Phil said.

"I'm sorry, Uncle Phil," I said. "But you can rely on my silence." He pressed my hand. I got into the car.

Devlin drove the car much more carefully than Loy. When we got to the end of the drive, he turned in the opposite direction. "I thought I'd take you to Maidstone," he said, as I began to protest. "You'll have a better choice of faster trains from there, than from Eskridge at this time on a Sunday."

"Thank you," I said.

We didn't talk for a while. Devlin's big hands were confident on the wheel as he motored through the country lanes along the Downs. I saw wild roses in the hedgerows, much prettier than Uncle Phil's rosebushes, but on the whole I prefer my flowers made up as bouquets. We were held up behind a tractor going around a sharp corner, and then overtook it and went up a hill. Devlin pulled into a lay-by at the top of the rise, with Kent spreading out below us in a patchwork of greens. He switched the engine off, and it was very quiet. I could hear birds singing and the tractor laboring up the hill behind us.

"Why are you stopping?" I asked.

"We're stopping because I can tell you're a lovely girl really, and I want to talk to you." He turned in his seat and smiled at me.

I jumped to the obvious conclusion. "Oh honestly," I said, exasperated. "I'd expect that sort of nonsense from Loy, but not from you."

"This isn't what you'd have got from Loy," he said, looking entirely sober now. "No, I reckon with Loy, you'd have got a much closer look at that corner back there than you'd have wanted, and probably ended up with your neck broken. That's why I offered to drive you."

I didn't quite know how to react to his slow voice saying this. "You mean Loy doesn't drive safely?" I asked, though I had already understood. I was horrified to find my voice shaking.

"He drives very well. Loy's a professional, and so am I. Your uncle Phil now, he's a nice man, a good man. He trusts you, and so does little Siddy. He tried to persuade you to help us out of your patriotic duty. And Malcolm, he tried to persuade you with facts and figures, and they're all real enough, no doubt. And young Nash, if he'd had a go, he'd have tried with sob stories, and Lord knows there are enough sob stories. They're good people, all of them. The best kind of English people. The kind of people you'd want running a country. Loy and I, we're not nice people."

Not English either, though he didn't have to say so, his voice made the point. I reached for the handle of the car door. Devlin put his hand on my arm. I didn't struggle, but I could tell by the feel of his hand how strong he was. Oddly, perversely, there was an almost erotic charge in the warmth of his hand and the strength of it. "Let me go!" I said.

"Let you go where, off into the farm country?" Devlin asked, quite gently. "Listen to me, Viola. We need you. I'm not threatening you, no, I'm not. Now I could, because we really can't afford to let you go, knowing what you know and maybe being afraid, like your uncle says. But you know names and place and time, and that's too much for you to know and for us to count on your word as a Larkin. I wouldn't think your word as a Larkin would count for all that much, not when you've changed your name and all."

"You have no idea how much my word counts, you animal!" I said. His hand was still holding my arm, not squeezing or hurting me, but holding on to me so I couldn't jump out of the car. He was right that there was nowhere to go. We were on top of the rise and there was nothing within running distance but fields, rolling away. All the farm buildings seemed far away and entirely out of reach.

"No, that's fair," he said. "I don't know. And I don't think Siddy or Lord Scott really can know either. Loy wouldn't be prepared to take the risk of letting you walk around knowing as much about us as you know, and I'm not sure he's wrong. But I thought I'd take a chance that I could persuade you to help, if that was the choice."

"Dead blowing up tyrants or dead in a ditch?" I asked, sarcastically.

"That's about the weight of it," he said.

Poor Antony would think his *Hamlet* was doomed if I died before rehearsal as well as Lauria. The thought gave me strength. "You don't dare," I said. "It'll draw too much attention to the production. Maybe Antony won't even put it on if I'm killed. It would be clear it was jinxed. He's very superstitious. You wouldn't be able to kill Hitler if there's no *Hamlet* to kill him in."

"He'll still be going to the Wagner. That's more dangerous, but it's the fall-back plan. Loy wanted to go for that as soon as he heard. But Siddy thought it was fate, you being cast as Hamlet. She wanted to get in touch with you as soon as Lauria told her Antony was going to ask you."

"Fate!" I said. It was so exactly like Siddy. I could hear her saying it.

"Well, fate it is now," he said. He smiled at me. "Why did you come along?"

"I thought Siddy was in some sort of trouble," I admitted. "I thought it was real trouble, not all this nonsense."

Devlin stopped smiling. He took a breath, and let it

out again. "Well," he said. "At least you have some family feeling. That's more to work with than if you were pure selfishness all the way through."

I had been terrified, but now I was furious. I just stared at him.

"I've sisters myself," he said, and he pulled me closer and gave me a most unsisterly kiss.

My first reaction as he moved towards me was to pretend to like it. I'd been kissed often enough on the stage, I was sure I could fake a response. But it would be a lie to say it was entirely unwelcome. For one thing, like his hand on my arm, it was, however wrong it might be, charged, exciting. For another it was oddly reassuring. If he meant to kill me, surely he wouldn't kiss me? At the same time I knew this was nonsense. Men raped women before killing them, never mind kissing them in a car. It wasn't at all like a stage kiss. It was firm without being rough, gentle without being timid, just like Devlin himself.

"Ah now, I shouldn't have done that," he said, as he moved away from me.

There was a tiny smear of lipstick on the side of his face. I suppressed an urge to wipe it away. He had let go of my arm. I didn't try to leap out of the car. "Because it will make it harder to kill me?" That was what I hoped, of course.

"Because you'll think I'm trying to seduce you into helping, and then you'll think you can go along with that and tell the police everything after," he said.

I was affronted. "If that had been a possibility, don't you think I'd have done that from the first moment? Agreed with Uncle Phil and then betrayed you? I gave my word. That might not mean anything to you, but it does to me."

"Ah, Viola," he said. "I can't trust you to keep quiet. I can't. That option doesn't exist, do you understand? I've seen too much in Ireland of people saying they won't talk and then talking. Your options are what you said before, dead in a ditch or dead blowing up tyrants. And isn't dead blowing up tyrants the better choice? For one thing, it doesn't happen for near enough two weeks, and we can have some fun in that time, while dead in a ditch happens now, today. For another, it might not matter to you how you're remembered after you're dead, but if you die in a ditch you'll be forgotten when the last person who saw your plays dies, and if you kill Hitler you'll likely be remembered forever. For a third, well, that way you might not die at all. This way's certain."

He had big capable hands, and blue eyes that always seemed to have a smile in the corner, and I couldn't doubt that he'd kill me as competently and with as little fuss as he drove the car.

"A fortnight . . ." I said, thinking for the first time about really doing it, really carrying a bomb into the Siddons. Being remembered for it didn't excite me. It would cast a shadow over my career, the same way nobody remembers anything about Mata Hari except that she was a spy. But a fortnight more of life, and after that I might survive. And even if the bomb did wreck the play, it wasn't the only play there would ever be, or even the only production of *Hamlet* there would ever be. "All right."

He didn't smile. "You won't be able to go home. We thought you could stay with Siddy . . ." He let the sentence trail, looking at me.

The thought of turning back to Coltham and tamely saying I'd changed my mind, and then staying with Siddy, who knew her friends were taking me off to kill me and who hadn't even got up to say good-bye, filled me with claustrophobia. "I have to learn my lines!" I said. "I have to learn my lines today. You might as well kill me here as brick me up with Siddy and expect me to be able to work. You can let me go home. If I don't, Mollie and Mrs. Tring will worry and probably call the police. They might call the police even if I told them I was staying with Siddy, they'd think she kidnapped me.

I'll do it for you, Devlin, and I won't talk, but you have to let me go home."

"You sound more desperate about that than about dying." He raised an eyebrow, and looked skeptical.

"Dying's grand and noble, and terrifying in the abstract, but not really real; even when it's about to become the dead in a ditch kind, death is an abstraction. Being shut up with Siddy is petty and appalling and all too well remembered," I said, fervently.

"You could stay with me," he offered. "I could drive you home and you could collect your script and whatever you need, and you could tell your friends where you were going to be, that you were spending time with a man. Would that be so unusual?"

"It would, actually, but they'd believe it much more readily, especially if you come in and wow them talking about *Saint Joan*," I said. It took every ounce of stage skill to keep my voice even as I said this, because I suspected he was about to kiss me again, and indeed he did, as soon as I'd finished speaking.

"I said we could have some fun together, and I think we could, don't you?"

He put his arm around me and held me against him. It didn't have anything to do with love, it couldn't, love was excluded from our relationship almost by definition. I'd always persuaded myself before that I was in love with anyone I felt like going to bed with, even if the love burned itself out as fast as the passion did. With Devlin there was never that illusion. He said he thought we could have some fun together, and I melted, I could hardly wait for decent privacy and a bed. Then, thinking about the night, I remembered. It was Sunday. "I still need to learn my lines. I need to learn my lines tonight!" I'd promised Antony I'd be word perfect by Monday morning.

"We'd better get on then, hadn't we?" Then, without starting the engine Devlin took off the brake and began to freewheel down the long winding hill. I didn't scream, or close my eyes, or flinch, just sat close beside him staring straight ahead until at the bottom the engine caught and he went into the next uphill stretch as if it had been nothing out of the ordinary. He looked down at me and smiled, the bastard, and I knew he'd meant it all along, just like bloody Shaw, meant it for a metaphor.

10

Carmichael left Jacobson and his men to organize the search for the Greens and headed towards the Yard. It was past noon, and he wanted to know if Peter Marshall had turned up at his ship. "No point in you waiting about, sergeant," he said to Royston as they drove down Great Russell Street. "I'm going to call my way through Gilmore's address book. I'll probably be all afternoon. You go back to her house and collect all her papers and have them brought here."

"Everything?" Royston confirmed. "Right, sir. I'll get on with it."

"Keep the car, it'll make it easier for ferrying them about," Carmichael said.

Royston raised an eyebrow at the irregularity. "Are you sure, sir?"

"Oh for heaven's sake, Royston, it'll save no end of time, and it's Sunday, nobody's going to be checking whether I'm in the car every moment. Regulations ought to let sergeants have the use of a car if they need it."

"Yes, sir," Royston said, dubiously, pulling up outside the deco monstrosity on High Holborn that was New

New Scotland Yard. Carmichael climbed out and waved him away.

There were no messages waiting so he went to his office and called the Portsmouth number. It seemed there was still no sign of Marshall, and Captain Beddow agreed to send someone up to London to attempt identification.

"Who was Marshall's best friend?" he asked.

"That would be Nash," Beddow replied. "But Nash is off on leave. He was also chummy with young Tambourne, who's here on duty. I'll send him up to London on the next train."

Carmichael confirmed train times and arranged to have Tambourne met at Waterloo at five-thirty and brought to the Yard. Then he called Hampstead and left a message for Jacobson there.

He sent the bombing leaflet through for identification and analysis. He asked the Sunday desk sergeant to see if the Yard could identify the ownership of the red Austin they suspected of being Marshall's. He asked for information and any records on Gilmore, Marshall, Gilmore's servants, and Antony Bannon. Then he couldn't put it off any longer. He pushed aside the piles of paper covering his desk sufficiently to clear a space large enough for a fresh legal pad of paper and Lauria Gilmore's address book and appointment diary. He proceeded to stare at them for a few moments, before opening the address book and picking up the phone.

By the time Royston came back with the papers he had reached *D*. Many of Gilmore's friends, including Antony Bannon, seemed to be away from their telephones on this beautiful Sunday afternoon. The rest seemed to be the theatrical mix he had been expecting, and only too glad to make appointments to see Inspector Carmichael in the coming week.

"Go to Waterloo for the five-thirty from Portsmouth, Royston, and pick up a young naval lieutenant called Tambourne. Come back here to collect me, and we'll all go and look at Marshall's body."

"At five-thirty?" Royston said, only the slightest hint of being hard done by in his voice.

Carmichael sighed. "I know it's working late, and on a Sunday, and I suppose I could have someone else do it, but even though I'm not expecting much joy out of the identification from what Jacobson was saying, I want to talk to Tambourne and find out what I can about Marshall. We'll probably need to go down to Portsmouth and talk to all his friends at some point. I can get someone else to go with me if you're in a hurry to get off."

"I am expected at home," Royston said. "But if it's all right with you, sir, I could pop round there now and tell Elvira what's up so she's not waiting for me, and then get back to Waterloo in plenty of time for five-thirty."

"You do that, Royston."

He was a good man, Carmichael thought, as Royston went. He shouldn't keep holding it against him that he had betrayed Carmichael to Penn-Barkis over the Thirkie case. In most ways, it was a shame Royston couldn't be promoted past his present position. He was as intelligent as any of the officers in the Yard, and had better police instincts than most of them. Impossible to contemplate, of course. Royston betrayed his social origins in every word he spoke.

Carmichael picked up the telephone and settled down to it once more.

At *M,* the desk sergeant came back with a positive identification of the Austin as belonging to Lieutenant Peter Marshall of Portsmouth. Carmichael thanked him, and went on. Nash, Robert, was listed under *N,* with the same Portsmouth number as Marshall. Tambourne's identification seemed to be very much a formality. Where was Nash on leave, he wondered, and where had he been on Saturday morning? He made a note.

He had reached *R* and filled up much of his week when Royston next put his head around the door.

"I've got Tambourne in the car," he said.

"I'll just get my hat, sergeant." Carmichael stood and

stretched. "Oh, and you were right, the car's Marshall's," he added.

"Makes this identification bit of a waste of time, doesn't it?" Royston said.

"I want to know why Marshall and Gilmore would build a bomb," Carmichael said. "This Lieutenant Tambourne might be able to help there. What's he like anyway?"

"Young," Royston said. "Tall."

Lieutenant Tambourne was a long-legged young man in naval blues who seemed to fill most of the backseat of the police Bentley. "I don't know why they sent me, I suppose I was the one Old Bed thought he could best spare," he confessed frankly.

"Captain Beddow said you were a friend of Marshall's," Carmichael said, twisting his neck to look at the young man as Royston drove them to the mortuary.

"Well we messed together," Tambourne said, dubiously. "Don't know that I'd say I was his friend."

"Who were his friends?"

"Well, he and Nash were thick as thieves. Apart from that, well, he was a matey fellow, on good terms with everyone, everyone will miss him, but he didn't have any other particular pals. I suppose Old B— I mean Captain Beddow must have thought we were friends because he and I used to play tennis together sometimes. The *Valiant*'s a training ship, you know, pretty much permanently at Portsmouth, and we have our own courts there. Marshall was very keen, but Nash doesn't play at all. He found out one day from something I said in the mess that I play a bit and nothing would do for him than to get up a game. Then we used to play any day it wasn't raining and neither of us was working. I wasn't in his class, he always beat me, but I could make him run sometimes, and he liked that." Tambourne pushed back a lick of hair that was falling into his eyes, in what was clearly a habitual gesture.

"What sort of person was he?" Carmichael asked.

"Open, friendly . . . good at tennis . . ." Tambourne didn't seem to understand what he was being asked.

"You're doing your National Service, aren't you?" Carmichael asked, to put him at ease.

"Yes, and in September I'm done with it and I'm off to Oxford, and I can't say I'll miss it."

"Marshall was career Navy though?"

"Oh yes. And his father and grandfather before him, I remember him saying. He was frightfully Hearts of Oak and all that. A little bit intimidating for some of the fellows. There was another National Service lieutenant who was just counting the days and couldn't get on with him at all. They used to have rows about, well, whether National Service was necessary for everyone, and whether Britain really needed a navy. But then the other man, Phelps, had funny notions. He'd been to some little school—" He shrugged apologetically.

"You were at Eton?" Carmichael suggested.

"Harrow," Tambourne said, apologetically.

Carmichael smiled, thinly. He himself had been at "some little school" so insignificant that it barely counted as a public school at all. "And Lieutenant Marshall?"

"Oh, he was at Eton right enough," Tambourne said cheerfully.

"What were his politics?" Carmichael asked.

Tambourne frowned. "You're not supposed to have politics in the Navy," he said. "And Marshall was career Navy. But as I was saying he was for King and Country all down the line. Always saying the country was going to the dogs, but for people like Marshall, it always is going to the dogs and at the same time worth laying your life on the line for. Not a cynic, if you know what I mean, not him and not Nash either."

Royston braked; they were at the mortuary.

Tambourne, when he unfolded himself from the car, proved to be even taller than he had looked, well over six feet. "How do they fit you in a ship, Lieutenant?" Royston asked.

Tambourne laughed. "Better than they could in an aeroplane at any rate. They wouldn't have me in the RAF. Look, can I ask you what's the procedure here? I've never done any of this before."

"We'll go with you to the room where the body we believe to be Peter Marshall's is being stored," Carmichael said. "Then you will either make the identification or fail to be able to make it. If you feel you can formally identify the body as that of Marshall, there'll be a statement for you to sign to that effect."

"So it's quite a quick business?" Carmichael nodded reassuringly. "And then what?"

Carmichael was surprised by the question. "Well, I may want to ask you a few more things, and then you'll be free to go."

"Do I need to go back to Portsmouth tonight? I brought a bag, because we didn't know how long it would take. I could have a whole evening and night in London and go up in the morning."

"That's between you and your commanding officer, but I'm certainly not about to tell him precisely how long the identification procedure took," Carmichael said.

"Thanks!"

There was a little garden beside the police mortuary, with a stone bench in it surrounded at this season by regimented rows of primulas and a little square of grass in need of cutting. Carmichael indicated the bench. "Let's sit down for a few minutes and get the questions over with first, and then you can head off as soon as we're done inside."

Tambourne obligingly sat on the bench, sticking his long legs out in front of him. Royston took out his notebook and began scribbling, no doubt setting down what he remembered of what had been said in the car.

The cold of the stone crept through Carmichael's trousers, despite the warmth of the early evening sun. "Did you know that Marshall knew Lauria Gilmore?" Carmichael began.

"Yes, actually. He knew her son during the war, they were on the same ship. He told me once when the subject of theater came up." Royston and Carmichael exchanged a look. Kinnerson again. "Her son introduced them during or immediately after the war, and they became friends. He always went to her plays. I knew he and Nash both used to see her sometimes in London." Tambourne smiled agreeably.

"Is Nash Eton too?"

"Oh yes." It seemed to strike Tambourne for the first time. "Nash is going to be absolutely gutted when he hears. They've been together since they were thirteen. They were like David and Jonathan."

"Someone should break it gently to Nash," Carmichael said. "Do you know where he is on leave?"

Tambourne shook his head. "Old Bed will know," he said. "Poor old Nash."

"And what was Marshall's job, on the ship?" Carmichael asked.

"Training. *Valiant*'s a training ship. Taking in raw recruits and turning out sailors, you know the drill." Tambourne was staring off into the distance.

"And was he good at it?"

He looked at Carmichael again. "Extremely good at it. All the men got on with him, and they always enjoyed his course."

"What exactly did he teach them?" Carmichael asked, patiently.

"Use of small craft. A surprising number of people don't know how to use a little boat to go out to the ship, or back to the dock. He'd teach the whole thing, rowing, small-scale sailing, knot-tying, inflating inflatables. Everyone enjoyed it. I enjoyed it myself when I took the course."

"Nothing to do with explosives?"

"Nothing at all." Tambourne seemed to understand the question after he'd answered it. "You think he had something to do with the bomb that blew him up? Because he wouldn't know anything about that, and even more he wouldn't do anything like that. He was all straight down the line King and Country stuff, true blue."

"There's nothing you can think of that would make him resort to building a bomb?" Carmichael asked gently.

"Nothing in the world. He wasn't a Jew or a terrorist! Marshall, my God, the last man in the world. He must have got caught up in the blast by accident. If it is him. Maybe something else has happened to Marshall and this body is some bomber."

"That's what you're here to tell us," Carmichael said, and stood. "We may as well get on inside before I ask you anything else that might just be wasting everyone's time."

The staff were expecting them. "The male body in the Gilmore case," Royston said. "Possible identification."

"It's not—" The attendant hesitated.

"We're all grown men," Carmichael said, and followed him down the corridor.

The room was chilly, especially after the warmth outside. The attendant pulled out a drawer.

The corpse was naked, as usual, and very mangled indeed. The head and upper body were particularly bad. Tambourne blanched and swallowed hard, as Carmichael had expected. "I can't possibly tell, nobody could possibly—," he said, then stopped. "You know, it is Marshall," he said, and turned aside and retched.

Carmichael had vomited until there was nothing left in him, the first time he saw a dead body, in France, in 1940. Then he'd vomited again the first time he'd seen a man he knew killed next to him, strafed from a Stuka. But before they'd got away from Dunkirk he'd become hardened to it, and years of police work had only made dead bodies that much more familiar. He didn't like the sight, but he didn't feel nauseated, just terribly aware of what a waste it was. How many secrets had this mangled thing that used to be Marshall taken with him into death? How long would it take Carmichael to discover them? He shook his head and looked back at Tambourne. "How do you know?" he asked.

Tambourne wiped his face with his handkerchief. "It's his legs," he said, his voice unsteady. "Nobody could know him by his face, but I played tennis with those legs a couple of times a week for the last nine months. Poor Marshall. Damn. Damn me. What a horrible way to go."

11

Devlin stopped at a call box in a tiny village some-where and made a call, no doubt to Coltham. I didn't run away, I didn't even try. I sat in the car and watched a hen scratch at some larkspur at the side of the road by a red brick barn. The thought that I was alive to see it was quite exhilarating. I felt almost drunk on the way the sunshine showed up the blue of the larkspur and the brown feathers of the hen. Devlin got back in and kissed me. He grinned when I asked who he was call-ing. "Got to let Loy know where his precious car is," he said.

We reached London and my flat at about half-past six. I had to give Devlin directions for the last half a mile. He parked neatly between two other cars. "You get your things, whatever you need for the next two weeks, and come straight down to the car," he said. "Then we'll have dinner and go home."

It occurred to me at once that if I was inside on my own I could lock the door and telephone the police. But not only would that be breaking my word to Uncle Phil, I didn't quite believe that Devlin wouldn't get me anyway.

My only hope was for him to trust me, my only hope of anything, of life, of another two weeks. I still thought I'd find a way out of actually doing it, but I thought I might be able to think of a plan later, when I knew what their plan was. I didn't entirely believe I was going to go through with the whole thing; I was going part of the way with them, to fool them, because I wanted Devlin, because I was afraid. I couldn't risk him thinking he hadn't entirely convinced me.

"It will be much easier if you come in," I said.

He smiled. "I don't want your flatmates to see more than they have to." He'd got out of me on the way home who I lived with and all about them.

"What, you're planning to watch me and be invisible? Because you know I'll probably be working with both of them at the theater? Mollie's probably going to re-place Lauria as Gertrude, and Mrs. Tring is my dresser. It'll seem much more normal if you come up, and I in-troduce you, and it'll also save me from having to ex-plain quite as much as I would if you don't. They won't believe I have a boyfriend if they never see you."

Devlin looked at me for a moment, and then shrugged. "If that's how you want it," he said.

"I won't say I'm staying with you until opening night," I said. "I'll just say for tonight, and then sort of let it extend. That'll be much easier."

"You know how to tell your own lies," Devlin said, amiably enough. "Is Loy's car safe out here?"

It wasn't of course. "We won't be long," I said, and opened the downstairs door with my key, then held it open for Devlin. He took it at once and let me go through first. I led the way up to the flat. I unlocked that door too, and called out that I was home.

Mollie came out of her room immediately. She was wearing her red butterfly dressing gown, which covered her from her neck to her ankles and made her look dramatic and oriental. "I've got the part!" she said.

And as easily as that I was back in the real world, the

world where the play was the most important thing and getting the part counted for everything. I hugged her. "Oh Mollie, that's wonderful," I said.

"I sobbed and sobbed for Antony," she said. Then she saw Devlin in the doorway. "Who's this?" she asked, frowning at me then glancing down at her dressing gown to make sure she was decent.

"This is Devlin Connelly," I said. "He very kindly ran me back to London. I'm going out for dinner with him. Come in properly, Devlin, and have a glass of wine or something while I get myself together. This is my flatmate Mollie Gaston."

"I saw you in *Dunkirk*," Devlin said, taking her hand. "I'm sure you'll make a beautiful Gertrude, but nobody will believe you're old enough to be Viola's mother."

"I'm going to have silver streaks and do older body language," Mollie said, but her eyes were on me, and she was still frowning. Well, it wasn't like me to turn up with strangers at odd hours. "Viola—"

"Where's Mrs. Tring?" I asked.

"It's Sunday night, she's gone to chapel," Mollie said. I should have thought that for myself.

"Do give Devlin a glass of wine while I duck into my room for a moment!" I said.

"Of course," Mollie said, and led Devlin off to the kitchen protesting that he didn't want anything and we were only stopping for a moment.

My script was already in my bag. I threw clothes and underwear and makeup and everything I thought I might need into a carpet bag. I knew I could ask Mollie or Mrs. Tring to bring anything I'd forgotten to the theater. I threw off the clothes I was wearing and put on my turquoise Parisian dress, the one that shows off my collarbones and which Mrs. Tring says is only barely respectable. I wanted to look nice for Devlin. I dug around in my underwear drawer and found my Dutch Cap, in its little box, and thrust that into my bag next to the script. I might live longer than the next two weeks, I might. I sprayed perfume everywhere, brushed my hair, pinned it back, and stuck one of Antony's pink roses into the pin. I looked at myself in the mirror. In *Buttered Toast* my cue had come at the end of a poem the young hero recited to Mollie as Lucinda. As he finished I came on as the maid, saying "Buttered toast?" and holding a plate of it out in front of me; it always got a huge laugh. But it was his lines that came into my head as I looked at myself in the mirror in my best dress, with the rose, and the Dutch Cap in my bag. "Though we cannot make our sun stand still, yet we will make him run!"

"Not more beautiful, that isn't possible, but beautiful for the evening," Devlin said, when I came into the kitchen. He was standing by the window, keeping an eye on the car. He looked relaxed and at ease. He had been busily charming Mollie, but Mollie wasn't entirely charmed. "We have to leave you alone for a moment, if you don't mind waiting, Mr. Connelly," she said, and dragged me into her room. So much for doing less explaining!

"What do you think you're doing?" she whispered as soon as the door was shut.

"What, you don't think he's gorgeous?" I asked.

"Charm of the Irish," she said, rolling her eyes. Mollie was part Irish herself, or so she sometimes said. "But this isn't like you! You never go out with men when you've got a part."

It was true. Men were for between-parts times, or when I was well into a successful run. I'd never normally start something new just when I was beginning to rehearse. "But look at him," I said, feebly enough, but it was all I had. "Don't worry. I'll be at the theater in the morning, word perfect."

"You'd better be, or I'm calling the police," she said. "Are you sure everything is all right?"

I thought about telling her. But what could she have done? She might even have approved—she'd certainly said now and then when she heard one of those stories about stone soap that she hated Hitler. Besides, Devlin could have easily killed us both if he thought we were a threat. "Everything's fine," I said. "Don't worry, Moll. I know what I'm doing. I'm pretty sure I won't be back tonight, we did some kissing in the car, but I've got my Cap."

"He's probably a Catholic," she said, direly.

He almost certainly was. "He needn't know I've got my Cap then," I said.

"There's something about him," she said, frowning. "Vi—"

"That's what I find so devastatingly attractive," I said. "I can look after myself."

She frowned, but stepped away from the door. I went out to Devlin.

As we went down to the car I realized that I was ridiculously overdressed for dinner, unless he changed too, and that meant going back to his place first. I hadn't thought about it, I'd only wanted to make myself look my best, or I might have wondered whether he had evening clothes, or if he did whether they might be at Coltham. "Am I overdressed?" I asked. "Because I can change again if so."

"I don't know what part you think you're dressing for," Devlin said, smiling. "I like what you have on, what there is of it. We're going to eat in a little Greek place I know in Whitechapel, and I don't suppose you have any clothes suitable for going there. Then we're going back to my place and you won't need any clothes at all."

There was something about the way he said this which made me—well, the conventional phrase is weak at the knees, but it wasn't my knees where I felt it. I got into the car and didn't even take the rose out of my hair. He drove through the light Sunday evening traffic to Whitechapel. He parked outside the glass window of a workmen's café. There were no women inside, and the men looked rough and unfriendly. I was horrified when

Devlin opened the door. "What will they think?" I whispered to him.

"They'll think you're slumming and you've picked me up," he said, quite casually. "They won't bother you, as long as you're with me."

It was strange how at home he managed to look anywhere he was. In Coltham, in the flat, and now here, he looked as if he fitted in. I didn't know if he'd brought me here to punish me for dressing up too much, or because he wanted to come here and liked the food and didn't think twice about what I was wearing. The food, when it came, was good, especially the lamb. They made good coffee too. I relaxed a little after a while when I saw nobody seemed to be giving me a second glance.

Afterwards we went back to his flat. He put Loy's car in a garage, which he then locked. The flat was on the ground floor of a boring modern cube put up where the older buildings had been bombed in the Blitz. The front door opened into a little hall with two doors off it, and the hall then opened out into a kitchen, and on the other side of the kitchen a tiny bathroom. It was all neat and clean but rather anonymous, clearly let furnished. Devlin hadn't made much mark on it. I wondered how long he had been living here. I already knew better than to ask.

Devlin opened the door on the left, which was a bedroom with a large bed. We went in, and Devlin carefully took all my clothes off and stroked me between my legs until I was almost howling with frustration then whispered in my ear that I ought to learn my lines. I actually did get my script out and tried to work on it, but he wouldn't stop touching me. I rolled onto my stomach, but he kept teasing me, stroking my neck and my arms, and eventually I swore that I knew the part all through already, which was nothing like true, but I thought there would be time for learning lines later, or early the next morning. So Devlin patiently untangled the rose from my hair, took off his own clothes, and enthusiastically, for a very long time, made love to me. It's hard to say how it was different from the other experiences of sex in my life before. It wasn't just that he knew what he was doing, though he did, he made love with the same casual competence with which he did everything else. It wasn't just that he expected to take complete control, though he did. I think it may have been that he had no hesitation, no diffidence. He knew what he wanted, and that surety, that knowledge, was what I wanted too.

At some point in that long night, long after midnight, I whispered those lines of the poem that had been in my head, and he squeezed me affectionately and surprised me by reciting the whole thing, out of his head, in the dark. After that I slept for a little, then woke and we did it all again. When I got out of bed, naked, in the morning light, desperate for the bathroom and with my legs feeling as if they would hardly carry me, Devlin opened both eyes a crack. "I'd love a cup of tea," he said.

I padded naked into the kitchen, and saw the shape of a man sitting at the kitchen table. I screamed, then saw it was Loy, reading a newspaper, and screamed again. Loy looked up over the paper and smiled at me. Devlin came running out of the bedroom, stark naked, with a gun in his hand. He saw us both and started to laugh.

I ducked into the bathroom and locked the door and sat in there listening to the two of them howling with laughter. I didn't find it the slightest bit funny, and wouldn't have even in the Frenchest of farces. I wanted to slap both of them. Devlin knocked on the door after a little while. "Are you all right?" he asked. "It's only Loy, and he's sorry he startled you. Are you coming out? I could use the bathroom myself."

"No," I said, grumpily. I had a leisurely bath, and eventually I improvised a couple of towels into sufficient covering to get me back to the bedroom. When I came out the two men were sitting at the kitchen table drinking tea. I ignored them and stalked into the bedroom, slamming the door behind me.

After a few minutes, in which he must have used the bathroom, Devlin came in. "I can see it must have been a shock, but why are you so angry, love?"

That "love" didn't mean he loved me, or even necessarily that he liked me, it was just what he quite naturally called everyone. "You sent me out there naked, knowing he was there," I said.

"Loy has a key, he lives here too, sometimes, but I didn't know he was there," he said. "He told me he'd bring my car here and take his back, but he didn't say when. I had no idea he was there. In any case, I've told him he'll have to find himself somewhere else. Apart from anything else, it's safer."

I was busy pulling on the black slacks and jersey I always wore for rehearsals. There were always things I couldn't say to Devlin. I couldn't ask him if it was like taking me to the café the night before, because I didn't know if he'd done that on purpose. I didn't even really know if he wanted me, or if he was only with me because I was convenient and needed looking after. I sat on the edge of the bed and looked at him. He must have dressed while I was in the bathroom. He looked a little concerned. "How long has Loy been there?" I asked.

Devlin looked uncomfortable. "I didn't want to ask him," he said. "Not long, I'm sure."

It wouldn't have to be very long at all to make me feel my privacy was quite thoroughly compromised.

"We had some fun, didn't we, darling?" he said, coaxingly, holding out his hand for me to come to him as if I was a dog or something.

"Some fun" didn't come near what I'd felt about that night, but I couldn't say that, there wasn't any way to say it. If I loved him I hated him too, and we were caught up together in this bomb business and it was all too much for me, especially on so little sleep. I just wanted to lie down and howl and be comforted.

"Oh well," he said, dropping his hand. "Come out and eat some breakfast then, and I'll drive you to the theater. Didn't you say you had to be there by ten? It's ten past nine now."

"All right. But if he makes one joke —"

Devlin held up a hand. "Loy's Loy," he said; that absolute loyalty.

And that was that.

12

Carmichael stood in the lift clutching a pile of reports and counted the brass buttons. Button *B* would take him down to the basement, where the files sat in their cabinets in dusty splendor. Button *G* let him straight out again on the ground floor, where Sergeant Stebbings sat in his cabinet watching all exits and entrances. Buttons *1* and *2* would take him to the upper regions where his colleagues worked, each in their own little offices. Button *3* was forensics. The report on the bomb and the bodies were probably waiting for him there. But it was the unavoidable top button, *4,* that he had to press. It was said that New New Scotland Yard cast a long shadow, and even respectable people crossed High Holborn to avoid walking through it. It was Penn-Barkis's office at the top of the building that cast that shadow. Carmichael had never liked seeing the Chief, and since the time he had taken this lift up to be browbeaten into acquiescence with what was wrong, he had avoided him as much as possible. This morning, as soon as he came in, Stebbings had told him the Chief wanted to see him first thing, and waved him towards the lift.

There were other things he could do. Penn-Barkis might let him resign. He lived on his pay, but he had a small amount saved, enough for a month or two frugal living, and there were other jobs, even for a man who'd been Scotland Yard since he was demobbed at the end of the war. Penn-Barkis shouldn't scare him, particularly not this time. He had the feeling Penn-Barkis was going to like what he had on the Gilmore case. He wished he could feel pleased about that and not uncomfortable. He took a deep breath and pushed button *4.*

The sun streamed straight in to Penn-Barkis's office, gilding the golfing cups behind the mahogany desk. A few dust motes danced guiltily in the beams. London lay spread out and shining beneath the windows as if Penn-Barkis were God, able to reach out his finger in the path of malefactors. As Carmichael came out of the lift, Penn-Barkis turned from the windows and walked over to his desk.

"So, sit down and tell me about this Gilmore business," he said.

Carmichael sat in the chair indicated, on the other side of the desk, exactly where he had sat the last time Penn-Barkis had wanted to hear about a case. "It seems she was making the bomb."

"You're sure of that?"

"As sure as it's possible to be when all the evidence has been blown to bits. The sappers seem quite sure." Carmichael took Curry's report from his pile. "Here's the evidence if you want to look at it."

Penn-Barkis took the report and turned one of the pages, then handed it back. "Bomb-making's a tricky business, apparently. Surprising more terrorists don't blow themselves sky-high. Any hints as to why she was doing it?"

"Nothing sure yet," Carmichael said. "It seems she may have been a communist—left leaning anyway. Two of her servants, Jews, have disappeared. I spent most of yesterday trying to trace them, but I've had no luck. The man with her turned out not to be Kinnerson, who's safe home in Amersham, but a naval lieutenant called Marshall who, as far as anyone knew, was all for King and Country."

"You've been through her papers?"

"Yes, a first pass yesterday morning, though it needs doing again more thoroughly. My next step, unless you disagree, sir, is to get the papers here and put someone on to going through them, while I check out her associates and Marshall's associates in the hope of finding out what they intended to do with the bomb."

Penn-Barkis raised his eyebrows. "Not much danger of them doing it anymore," he said.

"No, but our Prime Minister keeps making speeches warning us against the dangers of terrorists. I seem to have found some genuine ones, and it strikes me as worth bothering finding out what they thought they were up to. Also, they may have been part of a wider conspiracy, in which case—"

"Yes, yes." Penn-Barkis cut him off. "Give a statement to the press telling them the truth, as sensibly constituted." That meant leaving out details the police wouldn't want the public to know. "Then get on with it. But try to clear it up as quickly as possible. Dead bombers ought to be good news, and they're certainly no trouble. Take a couple of days on the connections in case, take until the end of the week if you need it, but don't waste time."

"Sir," Carmichael said, standing. It did no good to protest that he never wasted time.

"And don't let Royston use police cars to go home in the middle of a Sunday afternoon. He shouldn't be able to charm you into it. You know it's against regulations."

"No, sir," Carmichael said. He looked down at his boots. He had been in the wrong about the car, but the idea that Royston had charmed him into it, that he was susceptible to being charmed, was just Penn-Barkis twisting the knife.

He felt unsteady as he went down in the lift. He couldn't go on like this. He would resign when this case was over. He would talk to Jack, tell Jack about it and together they would make a plan.

In his own office he worked on the statement for the press. He had had much practice in the arcane art of couching his sentences in the careful passive and attributing everything good to the agency of Scotland Yard. He was surprised when his telephone rang.

"Carmichael," he said.

It was Sergeant Stebbings. "I thought you were in," he said. "There's a Mr. Kinnerson on the line for you."

"Put him through, please, sergeant." Carmichael took a fresh sheet of paper and wondered what Kinnerson wanted.

"Any news on my mother's death, Inspector?" Kinnerson asked.

"In fact we have made some progress," Carmichael said. He hesitated for a moment and then decided Kinnerson was entitled to hear what he was about to tell the press, but he would prefer to see his face when he heard. He didn't think he was involved, but he knew he had been keeping something back. "I would like to speak to you about it. Can you spare me an hour today?"

"As a matter of fact I have something I wanted to tell you too," Kinnerson said. "Lunch at my club?"

"What club is that?" Carmichael asked, astonished that Kinnerson would suggest anything so friendly. Asking him to lunch at his club indicated that Kinnerson saw him as a social equal. That wasn't at all how he had acted on Friday night.

"The Gresham," Kinnerson said.

The bankers' club, just what he would have expected. The food would be terrible, club food always was, but Carmichael certainly wasn't going to suggest anything else. "At noon then?" Carmichael asked.

"Certainly, Inspector. I'll look forward to seeing you."

Carmichael put the receiver down and sighed as he went back to his press release.

The Gresham was in the heart of the old City of London, the square mile of banking and finance that lay in the warren of tiny streets around St. Paul's Cathedral. It was squeezed between two banks on Pudding Lane, where the Great Fire of London was said to have started. The facade was Victorian, and so was the decor; heavy dark paneling, heavy leather-covered furniture, dark portraits in oils of lord mayors and pudgy aldermen. Carmichael gave his name and Kinnerson's to a gloomy clerk who took his hat and led him to the dining room.

Carmichael hated clubs. He belonged to one himself only for the convenience of having somewhere to collect his mail and meet people. At least his club, the Hamelin, was a little lighter in atmosphere and had younger members. Most of the members of the Gresham on show in the dining room seemed old enough to be stuffed and put in glass cases. Carmichael was not late, but Kinnerson was there before him. He rose as Carmichael reached the table. In these surroundings, Kinnerson looked less in control of the situation than he had in his home.

"I wanted to say again first how sorry I am about the misunderstanding on Friday evening," Carmichael said, as they both seated themselves. "I hope Mrs. Kinnerson has recovered from her distress?"

"She's still relieved I'm alive," Kinnerson said. "But let's not talk polite nonsense, Inspector Carmichael, we're both sensible men. Let's order and get that out of the way."

The waiter, a young man of typically Jewish looks, bowed at Kinnerson's elbow. "Brown Windsor soup or mulligatawny, fish or beef, apple pie," he rattled off.

"I'll take the Windsor soup and the fish," Kinnerson said. "And a half-bottle of Montrachet, I think, as we both have work to do this afternoon."

Carmichael nodded at the wine, and did his best to smile as he ordered the same. The Montrachet came immediately and the waiter poured and waited for them to sip. It was adequately chilled, and tart on the tongue. He set the bottle down on the table—1946, a good year. The label was written in cursive French on the left and angular German on the right.

"You had something to tell me about my mother's death, I believe?" Kinnerson said, as the waiter withdrew.

"Did you know your mother's friend Peter Marshall?" Carmichael asked.

"No." Kinnerson sounded very sure, and very sincere.

Carmichael supposed Tambourne could have been wrong, but tried again. "Lieutenant Peter Marshall?"

Kinnerson's eyes widened. "In that case I do know him, though I haven't seen him for years and wouldn't have thought of him as my mother's friend. Marshall and I were in the Navy together."

"When did you last see him?"

"I don't know." Kinnerson seemed perplexed. "He was at my wedding. I think I've had lunch with him a couple of times since then, here as a matter of fact. I send him Christmas cards. But the last time I saw him would be at least two years ago."

"You didn't know he was a friend of your mother's?" Carmichael took another sip of his wine.

"Now you mention it, I think she did mention now and then that she'd seen him, that he went to her first nights, that sort of thing. He and Nash were much more interested in theater than I was."

"Well, it seems he had lunch with her from time to time when he was in London, and he was with her on Saturday morning and the two of them were attempting to build a bomb, which subsequently killed them both."

Kinnerson's face gave nothing away. He took a large swallow of his Montrachet. "If I could have chosen, I'd

have had her die at the end of a performance as Cleopatra at the age of ninety, but I suppose blowing herself up
in an act of misguided idealism is much more like her
than being killed by someone else would be," he said.

"You don't seem very surprised," Carmichael said.

Kinnerson shrugged. "The idea had occurred to me
over the weekend. I've been thinking about it, and it
seemed the most likely thing. Not terribly likely, you
understand, but more likely than the other, if it wasn't
a complete accident."

"Have you any idea why your mother and your friend
would be building a bomb?"

"Presumably someone persuaded them it was a good
idea." Kinnerson shook his napkin onto his lap as the
waiter brought their soup.

"But who would have been their intended target?"

"I haven't the faintest idea. It's the wrong time of
year for Guy Fawkes, but perhaps the Houses of Parliament?" Kinnerson looked at him directly. "She wasn't
an especially sensible woman, you understand. And I
told you about her politics. Perhaps she heard the Prime
Minister talk about anarchists and bombs and decided
her politics were anarchist so she should take action."

Carmichael tasted his soup. It was even worse than he
had expected, and not very warm. "And Marshall? Was
he an anarchist?"

"Not when I knew him," Kinnerson said.

"You do sound remarkably unsurprised."

"That's not a crime, is it, Inspector?" Kinnerson's
eyes met his, still cool.

"Not a crime, but very unusual," Carmichael said.

"I didn't know anything about it in advance, I can assure you of that." For the first time, Kinnerson looked
uncomfortable. "You do believe me?"

Carmichael did, but he wasn't about to say so. In any
case, it wasn't what he believed that mattered. It wasn't
even what was true that mattered. He spooned up his
soup and changed the subject. "You mentioned politicians

she liked, Mr. MacDonald and Mr. Bevan; were there others she didn't like?"

Kinnerson grimaced. "Mr. Normanby. She loathed the whole Farthing Set if you want to know. She thought they tried to keep people down. That was her big thing, the idea that everyone should have chances, whoever they were. I can imagine her thinking she was Boedicea, if you can believe that."

"Were these thoughts what you wanted to tell me?" Carmichael asked.

"No. No, what I wanted to tell you wasn't about my mother at all. I'm not sure if you're the right person to tell, but you're the only person I know who might know who to pass it on to." Kinnerson pushed away his soup bowl.

"Go on?" Carmichael invited, neutrally.

"You know I work at Solomon Kahn," Kinnerson began.

Carmichael nodded. The waiter came and removed their soup, and deftly replaced it with plates of limp sole and gray mashed potatoes.

"I know this confidentially, but I feel someone ought to know. Mr. Kahn is moving large quantities of money out of the country. It isn't illegal, as far as I know— banks can do what they like with their money—but it does seem suspicious, especially when there's so much talk of Jewish conspiracies." Kinnerson looked at Carmichael and then away.

Carmichael was surprised. He also knew nothing about the state of the law on such things. It wasn't a matter for Scotland Yard. "How much money?" David Kahn, he remembered, had given money to an organization that smuggled Jews out of Nazi Europe.

"Hundreds of thousands of pounds," Kinnerson said. "Perhaps millions. Of course, we move money around all the time, but never so much, so fast."

"Where's it going? The Continent? The States?"

Kinnerson laughed. "You couldn't get it into either place—well, *you* could, but Solomon Kahn couldn't.

They won't take Jewish money, either place. Also, it would be subject to review. This is all going to Canada, which doesn't get any review, because it's part of the Commonwealth, so it's all under Imperial Preference, just the same as if it was going to another bank in England."

"And he's moved all that there this morning?" Carmichael couldn't see that it had anything to do with anything, but the sheer amount of the money made it interesting.

"Over the last two weeks," Kinnerson corrected him. "Since . . . I've noticed the amounts going, and today I decided to say something."

Over the last two weeks, Carmichael thought, then realized. Since Normanby came to power. Since Kahn's son had hidden or fled. "You think Kahn may be planning to move his bank to Canada?"

Kinnerson relaxed a little. "Either that or he's moving a lot of money out of the country ahead of a lot of customers. Or after them, if they're there already."

Were David and Lucy Kahn in Canada? Carmichael hoped they were. He hoped old Kahn would join them safely, and all the money as well. It wasn't illegal. He wasn't going to tell anyone. He wondered why Kinnerson had told him. Kinnerson had called him, wanting to tell him. He took a forkful of tepid over-cooked sole and studied the man across the table.

Kinnerson was a successful man, a man who had been to public school and in the Navy, a man who could afford to buy a house for his actress mother, but not a rich man, a man who needed to work for a living. Carmichael remembered the house, the nervous little wife. "He works for the Jews!" she had said. Had he suffered for working for the Jews? Would he have done it if there had been plenty of choice of jobs? Did Solomon Kahn pay better to attract men like Kinnerson? "Are you looking for a new job, Mr. Kinnerson?" Carmichael asked.

Kinnerson started. "I think I will be."

"You think Solomon Kahn is going to Canada and leaving you behind?"

"I'll find another position," Kinnerson said, confidently. "What's important now that my mother has done something foolish is to establish my good faith."

He held Carmichael's eyes a moment, and Carmichael was surprised to see that the confidence that was Kinnerson's natural state was assumed, that underneath the man was badly frightened. "Your good faith," he repeated.

"With you, Inspector," Kinnerson said, and gave an awkward little laugh.

Carmichael put it together. Kinnerson had guessed that his mother might have been building a bomb, and realized that he would look suspicious, and doubly suspicious because of his job, his association with the Jews. So he was selling out his employers in the hope of making himself seem trustworthy. That was why he had come to Carmichael instead of whatever the proper regulatory body was. Carmichael had no idea, but he was sure Kinnerson did. He didn't care about the money, and he could get another job, but he wanted to establish his good faith with Carmichael.

"You do believe me?" he asked.

"People like you usually treat the police like servants," Carmichael said.

"People like me aren't usually in this position," Kinnerson said. "I—my mother. My job. I do, in my job, sometimes have information in which a man who has a little money can make a little more money."

Carmichael felt sick suddenly and put down his fork. "This is not Nazi Europe," he said. "The innocent have nothing to fear from the British police. There's no need to bribe me with information or with money."

"You're saying what I'm sure you wish were true, Inspector," Kinnerson said. "And I am in fact innocent. But these days it seems safer to be sure."

13

Take a look at the theater," Devlin said as he pulled up on the Strand by the front-of-house entrance to the Siddons. The theater was dark, of course, as the last play had closed and we hadn't opened yet. "What it's like to get in and out of, where the exits and entrances are, where the boxes are, what the security's like, that sort of thing."

I looked at him blankly. "I don't know anything about that kind of thing."

"You can find out where all the doors are though," Devlin said. "On the day there'll be much more secu- rity, bound to be, so it might be as well to get the thing in well in advance, if there's somewhere to stash it."

"I'll do my best," I said. This morning I was ab- solutely sure I was just stringing them along, there was no way I was going to go through with it.

"That's my good girl," Devlin said, and leaned over to give me a kiss. "When are you going to get out?"

"I have no idea," I said, and I didn't. "First rehearsal can take any amount of time. With Antony—well, I don't suppose I'll be out of here before five at the earliest. I'll call you."

"No you won't," he said. "The fewer calls the better. I'll wait here from five on and pick you up."

"But it might be hours," I said. "And surely waiting here will be even more conspicuous." He'd driven me in his own car, a relatively ordinary Hillman, not Loy's flashy toy, but even that would be noticed waiting on the Strand for hours.

"I'll do it tonight. Just you try to find out what time rehearsals are going to be over normally," was all he said.

I kissed him good-bye and walked down the alley to the stage door. The doorman recognized me, and let me in without me needing to give my name. I smiled and tipped him. It's always good to keep such people sweet.

I had the star dressing room, which had my name on already. Mollie's room was next to mine. She was there already; she put her head out as I came by and offered me a cigarette. "Antony says Mrs. Tring can dress us both, if that's all right with you."

I remembered sharing dressing rooms with Mollie, when we were on tour. "That's perfect," I said, taking a light from her. "Are the costumes going to be complicated, did he say?"

"Elizabethan," she said. "Lots of changes for me, I don't know about you. And how are you this morning? You look exhausted."

"Like the cat who got the cream," I said, because it was all I could say. I gave her a smile; not a real smile, a theater smile. "He's meeting me after rehearsal. He's smitten."

"You're the one who's smitten," she said, accurately enough. "He's rich, I take it, with a car like that? What does he do?"

I had no idea what Devlin did, besides building bombs. "I haven't asked him," I said. "He wasn't rushing off anywhere this morning, he drove me to the theater."

"Idle rich," Mollie said, dropping her cigarette end and grinding it with her heel. "Well, I wish you joy of him, though he isn't at all your usual type."

"What is my usual type?" I asked.

"Oh, the useless type. Pals you kid yourself you're in love with, but who you easily detach yourself from when you're sick of them."

"Devlin isn't at all like that," I said, thinking of him.

"You watch out for him," she said. "I've never seen you this taken about a man, and never when you've got a part."

I stubbed out my own cigarette. "That reminds me, I need to go over my lines before Antony calls us up."

She rolled her eyes at me and went back into her dressing room.

I had about ten minutes' concentrated memorization, then Antony called everyone on stage.

That first rehearsal was bloody. I was nervous because I was tired and knew I didn't know my lines properly. Charlie kept fooling around, making jokes and trying to corpse everyone. Tim Curtis, who was a dear old queer, about ninety years old, and our Polonius, didn't take well to this at all. Antony had actually done something rather clever, and got Pat McKnight for Ophelia. The thing about Pat is that he looks rather like Charlie, only fair where Charlie's dark, and Antony's idea was that they'd have their hair done the same, and so would Tim, to bring out their being family. He also wanted Mollie and me to have our hair the same—different from the boys, but the same as each other—and our clothes were apparently going to echo too.

"Your clothes will be a kind of virginal echo of Mollie's," Antony said, addressing me but looking past me to the wardrobe mistress, who would make the clothes, or have them made. "More restrained colors, higher necks, that kind of thing."

As we only had two weeks, we were rehearsing on the stage from the start, though without any props, clothes, or scenery at first. Antony, naturally, wanted to do a cold run-through first, but before that he wanted to talk to everyone and arrange rehearsal schedules—because there's no point in having everyone at every rehearsal, though I would have to be at most of them. I told him I'd make any rehearsal he wanted, but it would be really useful if I knew in advance when I'd be able to get away. Antony isn't a total slave driver, and I think Mollie may have told him I had a new boyfriend, because he was quite reasonable about giving me a schedule and saying he wouldn't change it without warning.

Then he introduced us to Bettina, the wardrobe mistress, and the ASM and the stagehands, and then he said he wanted to talk to everyone individually about their characters. I boned up on my lines as best I could, during this, though he kept calling me over so I could "bond" with Charlie and Pat, and then with Doug James, who was Horatio.

I told Doug about my idea about Hamlet getting a Ph.D. and teaching and not wanting to go home, and he asked whether, in that case, I saw Horatio as a colleague or a pupil, and it struck me that there was something about their relationship where perhaps Horatio had been a pupil and was now nominally an equal but still used to deferring. Doug liked this a lot, and we went through some of our exchanges quickly.

"It especially makes sense with her being a woman," he said. "Because if she'd taught him, it would have reversed the usual male/female dynamic, she'd have been in charge, and even if, as Antony says, he wishes to be more than a friend, that would have been a reason for not speaking out."

"And yet the suppressed romantic thing is a reason for him coming home with her, when she heard that her father has died," I said. "He doesn't want to leave her."

"I'm so glad Antony decided on you and not Pam Brown, as he thought at first," Doug said.

So much for the only woman Antony could picture as

Hamlet, I thought. "It's lovely to be acting with you, too," I said.

"What do you think their subject was, at Wittenberg?" Doug asked.

"I hadn't thought."

"Well, I wonder if it might have been—well Horatio's at any rate, and Hamlet's too if she was teaching him—philosophy. If in the 'more things in Heaven and Earth' thing he meant to say our Philosophy, our subject of philosophy, if you see what I mean, rather than just Horatio's own personal philosophy."

"Oh I like that," I said. "It gives it extra meaning. I wonder if I could be reading some philosophy in the words scene. Who's a prominent philosopher I could be reading?"

"Plato?" Doug suggested.

"I'll ask Antony."

Antony was at that moment engaged with the Players, who would mostly rehearse alone after today and until the first full rehearsal, which was set for the following Wednesday afternoon. I stood at the front of the stage and looked out at the house.

The Siddons was a typical old London theater, a semicircle of seats facing a proscenium arch of stage. There was gilded scrolling, a little in need of upkeep, and the fronts of the circles and boxes were set with plaster cupids, and tragic and comic theatrical masks. The Royal Box, where presumably our potential victims would sit, was on my right as I looked up at it. It had a shield with the three gilded leopards. I couldn't see anywhere immediately appropriate to put a bomb. The best place would presumably be inside the box itself, though what reason anyone might have for going there was beyond me.

It was strange how at one moment I could be completely absorbed in the play, excited about a better understanding of my character and of Horatio, and at the next remember that there would be no play, that if I did what Devlin wanted, I would destroy it myself. Being in the theater it was easy to be entirely swept up in the play's reality, as being with Devlin I became swept up in his reality. For Devlin the most important thing in the world was killing the tyrants. For Antony and the others, the most important thing in the world was putting on *Hamlet*. Poor Hamlet couldn't decide whether or not to take the word of a ghost and kill her uncle, and she had my complete sympathy.

I did think, for a moment at the front of the stage, waiting for Antony, that I could walk out now. Devlin wouldn't be waiting for me. I could go home, get my passport, and be in France by the time Devlin came back to the theater. I needn't break my word or tell anyone anything, I could just disappear. But what could I do in France? The Reich had no need of English actresses. I couldn't imagine what I could possibly do there.

Then Antony was free, and he agreed that my book should be Plato and made a note of that and the way to play the philosophy line. He then began the walk-through.

I managed most of my lines, with only a little prompting. I wasn't the only one who didn't know them. We were all terrible, as you'd expect. Mollie, with much more excuse for not knowing her lines, was word perfect, but her conception of how she wanted to play Gertrude and Antony's weren't entirely congruent. As Antony was playing Claudius as well as directing, this meant that their scenes were being constantly interrupted. We stumbled and stammered our way to the end of the play, taking about six hours to get through what we hoped would come in under three on the night. Charlie corpsed both me and Mollie in the fight scene, to Antony's great annoyance. It was well after six when we finished.

"Well, I've seen worse first rehearsals," Antony said, picking himself up at the end. "But I don't know when," he added. "We've got less than two weeks to get this mess into shape. We've got eleven days before the dress rehearsal, twelve days before the first night. Pick up your schedules from Jackie, she'll have them ready for you, for God's sake learn your lines"—this with a glance at me—"and get back here tomorrow ready to give all of yourselves to it."

Jackie, his long-suffering assistant, came up out of the pit and handed round the schedules. She'd found time somehow, between dealing with Antony's tantrums and writing down his instructions, to get them typed up. I stuffed mine into my bag. I was aching with tiredness. Hamlet is an extremely physically demanding role, and we'd repeated the swordfight several times, for the blocking.

"Are you sure it wouldn't be better to come home and get some sleep?" Mollie murmured.

If it had been up to me, I wouldn't have hesitated. Wonderful as Devlin was, I'd have traded him right then for a bath, one of Mrs. Tring's dinners, my own bed, and the chance to go over my lines. As it was I had no choice. "He'll be waiting for me," I said.

Mollie shook her head and went off. I collected my bag from my dressing room and waited a moment before following her.

The doorman smiled and opened the door for me.

"Is this the only exit from this theater, apart from the front-of-house?" I asked.

He blinked at me. "Well, there's the back entrance, like, which we use for bringing in big things on a dolly—flats sometimes, or pieces of scenery that get built elsewhere that are too big for a normal door. It's always kept double-locked when it's not in use. Don't you worry that anyone will be getting in to bother you in your changing room, miss."

"Oh, thank you," I said. "I know it's silly but I always do worry and want to make sure."

"It's double-locked, and nobody has the keys except Nobby and me." Nobby was the stage manager.

"That sounds safe enough," I said, and thought that while he believed I was worried about people getting into my dressing room I'd keep on with it. "And there aren't any unusual ways of getting around behind from front-of-house, are there?"

"Just the usual pass door or up the steps onto the stage, when the steps are there, miss. And front-of-house is locked, usually, and when it's open before a performance there's always a doorman there too."

"Thank you so much for reassuring me," I said, and tipped him again. I walked up the alley to where I could see that Devlin was waiting.

"Your friend Mollie told me to let you get some sleep tonight," he said. He was smiling.

I was mortified. "She is a bit overprotective," I said.

"Well, maybe I will and maybe I won't. It all depends. Can you cook?"

"I can't cook at all," I admitted. I never had any chance to learn when I was young, and Mrs. Tring did all the cooking for me and Mollie.

"Then you'll have to clean up after my cooking," he said, and drove off without another word.

14

Carmichael realized as soon as he came through the door that it was a bad time to try to talk to Jack. The trouble was that it was always a bad time. Oh, they had their good times, the times when the flat felt like a magical haven of calm in a turbulent world, the times when Jack got up to make his breakfast, when they shared a pot of special tea, when Carmichael felt blessed with his luck and didn't want to take risks with it. Then there were the other times, when Jack was restless, jealous, when he accused Carmichael of treating him like a servant, which strictly he was. There was nobody as sympathetic as Jack on a good day, and nobody as self-centered as him on a bad one.

Jack came out of the kitchen as Carmichael turned his key in the lock, and it was immediately obvious from his face that this wasn't one of the good times.

"I need to talk to you," Carmichael said, hanging up his coat and hat.

"And I need to talk to you," Jack echoed. "Can't we go out? We never go out. Can't we go out to eat and then go dancing? You're always away, or working late, or if you're here you're tired out."

This was a very familiar complaint, and no easier to take because it happened to be true. The real trouble was that Jack was starved of excitement. He went nowhere and saw nobody. An occasional meal in a restaurant, with Carmichael constantly worrying that they would be recognized; an occasional dance in a dance hall, shuffling around the floor with tired tarts paid sixpence for the privilege; an even more occasional party with Jack's friends, who Carmichael loathed; or a trip to the theater or cinema—these had been the highlights of Jack's life for the last eight years, since the end of the war, since he and Carmichael had set up house together. Carmichael's work brought him as much excitement and stimulation as he wanted. When he came home he wanted to relax. Only too often, Jack had spent a boring day at home and wanted some fun.

"Not tonight. I need to talk to you."

"We could talk in a restaurant," Jack said, putting his head on Carmichael's shoulder.

"I eat in too many restaurants as it is," Carmichael said, ruffling Jack's hair. "When I come home, I want your cooking."

"I don't know why you don't get married if what you want is home-cooked meals all the time," Jack said.

"I don't get married because I don't like women and I do love you," Carmichael said, evenly. This too was a familiar argument. He knew Jack's lines as well as his own. "Never mind the food, come and sit down. I want to talk about something different."

Jack followed him into the room they called the lounge. There was a divan and a coffee table and a cabinet with a large radiogram and a tiny television set Jack had coaxed Carmichael into buying a year ago for more than they could afford. On the coffee table was a tray with glasses and a bottle of Haig. Without waiting, Jack poured two small pegs and handed one to Carmichael. Then he perched on the other end of the divan.

Carmichael took a sip of the whisky. He would have preferred a cup of tea and some dinner, but he didn't want to press the issue. He fixed his eyes on the little pile of Jack's books on the coffee table. The *Alexiad* of Anna Comnena was on the top, and underneath it three hefty books with the word *Byzantine* or *Byzantium* in their titles. It was Jack's latest enthusiasm. "How would it be if I left the Yard?" he asked.

Jack took down half his peg in one swallow. "And did what?" he asked.

"I don't know," Carmichael said. "Something else. Something where I wouldn't constantly feel I was being forced into an impossible position."

"But you love your job!" Jack leaned forward. He was twenty-eight, but there was still something boyish in the way his sandy hair fell across his forehead.

"I used to." Carmichael sighed. "There's something I didn't tell you. At the end of the Thirkie case, I had all the evidence, everything, and I took it to Penn-Barkis and he told me to forget it, Kahn had done it. And he threatened me, he said he knew what I was, and if I didn't forget it and agree that Kahn had done it, that he'd expose me, prosecute me, fire me, ruin my life even if I didn't go to prison."

Jack looked scared, and guilty. "You were always saying they'd find out about us, but I didn't believe it."

"I don't think we were especially indiscreet," Carmichael said. "I think someone worked something out, and then investigated. It's not your fault. I relied on nobody asking too many questions. It's tacitly got away with all the time, because nobody wants to know. If somebody did want to know, somebody high up, they could find out."

"Penn-Barkis wanted to know?" Jack looked even more scared now.

"Penn-Barkis or someone higher," Carmichael said. "There were people involved in the Thirkie case who are right at the top. The Home Secretary. The Prime Minister. They didn't want me jumping to the right conclusions and exposing them. They may even have known before and sent me especially because they knew they had a lever to use against me if they needed it." This bitter thought had been a torment to him ever since.

"But you went along with it? You did what they wanted? You said Kahn had done it, and Kahn hadn't done it?"

"Kahn was as innocent as a baby. The person who did it was our dear Prime Minister, who talks on the BBC as if butter wouldn't melt, but who is to my certain knowledge Thirkie's murderer. And for what it's worth, he also ordered the murder of several other innocent people." It was a relief to say it, to have someone else know. "There was a hairdresser called Agnes Timms who was shot, and Lady Thirkie, the dowager Lady Thirkie, was killed because she wouldn't cover it up for them. I met her. I liked her. But I went along and I helped cover what they wanted covered, and let them have the scare they wanted that put them securely into power, and now they know I'll do what they want."

"Why didn't you tell me before?" Jack asked, accusingly.

"I'm sorry. I was ashamed of it, and it never seemed like the right moment," Carmichael said. "I realized today there was never going to be a right moment, and the fact I hadn't told you was going to get bigger and bigger."

"You should have said."

"I know." Carmichael put his hand on Jack's knee. "But listen. Today in his office Penn-Barkis taunted me with being queer, just a little bit, and I have to get out of there. I have no integrity left, Jack, he's bought me and he knows he can do what he wants with me."

"Would he let you leave?" Jack asked.

"I think so." Carmichael sat back and sipped his whisky, consideringly. "I think if I resign at the end of this case, which is completely separate, it won't look as if it has anything to do with the Thirkie murder. In those circumstances I think he'd be prepared to let me go into obscurity."

"But what would we do? Where would the money come from?" Jack finished his whisky and put the glass down.

"We might have to cut back a bit. But there ought to be firms that would hire me. All my experience is police, but at least that shows I'm trustworthy. Or I could try going back into the Army."

"No!"

"That would be a last resort," Carmichael said, gently. "But I'll always think well of the Army. It brought us together."

"Brought us together and wouldn't let us have a bloody minute to be together," Jack said, bitterly.

Jack had been assigned as Carmichael's batman, before they went to France. Carmichael was attracted, and more than attracted, not only by the young man's beauty but by his gentleness and courage. He had seen Jack wading in to a fight to stop a baby-faced recruit being bullied, and had loved him for it even as he stopped the fight and put them all on fatigues. But he would never have spoken, never have said anything inappropriate if it hadn't been for Dunkirk.

Jack had been beside him in the boat when they were strafed by a Stuka. They had been under fire before, all of them, but there was something peculiarly horrible in being sitting targets in the open boat. They were too tightly packed together to be able to dodge, even if it would have done any good. The machine-gun bullets hit the sea, and then the side of the boat, then the arm and head of one of the men beside them. The plane turned for another run, and they had thought they were facing their final moments. In that moment, without the slightest bit of fuss, as if it was the most natural thing in the world, Jack had got up and flung himself in front of Carmichael.

A big gun on a corvette nearby hit the Stuka neatly as it turned, and they saw it plunge into the sea in front of them, the waves it made rocking their little boat. Jack sat back into his place, and Carmichael busied himself with some others throwing the dead man into the sea. When they sat down again, he had put his arm around Jack. It had seemed natural, not only to them but apparently to the others on the boat, a mixed crew from all the regiments of the British Expeditionary Force, with one or two French poilus among them. Nobody said anything. They had sat like that for the hours of the Channel crossing, hardly speaking, but acutely aware of the touch and of each other.

The next time Carmichael was alone with Jack, in the camp at Pevensey where they were hastily assigned, he put out his hand and tried to thank him for what he had done. Jack had taken his hand, looked into his eyes, and taken him in his arms. If Carmichael had acted he would never have ceased to reproach himself for taking advantage. But it was Jack, younger but far more experienced and much less inhibited, who acted, and Carmichael followed. All the time until the end of the war, moving from one camp in England to another, constantly interrupted by drills and air raids and men wanting orders, they had talked and dreamed of the time when they could set up house together in peace and secret comfort.

"My man," Carmichael said now, softly. It was their old joke, old endearment. It was what rich men called their valets, their servants who saw to their needs, and Carmichael could refer to Jack as his man to anyone. They had found each other and miraculously come together across all the barriers of class and gender. "My man," he said again.

"Not the army, P. A.," Jack said, sliding across the divan to lean against Carmichael.

"They probably wouldn't have me anyway," Carmichael said. "I'm getting old for that game. No, I'll look about for an office job. Nine to five, no traveling, home on time every day, wouldn't that suit you?"

"It wouldn't really be any different, except that you'd be bored too," Jack said. "We'd still be stuck in this flat, we still couldn't ever hold hands coming out of the pictures or do anything together without being afraid. They'd fire you from a job like that for being queer, if they found out."

"How about if I looked for a job in colonial administration then?" Carmichael stroked Jack's hair back off his face and looked down at him tenderly. "India, or Africa? The Exotic East? Burma, maybe? I've heard that in Burma the people don't care about homosexuality."

"You bet your life the English people do," Jack said. "There isn't any magic place we can go that will make any difference. There's nowhere in the world where people like us can live openly like anyone else, have friends, ordinary friends, act normally. You and I love each other but we get sick of each other because we're too much cooped up alone."

"Come on, you're always telling me stories about rich queers who live on the Riviera perfectly openly."

"Along with stories about poor queers being sent to Hitler's camps to be worked to death. I flat out won't go to the Continent, P. A." Jack sat up, fully in earnest. "India or Africa if you say so, but not to Europe. We should have stopped Hitler when we had the bloody chance."

"You and Winston Churchill and Crazy Lord Scott," Carmichael said, fondly. "Nobody's suggesting going to Europe. But I think it might be getting as bad as that here, by and by. We might look at Canada, or Australia?"

"I'll miss London," Jack said, settling back against Carmichael. "I'll miss the libraries and the cinemas and my friends. But if you decide you have to go, I'll go where you go, you know that."

15

After that, things settled into a kind of pattern and went on like that for a few days. I rehearsed all day, then in the evening Devlin met me at the theater, drove me home, cooked me dinner, and I cleaned up after him and after that we went to bed. I kept on moving between the three worlds—Devlin's world where I was going to blow up tyrants and I loved him but had to be careful not to say so, Antony's world where I was going to act in a play, and Hamlet's world where I was going to catch the conscience of a king and die in a duel with Laertes. You could say I was acting with Devlin, but I was also acting with Antony, and certainly when, as I was more and more, I was entirely caught up in Hamlet.

When Malcolm had said I was rooted in shallow soil, like all my sisters, what he'd meant was that he didn't think I was sane all the way through. Hamlet certainly wasn't sane all the time, and the more I thought about what he said, and the more I moved between the three worlds, the more right it seemed. Hamlet's upbringing lacked sisters, and mine had all too many of them, but neither of them had made us like other people.

We were working a lot on the Ophelia scene, which is the part of the play where the balance is most changed by the gender swapping. Antony had Pat standing above me, leaning over me, as he threw our sexual past in my face and I gave my responses desperately, and then starting to circle me, holding the gifts out of my reach. We kept the nunnery line in the end, because we decided it worked if Hamlet said it as if she thought Ophelia was going to have as much luck finding a partner in a nunnery as with her. I kept dreaming about this, but in my dreams, Ophelia was not Pat, but Devlin, who changed into Loy as people do in dreams, and began giving Ophelia's mad speech, "They say the owl is a baker's daughter," and becoming an owl and flying around the theater. All my dreams were terribly strange. Perhaps a trick cyclist would be able to explain it, or perhaps it was because I wasn't sleeping very much.

The next thing that really happened was on the Thursday night, when Loy and Siddy came to see us.

Devlin must have known they were coming because he'd bought enough lamb. He cooked very precisely, buying all the ingredients he needed and using them all up. If he wanted a handful of parsley, he'd buy a handful in Covent Garden, he didn't keep any in the cupboard. If he was cooking with wine, which he was that day, he'd use what he needed and we'd drink the rest of the bottle. Everything was always ready at the same time, and it was usually delicious. That night he made lamb stroganoff with a mushroom risotto, and as I was laying the table the door opened.

I hadn't seen Loy since the morning he'd caught me naked in the kitchen. He'd obviously listened to what Devlin said about sleeping elsewhere. But he'd kept his key, so he just walked in without knocking or anything. I didn't like that at all. Siddy was behind him. She looked defiant somehow, the way she looked when she used Mamma's diamonds to carve hammer-and-sickles into every window pane of Carnforth. (Actually, that wasn't entirely her fault. I mean Pip did start it by using her engagement diamond to draw a swastika on the drawing room window. And Pip was four years older, and should have known better.)

Devlin glanced up as they came in. Loy nodded to him. "No trouble," he said. "They don't know they're born, compared to the other side of the water."

Siddy blew out smoke and did her eye-sliding thing at me. "How are you doing?"

"I'm very well, no thanks to you," I said, and laid extra plates and knives and forks on the kitchen table.

I was angry with Siddy. I felt she'd betrayed me into all this. I didn't blame Devlin, or even Loy; they had acted as they had to act once I was involved. I blamed Siddy for saying it was fate and dragging me in.

Devlin dished up the dinner, and I poured out the white wine that was left in the bottle. It didn't go far between four.

"This is good," Loy said when he tasted the meat.

"It's a sweet little oven. I'll be halfway sorry to leave this place," Devlin said.

"Why do you have to leave?" I asked.

"It'll be burned, after the job," he said, then saw my face. "Oh, not literally burned, love, burned out. Traceable. They're sure to find out you were living here. But then I'll be burned too." He shrugged.

"You're burned, Dev?" Loy asked, concerned.

"Mollie Gaston knows me, and half the theater's seen me picking Vi up after rehearsal. My face and papers wouldn't stand up to too much investigation. I'll have to go home and lie low for a while. No harm done. It's about time I stopped taking so many chances."

Loy frowned and chewed.

"You actually think there's going to be something past the job?" I said.

Devlin gave me one of his lovely smiles. "Well, there might be. It all depends how we do it, and how innocent you look."

"If they're sure to find this flat and find out about you, then they'll know I'm not innocent."

"There's always the 'don't they know who Pappa is' defense," Siddy put in. She wasn't eating, just pushing her food around with her fork. "You are a peer's daughter after all."

"Do they hang peer's daughters, or strike off their heads with an axe like Anne Boleyn?" Loy asked, raising an eyebrow and leaning his elbow on the table.

"How about Irish baronets?" I riposted. I'd asked Mrs. Tring who he was, and she'd told me he was a baronet who had done something brave in the war. "They can line up the three of us on the block, while poor Devlin hangs in lonely solitude."

"It all depends how we do it," Devlin said again. "If we make it look as if it was done by the dangerous Jewish communists Normanby's been ranting about, they may not even bother to examine the people in the theater. But if we have to do it in a way that points to you, then they're going to find this flat and find out about me, though I'll be gone. You could be gone too, or you could stand there and look guilty, or you could stand there and look innocent."

"You could also play 'my boyfriend set me up,'" Siddy said.

"When he said to put this bomb in Hitler's box, I had no idea it was going to explode!" Loy said in a squeaky falsetto.

"The trouble with that one is that it won't play very well late on. You need to start coming outraged innocence from the first moment, or it doesn't work at all," Devlin said. "Not understanding what you did is not a fallback position from knowing nothing."

I ate a mouthful of my dinner. It was delicious, tender and flavorful, subtle and sophisticated. I'd have swapped it in a heartbeat for one of Mrs. Tring's corned beef hashes.

"So how are we going to do it?" Siddy asked. She

pushed her plate away almost untouched and lit a cigarette.

"What's the layout like?" Loy asked, turning to me.

After asking me to find out, the first day, Devlin hadn't said a word to me about it. "There are two doors, well, three, but the third one's double-locked and only used for bringing large pieces of scenery in. There's a doorman on the stage door all the time the theater's open, and another on the front-of-house when that door's open, which it usually isn't, except for performances. All the public come in through the one front-of-house door, which opens onto a lobby with a ticket office, and doors from that into the stalls, stairs straight up to the circle, and smaller stairs going all the way up to the upper circle and the ha'pennies."

"The ha'pennies?" said Loy, raising an eyebrow.

"The very top circle, the cheapest seats," Devlin put in. "The seats cost more than a ha'penny now, of course. They also call it that because you're so high up."

"To get to the boxes you go up to the upper circle and around. There are four boxes, two on each side. The Royal Box, which is pretty much bound to be where they sit, is on the left of the theater, stage right. It's bigger and more gilded than the other boxes. There's nothing underneath it that I can see, other than the side stalls. I think we'd have to put something right inside the box."

"That's not good," Siddy said. "They're sure to check it pretty thoroughly."

"What's the outside of the box like?" Loy asked. "The front of it?"

"It curves, it's white, and it has a gilded shield on it," I said.

"Could you fasten something onto it?"

"I suppose so, I mean maybe someone could, but it would be extremely conspicuous." I couldn't picture it at all.

Loy looked at Devlin expectantly. "The trouble is getting the charge right," Devlin said. "If it's inside the box, that's easy. If it's fastened to the outside, then if we make it big enough to be sure to kill them, then there's going to be a lot of collateral."

"It'll show if it's on the outside," I repeated.

"Not if it's under a flag," Devlin said. "He never goes far without his flags."

I thought of the hundreds of swastika flags you always saw in pictures from Germany. "How can you be sure they'll put a flag there, even so?"

"They're going to put two, a Union Jack and a swastika, together. It couldn't be better if we'd planned it," Loy said.

"Privileged information, Vile, they're not about to tell you how they know," Siddy said. "But the truth is there's a chap in the Foreign Office in Moscow's pay who's helping us."

"Shut up. I know too much already," I said. I was actually relieved to discover that there was more to the conspiracy than the people I'd already met.

"How easy would it be for you to get up to the front of the box, during a rehearsal?" Loy asked.

"Impossible," I said. "It's twelve feet up in the air. The only way would be a ladder. It would be fairly easy for me to go into the box. Antony has us sit in the stalls while we're waiting to be rehearsed, watching the others. I could quite easily go out of the back of the stalls and up to the circle and through into the box, and I suppose I could lean out and get to the front of it that way, though someone on stage would probably see me."

"Wouldn't they see you going up to the box?" Siddy asked. She still looked a little suspicious of me, though the men both seemed quite trusting. They were professionals, but then they didn't know me as well.

"They might, but if they did I suppose it wouldn't seem like an impossibly eccentric thing to be doing. I mean we're supposed to sit quietly and watch, but getting up and wandering about quietly would come under the category of stretching our legs."

"What they let you do now and what they let you do next week before the performance might well be different things," Loy said.

"Would they let me in, do you think?" Devlin asked. "They know I'm your boyfriend, and I'm burned anyway. Would they let me come in and sit and watch, and maybe go up to the box?"

"I could ask Antony," I said, dubiously. "You'd have to be as quiet as a mouse when he's directing. And he might ask Jackie or someone to take charge of you."

"Let's try that tomorrow," Devlin said. "I'd like to have a look at the place for myself."

"Wait a moment, how soon can we get it in?" Loy asked. "How far ahead of the time? Because if we could get it in tomorrow, or before they even think we know they're going to be there, it would be something their security has already noted."

"Unless their security finds it," Devlin said.

"It should be either a long time before or immediately before," Siddy said. She got up and walked around the kitchen, peering into empty cupboards.

"It depends exactly what we use," Devlin said. He leaned back looking comfortable, in complete contrast to Siddy's twitchiness and Loy's alertness. "Most times the simplest thing is to use an alarm-clock timer, and that means you can't set it more than twelve hours before. But we could have it in place well before that, if Vi can get up to the box on the day and wind the clock."

I flinched. They all looked at me. "If I were caught winding it, it would be the chop without any tyrant slaying," I said.

"Would you be nervous, then?" Devlin asked.

"She'd be bound to be," Siddy said, for once seeming sympathetic. Her pacing had brought her behind my chair; she put a hand on my shoulder.

"Vi's been very calm so far," Devlin said.

"Vi's been half-believing she could get out of it at the last minute, so far," Siddy said.

I twisted and looked up at her, annoyed that she had guessed. "I'm not!"

"I know how you are when you're pretending, and how you are when you're committed. You're pretending." All those years of games, of alliances and betrayals, sister against sister, against parents and servants, all of us in that crucible atmosphere where adult supervision was brief and arbitrary, where we were supposed to be educating ourselves we had at least learned each other.

"Not pretending," I protested, not sure myself as I spoke if I were faking sincerity or meaning it now. "But it all seems so—unreal. Dramatic." There had been moments it had felt only too real. In the car, freewheeling, and when Devlin came out of the bedroom with the gun. I hadn't seen that again, but I knew it must be there all the time, hidden somewhere in his easy reach.

"It's real enough," Loy said. He turned to Devlin. "I thought you said—"

"Vi will do what she needs to do when she needs to do it," Devlin said, evenly.

Nobody said anything for a moment. I ate some more of my rapidly cooling dinner. Loy swallowed down the last of his wine. "Enough of this gnat's piss," he said, and brought a fifth of whiskey out of his pocket. He poured for himself and Devlin, in the wineglasses. Siddy sat down and pushed her glass forward. Loy hesitated, and poured for her too. I thought how she had said on the phone that the thought of her being drunk was a good joke. Loy looked at me, his head cocked.

"No," I said.

Siddy cupped the wineglass in both hands and sniffed, then tasted the whiskey with her tongue, catlike. "It's your beastly Irish stuff," she said, putting it down on the table.

"There's others will drink it if you won't," Loy said, pouring it into his own glass. Siddy laughed, a little shrilly.

"If it isn't a clock, if getting into the box on the day to

wind it might be difficult, it will have to be a detonator," Devlin said, as if he were going straight on with what he'd been saying before. He'd finished his dinner and put his knife and fork neatly together bisecting the empty plate. It was my job to wash the dishes, but I didn't want to do it in front of Siddy and Loy, especially Siddy.

"I think they'd notice a long fuse sizzling away like in a pirate film," Loy said.

Devlin laughed. "I was thinking of a radio detonator. That would be better than a clock in some ways. For one thing, it's silent ahead of time, and even the quietest clock ticks and draws attention to itself. Also, it means the timing is more exactly controlled. With a timer there are always possibilities, an early interval, someone leaving to go to the toilet. With a detonator we can pick our moment."

"You say we," Loy said. "Who?"

He wanted it to be him, I could see it in the set of his body. Devlin took a slow pull of his whiskey and smiled at Loy. "Vi," he said.

"Oh no!" I said.

"You'll be on stage, you'll be able to see everything in the box, and you'll have a nice straight line of sight," Devlin said, as if that settled it.

"But if she doesn't do it the whole thing will be wasted!" Loy said.

"She'll do it," Devlin said.

"I might have a straight line of sight, but I'll also be trying to act," I said. "I can't be acting Hamlet and thinking about lines of sight and whether they're all in their box! And I can't be carrying around a great big detonator or whatever it is! Anyway, you don't know how dark the house looks from the stage. It's just a dazzle of darkness against the lights. They could all be in the bathroom and I wouldn't know."

"Do it when you stab Polonius through the arras," Devlin said. "It'll be a little box. It can go in your pocket."

"I won't have pockets!"

"I'll make it as small as I can and you'll easily be able to hide it."

"Let me do it," Loy said. "You and Vi get the bomb into the theater, and I'll sit in the audience and blow the detonator."

"You can be backup, the way we discussed before," Devlin said.

Loy frowned, but nodded. He sipped his whiskey.

"What about afterwards?" I asked. "I can't see me saying my boyfriend told me to squeeze this trigger and I didn't think it would do any harm. How would I get rid of it?"

"We could put it inside something nobody would look inside, something you could get rid of afterwards," Devlin said.

"Yorick's skull," Siddy said, and gave a horrified giggle.

16

Carmichael spent the days between Tuesday and Thursday trying to get hold of the Greens, Nash, and Bannon, and talking to those of Gilmore's friends he could find. His picture of the actress didn't much change, and his idea of her motivation in building a bomb didn't clarify much either. He discovered that the bomb-making pamphlet was one produced during the war for use by the civilian population after the projected German invasion. Jacobson and the Hampstead police interviewed the Greens' Jewish connections, without finding any sign of the Greens themselves. Mrs. Channing was pulled in and questioned, but stuck to her story that she wasn't going to allow Jews in her respectable establishment. She broke down when confronted with the evidence of her husband's Jewishness, and cursed Jacobson as a traitor, but either did not know or would not reveal the location of the Greens. There wasn't anything to charge her with, so they had to let her go.

On Thursday, after a flurry of messages and miscommunications, he managed to speak to Bannon's secretary directly. She established that Bannon was always at

rehearsal, but that he would see Carmichael at rehearsal
on Friday morning.

The papers made the most of Carmichael's story, and
vilified Gilmore even more than they had praised her
before. They couldn't find as much to say about Marshall, but they did their best, calling him a traitor and
a man in the pay of Moscow. Meanwhile, appeals for
Nash to come forward were unavailing. "If he were innocent he'd have been here by now, leave or no leave,"
Carmichael said to Royston. "I want to look through
Marshall's things. I'm either going down to Portsmouth
or I'm going to get Tambourne up here again to tell me
about Nash."

Carmichael called Beddow, who preferred to send
Tambourne up, and Tambourne seemed quite enthusias-
tic at the thought of another night in London. "I doubt
I'll be able to help much, though," he said.

Carmichael took him to one of the nicer interview
rooms in the Yard. Tambourne looked around warily, as if
he believed the stories about truncheons and castor oil
and lead-lined hoses. It was windowless, like most of the
rooms, but furnished with table and chairs and lit with
strong electric light. He sat down, and Royston brought
the strong stewed tea that was all the Yard could produce.
There was also a plate of pink wafer biscuits. Royston set
cups in front of all of them and took out his notebook.

"So, you told us about Marshall, now tell us about
Nash," Carmichael began.

"I brought this," Tambourne said, and passed over a
snap. It showed two men in naval uniforms sitting in a canoe. They both had the sun in their eyes. One of them was
laughing, the other was holding up a cup of some kind.
"That's Nash with the cup. It's this year's Portsmouth
Harbour canoe races. They won the two-man."

"Did you take this, sir?" Royston asked, as Carmichael
wordlessly passed the snap across.

"Yes," Tambourne said. "With my little Brownie. It's
the only one I have of the two of them. There's also this

one." He handed over another snap. Marshall, dressed for tennis, with a black Labrador. It was clearly a shot of the dog, not the man.

"Whose is the dog?" Carmichael asked.

"Mine, that is to say my sister's," Tambourne said, embarrassed. "You can't have pets in the Navy. Dot brought Sally over to see me one weekend, and brought her down to the courts. This was just a few weeks ago, the weekend of the Thirkie murder."

"She looks like a lovely dog," Royston said, diplomatically.

Carmichael looked again at the picture of the two men in the canoe. They were wearing caps, but it was possible to see that Marshall was fair and Nash dark. Other than that they looked almost indistinguishable not only from each other but from half the middle-class young men in England. There they had been, winning a two-man canoe race and petting dogs in all innocence, and where were they now?

"Nash seems to have gone into hiding. He doesn't seem to have any family, and Captain Beddow doesn't know where he is," Carmichael said.

"He's still on leave until Saturday," Tambourne pointed out. "He might be somewhere where he hasn't seen the papers, or heard the wireless."

"I thought serving officers weren't supposed to leave the country without permission?" Carmichael asked.

"No, that's right, but he could have gone over to Paris for a few days even so. Or he could be fishing somewhere remote in Scotland," Tambourne suggested, clearly racking his brains. "No, it isn't very likely. You're probably right that he's in hiding. I don't have any idea where, though."

"I take it he didn't confide in you his plans for his leave?"

"No," Tambourne said. "I really didn't know Nash all that well."

"It seems nobody knew him well except Marshall, or

Marshall well except Nash." Carmichael sighed. "Do you think Nash would have known what Marshall was up to?"

"Yes," Tambourne said, very definitely. "I find it hard to believe that Marshall was building a bomb, but since it seems he was, then I'm sure Nash knew about it as well, and was probably involved."

There hadn't been any meetings with Nash indicated in Gilmore's appointment book. But all her appointments were indicated with one set of initials, even if she'd been meeting more than one person; Carmichael had learned that from his meetings with her friends. Nash could have been present at the bomb-making meeting, and survived somehow to escape afterwards.

"Was Nash involved in explosives?" Royston asked.

"No. He's an ASDIC man. Radar, you know?"

"And his politics? The same as Marshall's?"

"Very much the same to all appearances," Tambourne said. He stretched out his long legs and leaned back in his chair. "Nash was quieter than Marshall, and he didn't play tennis. He was dark-haired and essentially Etonian. Reserved. English. Good at his job, and good at teaching it to the recruits, as far as I know. He wasn't as outgoing as Marshall."

"They were very close, you said," Carmichael said. "Do you think there's any possibility they might have been more than friends?"

"Good God, no!" Tambourne sat up straight and knocked over his tea. He snatched for the cup before it broke, but the tea soaked the plate of biscuits. "I'm so sorry."

"Don't worry, the biscuits are no loss anyway. Nobody ever eats them, I can't think why they always send them with tea," Carmichael said soothingly.

Royston fetched a cloth and dried the table. They settled down again. Tambourne tried to answer again more temperately. "I know the traditions of the Navy are supposed to be rum, sodomy, and the lash, as Mr. Churchill put it, but really, Inspector, you mustn't think that's literally true these days. Marshall and Nash were good friends, but there wouldn't have been anything unnatural."

Not that Tambourne knew about anyway. "So why do you think they were building a bomb?" he asked.

"It seems like something from an illustrated paper," Tambourne said. "All I can think, since you have evidence it's real, is that they must have been secret communists. I've been thinking about it, and it's the only thing that fits. It seems Miss Gilmore was some kind of socialist, according to the latest reports in the *Telegraph.* Marshall, well, all the true blue stuff must have been a facade, though it was a very good facade, it certainly fooled me. He and Nash must have been secret communists for years, underneath, and waiting their moment."

Royston scratched his head, but wrote it down.

"Why would this be their moment?" Carmichael asked.

"Because of Mr. Normanby coming to power," Tambourne said. "I mean he's the very opposite of a communist, so they wouldn't like him at all. They didn't like him, Nash didn't anyway. He called the new organization a coup, in the mess. Marshall shut him up. I thought it was because of not talking politics, but it might have been because of this."

"So what do you think would have been the target of their bomb?" Royston asked.

"Well if they really are communists, they'd bomb anyone just for the fun of it. Look at that old lady in Wales. But I'd have thought probably the Prime Minister, if there was any way of getting at him."

"Gilmore and Marshall aren't going to be bombing anyone now they've blown themselves up," Carmichael said. "Nash, on the other hand, is still out there. Do you think, from what you know of him, he'd carry on with a plan after the others were killed?"

Tambourne hesitated. "Well I would say yes, absolutely

he would," he said. "But ever so much of what I knew of Nash must have been a facade, a lie, if he's really a communist. So I don't know that what I think he'd do is worth anything at all. I didn't know him well anyway, and if he was capable of really being a communist while pretending the views he did pretend, then he could have pretended anything at all."

There was a little silence after this. "Do you know anything about his family?" Carmichael asked.

"I think they were killed in the Blitz," Tambourne offered.

"Marshall's parents were killed in the Blitz," Carmichael said.

"Oh, that's right." Tambourne looked embarrassed. "I don't know anything about Nash's family then."

After he left, Carmichael went through Marshall's possessions. They had been hastily packed by someone, a rating, or perhaps Tambourne himself, who seemed to get all the jobs nobody else wanted. Marshall had a good supply of uniforms, and two civilian suits, both from good London tailors. He also owned a large supply of wool sweaters in blue and navy blue. Carmichael supposed he would need those for chilly days on the water. He listed them all diligently. There were white tennis clothes, slightly grass-stained. There were socks, neatly rolled, whether by Marshall or someone else, and a heap of white Y-front underpants, not rolled at all. There was a framed photograph of a sailing ship, and another of a bride and groom, by the style of the clothes probably Marshall's parents.

There were a series of silver cups, all won for racing, including one for the two-man canoe race for 1949, which must be the one Nash had been holding in the photograph. There was a tennis racket in a press. It didn't seem much, for a whole life. Marshall had been the same age as Kinnerson, and Kinnerson had a wife and a house. It seemed strange that these few things were all that Marshall had left. He opened a little wooden box that contained cufflinks and a tie pin and put it back inside the cup that recorded Marshall of *Valiant*'s victory in the Portsmouth single canoe races for 1945. How long had Marshall been stuck down in Portsmouth teaching ratings to row? Tambourne had seemed tired of it after less than a year.

There was a little pile of books, editions of Kipling, Chesterton, Swinburne, Arnold, Hardy's poems. There was no address book, but there were two hard-bound notebooks. One of them was quite full of jottings concerning the progress of the ratings at boatmanship. The other contained handwritten poetry.

Carmichael flicked through it. None of it was terribly good. Most of the poems were full of crossings out and arrows indicating that one line was supposed to come before another, followed by a clean version, presumably Marshall's final choice. The subjects were mostly pastoral, ships, the water. He flicked faster, then his eye was caught by a sonnet, entitled "The Farthing Peace."

> *Our fathers taught us that the world was free*
> *Willed it to us in their history*
> *Taught us to rule it and ask no praise*
> *Walking as tall as the Lord of Days.*
> *Then the sirens called and they ran away*
> *Claimed what they had said had been meant in play*
> *Asked how had we taken so seriously*
> *The laws they had made, and they bade us flee.*
> *We fought, then we fled, when we met defeat,*
> *They appeased it as peace, claimed the victor's seat,*
> *Starved us of money, and men, and might,*
> *And pinched us and prodded us into the night.*
> *Till they found, when they ended beneath the sod,*
> *Just what was meant by a Jealous God.*

He too had felt like that, when the peace was made. He had thought the Farthing Peace hollow, had wondered what they had fought for at all, why they had endured the Blitz if they were going to call it a draw with nothing accomplished and claim it as Peace with Honour. Then as the years had gone on without the war being renewed, he had grown reconciled. England will always be England, he had told himself. He wondered when Marshall had written his sonnet. None of the poetry was dated.

He continued flicking through the other lyrics. None were as overtly political, and none of them struck him as even slightly communist. Perhaps Marshall had been the ordinary patriot he seemed. You didn't need to be a communist to be opposed to Normanby, or perhaps even to wish to blow him up. Appeased it as peace, indeed. He noted the notebooks on his inventory, and went on.

17

After they left, Devlin and I talked for a long time about bombs, which he knew a lot about and I didn't know anything. But I did know about the inside of the Siddons, and I was adamant that I didn't want to have to press a button hidden in Yorick's skull, or anywhere, to blow up the box. "I'd rather wind a clock," I said. "At least I could get that out of the way beforehand. I'll do it, Devlin, but I can't do it while I'm acting, I can't come out of Hamlet to do it."

He didn't like it but he believed me in the end. "Is there anywhere else in the theater with a line of sight on the Royal Box?" he asked.

I wasn't sure at first what he meant by a line of sight, but it turned out after some explanation that all he meant was a straight line that didn't go around any corners. "Radio's like light," he said. "In fact I was told that it is light in long wavelengths that you can't see. Radio can go through walls, like the front of the box, but it can't go around corners. It's like getting reception on the wireless. You have to get the antenna in a line. We won't be able to mess about with antennae."

"I'm not sure there is anywhere else, then," I said, despondently. I pictured the theater, and the box, and drew a sketch for Devlin, which he studied and then dropped into the half-full glass ashtray, and set it on fire with a match. He always did that kind of thing, making sure not to leave evidence, not as if he were taking extraordinary precautions but quite as if it was the most natural thing in the world.

As it was flaming out to ashes, he said, "Maybe the opposite box has a line of sight. Or there might be a seat up on the other side up in the ha'pennies. I'll be able to tell when I've been in. But if my going in is a once-off thing, it would be better if we leave it until I've made the bomb and can take it in and place it."

"You're going to make the bomb?" I asked, horrified.

Devlin put his hand on mine and smiled. "Don't worry so much, darling," he said. "I'm a professional, I told you that. I won't blow myself to bits. I never have yet."

"But where will you make it?" I asked.

He jerked his head at the spare bedroom, where he had said Loy used to sleep. "There are ways of finding places where bombs have been made, but this place is burned anyway, so I'll make it here," he said.

"Be careful!" I said, hopelessly.

He laughed. "I'm not an actress working from an old recipe, love. I know what I'm doing. Now, what are the chances we could have the opposite box? Would it be taken, usually, for a first night?"

"Oh yes," I said. "Always. And if it isn't really taken, Antony would paper it." Devlin looked inquiring. "I mean he'd find some nice friends of his in evening clothes to sit in it and applaud wildly. If you're an actor and not working, it's easy to get tickets for shows that aren't sellouts, especially first nights."

"So we ought to book it early if it turns out we want it," Devlin said. "Of course, it may be booked already. If there's a seat up in the ha'pennies, that would just mean having a ticket and getting there early—they don't sell particular seats up there, do they?"

"No, that's right," I said. "You've sat up there?"

"Many a time," he said. "Up rubbing knees with the gods in the ha'pennies." He smiled. "More my mark than sitting with the peer's daughters in the upper circle."

I ignored this and started to clear the dirty dishes from the table.

"The only other possible place would be standing up in the stalls, and that would be very obvious. Hitler's bodyguards would be bound to spot that and might even shoot before he has a chance to push the detonator." He stared over at nothing where I'd been sitting. I took his glass and his plate without him moving. "No, I'll have to do it myself if it comes to that. I can't trust Loy not to stand there longer than he needs to, just for the thrill of it."

"He won't like that," I said, scraping the plates into the bin. I noticed again how little Siddy had eaten.

Devlin turned and smiled up at me, his slow confident smile. "Don't worry about Loy, darling. I can deal with him."

"I wish you didn't have to," I said, running hot water into the sink. I'd disliked Loy more than ever that evening. It wasn't just his arrogance; everything about him set my teeth on edge. "And I'm sure he's bad for Siddy."

"It's not a very happy alliance, that one," Devlin agreed.

"How long have they been together?" I asked, unsure if he'd answer or just clam up.

"Couple of years, off and on," he said. He was being more forthcoming than usual. Maybe it was the whiskey. "Since she got divorced from Lord Russell. Thing is that Siddy can give Loy something he needs."

"I'd think he could get all the women he wants," I said, not looking at Devlin, concentrating on rinsing the glasses under the hot tap.

"Yes, he can, and that doesn't do him any good,"

Devlin said. "What Siddy can give him is Moscow's approval."

I did turn around then. "She really is a communist? Not playing at it? A real card-carrying Stalin-approved communist?"

"I thought you knew that, darling," Devlin said, looking wary. "You knew she'd been over there."

"She's been to Germany too, that doesn't make her a Nazi," I said, turning back to the sink and thumping the plates into the water. "She says she's a communist, but she's been saying that since she was six years old."

"She's made herself what she wanted to be then," Devlin said. "Moscow gives her things, and she can give them to Loy. Jobs, information. It keeps him with her."

"I don't like him," I said, scrubbing viciously at a plate.

Devlin sat back in his chair. "There's something you don't understand about Loy."

"I don't understand *anything* about him," I said, vehemently.

Devlin laughed. "You know he's an Ulster baronet?" That confirmed what Mrs. Tring had told me. "He owns Arranish Hall, in Ulster. His background is like yours, not like mine. When he dies, they'll put him in the family tomb with his names and dates and gold coins on his eyes, not just shovel him into a pauper's grave with a pair of ha'pennies. Yet he has no money, no more than I do, just the name, and the title, and the memory of what it means. And he has one more thing, you know he has a medal, a George Cross? You know how he got it?"

"Something frightfully heroic in the war," I said, sullenly. Devlin had used an enormous number of pans and spoons making dinner today.

"Well, you know why he was in your war at all? He's got an Irish passport and the Republic never got involved; he could have stayed safe at home."

This wasn't what I'd expected him to ask. "For a bit of fun?" I suggested, attacking the rice pan.

"That's what he says now. But the truth is he was caught with a bomb, in the summer campaign of 1939, the IRA campaign in Britain that is, and because he is who he is, because of who his pappa was, like Siddy said to you, the judge gave him a choice of enlisting or going to jail, so he enlisted."

"Had you made the bomb?" I asked, as quietly and as calmly as I could.

"I had," Devlin admitted. "Loy and I go back a long way. But the reason he was caught with it, and probably the reason he got that medal too, is because he likes riding the thrill too much. He could have got the bomb in and got out of there quite safely, but that wasn't good enough for him, he had to skirt the edge and feel the thrill, and get caught. Now I know Loy. There's no risk he won't take, and he's Sir Aloysius when it comes to it, and he knows Lord Scott and Lord Scott's promising us the moon and the stars for doing this job. I'd trust Loy to take any risk. What I wouldn't trust him for is to do a job the safest surest way and avoid the risks. He courts risks. Like that flashy SS 300 he drives."

"Why are you doing this, Devlin?" I asked, putting the heavy rice pan on the draining board. "Uncle Phil's doing it to get control of the country, and Siddy's doing it for Stalin and the Dear Workers and Loy's doing it for the thrill, and I'm doing it because you're making me, but why are you doing it?"

"Well, it's not for what your uncle Phil is promising us, whatever he thinks," he said. "And it's not because I don't know how to do anything else, which Loy threw in my face one time when I wouldn't let him risk killing us all. I may be a professional, but I've never done a bombing I didn't believe in. This time, Vi, this time may be the most important of all, and for Ireland as well." He looked at me over by the sink as if I were a dog he was hoping to train. "I don't know if you'll understand, but there's a thing it's hard to give a name. It's what we fought for in Ireland when you wouldn't give it to us, and it's what's been lost on the Continent—I could call it freedom, or self-determination, but that's too abstract. It's the idea that one man's as good as the next, before the law, whoever he is. It's the idea behind the French Revolution, but it's lost now in France, where old Petain licks Hitler's boots. It's the idea that built America, but they're too frightened over there now even to elect old Joe Kennedy instead of Lindbergh with his talk of keeping down the Jews and the blacks."

He shook his head. "This isn't going in, is it, love? You grew up in privilege and rebelled so far as to go into the world of the stage, a completely unreal world, but you've got no understanding of what I'm talking about."

"I don't know," I said, honestly enough. "I do care about individual liberty. I didn't want what Mamma wanted for me and I didn't do it, and I've paid my own way and worked hard since I left home. But I don't think liberty is something you get by blowing people up. It seems to me something that comes along when you give people the choice."

Devlin leaned forward and took my hands. "When people have choices, yes, but that's just what Hitler's taken away, and Normanby wants to do the same here—and if he does it, you can bet that dear old Eamon de Valera will go down the same road in Ireland. Right now it's choice for the Jews and the communists, and who knows whose choice he'll be taking away next? In Germany you know, all the children join the Hitler Youth and are encouraged to denounce their parents. They do real military service, not like the feeble National Service you have here. The very idea of choice has been almost forgotten in fifteen years of Hitler—even without what's going on with the Jews, which you might not believe but which I do. Siddy isn't the only one who's seen them. How long before we have camps here? How long before the Lord Chamberlain says you can't put on a play not because it has too much bosom but because it says something against the government?"

"There aren't many plays that say things against the government," I said, feebly.

"That's the pity of it, my dear," he said. "Plays help people think, give them ideas. Think of your ordinary working chap up in the ha'pennies seeing *Saint Joan* and thinking there is more to life than his daily work, there are things worth fighting for."

I sagged against the sink. "Oh Devlin, please don't go on about the Dear Workers, I can't stand it."

"No? But it is those ordinary people who matter, their choices. Look at your friend Mollie. I like Mollie." I was instantly jealous. He had never said he liked me, and I wasn't sure he did. "She was modestly educated, she had no money of her own, she came to London and made her own fortune from her own God-given gifts. Who'd live in a country that said she shouldn't do more than wash dishes?"

I pulled my hands out of the dirty water. "I'm not sure she'd be any better off in Russia than Germany. I don't think Stalin's any better than Hitler," I said.

"He's a lot further away," Devlin said. "The enemy of my enemy is my friend. And he at least pays lip service to the idea of equality, even if there are purges from time to time. I wouldn't be very keen on the idea of a close alliance with Russia, and I wouldn't want to live there, but for the time being we have goals in common. At least the Red Army are fighting Hitler, and they're the only ones who are."

"They're both tyrants if it comes down to it," I said.

"And that's what Normanby's trying to make himself, with all this hysteria about terrorists and the new laws. And you just swallow it, maybe with a little grimace, but down it goes like cough medicine. England is like a country of sleepwalkers, walking over the edge of a cliff, and has been these last eight years. You're prosperous, you're content, and you don't care what's going on the other side of the Channel as long as you can keep on having boat races and horse shows and coming up to

London to see a show, or for the workers, dog races and days on the beach at Southend."

"It's not my fault," I said, almost frightened by his vehemence.

He stood up. "It's not your fault, no, love, but it is your responsibility, and that you can't see that is your fault," he said. He took two steps over to the sink and put his arm around me. "Bed now," he said.

"But I haven't finished the dishes," I protested.

"They'll wait," he said, pulling off my rubber gloves. "Come with me now."

And I did.

18

The Siddons was a slightly shabby eighteenth-century theater on the Strand, opposite the Strand Palace Hotel, where Carmichael had once successfully apprehended a jewel thief. He didn't think he'd ever been to the Siddons. It tended to show highbrow and slightly depressing plays. The facade was painted to be enticing, but in the full sunlight it looked a little overblown. "Have you ever been inside here, sergeant?" he asked Royston.

"Saw a French thing about a miser here a few years ago with my Mrs.," Royston said. "Very funny."

The front doors to the theater were firmly closed. There was a man up a ladder fixing letters on the theater's marquee. "Ask him where we go in," Carmichael instructed Royston.

"Oy," Royston called, and when he had the man's attention, "how do we get inside?"

"Theater's closed for rehearsals," the man called down.

"We've an appointment with Mr. Bannon," Carmichael said.

The man peered down at them. "Oh. Well, go around the back to the stage door, then."

"Where's that?" Royston asked.

"The stage door," the man repeated, more loudly, in the tone used for addressing idiots and foreigners. He pointed down an alley.

"After you, sergeant," Carmichael said.

The back of the theater was black, dingy, and run-down. Evidently all the attractions were kept for the front. The stage door was opened to their knock by a uniformed doorman.

"We have an appointment to see Mr. Bannon," Carmichael said.

"He's rehearsing," the doorman said, dubiously, looking them up and down.

"Tell him Inspector Carmichael and Sergeant Royston, of Scotland Yard," Royston said.

"Well, you'd better come in then," the doorman said, ungraciously.

"Did you know Lauria Gilmore?" Carmichael asked.

"Seen her a time or two," the doorman said. "And she wasn't a communist, no matter what they're saying. She used to tip well, and everybody knows communists don't tip."

"So where do we go?" Carmichael asked.

"Down the corridor, past all the doors, straight on through the pass door, and straight on again until you come to the other pass door at the end. Then go down the stairs. That'll put you in the stalls. Mr. Bannon will either be there, or on the stage, depending if he's acting or directing, and if he's on the stage you can call up to him. But I wouldn't if I were you. Jackie, that's his assistant, she'll be in the stalls. I'd have a word with her and she'll pick her moment to interrupt."

"Thank you," Carmichael said.

As they walked down the ill-lit passage, he murmured to Royston, "Did you know that communists don't tip?"

"I'd heard it before, sir," Royston admitted. "Apparently they see it as a sign of thinking people are below them. An insult to the worker, that kind of thing."

"So nobody tips in Red Russia?"

"Ah. I heard that in Red Russia there's a lot of outright bribing going on if you want to get things done. It's communists here make a point of thanking people under them, but not tipping." Royston pushed open the first pass door. "It doesn't make them very popular, as you might imagine."

"Is it actually true?" Carmichael asked, going through into another dimly lit stretch of corridor. There was a strange smell compounded of greasepaint and sweat.

"Now that I couldn't tell you. I've never known any communists socially. If you really wanted to know you could go down to the Scrubs, where they're keeping the communists they've rounded up recently, and try asking. No shortage of them. I hear they arrested another lot of them yesterday, ones who'd come around protesting about their paper being closed down."

"That's not a crime, surely?" Carmichael asked mildly.

Royston laughed.

"I was just wondering what it said about Gilmore that she did tip," Carmichael went on.

Royston put his hand on the second pass door, and stopped. "Remember what Kinnerson said in the first place? She'd come up from underneath, she knew what it was like to struggle, she thought people ought to have a chance? Well then, even if she was a communist, she'd know how important tips are to people who need them."

"Let's go through, sergeant," Carmichael said.

They both blinked when they came through the pass door. They were at the top of a flight of stairs that led down into the orchestra pit and the stalls. Beside them, the stage was brilliantly lit in lurid green, which changed a moment after to bright white, and then a brilliant gold. Someone shouted something, and it went to red, and then faded to pink.

As they picked their way down the stairs, a woman hurried over to them. "Are you Scotland Yard?" she asked. "I'm Jackie, we spoke yesterday. Antony's just working on the lighting before the rehearsal starts properly, but if you wouldn't mind waiting a moment, he'll come and talk to you."

"Would it be possible to talk to some of the other cast members who knew Miss Gilmore and who aren't rehearsing at the moment?" Carmichael asked.

"Well, yes, if you're quiet," Jackie said, with an anxious glance at the stage, which was now lit in mottled green and white. A dark-haired woman, illuminated, burlesqued a pose.

"No, that's for the ghost!" someone bellowed.

"Oh dear," Jackie said. "Now who—oh, here's Pat. Pat, would you like to talk to these policemen about Lauria for a moment? I must go and calm Antony down."

Pat was a young man with pale hair cut strikingly in a fringe across his forehead and long over his ears. It wasn't possible, in the strange light, to tell what color anything was. His face looked bilious, but he was smiling. "I'm Pat McKnight," he said. "I knew Lauria, but not well. We were in *Fallen Angels* together."

This was a conversation Carmichael had had several times with different people over the last few days. He proceeded to sit in the front row of the stalls and have it again.

After a while the light steadied and settled on white. Jackie came back, bringing with her a middle-aged man of what Carmichael thought of as an Italian type, wearing long green and gold robes trimmed with fur. Carmichael rose. "Mr. Bannon?" he asked. "I'm Inspector Carmichael, and this is Sergeant Royston."

"Inspector. I'm sorry you've had to wait." Bannon had a plummy theatrical voice.

"Let me take your robe, Antony," Jackie said. "You don't want to trail it in the dust down here."

"Take it to Bettina and get it shortened right away,"

Bannon said, shrugging it off. Underneath he was wearing slacks and a pullover. Jackie left, carrying the robe casually over her arm, and Pat McKnight scurried off after her. Bannon flung himself down, and Carmichael sat beside him. "It's an absolute madhouse here today. We've a week left before we open, and everything's chaos."

"I'm sorry to take up your time when you're so busy," Carmichael said. Royston pulled out his notebook. "But I need to ask you about Lauria Gilmore."

"Wonderful actress. Terrible loss to the theater. We've replaced her with Mollie Gaston, who hasn't a tenth of her talent."

"Had you heard she was building a bomb?" Carmichael asked.

"Yes." Bannon frowned. "I heard that, but I don't believe it. I expect the evidence shows the bomb was inside the house, but is there anything to prove that the other man, the lieutenant, hadn't brought it there with the intention of killing her? I think this talk of Jewish plots and communist plots has made everyone think, quite naturally no doubt, that every murder must be such a plot. I think perhaps the lieutenant was in love with Lauria, she agreed to meet him, he turned up with the bomb to threaten her, said he'd kill them both if she didn't love him, murder-suicide. Perhaps she thought he was bluffing, or perhaps he wasn't as expert with his homemade bomb as he thought he was."

How fantastic, Carmichael thought. "Why take a bomb when a pistol would do as well or better?" he asked.

Bannon looked annoyed at having his theory questioned. "Perhaps he couldn't easily get hold of a gun. Or perhaps he too had been influenced by all this hysteria about bombs in the press, and believed a bomb was the modern weapon of choice?"

"Perhaps this will all turn out to be the answer," Carmichael said, humoring him. "But for a moment, consider, from your knowledge of Miss Gilmore, if you can think of any circumstances in which she would have wanted to have made a bomb?"

"None," Bannon said immediately. "It's ridiculous. No, I don't have any idea why she might have been doing that."

"You invited her to lunch with you last Friday," Carmichael said.

"And she came, of course. Lunch at the Venezia. That was to offer her the part. Gertrude, of course."

One more theatrically obsessed actor, Carmichael thought. There probably wasn't any more to be got out of Bannon than Gilmore's other friends, though his denial was more severe than most. "You were probably the last person other than her servants and Marshall to talk to her. What mood was she in? What did you discuss over lunch?"

"She was happy. Thrilled with the part. And of course we discussed the play. The rest of the cast. I had wanted Pamela Brown for Hamlet, but she was adamant she didn't want to play cross-cast. Lauria and I discussed several other possibilities, and she helped me decide for sure on Viola Lark."

"Was that all you discussed?" Carmichael asked.

"Well, I did confide in her one other thing, which I'm not sure I ought to tell you as it hasn't been announced yet." Bannon looked a little guilty.

"You should certainly tell us," Carmichael said. "Anything you said, that she said, could have bearing on her motives. It's very important that you cooperate with us."

"Yes, Inspector," Bannon said, licking his lips nervously. "It's just I'd been told not to tell anyone, but I was so proud. You must have heard that Hitler's going to be in London. He's coming over to see *Parsifal,* and while he's here he's going to have meetings with the king and the Prime Minister, and he's also going to come here, on first night, with the Prime Minister, to see *Hamlet.*

It'll be announced soon, the Fuhrer seeing English culture at its best, but I was asked not to tell anyone before the announcement."

"And you told Gilmore?" Carmichael could hardly believe it. He had told her, and she had immediately gone home to make an appointment with Marshall to begin building a bomb. He met Royston's eyes, and Royston shook his head a little in incredulity.

"I was so proud," Bannon repeated. "They chose my play. My *Hamlet*. Anyone would be proud."

"Have you told anyone else?" Carmichael asked.

"No," Bannon said, in such a way that Carmichael was sure that at the very least the whole cast knew.

"How did Gilmore react to the news about the celebrities coming to the first night?" Royston asked.

Bannon peered past Carmichael and looked at Royston as if he'd forgotten he was there. "She seemed very pleased, very excited, just as I'd expect. She asked if the Fuhrer spoke English, and I said I didn't think he did, and she said Shakespeare rose beyond language. She asked where they'd sit, and I told her it would be in the Royal Box."

"Where's that?" Carmichael asked. Bannon pointed up and back. Carmichael stood and turned and looked up at a bowed box. Carmichael imagined it blowing up, turning Hitler and Mark Normanby into bloody bodies like Marshall's, changing the history of the world.

"She was right, wasn't she?" Bannon asked.

"I don't know," Carmichael said.

" 'To be or not to be,' you don't need to understand English to understand that. It is more than the language, it is the human condition. And besides, it'll be a very visual production, the ballet, the swordfights—and we're going to provide a special program in German explaining the plot."

Carmichael turned to sit down again, and as he did so a girl and a man came down the stairs from the pass door. The girl was beautiful in a crisply aristocratic way, her blonde hair glossy, her features crisply defined. He had seen her, photographed in gentler focus, on the covers of magazines, and knew she was Viola Lark, previously Larkin, of the notorious Larkins of Carnforth. He thought now, as he had thought before, that there was something a little unstable about her. The man behind her looked like a bruiser; he wondered if he was a bodyguard.

She came directly towards them. She ignored Carmichael and Royston entirely. The man with her nodded to them in a friendly way. "Oh, Antony, Jackie said you were down here. I wanted to ask if it's all right if Devlin sits in on the rehearsal today. He'll be as silent as the grave, I promise."

"Oh Viola, you know I don't like this kind of thing," Bannon said. "Yes, I suppose he can, but don't make a habit of it. Pleased to meet you, Devlin."

Devlin shook Bannon's hand. "Oh, and these are Inspector Carmichael and Sergeant Um. Viola Lark and her boyfriend Devlin."

Carmichael had been looking at Viola, and he saw fear in her eyes for a moment, before it was glossed over by an actor's smooth confidence. She shook his hand without a tremor. "Devlin Connelly," her boyfriend said, revealing a strong Irish accent. Carmichael shook his hand too.

"Did you know Lauria Gilmore?" he asked him, to be sure.

"I never had the pleasure, Inspector," he said.

"I acted with her in *The Importance of Being Earnest,* but I didn't know her well," Viola said. There was no trace now of the nervousness or fear or whatever it had been. He almost wondered if he had imagined it.

"I saw that production," Carmichael said. "Just after the war, wasn't it? And you were Cecily?"

"That's right," she said. "I hadn't really seen much of Lauria since. I was looking forward to working with her again, and horrified when I heard about the bomb."

"We all were, Viola," Bannon said.

Connelly, Carmichael noticed, was looking where he had been looking, up to the Royal Box. He saw Carmichael looking at him, and smiled. "Fancy place this," he said.

"It's one of the most beautiful theaters in London, I always think," Bannon said. "Now, Inspector, have you finished with me? Because I really should be getting this rehearsal going."

"I'm finished with you for the time being, but if I think of anything else I want to ask you, would it be all right if I came back? You're a hard man to catch on the telephone."

"I'm here most of the time. Fix it up with Jackie if you want to see me." He turned away as if they had already left. "Now Devlin, you really must sit still here and be quiet, and not do anything to distract anyone. And if I find that Viola is nervous or off her form because she knows you're here, I'll send you out straight away. I won't give warnings, I won't hesitate." Connelly was twice Antony's size, and it was comical to see Bannon addressing him like a schoolboy.

"I'm hearing you clearly, Antony," Connelly said. He sounded amused, and when his eyes met Carmichael's there was a twinkle in them.

"Do we go out through the pass door, or can we get out at the front?" Carmichael asked.

"Just go back the way you came in, if you don't mind," Bannon said. "I could have them open up the front-of-house for you, but there isn't really any point. Just straight along the corridor. Shall I send Jackie with you?"

"We can find our way," Carmichael said. "Come on, sergeant. Good-bye Miss Lark, Mr. Connelly. Thank you, Mr. Bannon, you've really been most helpful."

Bannon looked blank, as if he wasn't at all sure how he might have helped. Viola Lark looked arrogant and impervious. He wondered how she had wound up involved with Connelly, who at least seemed as if he had a sense of humor.

They walked to the steps and through the pass door. Carmichael turned around for a last glance at the Royal Box and the assassination that had been averted by Gilmore's incompetence. "Well," Royston said as the door closed behind them. "Well!"

19

I had no trouble getting Devlin past the doorman. He'd seen me getting out of the car enough times, and we wandered up to him hand in hand. He didn't even ask his name. I showed him my dressing room, and Mollie's, which was empty because Mollie wasn't due in until the afternoon. We were doing my mad scenes and the Ophelia scenes that morning, so we didn't need Gertrude. Mollie had a little posy by her mirror, white carnations and a bit of fern, and Devlin asked about that. "By first night all our dressing rooms will look like flower shops," I said. "I don't know who sent Mollie that, some admirer probably."

He didn't say anything, just nodded, and walked behind me down the corridor.

As soon as we came out into the wings I knew it was a bad day to have brought Devlin into the theater. There was a change in the atmosphere, an awkwardness in the way people were standing about that told me something was wrong. Pat was leaning against a flat smoking. His eyes rested on Devlin a moment as we came past, and I saw admiration but also something else, a kind of spec-

ulation. "Where's Antoine?" I said. Pronouncing his name
as if it were French was the way we'd been teasing Antony
the last couple of days.

"Ask Jackie," Pat said.

Jackie was making notes. She looked up when she
heard her name. "He's in the pit," she said. "You'd better
go down if you want him."

I took Devlin back and down the stairs through the
pass door. Antony was sitting in the front row, casually,
with a couple of men next to him. As we walked towards
them I looked back at Devlin and saw that he was looking up at the boxes, calmly assessing already.

I don't know what I said to Antony after he told me
they were policemen. I felt sick, and I just acted over it
all as best I could. At least the stage gives you practice
for that sort of thing. They went quite quickly, thank
heavens, and before I knew it I was in position with Pat,
and Devlin was sitting with Jackie in the front row of
the stalls.

I knew my lines quite thoroughly by this time.
Antony had been lighting all morning, which had put
him into a foul mood, like always. He wanted me to run
through my soliloquy first and then go straight on with
Ophelia. He was considering having Ophelia watch me
all the time, to make him generally less sympathetic,
and so Pat stood at the back of the stage ominously
when I came down to the front to address the audience.
I had to hold a prop rose and twist it in my hands. The
rose had come, a ghastly silk thing, and Antony had
me make various moves with it.

"How does it look, Jackie?" he called. I looked out
into the pit. I couldn't see Jackie or Devlin now; we had
the proper stage lights that make everything else seem
like the inside of a dark hollow shell.

"Ghastly," Jackie called back. "You can tell it's a fake.
Fake flowers are never convincing. We could have a real
one if you like."

"The trouble with a real one is that it might die on

stage, and also it would be different every night, with thorns in different places. The thorns on this are quite blunt," I said, in an ordinary voice but pitched to carry.

"There's color matching too," Antony said. "Well, let's have the speech."

Three words in, he stopped me and rearranged my hands. I began again; this time I got to the second line. I couldn't help wondering what kind of impression this was making on Devlin. He had seen me act, but acting is different from taking direction. I did what Antony asked, even when he snapped, changing my emphases until they were just as he wanted.

Then I did the speech again from the top, only being stopped twice, while he arranged Pat. "This is the heart of the play," Antony said. It was also the bit of the play everybody knows by heart, and therefore the most tedious. It would have been hard to make it sound fresh and natural in any conditions, and that morning, with Devlin out there, I couldn't leave myself behind and sink into Hamlet as I usually did.

"Once again, from the top, both of you, and don't forget to move forward, Viola," Antony said.

As I started again, I felt all the audience attention, such as it was, leave me. I kept on, but the auditorium felt hollow. It's a truism that it's different acting with an audience, and with a full house rather than an empty house, but I'd never before felt the difference made by losing the attention of a bare half-dozen people.

"Sorry, but someone else to see you, Antony," Jackie called.

I stopped on "sea of troubles," absolutely amazed. Jackie never interrupted like that.

"Is this Piccadilly Circus?" Antony asked, with rhetorical fury. He went stamping down through the wings and the pass door, calling for house lights.

I realized then that someone must have come in through the pass door and down the steps, someone who had taken all the attention. I should have stayed where I was, but I was curious as to who it could possibly be, so I followed Antony. Pat gave me a grin and trailed along behind me.

There were three men. One of them was bland and English, one of them had only one arm and a very German face, and the third man was the one who knew how to make an unlit entrance well enough to take everyone's eyes from the stage. He was over six feet tall and wearing a black German uniform with silver eagles on the shoulders—and one thing you absolutely have to give the Nazis, whatever you think of them, they do have a simply splendid sense of style. His face was chiseled, and his hair was graying a touch at the temples in a most distinguished way. Yet, although he was a splendid physical specimen, he chilled me entirely.

We got down just as Antony was shaking hands, and though he didn't look pleased, he had to introduce us as well. "This is my star couple, my Hamlet and my Ophelia, Viola Lark and Pat McKnight," he said. "Viola, this is Mr. Um, of the Foreign Office, and Herr Schnell, of—the German Embassy, is it? And this is Captain Keiler of the SS."

Pat and I shook hands with Mr. Um and with Herr Schnell. The latter shook left-handed, as his right arm was an empty sleeve pinned to his side. I noticed several ribbons and medals on his uniformed chest but didn't recognize them. Then it was Keiler's turn. His eyes reminded me of the boy in the fairy tale who has swallowed a splinter of magic ice and is slowly turning to ice from the inside out.

"Heil Hitler!" he snapped, then he clicked his heels together and bowed over my hand. "Lady Viola, I know your sister Lady Celia of course. She tells me she has not seen you for a long time, and she longs to see you act."

The Lady Viola bit was a mistake all Continentals tended to make, and I have to say Pip, Celia that is, hadn't done a thing to discourage it. Dodo told me that when they went over there for the wedding Mamma nearly had apoplexy because they were calling Pip Lady Carnforth, which is Mamma's own title, and when Mamma straightened them out on that, they started calling Pip Lady Celia, though of course she's only an honourable, like all of us. I wondered if Pip was sick of it now, after ten years in Germany. "How kind of her," I said. "What a pity she won't be here to see me play Hamlet in front of the Fuhrer."

Captain Keiler's blue eyes registered a little confusion. "But she will," he said. "She accompanies Reichsmarshall Himmler, naturally. Had you not been told?"

"I'm always the last to know anything," I said, with a foolish little laugh, thinking that I must tell Siddy and Uncle Phil at once, and feeling a tremendous sense of relief because now it would all have to be canceled. Devlin and Loy might want to go ahead with the assassination, but Siddy and Uncle Phil were in charge and wouldn't risk hurting Pip. "I'm delighted to hear this news now." I smiled a genuine smile at Captain Keiler, whose expression softened a little before he looked back to Antony.

Mr. Um of the Foreign Office chose this moment to assert himself. "We've come to look over the security arrangements," he said.

Herr Schnell nodded. "We've come to ensure the security arrangements are adequate."

"We have come to take over the security arrangements," Captain Keiler said, clarifying.

Antony frowned. "There have never been any problems with security in the Siddons."

"There have never been the Fuhrer, the Reichsmarshall, and the Prime Minister of England together in the Siddons before," Captain Keiler said. He was smiling now as if someone had issued him a smile and told him to wear it along with the eagles and the creased pants. "The usual arrangements are doubtless adequate for the usual situation, but this is to be an unusual situation. I would like you to show me what is proposed, and if I have any changes to make, I will make arrangements. To begin with, where will the Fuhrer be sitting?"

"Do we have to do this now?" Antony asked. "We were in the middle of rehearsal."

"Carry on with your rehearsal," Captain Keiler said, generously. "I need someone to show me, only, and I will not disturb."

Antony looked at Jackie. "I'll show you," she said. "To answer your question, the Fuhrer will sit up there." She indicated the Royal Box.

"Ah yes," Mr. Um put in. "And we have arranged for flags to be hung in front of it, there, over the shield, and flowers along the top."

"The British flag and the German to be exactly the same size," Herr Schnell put in anxiously. "That has been agreed."

"Yes, that's entirely agreed, old chap, exactly the same size," Mr. Um said, reassuringly, just as Siddy and Loy had already told me.

Keiler didn't seem interested in flags; he was looking up assessingly, trying to see if there was anywhere underneath to put a bomb, probably. It was then I remembered Devlin, and looked around for him. He had done the sensible thing and stayed where he was. He smiled at me quite calmly when our eyes met. If that had been me, I'd probably have done something stupid like made a dash for it when the Germans came in, but Devlin sat tight, unruffled.

"I'll take you up, shall I?" Jackie asked.

"Afterwards I will need to see where he will come in, and where he will leave, and where all the exits are," Captain Keiler said. He turned to Antony. "From Wednesday I will be posting guards of our own at the doors, you understand, all doors, so tell your actors to have their cards with them for coming and going. Also"—he turned back to me—"Herr Schnell, with your permission, allow me to invite Lady Viola to the reception at

the Embassy on Tuesday evening. It will be a simple reception for welcoming the Fuhrer and Herr Reichsmarshall Himmler, and of course Lady Celia will be
there, and I believe some others of your beautiful
sisters."

"I think an invitation has been sent to—sent already,"
Herr Schnell said. He obviously knew the proper form
of my name, but equally obviously didn't want to use it
and risk embarrassing Keiler. "If not, then that over-
sight will be corrected immediately."

"Thank you, I'm honored," I said, which was about
the only possible thing to say in the circumstances, unless I decided to cackle like Richard III and shout that
they wouldn't be inviting me if they knew what I knew.

"If you'll come this way," Jackie said, and shepherded
them along. Devlin drew his feet back as they passed
him, but not an eye hesitated over him. He wouldn't be
able to scout out the theater. But it wasn't necessary any
longer. They'd have to bomb them in Covent Garden,
and that wouldn't be my affair. Devlin would let me go
home. I wondered if he would want to keep seeing me.

"All these terrible interruptions, Piccadilly Circus is
nothing to it," Pat murmured in my ear, unkindly imitating Antony. I would normally have laughed, but I didn't
have it in me at that moment.

"Come on, let's get back to it," was all Antony said.
The rehearsal dragged on, with me at my least inspired,
until Antony let us go for lunch. Devlin came out with
me. There was a German soldier standing next to the
doorman at the stage door. He was very young, and he
had a rifle. He looked at our papers conscientiously and
let us pass.

"I have to speak to Siddy, soon," I said to Devlin as
we walked out onto the Strand. It was a beautiful day,
the kind of day when you want to get out of London and
walk out in the hills somewhere.

"You'll be seeing her, and all of them, tomorrow,"
Devlin said. "Coltham again, for the weekend."

"Rehearsals!" I said. "What are you thinking?"

Devlin just blinked at me.

"You think I'm the kind of person who has country house weekends and doesn't need to work, but you're totally wrong. I gave that up years ago. Why don't you see that, when you see me working like a dog?"

"Where's your schedule?" he asked, without answering.

I took it out of my bag. The next day, Saturday, was impossible, I was needed at the theater all day and on into the evening. "You've Sunday afternoon free," he observed. Antony was rehearsing the Players. "I'll take you down to Coltham in time for tea. You'll see Siddy. But I heard what you want to tell her, and I can assure you she knows already."

I rolled my eyes because I didn't believe him.

20

It almost isn't worth driving back to the Yard from here, sir," Royston said.

"If we leave the car we'll only have to come back for it," Carmichael said, opening his door. "Penn-Barkis told me off for letting you use it on Sunday, you know."

Royston's already red face blushed to beetroot. "It wasn't me, I didn't say a word," he said.

"Then somebody saw you," Carmichael said, lightly. He hadn't meant to remind Royston of his betrayal. "But now. Worth it or not, drive me to the Yard."

"Yes, sir," Royston said.

They drove the half mile along the Strand, around the Aldwych and up the Kingsway in stately silence. Carmichael opened the door to get out, leaving Royston sitting in silent misery. Carmichael took pity on him. "As I said before, if I hadn't done anything wrong, you'd have had nothing to tell. Don't worry about it, sergeant. This is a new case, and if I'm not wrong, we've almost cleared it up."

"Apart from Nash and the Greens," Royston said.

Nash, and the Greens, yes. They were loose ends that

couldn't be left. Carmichael thought about Nash as he walked up the steps. The Greens were Jewish, and could have just run for no better reason than being afraid, like David Kahn. But there was no explanation for Nash. Nash must know whatever Marshall knew. How long could he stay in hiding? And where was he? Carmichael pushed open the doors and saw, in the glass booth that passed for a desk, the jowly face of Sergeant Humphries. He nodded a greeting. Was it Stebbings's day off? Or perhaps he was ill? "Morning, sergeant, where's Sergeant Stebbings this fine morning?"

Humphries rolled his eyes. "Gone to his daughter's wedding, in Brighton. He'll be back at work Monday morning. Sergeant Pomfret will be here Sunday, like always. I ought to issue a bulletin, or put up a sign, because everyone coming in has been asking. He's not the only one capable of sitting in this glass case, you know."

Carmichael laughed. "I should think he's worn that chair pretty smooth by now."

Humphries, who must have weighed several stone more than Stebbings, obligingly shifted his weight about and made the chair creak. "Very comfortable," he said.

"I want to see the Chief if he's time for me. He's probably half-expecting me."

Humphries looked ponderously down his list. "Nothing here, but I'll ask if you can see him and call through."

As Carmichael was turning to go, a young woman came tentatively through the doors and up the steps towards the desk. She was tall and dark-haired, and wore a green dress sprigged with spring flowers, like a meadow. Carmichael watched her hesitate and advance towards the desk. He wondered why she was here. The general public didn't like coming to the Yard. They didn't even like falling under its shadow, and crossed the road to avoid it. She certainly didn't seem like a criminal. Someone's witness, Carmichael thought, and went off to his room.

He read with some surprise the report on Mercedes

Carlos. It had taken some time to come through, because it had required inquiries in Spain, but he had expected it would be completely routine. On the contrary, it seemed her parents were Anarchists who had fought against Franco in the Civil War, her brother was missing, and she had been smuggled back to Britain by Gilmore in the guise of a maid after her Spanish tour. He stared at the paper, astonished. Anything less like an anarchist than Mercedes Carl with her piled-up hair and confiding way of speaking he couldn't imagine. He counted on his fingers and worked out that she would have been twelve or thirteen at the end of the Spanish Civil War. Whatever her parents were, she had been just a child. She had looked afraid, he remembered, when he had asked her if she'd go back to Spain now that Gilmore was dead. He would have sworn she was genuine. She had stayed put, when the Greens had run. He would have to speak to her again.

The telephone rang. "Humphries," Humphries said at the end of the line. "Got a young lady here wants to see you; well, wants to see someone in connection with the Gilmore bomb."

"Not a nut, you're sure, sergeant?" Carmichael asked. There were always a few loons turning up in a murder case. Mediums with messages from the dead, people who had seen suspects where suspects couldn't have been, people coming in to confess who regularly confessed to everything. He would have trusted Stebbings to weed out a nut.

"I'm pretty sure not, sir," Humphries said.

"Oh all right. Put her in the little interview room, I'll see her. And send Royston in, if you can find him," Carmichael said.

As he made his way through the gray corridors to the interview room, his hopes rose. Perhaps she was Nash's girlfriend and had been hiding him. He ran into Royston just outside the door and they went in together.

It was the tall girl in the green dress. She was sitting

in one of the uncomfortable chairs when Carmichael came in, and she jumped to her feet. Close up it was clear that despite her height she was younger than he'd thought, perhaps no more than eighteen or nineteen. She'd be a bit young for Nash, but men often did like young girlfriends. "Inspector Carmichael, Sergeant Royston," he said, offering his hand.

"Rachel Grunwald," she said, and shook hands with both of them.

Not Nash's girlfriend then. Carmichael found himself reassessing her. She didn't look Jewish, and her voice was an educated London one. "Sit down, please, and show me your papers, and tell me why you've come."

She pulled her papers out of the little leather bag she carried. He glanced at them. Yes, Jewish. Rachel Ann Grunwald, born 1930, Amsterdam, British resident, not citizen. He passed them to Royston, who diligently wrote it all down.

"It's about my uncle and aunt," she said, sitting down.

"And your uncle and aunt are?"

"Well, their real name is Grunwald too, but they call themselves Green." She hesitated, and Carmichael did his best to look noncommittal and encouraging. "My uncle changed it when he got married. Aunt Louise thought it was more English. It was Grunwald in 1940 when we all came over here. They both worked for Lauria Gilmore."

"They're missing," Carmichael said.

"I know." She swallowed hard. Royston passed her back her papers and she stuffed them into her bag without looking, keeping her eyes on Carmichael. "They've been moving from family to family since last Saturday night, trying to get to my father. My uncle was the youngest of the family. My father was the oldest. He feels— my father feels—protective towards him. Father brought him out of Holland with us. Uncle Hem was twenty-four, a university student at the time. I was ten. My brothers and sisters were even younger. And my uncle believes my father can work miracles. He thinks he can get him away again. But he can't. He's mad to risk it. We're not the sort of people who know about those things, and we can't afford it. It might be all right for rich people who can live anywhere, or people who have nothing to lose, but not for people like us. We already lost it all once, when we left Holland. I said to my father that he's endangering us all, if he helps Uncle Hem, and he's bound to be caught. But he says I'm just a girl and what do I know about it?"

Carmichael untangled this. "So your uncle Mr. Green is seeking aid from your father, Mr. Grunwald, and you feel your father is inclined to give it, despite the risk to the rest of his family?"

"I don't know what my uncle's done. I don't know if he was involved in the bomb. But if I tell you where they are, will you arrest them now, and stop my father getting himself involved? He's trying to see dangerous people, and he doesn't know any of them or the first thing about how to go about it and he's going to get himself arrested. Then they'll pack us all straight back to Holland, and you know what that means! But you mustn't tell my father it was me who told you."

Carmichael looked at her. There wasn't any "if" left in the matter of her telling him, whether she realized it or not, nor was she in a position to make bargains. "When I know where they are, I'll undertake to have them arrested immediately. They're not at your home?"

"No. There isn't anywhere to hide them there. Too many children." She shrugged. "They're at 141 Acacia Gardens, Golders Green. They're in the attic, my father says."

Royston wrote down the address. Carmichael watched him then looked back to the girl. "What does your father do, Miss Grunwald?"

She seemed a little disconcerted by the question. "He's a doctor. He was a doctor in Holland, and now again here."

Yes, she looked like a doctor's daughter. "And how many brothers and sisters do you have?"

"There are five of us," she said. "I don't quite see why you're asking this?"

"And is your mother alive?" Carmichael continued.

"Yes, of course she is!" Rachel Grunwald looked frightened now.

"So you think your father is risking the seven of you for the two Greens, and that he's making a bad bargain?"

She looked at Royston, who was writing, and back at Carmichael. "Yes. That's exactly what I think."

"Do you like your uncle and aunt?"

She pushed back her smooth dark hair. "To be perfectly frank, no. Uncle Hem has never made anything of himself, he's a servant still, after all these years. And my aunt Louise is always putting on airs about being born British, as if it makes any difference, when I'm as English as she is after all this time. And they're so Jewish! I mean we keep the Sabbath and have two sets of dishes, but that's not good enough for them. And now building a bomb, or whatever they were doing. They're mad. I just don't want them to drag me and my family down with them."

"Well, thank you, Miss Grunwald, you've been very helpful," Carmichael said, standing up.

"And you won't tell my father I came here?" she asked.

"I can't make any promises, but I'll do what I can," Carmichael said, in the old formula of the Yard. It reassured the girl, and she went out, clutching her bag.

"Sickening, somehow," Royston said, shutting the door behind her.

"However sickening, get a team of nice solid constables together and go and pick up the Greens, and whoever's hiding them. We'll need to talk to Mr. Grunwald too, to see what sort of feelers he's been putting out to try to find the Jewish terrorist underground. But get the

Greens, right now, before she thinks better of it and tips them off."

"Not coming yourself, sir?" Royston asked.

"I have to see the Chief about the Hitler box thing," Carmichael said. "He might be waiting for me now."

Indeed, Humphries sent Carmichael upstairs to Penn-Barkis. The lift once more wafted him to the top of the building, and the astonishing view of the kingdoms of London spread out before him, looking particularly enticing in the sunshine.

"News on the Gilmore bomb?" Penn-Barkis greeted him. "I hope so."

"Yes, quite a bit of news," Carmichael was pleased to report. "I know what they were going to do with it. It seems when Mr. Hitler's in London next week, he's to see *Hamlet,* with Mr. Normanby, and it's the production Gilmore was going to be in."

Penn-Barkis nodded briskly. "Good work. Is there proof?"

Carmichael shook his head. "Balance of probability only."

"Well, they're dead," Penn-Barkis said. "The play can go on uninterrupted."

"There is the question of Nash," Carmichael said.

"Who's Nash?" Penn-Barkis frowned.

"Marshall's friend, the one who has disappeared. He and Marshall were apparently like David and Jonathan."

The implications of Penn-Barkis's sneer angered Carmichael, but he plowed on regardless.

"There are Gilmore's servants as well, the Greens, the ones who vanished, but we've got a line on them. In fact, Royston should be picking them up as we speak. But I'm worried about Nash."

"You mean you think he might try to carry on where Marshall left off?" Penn-Barkis asked.

Carmichael hesitated. "I suppose it's a possibility. I expect Marshall and Gilmore being blown to kingdom come put an end to it, but I can't rule it out altogether."

"Do you think we ought to warn the security services, and the Germans for that matter? We could cancel the visit to the theater. But it is being announced today, it's too late to cancel without publicity. Is there enough of a risk to make it worth it? It's a big thing, canceling something like that, makes it look as if we can't handle our own people, in front of the Germans, who certainly do know how. Bit of a black eye for us, really."

"I don't want to decide that now," Carmichael said. "I want to talk to the Greens, who may know something about Nash and about the plot. Probably, without Gilmore to get the thing inside, the plot will be off anyway. But if we have to cancel, since there would be publicity whenever it happened, we can get them to cancel right up to the last minute, can't we, and there's still a week."

"A week, yes, plenty of time," Penn-Barkis said. "Very well. Don't tell the press anything, let them think you're still investigating. We don't want to tip Nash off. And we'll increase security on the theater, and on Covent Garden as well in case they change their venue with the loss of the actress."

"Yes, sir," Carmichael said.

"Good work, Inspector," Penn-Barkis said. "Take the weekend off. Rest. You can afford the time. Go to a show. Relax."

"Yes, sir," Carmichael said again, more decided than ever that he would hand in his resignation at the end of this case.

21

I don't have to explain, do I, that when we went to Coltham Siddy and Uncle Phil were of exactly the same mind as Devlin and everything was perfectly bloody? I can hardly bear to think about it. I've already written far too much, there's no need for me to go into the details of all that. We all sat there in Coltham, all the same people as the week before but in the Chinese parlor, because it was raining, and ate scones and seed cake and little delicate cucumber sandwiches, and they tried to explain to me that a sister more or less made no difference, if you could get rid of a couple of dictators at the same time. Siddy at least had the grace to look as if her conscience was a bit troubled by it.

I've said I almost never saw my family and kept up with them from Mrs. Tring reading the society papers. That's true. I often went for months without seeing any of them. I saw Dodo most often, once or twice a year when she came up to London for the day. I hadn't seen Pip for years. I could dislike them quite intensely—at that moment, I almost hated Siddy. But we'd all been brought up together in a way quite unlike the way normal people are brought up, even people of our class, and that made a bond. Whether I saw them or not, whether I wanted to see them or not, they were my sisters and I cared about them. From one angle, I could see how ghastly they were, and that was the angle on which I had changed my name and made my life in the theater. There was another angle though, a very deep one, and from that angle everyone else came and went but my sisters were the only ones who were real.

There were six of us. Pappa wanted a son, and so he made Mamma keep on having babies, as fast as she could until she just couldn't do it anymore, and they kept being girl after girl. There's a story that when Ma was carrying Rosie she made Pa promise that this was the last, and he'd agreed because he was sure it was a boy this time. A gypsy told him. Then when Rosie was born they both wept, Ma with relief and Pa with disappointment, and afterwards he would never allow gypsies to camp in Gypsy Hollow.

The title, and Carnforth Castle, will go to some boring Larkin cousins in Northumberland. You'd think this was a tragedy and the end of a way of life the way Pa carries on, but it happens every couple of generations in every family in England and somehow everything stays the same. For that matter, Grandfather was the nephew of the previous Lord Carnforth, and Pa himself was a younger son. If Uncle Bartie hadn't been killed at Ypres he'd not have inherited. In fact, Pa was in line to inherit anyway, because according to some letters Tess found inside *The Symposium* our sainted uncle was as bent as a paperclip. But if he'd had to wait for Bartie to die in the usual way, we wouldn't have been brought up at Carnforth.

Carnforth isn't much like Elsinore really. It's in Oxfordshire, about twenty miles from Oxford itself. They call it a castle, but there's only really the keep and one tower that's medieval. Most of the house is eighteenth century. The medieval castle was built by some Norman

Larkins who tramped over tediously from the Continent with William the Conqueror. They lived in it through the Middle Ages, no doubt finding it drafty and inconvenient, assuming the rest of it was like the bits that are left. The Elizabethan Larkins had the good sense to move to London where they could go to see original Shakespeare plays, and let the castle decay. I always say I'm a throwback to them. After the civil war, unfortunately, the Restoration Larkins decided to go back to Carnforth. Perhaps they didn't get on with Nell Gwyn. They built a charming manor house beside the falling-down castle. That manor house burned down at the end of the eighteenth century, just in time to be regarded as charming ruins by the Regency Larkins, who rebuilt the castle. There's a painting of the Restoration house in the billiard room, and one room of it survives as a sort of barn. We used to spend a lot of time in it.

People think it must be frightfully grand living somewhere your ancestors have always lived, but they don't think of the horrors of eighteenth-century kitchens, miles from the dining room so that the food is always cold. They don't think of trying to heat the Hall—that's the old keep, the central part of the house, where you come in. Most of all they don't imagine being cooped up there for eighteen years seeing almost nobody but your family.

We didn't go to school. Pappa had the theory that school made girls vulgar and ordinary. Nor did we have a governess. Pappa thought Mamma quite adequate to teach us, not really considering that she had never had much of an education herself. Mamma did teach us all to read, more or less, but her lessons never got much beyond that. Fortunately there was an excellent library, mostly bought by the yard by our grandfather. None of the books were modern, except for Pappa's collection of books on the Great War, but it was possible to read anything worth reading that had been written before 1875. Those of us given to reading read a lot. Tess did, and I

did, but Pip hardly opened a book and I don't believe
Rosie ever did. For me, it was something to do. I sometimes say it was good training for an actress. I read
widely. I learned to memorize and to recite—Pappa was
awfully fond of having us learn poetry. I had most of
Marmion by heart before I was ten.

Beyond that we played complicated games of our own
devising, inside and out. We loved animals. We had pets,
which we adored, and wept when they died. We carried
out a surreptitious war with the gamekeeper, who laid
traps for wild animals. We were always on the side of the
animal. We were close to animal ourselves. We never
went to London, and though we had visitors they didn't
pay much attention to us. Why should they? We were
children. They would say we'd grown and hear us recite
and then we'd vanish back to our own lives and they'd
sigh with Pappa over his lack of sons. We seldom met
children of our own social class, though we were incul-
cated with a great deal of information about the social
class of the children of the Oxfordshire peasants we did
meet, enough to stop us making any friends. Mamma
and Pappa were the ultimate authorities, inestimably
above us, almost like gods. The servants and villagers
could be allies or enemies, but were inestimably below
us. The only people on our own level were each other.

We were six sisters, with only an eleven-year age gap
between Tess, whose real name was Olivia, born in
1914, and Rosie, born in 1925. When people talk about
us as sisters they always want to talk about what happened to us afterwards, when we were grown up. What
they couldn't see was what counted was what happened
when we were children, at Carnforth, in that hothouse
atmosphere when we couldn't get away from each
other, when we were each others' only companions, and
rivals, when we loved and hated one another and
couldn't imagine life without the others. The jokes we
heard, the words we made up, everything in our lives
was defined by each other. Pip, Celia, was born a year

after Tess in 1915. Perhaps Pa couldn't get leave because I wasn't born until 1917, when he spent a year as Lord Lieutenant in Dublin recovering from wounds gained at the Somme. He was fit to go back to France again the year after. He loved his time on the Western Front and said afterwards it was terrific fun, and spent much of his time reading books about it and correcting them in red ink. He didn't write to the authors pointing out their errors, as Tess suggested he should; he thought it quite adequate, however egregious their mistakes, to correct them by hand in his own copy. Siddy was born in 1919, Dodo, whose real name was Miranda, in 1922, and Rosie in 1925.

In our shifting alliances, I seldom aligned myself with Pip or Siddy, my nearest agemates. More often I would be with poor Tess, or with the little ones, especially Dodo. Pip and Siddy were each other's inseparable favorites. We had our times of tormenting each other, and our times of truce, and there was always the option of "ginns," which we never abused.

We all had our own spheres, our things, where we were the experts, that we cared about passionately and defended from the others. These things distinguished us from one another, were claimed and staked-out territories as much as anything. It was almost arbitrary what they were, and how far away from each other they were, in childhood at least. My godmother, my mother's cousin Bea, took me to see *Romeo and Juliet* when I was ten, and thereafter I aimed my life towards the theater. Theater became my thing, my sphere, as communism was Siddy's and academia Tess's. Dodo's thing was art, painting; Rosie's was horses; and Pip's was Pappa. It became fascism later, when she was older and fascism was invented, but there's not so much difference as there might appear. It had to do with power. Pappa was the most powerful person in our world—physically powerful, and having all the real power as well. She was fascinated by that. I don't think Pip ever read a book that wasn't about a Great Man.

She read about Napoleon and Alexander, she read some of Pappa's war books, because they were, in her mind, about him. She was frankly oedipal about Pappa. She said once, at the tea table, that she'd marry him when Mamma died. She must have been about seven, which would have made me five. I remember Mamma continued pouring tea quite serenely and saying something about the funny things children say. This may be a false memory, because it was a story Mamma found funny and repeated later.

In later life, these territories marking us off from each other became our real lives. We were strange obsessive children, and we became strange obsessive adults. Tess went to Oxford and had her debutante year and got married appropriately, safely, to Sir James Thirkie, baronet. Pip demanded, and got, a finishing year abroad to learn German, did learn German, contrived to meet Hitler and managed to hook a leading Nazi as a husband. During the war, when German bombers were flattening London, and killing poor Tess in her shelter for government wives, we felt bad about Pip's position, but all was forgiven later, as all was forgiven the Germans generally. I became an actress. Siddy came out, married, had a baby, divorced, caused scandal by leaving the baby with her husband, visited Moscow and became a real communist, married again, and rapidly divorced again. Dodo paints, and has the occasional exhibition, is married to a prominent scientist who has something to do with atomic research, and has two delightful children. Rosie, whose obsession was the most normal, came out, rode to hounds, met and married the Duke of Lancashire and produced sons. She steeplechases, breeds racehorses, and hunts in the Shires every autumn.

My sisters—I don't necessarily like them, and I'd rather be stuck with pins than spend a week alone with any of them, but I love them. They are necessary to my world. I felt diminished when Tess died. I went to the funeral, even though it was up in Yorkshire and meant hours on a blacked-out train. When I got there, old Lady

Thirkie was charming to me, Sir James seemed very withdrawn, Pappa grunted, and Mamma barely acknowledged my existence. It was a funny kind of funeral, as they didn't really have a body. We were all there, the five surviving sisters as the newspapers put it. Poor Tess. I miss her still. I still couldn't really believe Siddy could write Pip off that way.

It's what the trick cyclists say, isn't it, tell me about your childhood? I wonder if they'd see how ours made sense of us? I wonder if they'd think any of us emerged from it sane?

Back in the Chinese parlor of Coltham, on Sunday afternoon, Lieutenant Nash poured me more tea. "I know it makes it harder," he said. "But you knew there would be other people in the box, aides and bodyguards and people like that."

"I wasn't thinking about them," I said, though I could see they had already been on poor Lieutenant Nash's conscience. He was just the kind of person to fret about them. "I suppose I should have been. I'm finding it difficult enough to think of killing Mr. Hitler and Mr. Normanby, let alone more comparatively innocent people, and now you want me to kill my own sister."

"You won't have to actually do it," Loy said. "I'll do it." He was leaning back beside Siddy on a splendid golden Chinese sofa with black carved dragon arms. He looked relaxed and comfortable as he suggested doing murder.

"Line of sight—" Devlin began, but Loy cut him off.

"In a theater like that, radio bounces off everywhere, you don't need as exact a line of sight as you think. If I sit up in the ha'pennies, towards the back, I'll have as good a line of sight as anywhere, apart from the stage." He popped a triangular sandwich into his mouth and began to chew.

Nash looked at them angrily. He was on the edge of his seat. "Can't you see that isn't the point?" he asked. "Miss Larkin isn't distressed at the thought of whose finger will

be on the trigger, but at the thought of killing her sister."
He turned back to me. "All I can say is that sometimes to
achieve something good, it is necessary to do something
bad."

"The end justifies the means?" I asked. "Well, no. It
doesn't. I think the world can replace those dictators
much more easily than I can replace a sister, and I think
it will. This country has been slowly drifting towards
fascism ever since the Farthing Peace—before that
even, throughout the thirties. There isn't anything we
can do to stop it if it's what most people want."

"It isn't what most people want," Uncle Phil said. He
leaned towards me across the table. "Look at the protests
against the identity cards."

"A handful of Jews and communists and Quakers and
people like that?" I asked. "The majority of ordinary
people don't care or actively like the idea of our having
a proper leader, a fuhrer to sort us out. If we kill Hitler,
Germany will immediately replace him with another
just like him, and that goes double for Normanby."

"You said this before," Devlin said.

I looked at him. "I'll say it again. It doesn't matter
how many times I say it. It won't make any difference. If
I felt very strongly about doing it I might be prepared to
kill Pip in the way of it, but I don't. Oh, I'll do it. I
haven't forgotten what you said to me in the car last
week. But I hate it. I don't think it's justified by anything
at all."

Devlin smiled. Uncle Phil stared at the wall as if the
painted turquoise phoenixes and dragons had wisdom
for him. Siddy stubbed out a half-smoked cigarette, and
turned for Loy to light her another. Nash looked pained.
"It isn't easy," he said. "I didn't make this decision easily myself. Pete already died for this, and Lauria too. But
they were volunteers, and Miss Larkin isn't. It seems to
me there comes a point where we become as bad as our
enemies. What about the Covent Garden option?"

Everyone's eyes went to Loy. He enjoyed it, I could

tell, he leaned back and blew out smoke slowly. "Well, it would be a suicide mission," he said. "We don't have anyone on the inside, and couldn't get anyone in. A bomb wouldn't be possible. A gun should be, but there's no chance of surviving it. We do know, from our FO contact, where Hitler will be sitting. But even if we could take him, it would be only half the job. Normanby won't be with him, he'll be accompanied by Lord Eversley on that occasion."

"I'll do it," Nash said. "I'm a decent shot and I'm prepared to risk it."

"We need you afterwards, Bob," Malcolm said. "We need your contacts in the Forces to ensure there isn't a military uprising." Uncle Phil put his hand on Nash's arm. Nash looked as distressed as any stiff-upper-lipped English face can look.

"I'm more than a decent shot," Loy said, his last words imitating Nash's tones and accent unkindly. "And I'm prepared to risk it if necessary. It's the emergency back-up plan. It's half the job, and it's suicide. The *Hamlet* bomb does the whole job, and we can walk away from it."

Siddy looked at me. "Pip does more than condone evil," she said. "She almost worships it. She knows what's going on. I'd rather do this without hurting her, but she's not the sister you remember."

"No more than you are?" I asked, cruelly. "No, she is, and you are. You two locked me in the barn once. Do you remember? You said Pums was there and needed me, and when I went there was no cat, just the dark night and the empty barn, and you locked the doors and I heard both of you laughing as you ran away. It's clear you haven't changed a bit, either of you."

22

Monday morning, Carmichael was at the Yard early. Sergeant Stebbings was back at his usual post, looking as if he had never left. "How did the wedding go?" Carmichael asked.

"Well enough," Stebbings said. "Nothing special for you this morning."

"Nothing on Nash?"

"Not a sausage."

Carmichael frowned. He was increasingly convinced that if he found Nash he'd have solved the case. "I came in to ask where the Greens are. They were being picked up on Friday afternoon. The Chief said I could take the weekend off, and I did, but I want to have a go at them this morning."

Stebbings looked through his papers, slowly. "Nothing here," he said. "I don't know anything about it."

"Maybe it's on my desk," Carmichael said, without much hope. "Is Royston in?"

"Due in at nine," Stebbings said.

"Well, send him in to me when he gets here," Carmichael said.

His office was as piled up with papers as it always was, but there was nothing new except the day's issue of the *Times*. Carmichael lifted it from the top of a stack and read through the headlines: Hitler due to arrive in England on historic visit; Winston Churchill calls the American-style fixed terms unconstitutional; protesters clash with Ironsides and are arrested; battle for Kursk. He threw the paper towards the basket, missed, picked it up again and dropped it in carefully. He looked at his desk and sighed. Well, as he was in early with nothing much to do, he might as well go through the piles. The report on Mercedes Carl he put on one side. He would have to go out to Hampstead to see her again, if she was still there. If she was, it was almost proof of her innocence. He sighed. He got rid of old newspapers, old reports, old envelopes, filling his wastepaper basket.

He read a report he had read before, relating to the Farthing case, saying some of Lady Eversley's stolen jewelry had been identified in Portsmouth and Hove. A gold hairbrush had been sold by a middle-aged woman, and a bracelet and some earrings by a young woman in a headscarf. Lucy Kahn, Carmichael thought, and wondered what she had been doing in Portsmouth. Seeing Nash and Marshall? Was it possible? No, it must be pure coincidence.

Royston put his head around the door, knocking as he did. "The Greens are in the Scrubs, sir," he said.

"In the Scrubs? Is every police station in London full?" Carmichael asked in surprise.

"Pretty much, sir, yes, so far as I can make out. Jews, terrorists, protesters. They're talking about building new prisons; Mr. Normanby is anyway."

"Well, let's go to the Scrubs and see them." Carmichael stood. "Bring the car around to the front."

Clouds were chasing each other past the sun. They crawled along, hardly faster than walking pace, behind a red double-decker bus. "Did you hear about Sergeant Stebbings's daughter's wedding?" Royston asked as he overtook the bus. "Wedding car broke down on the way to the ceremony, so Stebbings flagged down a passing police car, daughter and all, so she turned up at the church in her long white gown getting out of a patrol car, and everyone thought they'd done it on purpose."

Carmichael laughed. "Who told you that?"

"Oh, Sergeant Stebbings himself," Royston said. "He could see the joke, though it's always hard to tell with his voice that never cracks."

Carmichael bit back an inappropriate urge to complain that Stebbings had told Royston and said nothing to him.

They were in a sunny patch when they drew up at His Majesty's Prison Wormwood Scrubs. Sunshine did not improve its pink and white castle-style entrance. "Not a pretty sight," Royston said. "Have you been in the Scrubs before, sir?"

"Once," Carmichael said. "In the Bradshaw business. I came here to talk to Ben Bradshaw after he'd been convicted but before the rest of them had."

Royston nodded. "Was it bad inside?"

"About like any prison, sergeant," Carmichael said, and led the way to the gate.

They showed their Scotland Yard identification at the candy-striped gate, and again inside, and were shown politely to a bare room painted chocolate brown to waist height and a banana yellow above. The only furniture consisted of two low benches. "There's this room, which is the interview room, or the visitor's room with a partition," the warder said.

"This will do, thank you. Please bring the Greens now."

"It's only Green we have," the warder said.

"Well where's Mrs. Green then?" Royston asked.

"I don't have any information about that," the warder said, cringing at the sergeant's tone. "But we're not set up for women here, let alone married couples."

"Bring us Mr. Green," Carmichael said, wearily. The

warder left. Carmichael paced from one end of the room to the other. There were no windows, and the bare bulb of the electric light swung several feet above their heads. "How did you know Mr. Green was here, Royston?" he asked after a while.

"They told me in Hampstead when I tried to get them into the cells at the station on Friday," Royston said.

"So Jacobson, or someone at Hampstead, might know where Mrs. Green has been taken?"

"Very likely, sir."

"Did you charge them?"

"Inspector Jacobson booked them all under the new terrorism laws, because otherwise they'd need to be charged in three days, and it was Friday. There's no doubt if they were involved with the bomb that it was terrorism, and that the other people, the Levis, were sheltering them. And this way they can be held for a month before charging, if it's necessary."

"Thank goodness he had the sense, because it might have been very difficult charging them today if we've lost Mrs. Green."

Royston laughed, and the door opened to admit the warder, accompanied by another uniformed warder and a little man in a crumpled brown suit. Mr. Green had been left his own clothes, as he was a prisoner on remand, not yet convicted.

"Thank you, please wait outside, I'll call you when he needs to go back to his cell," Carmichael said. The warders looked as if they would have liked to dispute this order, but nodded, forced Green down on one of the benches, and left.

"I am Inspector Carmichael of Scotland Yard, and this is Sergeant Royston," Carmichael began. Royston took out his notebook and sat down on the other bench. Carmichael remained on his feet. "Well, Mr. Green, or do you prefer Grunwald?"

"Green, please sir," Green said, looking up at

Carmichael. He did have an accent, not very heavy, the kind of accent Carmichael thought of as a Jewish servant accent. "Where is Louise? Is she all right?"

Carmichael and Royston exchanged glances. "Your wife is in custody, but she's all right. I can't tell you where she is," Carmichael said. "Now, please just confirm a few facts for me. You are Hem Green, formerly servant to Miss Gilmore?"

"Yes."

"You are a Jew?"

"Yes."

"You came to this country in 1940, under the name of Grunwald, married a Jewish woman of British birth in 1942, and changed your name to Green. You have been employed by Lauria Gilmore ever since."

"Yes, that's right."

"Your brother is Dr. Grunwald, of Golders Green?"

"Yes . . ." Green licked his lips nervously. "He knows nothing about this."

"We'll find out what Dr. Grunwald knows," Carmichael said.

"Why am I here?"

"You're here specifically because the police stations are full, and you're under arrest because of suspicion of complicity in the bomb Lauria Gilmore was building in her Hampstead house."

Green shut his eyes for a moment, then opened them again and looked Carmichael full in the face. "Can we make a deal?" he asked.

"A deal? What kind of deal?"

"If I tell you everything I know, will you let Louise go? And the Levis? They're all innocent. And I'll serve a term in an English prison for what I've done, but you won't send me back to Holland."

"I don't think I can agree to that, Mr. Green," Carmichael said. "Conspiracy to terrorism is a capital charge."

"Well then hang me if you must, but don't send me back to the Reich. At least it would be a clean death, not like in the camps. At least you can't send Louise there."

"If you were deported to Holland your wife would go with you," Royston said, unexpectedly.

Green's eyes snapped to him. "But she's British born!"

"I shouldn't think that would make much difference," Royston said. "If we sent you and Louise and the Levis off to a work camp in Poland or Czechoslovakia who would know the difference? You're not in a position to make bargains, Mr. Green. But we might—might, I say—agree not to send her off and to hang you here, if you're very cooperative."

"What was the intended object of the bomb?" Carmichael asked, softly.

Green looked up, despair and defeat visible in the slump of his shoulders and the creases of his face. "Hitler," he said, quietly, and swallowed. "She wanted to blow up Hitler when he came to her theater."

"Well, that's a good answer, it confirms what we already knew," Carmichael said. "And who was involved in the conspiracy altogether?"

"Lauria, Peter Marshall, and myself," Green said.

"Not your wife?" Royston asked.

"No. She knows now, I had to tell her, but she didn't know anything at the time."

"That's hard to believe," Carmichael said. "I doubt a jury would believe it unless you're much more forthcoming than you have been. You offer us an absurdly small conspiracy, with everyone except you dead. And we already know some of the others. Lieutenant Nash, for instance."

"You know about Bob?" Green looked surprised. "Well, Bob, yes. And if you know him you must know about Lord Scott, and Mr. Nesbitt, his secretary. Apart from them there's an Irishman I only met once, Sir Aloysius, and his girlfriend, Siddy. I don't know her proper name."

Royston was writing rapidly.

"Is that the truth?" Carmichael asked.

"It's the truth!" Green protested.

"And all these people were in favor of blowing up Hitler? Lord Scott? Sir Aloysius? Sir Aloysius what?"

"I don't know. He's Irish, tall and dark, he drives a sports car. He wears silk scarves and handmade suits. He talks in a sarcastic kind of way."

"And what about his girlfriend?" Royston asked. He had caught up with his notes.

Green looked around at him wildly. "I said, I don't know her name. She goes by Siddy, but that isn't a girl's name. She's got short blonde hair and she smokes all the time and she's got an expensive voice, a bray like they do."

"How old?" Royston asked.

"I don't know—twenty-five?" Green shook his head.

"And Sir Aloysius? How old?"

"Thirty-five, maybe older. He looks like a sportsman, fit but maybe getting a bit old for it."

"And all these people were involved in the conspiracy, but your wife wasn't?" Carmichael asked, as Royston began to write again.

"No! Louise didn't know anything about it. She wouldn't have approved."

"And Miss Carl didn't know about it?"

"Mercedes?" Green was startled. "Who would tell anything important to someone with more hair than wits?"

"Did you know Miss Carl's parents were anarchists in the Spanish Civil War?" Carmichael asked.

Green blinked. "I knew they were something that had got her into trouble in Spain. Lauria told us that when she brought her home. I didn't know they were anarchists. But Mercedes must have been just a baby."

"She knew nothing of your conspiracy in any case?"

"Nothing at all," Green confirmed. "She wasn't even there. She had Friday off to see her young man. Lauria was always giving her time off, whatever she wanted. She was much too soft with her."

"How did it work that Miss Carl and Mrs. Green didn't know anything about it when you were all in the same house?" Carmichael asked. "There must have been a lot of coming and going of conspirators."

"No, not really." Green looked relieved. "Sometimes Lauria would call me in as if she wanted something and I'd stay to talk about it, that's all."

Royston looked up again. "How long did the conspiracy last?"

"It wasn't really a conspiracy like you think." Green held up a hand. "I know you mean in the legal sense it was a conspiracy, but it wasn't like we were having secret meetings and passwords or anything. They were just friends of Lauria's. She'd known them all for a long time, except for Sir Aloysius and his girl. She knew they thought the way she did, that's all. When she came home from lunch with Bannon on Friday she called me in and said there was this wonderful chance. She told me to shut the door, and not to tell Louise. She knew Louise would panic. She told me she had a chance to kill Hitler, and she and Marshall were going to make a bomb."

"On Friday after lunch?" Carmichael said, just to confirm. "That was the first you heard of it?"

Green nodded. "She'd just heard about Hitler going to the theater. It was all quite impromptu, you see."

"An improvised bomb, not an organized terrorist group, you mean?" Carmichael asked, sympathetically, wanting to draw Green out.

"Yes. You don't have to be a terrorist to want to kill Hitler."

"So what did she want you to do?" Royston asked.

"She wanted me to make a case for it."

"A case?" Carmichael asked, puzzled.

"A wooden case, like a strut, painted white so it would look like part of the box. I said I would, and she said I could start on Sunday, once she had the bomb made, and to make it look to Louise like part of my ordinary carpentry for the house."

"Did you know how she was going to make the bomb?"

He looked uncomfortable. "No more she didn't know herself. She asked them all round for dinner, to find that out. At first it was only going to be five; with Lauria, Lord Scott and Mr. Nesbitt, and Peter and Bob. Then she called me in again and said Sir Aloysius and his girl would be there too, so they were seven for dinner. Louise was fuming, she'd started preparing already."

"So the conspiracy only had one meeting?" Carmichael looked at Royston, who was writing diligently.

"On the Friday night. They had dinner. Now we were supposed to be off after dinner, it being Friday night, but I asked Lauria if she wanted me to do anything on Saturday, and she said no, to go to the synagogue as usual."

"Were you there when the rest of the conspiracy were eating their dinner?" Royston asked.

"I was there to serve them." Green looked at Carmichael. "It really wasn't like a conspiracy like you read in the papers. It was only because Lauria had this idea, and they took it up."

Carmichael nodded. "What did they discuss at dinner?"

"Well, Lauria had told them about it on the phone. Bob had brought this old set of instructions, from the war, about making bombs, and he and Peter were very keen to use it. Sir Aloysius said that was amateur and to wait until he'd got hold of a friend of his who knew all about it. Lord Scott said better not to involve more people than absolutely necessary. They agreed that Lauria and Peter and Bob would have a go at making the bomb on the Saturday morning."

"Nash was there?" Royston asked.

"He was there when Louise and I went off at nine," Green confirmed.

"Did they stay the night?"

Green looked shocked. "Certainly not. They went off home."

"To Portsmouth?" Carmichael asked.

"No. Peter had a little London flat. We saw Bob and Peter frequently, they were friends of Lauria's since the war. They'd often dine with her, or take her out somewhere."

"Was she particularly close to one of them?" Carmichael asked. They were Kinnerson's age, he remembered, rather old for lieutenants, but surely too young for Gilmore.

Green laughed. "They were particularly close to one another," he said. "You get a lot of that in the theater, and Lauria didn't mind."

Royston tutted. Carmichael went straight on. "So what was the position with the conspiracy when you last spoke to them?"

"That Lauria and Peter and Bob were going to make a bomb, that I'd make a case for it, then Lauria was going to smuggle it into the theater and blow up Hitler and Mr. Normanby, and then afterwards Lord Scott would see that things went right."

"By right, meaning the way you wanted them?" Royston asked, sarcastically.

"Meaning in the enviable tradition of British democracy," Green said, with dignity, in his accented English.

"What was Lord Scott expecting to get out of this?" Carmichael asked.

Green shook his head. "I didn't ask."

"Was he a close friend of Miss Gilmore?"

"Not all that close. She went to his parties, he sometimes came to dinner, or took her out. They had known each other for a long time, since she was a pretty young actress. I think they might have been close, in your sense, meaning she might have been his mistress, a long time ago, but for years it has just been a friendship."

"And what about Sir Aloysius?" Carmichael asked.

"I don't know anything about him at all, other than his name and what he looks like, which I've told you. I never saw him before. I don't think Lauria knew him either, because she called him by his title, which she wouldn't with someone she knew well. Lots of lords and ladies and sirs she knew well enough to call by their names, but not him."

"And you contend that this impromptu conspiracy sprang up on Friday afternoon and was ended on Saturday morning with the explosion?" Carmichael gave Green a hard stare.

"Yes. Yes, that's the truth." Green looked desperately at Royston, found no sympathy, and looked back at Carmichael.

"Why didn't you seek their help when you ran?"

Green put his hands to his face. "I wanted to go to Lord Scott, but Louise wouldn't have it," he said. "She thought we should stay with our own sort. She didn't think lords and sirs would want to be bothered with me, and likely enough she was right, even if that Siddy did shake my hand. What did it cost to shake your hand, Louise said, compared to hiding us and keeping us safe."

"And what did you intend to do?"

"Get to Canada or Australia," Green said. "Louise, she didn't know anything about it, and she's English—Jewish like me, but English—she doesn't know what it can be like, how bad it can be. Let her go, sir, let her go back to her parents. She never did anything except hide in a few attics with me for a week."

"You keep on cooperating, and we'll see what we can do," Carmichael said.

They asked him all the questions again, and everything else they could think of; they kept it up until Green was hoarse and Royston was running out of paper, but they didn't get any more out of him and he didn't change his story.

23

Monday morning, at rehearsal, in between endless attempts at getting our scene right, Mollie explained that she was worried about what I was going to wear to the reception. She'd brought me in the engraved invitation; it had arrived at the flat that morning. There was a swastika embossed into the card. We were rehearsing the bedroom scene, where I confront Gertrude about Claudius's true nature and then accidentally kill Polonius, who is spying on us from behind an arras. I claim to think he's a rat, and in fact think he's Claudius. The emotions were all in the right places, but Antony kept stopping us so that he could rearrange the arras. It was a sort of screen, like a big fire screen, and he had it downstage at an angle so that the audience could see Polonius crouching behind it all the time. It persisted in not falling in the right direction when I stabbed through it. I had to repeat my "rat" line and stab about a hundred times, with pauses for Antony to call the stagehands and fuss with the stupid arras.

"What are you going to wear to this reception at the German Embassy?" Mollie asked, during one of these pauses. She was sitting up in bed, propped on pillows. Her hair had been trimmed and streaked silver in a way that suited her very well, the essence of mature but sexy. I thought she'd be a great hit. For the actual scene, she'd be wearing a revealing red and black nightdress, and I'd have a virginally white nightdress that covered me from my neck to my ankles and wrists. Antony wasn't always subtle. For now, I was perched on the end of the bed in my usual rehearsal clothes.

I laughed. "You sound like Buttons fretting about Cinderella in a panto."

"I do not!" Mollie said, in her deep voice. She had played in panto, starting off. With her silver-streaked hair, if she did it now she'd have to be a witch.

"Once more!" Antony called. Thinking about what I was going to wear to the Embassy reception, I spoke my line, again, leapt off the bed, again, snatched the fencing foil, again, and drove it through the arras, again. The arras fell, again on top of poor Tim.

"Back," Antony called wearily.

"How about a curtain?" Tim asked. "We had a curtain when I played Polonius in Bristol." We had all heard more than enough about the time Tim had played Polonius in Bristol by now.

"Curtains have been done," Antony said, crisply and unarguably.

I got back onto the end of the bed. "So what are you going to wear?" Mollie asked.

I had decided during my sword thrust. "My turquoise Parisian dress."

"But that's three years old," Mollie protested. "You should ask Antony for an hour and run out to Marshall and Snelgrove or Harvey Nichols and buy a new dress. Something new and fashionable. If you got black, or dark red, I could lend you my sea-green scarf, and you could fasten it with your pearl clip. You'd look like Lady Mary Romsey in this week's *Tatler*."

I sighed. I remembered Lady Mary when she was a

pudgy five-year-old bridesmaid at Tess's wedding. "It doesn't matter what I wear, I can't possibly compete. Siddy's got a new Molyneux. Every woman there will have dresses made especially for them, from this year's Paris collections, or by the court couturiers here in London. I can't buy something today or tomorrow that wouldn't look like cheap trash by comparison, no matter what I spend. With people like that, you've lost if you try to copy them. I may as well wear a three-year-old good dress as a new bad one. At least this way they might think I simply get terribly fond of my old clothes."

Mollie didn't laugh.

"It's not as if I'm trying to meet someone," I said.

"I wish you would. I think Devlin has bewitched you or something. I've never seen you like this about a man."

"Again!" Antony called. "And this time, Viola, as you thrust, put your left hand on the edge of the arras and give it a little push leftwards."

I went through the motions again, and this time the arras, which was on casters, went sailing off into the wings. I corpsed, and so did Tim.

"A little push, I said, not a great shove!" Antony screamed.

I went back to the bed as the stagehands started fussing with the arras again. "Devlin—" I started.

"Never mind Devlin," Mollie said. "I shouldn't have said anything. You're ga-ga over him and that's the end of it. But I've thought what to do about clothes. You could wear your first act costume. It was made for you. And while it isn't in fashion, it isn't out of it either, it's timelessly Elizabethan. And I know it's finished, because I saw you trying it on."

My first act costume was a dark blue velvet gown trimmed with gold, high necked—all my Hamlet clothes were high necked—close fitting and embroidered to the waist, then flaring out below to give me room to do all the things I had to do. The only time I wore doublet and hose was at the end, because even Antony could see that I couldn't fence in a skirt. "It would look awfully odd," I said. It was a rich dark blue and this year's colors were all beiges and pastels.

"It would advertise the play," Mollie said. "It would remind people you're Viola Lark, not just the Larkin sister who acts."

"That's true," I said, struck by the thought. "I'll have to ask Antony if I can take it out."

Antony was raving at the arras.

"Catch him at a good moment and he'll see how it's almost as good for the play as Hitler coming," Mollie said.

I went down to look at the dress when Antony gave us a ten-minute. It didn't look quite as good close up as it would from front-of-house, but then it wasn't meant to. It looked like a costume. I stroked the sleeve. It was cheap stuff, dyed too brightly, it wouldn't wear. Still, it didn't need to. There hadn't been a play since the war that had run more than a year. Besides, I reminded myself, this play wasn't going to run at all. The dress might as well get an airing. I went to find Antony.

Nothing else happened that day but a lot more rehearsing. I spent the night with Devlin, as usual, but we didn't talk much. On Tuesday morning I had my hair trimmed and marcelled into the Mollie-lookalike cut. I almost didn't recognize my face without my hair flying everywhere. I wondered as I looked at the mirror whether I'd have been happier with a wig, but it was too late. Antony loved it, anyway. When I got to the theater he said admiring things about the shapes of my earlobes.

I left Mollie at the theater at half-past five in order to be dressed and ready for the reception at seven. I didn't go back to Devlin's for once; he'd agreed I could dress at my own flat. I had a bath, with rose petals in the water—the last of Antony's roses. I enjoyed the luxury of soaking with them. Then I was worried that I'd have unsettled my hair, but they'd clearly put enough of the marcel stuff on to lacquer it to my head; hardly a hair had loosened.

Mrs. Tring was there when I came out of the bathroom. She came out of the kitchen when she saw me, a dishcloth in her hand. "I hope you don't want dinner," she said. "It's chops, and chops don't stretch."

"I remember when you stretched one chop into a meal for four," I said.

"That was a chop and some bacon, and pies take time, in case you didn't know."

I laughed. "I don't want dinner anyway, there's bound to be food at this stupid reception I'm going to."

"Is that why you've done that to your hair?"

"No, that's for the part. It's supposed to look like Mollie's. You'll see when you see us together, or at the worst at the dress rehearsal."

"Not a bit like Mollie's if you ask me. And she has those streaks in it. Be going gray soon enough, I said to her, no need to bring it on sooner. Wigs were good enough in my day, or finding someone who has gray hair natural."

"Will you help me on with my dress now?" I asked. "After I've done my face that is."

"I'll do your face too if you like," she said, going back into the kitchen and coming out empty-handed. "You never remember how light you have to keep it when it's not for the stage. How do you want it? Debutante?"

I sat down in front of the mirror in my bedroom, still wrapped in my towel, and she stood behind me. It was like every dressing room we'd ever been in. "Not debutante," I said to her reflection. "As if I was going to be on a magazine cover over the title 'Glamorous Viola Lark Stars in *Hamlet* This Month at the Siddons.'"

"You should be so lucky," Mrs. Tring said, and in about ten minutes transformed my face into exactly what I wanted. I looked ten years younger. "For the part, we'll have you paler, but for this ball you'd do better with some color." She dabbed low down on my cheeks, and then higher, bringing out the angles. "What are you wearing?"

"My act one dress," I said. She'd seen it already on the bed, not to mention at the theater when we did the dress parade on Saturday.

She pursed her lips. "Well, that'll certainly show. Touch of violet on your lids then, bring out the blue." I obediently shut my eyes. "And since your ears are showing, how about those pearl drops your auntie the Marchioness gave you?"

"She's my mother's cousin, not my aunt," I said, as Mrs. Tring clipped them on. They hurt, and I knew the pressure would be agonizing by the end of the evening. "Dress," I said, looking critically at my face.

"Perfume first," Mrs. Tring reminded me. "Then I must get back to my chops, Mollie will be home soon and expecting dinner ready."

The reception started at seven, so I timed my arrival for half-past. The German Embassy was in Carlton House Terrace, by Pall Mall. It's strange how many Londons there are and how they overlap in some places but not at all in others. There's the debutante London, which is mostly Mayfair and Knightsbridge, in which the embassies and Pall Mall are included. Then there's theater London, which overlaps at the West End, but only there, and which includes bedsits and fix-ups in Muswell Hill and Clapham that I once hadn't known existed. There's financial London, around St. Paul's and the City. There's the London of the swarming poor, still almost Dickensian. All of these pass each other in some streets, rub shoulders in others, and leave certain areas untouched. I had lived for a year in debutante London, intriguing for invitations to parties only to pronounce them awful squeezes once I was there. Now I lived in theater London and Pall Mall was so firmly set within debutante London I hadn't been near it for years.

When the taxi drew up at the Embassy I was surprised. The outside looked like a pair of restrained Regency frontages, hung about with swastika flags and guarded by storm troopers, but much less intimidating than I had been expecting. Inside was completely different. Clearly the entire building had been made over by some mad devotee of monumental Bauhaus. I gave my name at the door, and yielded up my invitation. A storm trooper searched my bag, finding nothing but makeup, a hairbrush, and a little purse with taxi money. He was polite but thorough. There would have been no smuggling a bomb in here.

After that I was taken up a line of heel-clicking, saluting, hand-kissing Germans until I finally reached the pinnacle at the top of the stairs and was introduced to Herr Hitler himself. He had very intense blue eyes that seemed almost mesmeric. I had seen hundreds of photographs of him, of course, but none of them captured that charismatic quality he had in person. He didn't have the arrogance of most of the Germans I had met, Captain Keiler quite definitely included. He had a kind of humility that was quite charming. I instinctively liked him.

He didn't speak English, but Herr Schnell stood next to him ready to translate. "The Fuhrer says, another of the beautiful Larkin sisters," he said. "But he wants to know, why do you call yourself Lark?"

"Because I am an actress," I said, and Schnell translated.

"What is a lark?" Hitler asked and Schnell passed the question on to me.

"A bird," I said.

Schnell frowned. "What bird?"

"I don't know the German name, but in French it is *alouetta*."

He translated this. "Why is it that in England all the pretty girls learn French and not German?" was the response to this.

"When I was young they learned French, but they learn German these days," I said. This wasn't entirely true. It's true that they learn German now, but my own French was pretty minimal, barely enough for shopping. I only knew a lark was *alouetta* because of the song, which Pappa used to sing. I think he'd learned it in the trenches.

"You are still young," the Fuhrer said, gallantly. "I look forward to seeing you act."

"Even though you won't understand a word of it?" I asked.

"I know the play. And besides, Shakespeare transcends language." While Schnell translated this, the Fuhrer took up position as if cradling a skull, and said, quite distinctly in English, "Alas, poor Yorick."

"I hope you enjoy it," I said.

"We will speak again at the theater afterwards," the Fuhrer said, and as he translated this Herr Schnell signaled to me to pass on.

That's all the conversation I ever had with Adolf Hitler, Fuhrer of Europe, and it really couldn't have been more trivial.

I went on, down a flight of stairs. At the bottom was Pip, acting hostess. Her hair was marcel waved like mine, but with gray streaks like Mollie's, only in her case they were natural. She was wearing a floating apricot dress in several layers. "My God, Fats, you do look different," she greeted me.

"It's my act one costume for Hamlet," I said.

She laughed. "Well drift on. I'll come and find you in a bit. I have to do my hostess duties for a little while yet."

"Don't you find it a terrible bore?"

"Not in the least. The Fuhrer isn't married you know, so Magda Goebbels and I take it in turns to do the formal entertaining for him. But he moves us around all the time, it's his incentive system, and I've been stuck in Prague for the last year."

"Siddy tells me you're practically the queen of Czechoslovakia," I said.

"Well, being first alone in Prague is nothing like as good as sharing first place in Berlin. Or London, for that matter. I'm hoping to use this trip to get Heinie back to Berlin in the next rotation." Pip smiled at a stranger coming down the stairs. "Go on. I'm dying to have a proper chinnie with you, but I can't now. I'll find you in the crush as soon as I'm free."

Siddy was dancing with Captain Keiler. She'd had her hair done too, trimmed sharply along her jaw. It made her look more catlike than ever when she looked at me sideways. I wondered if she'd brought Loy. I took a glass of hock from a passing waiter and stood against the wall. There were people there I knew, from years ago, but nobody I wanted to talk to. I wanted to talk to Pip, to have a chinnie as she put it in our old term, meaning a chin-wag, a cozy chat. I knew she'd be hours yet standing welcoming people. I drank my hock. I saw the man from the Foreign Office who had come to the theater spot me from across the room and make his way towards me.

"You look most striking, Miss Lark," he said.

"It's my costume from act one," I said. I could see I was going to be saying it a lot.

"How original of you," he said.

"Well, when it comes to it, I'd much rather be here in costume as an actor than as a poor relation in a three-year-old dress," I confided.

He smiled. I saw that he was drunk already. "Ah, but we're all poor relations here, all of us English. Don't you feel it? The real centers of culture and economics are on the Continent, and we know it. The Empire's a fading dream, it has been all this century. The countries of the future are Germany and Russia, where they're prepared to try new things. We only copy them."

"America?" I asked, to be perverse.

"If they could ever pull themselves out of their series

of depressions they might make something of themselves," he said. "But no, it's the countries of the Continent we need to look to, the Reich and the Soviets. They're the ones we have to choose to steer our star."

"I'm sure you're right," I said, and carefully didn't ask him which of those two titans he favored. If he was Siddy's little man at the FO, then it would be Russia. I didn't care and I didn't want to know. To my astonishment, I caught sight of Dodo by the buffet, swathed in beige lace and looking like a hippo. "Excuse me, I must go and talk to my sister," I said.

"She's dancing," the FO man said.

"My other sister," I said, confusing him utterly.

I loaded a plate with lobster mayonnaise and vol-au-vents. There was sauerkraut, but nobody seemed to be taking it. Dodo saw me and grinned and we ducked into a corner with our loaded plates. "What are you doing here?" I asked her.

"Well, I thought I was here to talk to Pip, but it seems that actually some German scientists want desperately to talk to Walter about atoms. Heinie kept on about it at dinner. They want us to go to Germany and for Walter to work on atoms for them. You know I don't understand his work, though I was frightfully proud when he made that discovery and got all the attention."

"Are you going to go?" I asked.

"Walter's been stalling so far," she said. "I think he'd like to, really, to have the funding for research Heinie was promising. But we have to think about whether it's the best thing for the children. I suppose I can paint anywhere, it might even be good for my painting to see new places, but I am so very fond of the English landscape. I think I might feel exiled from my roots if I lived there and tried to paint it. I never really enjoy holidays abroad. Then I'd be near Pip, of course, but so far away from all the rest of you—and I don't think I'd fit into society in the Reich, I don't fancy queening it the way Pip does, I'm more of a home and children kind. Of course, that's what they're supposed to be for isn't it, *kinder* and *kush* and all that, but then there's the painting. And another thing, I don't speak German and I've always been hopeless with foreign languages."

"Don't go," I said. "I'd miss you terribly, and it's clear you don't want to."

"I don't, but it might be such a chance for Walter," she said, looking fretful. "Oh do come and talk to him, Fats, you've always been cleverer than me."

"What has cleverness got to do with anything? Your instincts are telling you not to go, and if you say that to Walter he can weigh that for himself."

"Walter doesn't count much on instincts," she said, sadly, and dropped a large blob of lobster mayonnaise right onto the bodice of her beige lace dress.

24

"Lord Scott isn't someone we can just arrest," Carmichael said, as they drove back to the Yard.

"He's one of Churchill's lot, isn't he?" Royston asked. "Gah, they're all as bad as each other."

"He's certainly not one of the Farthing Set. We'll need to get warrants, and whether the Chief will give them to us on a servant's word . . ." Carmichael sighed.

"You believed him though, didn't you, sir?" Royston stopped at a red light and Carmichael felt the pressure of the sergeant's earnest gaze.

"Yes, I believed him, for what that's worth. There wasn't any malice in the way he named names, and he confirmed Nash. I said Lieutenant and he came right back with Bob. If he'd been making them up he'd have had more on the mysterious Sir Aloysius."

"Oh, don't you know him?" The light changed and Royston drove off. "Unless there's more than one Irish Sir Aloysius, which I suppose there might be. I was thinking he must be Sir Aloysius Farrell, George Cross, the Hero of Calais."

"The name does ring a vague bell," Carmichael said.

"Was he the young officer who got the Guards out at the last minute?"

"That's the one. He was all over the papers at the time."

"But why the devil would someone like that be involved in this conspiracy?"

"Why would Lord Scott? Or Marshall and Nash for that matter? Or Gilmore? They want to get power for themselves by killing Mr. Normanby. Exactly the same as the Farthing thing but the other way around. That's why I said they're one as bad as the other."

They inched their way in silence for a while through the early evening traffic; black taxis, red buses, cars of all descriptions. "I'll ask for reports on all of them tonight, but it'll be too late to get warrants until tomorrow, and I'll have to see the Chief," Carmichael said. "You have any idea about the girl, Siddy?"

"Sorry, sir," Royston said. "Funny name for a girl. If we can't find her any other way we could check all the birth records for girls called Sydney for about the right dates. Can't be many."

"I don't envy the constable who gets that job. But it's more likely a nickname. Or Sydney could be her surname."

"Or Siddons, like the theater," Royston put in.

"If we get Sir Aloysius, he'll probably lead us to her. She probably isn't important anyway."

They drew up at the Yard. "Park the car and get off home, I'll see you here bright and early tomorrow," Carmichael said, getting out.

Stebbings was still at the desk. "Hello, sergeant, is the Chief still here?"

"Just gone off, sir," Stebbings said.

"Well, I need a number of things." Stebbings took up a pencil and waited. "I need to know where Mrs. Louise Green is. She was arrested Friday, booked at Hampstead under the Defence of the Realm Act. Then I want urgent reports on Lord Scott, his secretary Mr. Nesbitt, Sir

Aloysius Farrell, and any other Irish Sir Aloysiuses there may be. Next, I want an appointment with the Chief first thing in the morning, on a matter of warrants for arrests for the Gilmore bomb."

"Yes, sir," Stebbings said. "We should have all of that for you by the morning, sir."

Carmichael turned and left, feeling curiously deflated. Jack would be waiting for him, he thought as he headed towards Holborn tube station, and he could make him happy for once by being home on time and taking him out for dinner.

Tuesday morning at eight-thirty, Carmichael was back at the Yard. "Reports are on your desk, and you have an appointment with the Chief at nine," Sergeant Stebbings said.

"Thank you, sergeant."

Stebbings didn't respond.

Lord Scott's report reminded Carmichael very much of the ones he'd been sent at Farthing. Scott was an aristocrat and a politician. Philip John Scott, born in 1889 with a silver spoon in his mouth at Coltham Court, eldest son of the previous Lord Scott and his wife Honoria Mary. Educated Harrow and Oxford, fought and was wounded in the Great War, married in 1921 to Pamela Dixon, of the American millionaire Dixons. One son, Benjamin Charles, born 1923; two daughters, Diana Honoria, born 1925, and Susan Pamela, born 1927. Pamela died in the Blitz, Lord Scott never remarried. He had sat in the House of Lords for the last thirty years, meddling in the country's affairs. He had held minor office under Baldwin, again under Chamberlain, and had risen to the heights of being briefly minister for munitions under Churchill during the war. Since then, he had remained a Churchillian, hostile to the Farthing Peace. He had been Chancellor of the Duchy of Lancaster under Eden, which could mean anything or nothing, and held no current post.

He turned to Sir Aloysius Farrell, expecting more of

the same. It began similarly. Sir Aloysius was born in 1914, the son of an Irish baronet and his wife Agnes. His father had died in 1916 on the Somme, so he had inherited the title very early. Unlike Lord Scott, there had been no money—the report didn't outright say as much, but Carmichael could tell from the name of the school young Sir Aloysius had attended. If they could have afforded it, he'd have been at Harrow, Eton, Winchester, Rugby, or perhaps Stonyhurst if they were Catholics. Instead he went to somewhere called St. Michael's in Bournemouth. It wasn't even one of the second-tier public schools. Carmichael had been to a school like that himself, a minor school that aspired.

Sir Aloysius had left school as soon as he could, and who could blame him, in 1930. He had gone straight into the Army and spent three years as a lieutenant. Then he had come to the end of his term of enlistment in 1933 and left. He was next heard of in court in Ireland being reprimanded in an IRA case, in 1935. Then, in the summer of 1939, he was arrested in London with a bomb in his possession, clearly part of the IRA bombing campaign of that summer. He had been offered the choice of prison or returning to the Army, and he had naturally chosen the Army. This led him to Calais as part of a sacrifice Churchill was making, landing a battalion in Calais to distract Hitler from the evacuation of Dunkirk. Against all odds, when all his superior officers had been killed, Sir Aloysius had managed to rally the remnants of the battalion and get them out of Calais and back to England on a half-sinking French cruiser he had commandeered. He remained in the Army until the end of the war, and then disappeared as far as the record went—no more arrests, no marriage, no visible career. His mother had died in 1944. His residence was listed as Arranish Hall, Ulster.

There's a bomber if you like, Carmichael thought, stunned. The only wonder was that they'd made such an amateur bomb and blown themselves up. The IRA usually knew what they were doing. But Green had said that Sir Aloysius had wanted them to wait until he could get hold of a friend who could help.

The phone rang. "Nine o'clock," Stebbings said. "The Chief's expecting you."

Carmichael rose, clutching the papers, and made his way to the lift.

"What's all this about?" Penn-Barkis asked as soon as Carmichael stepped into his room.

"Green has fingered the other conspirators in the Gilmore case," Carmichael said.

"Who is Green?" Penn-Barkis gestured impatiently to a chair; Carmichael sat.

"Green is Gilmore's servant. I wanted to see you, sir, because this is potentially sensitive; some of the people he fingered are titled. We'll need proper warrants."

"Are you sure the servant isn't just spinning you a tarrydiddle? It could be a lot of trouble if we wrongfully arrest prominent people." Penn-Barkis frowned.

"Yes, sir, I know, sir," Carmichael said. "But Green's very anxious to ensure his wife's safety. He says she's quite innocent, and he's terrified that she'll be sent to the Continent and to a camp. I don't believe he was lying when the only hope of her safety is through us."

"Where is she?"

Carmichael realized he still didn't know. "She's in custody, but I'm not sure where. I asked Stebbings yesterday to find out, but the information wasn't on my desk this morning. Green's in the Scrubs, and she'll be in one of the women's prisons."

"Oh very well, go on." Penn-Barkis steepled his fingers and looked at Carmichael over them.

"One of the fellow conspirators is Nash, who we knew about, if you remember, sir, Marshall's friend. It seems likely he was in the house at the time of the explosion. We already knew about him, though we still don't know where he is. The others are Lord Scott—"

"Lord Scott!" Penn-Barkis interrupted. "You want to arrest Lord Scott?"

"Yes, sir," Carmichael said, doing his best to keep his voice calm. "You have to remember this is a case where the conspiracy was attempting to blow up the Prime Minister."

"I suppose Lord Scott would have something to gain from that," Penn-Barkis conceded. "Go on."

"The other major figure is Sir Aloysius Farrell. Green didn't know his full name, just Sir Aloysius and that he was Irish, but there don't seem to be any other candidates, especially when you consider that Farrell has IRA connections going back fifteen years. He's a bomber, sir, he was caught with an IRA bomb in 1939. We need to find him and pull him in." Carmichael offered the report, which Penn-Barkis took and glanced at.

"Anyone else?" he asked.

"A girlfriend of Farrell's called Siddy; we don't know anything at all about her."

Penn-Barkis dismissed her with a wave of his hand.

"Lord Scott's secretary, Mr. Nesbitt. We can pull him in with Scott, if we can get Scott."

"We can get a warrant for Lord Scott's arrest," Penn-Barkis said. "The difficulty is that he's the kind of man who has friends in high places, within the system. If we applied for a warrant, it's possible that someone would tip him off. Yet if we arrest him without one he might contrive to get a magistrate to release him." He sat in silence for a moment, staring out of the window at London spread out below him, then he picked up the telephone. "Put me through to the Home Office," he barked into the instrument. There was a pause. "Yes, Penn-Barkis here, I need to speak to Lord Timothy. Yes. Yes. Yes, it is urgent. Well, could you ask her to ask him to call me? Certainly, yes, thank you." He put the receiver down again and smiled at Carmichael. "I'll be in touch when I've had a word with the Home Secretary," he said.

Carmichael stayed where he was, despite the clear dismissal. "And Sir Aloysius?"

"Get a warrant right away and bring him in," Penn-Barkis said.

"The problem is that we don't have the faintest idea where he is. He has a house in Ireland, but—"

"No, he won't be likely to be there," the Chief agreed. "Well, this is where the new identification cards really come into their own. For one thing, when he applied for them he must have given an address, though he could have given his Irish one. But beyond that anyone who stays at a hotel, or who rents any kind of accommodation has to show them, and the hotel keepers and landlords have to keep records, and send them to us. If he's in London, which I think is a reasonable assumption, we should be able to find him by a search through our own papers. Put somebody on that right away. I said all along that this system would make our lives easier."

"Yes, sir," Carmichael said, and stood.

"Let me know if you're leaving the building," Penn-Barkis said.

"Yes, sir." Carmichael walked over to the lift. As he stepped in, he heard the telephone ring.

Royston was waiting in his office. "Sir Aloysius is an IRA bomber," Carmichael said.

Royston blinked. "I thought he was a war hero?"

"He's both," Carmichael said. "And I've got a lovely job for you. Check the address Sir Aloysius gave when he got his new papers. Also, go through all the files on hotels and rentals for the last month and see if you can find out where he is. Check under *A* as well as *F,* sometimes clerks get confused by a title."

"I already did that for Nash," he objected.

"That reminds me, you can do it for Marshall too. Marshall and Nash had a place in London, remember?"

"But don't we have the telephone number for it?" Royston asked.

"You're absolutely right, sergeant, and I'd entirely forgotten. I called it that first morning, and then gave up on it and called Portsmouth and never thought of it again. You go and get on with Sir Aloysius the Bomber and I'll find out from the Post Office where the place is that the telephone number belongs to."

The Post Office were obliging, and gave him an address in Chalk Farm. He itched to be off there at once, but waited for Royston and Penn-Barkis. Royston came back first. "Nothing," he said. "Not a sausage, under *A* or *F*. Probably staying with friends, or the room is in the name of that Siddy girl."

"And what address did he give when he got his papers?"

"Arranish House, Ulster. But he got the papers issued in London."

"No help at all. He must be trying to hide. But the man must have friends, relations, who know where he is." Carmichael glared at the report.

"Maybe one of them will turn him in, like the Greens," Royston said. "There is another possibility. I had a word with Jenkinson, who knows about the Irish side of things, and he said that if he's Irish he might have an Irish passport, which would do for checking in at a hotel. No different from using his card, you might say, but it seems that in the Republic they're not sufficiently careful about handing out passports, and if he's an IRA man he might have more than one, in different names."

Carmichael groaned. "Wonderful," he said. His telephone rang. He picked it up. "Carmichael."

"Penn-Barkis here, Inspector, and the Home Secretary wants to see you, to go through the evidence. You have an appointment with him at ten tomorrow morning, in the Home Office. Don't take any action in the matter of Lord Scott until after you've spoken to Lord Timothy."

"Yes, sir," Carmichael said.

"Have you made any progress in finding Sir Aloysius?"

"No, quite the opposite. He doesn't have a hotel or a lodging. He must be deliberately hiding. Can we get a warrant in any case, sir, so I can arrest him if he turns up? Or I could just pull him in. I don't think he has the connections Lord Scott does. The good news is that I have found a possible place Nash might be. I'll check that now, sir."

"Very good, but keep working on Sir Aloysius," Penn-Barkis said, and the line went dead.

"I've been thinking, maybe he's staying with Nash at Nash's place," Royston said.

"Let's hope so, sergeant."

They set off for Chalk Farm with high hopes. The address proved to be on the top floor of a purpose-built 1930s building of six flats. The entrance hall was painted cream and had a set of six mailboxes and six bells. There was no name on the bell of 6, nor any answer when they rang the bell downstairs. They climbed two flights of pale green stairs, and arrived at a little landing, with two doors facing each other. Royston shrugged and knocked on the one marked 6. There was no reply.

"May as well try the other and see if they know anything," he said, and knocked across the hallway at 5.

The door to 5 was opened at once by a fat woman with her hair in curlers and a cigarette in the corner of her mouth. "Whatever it is, I don't want any," she said.

"We're not selling anything, we're looking for the occupants of number six," Carmichael said.

"They're not there," she said.

"Do you know where they are?" Royston asked.

"Down to Portsmouth I expect. They're only coming and going here, you know." She blew out smoke.

"When did you last see them?" Royston asked.

She squinted suspiciously. "Why are you asking so many questions?"

"We're police," Carmichael said, wearily, deciding it was probably most productive to gratify her curiosity a little. "There's a possibility they're mixed up in something criminal. Do you remember the last time you saw them?"

"There's never been nothing like that," she protested. "Couple of nice polite young men they are, and only sharing the flat because of the expense. They're hardly ever even here together, the way they get their leave, see. No, you don't want to think that about them."

Carmichael wondered if his own neighbors would be prepared to go to such lengths lying for him if it came to it.

"It's nothing like that," Royston said. "Matter of murder."

She took a last drag on her cigarette and stubbed it out on the wall. "Murder?" she asked, as if it were an entry on a menu she didn't think she'd choose. "Well I never."

"When did you last see them?" Carmichael repeated patiently.

"Not this weekend, the weekend before," she said. "One of them was here, the dark one, and the fair one came down and joined him on the Friday."

"And when did they leave?" Royston asked.

"I saw the fair one leave on the Sunday morning when we were all on our way out to church. He said good-bye very politely, like always. I don't know when the dark one left, either when we were in church or before sometime. I haven't seen either of them since, but it isn't unusual, sometimes they won't come down here for weeks at a time. They're sailors, and they have to wait till they have leave, but when they do, they want to be in London, only natural isn't it?"

"Do you have a key to six?"

"No, why would I?" She bristled.

"You're obviously a friend of theirs, and they were away a lot, they might have left you their key so you could let meter men in and that kind of thing," Royston said.

"All the meters for the building are together downstairs," she said. "There isn't any need for anything like that. I haven't got a key, not that I would have minded if they had ever asked me. Very nice polite gentlemen, never no noise, and they keep to themselves."

"You're sure neither of them have been hiding in the flat?" Carmichael asked, losing hope but not prepared yet to surrender it entirely.

"I'd have seen them going in and out," she insisted. "And the walls are that thin, if they'd been there I'd have heard something, I always do, moving about, and the water running."

"Thank you, you've been very helpful," Carmichael said.

They walked down the first set of stairs. Carmichael stopped on the first floor and knocked on *4*.

"What are you doing, sir?" Royston asked.

"Checking her story, just in case she was being all too helpful to Nash, nice polite boy," Carmichael said.

The woman in *4* was sharp-nosed and hostile. "What do you want?" she asked.

"Police, we're inquiring about the occupants of number six," Royston said. "When did you last see them?"

"Last heard them tramping about last Sunday morning," she said. "Is that all?"

It was all. "We can get a warrant to break in and check the place," Carmichael said as they got back into the car. "But I hardly have the heart for it. Nash isn't there, and hasn't been since last Sunday, though he could have been quite safely until today. I wish I knew how that man had contrived to vanish."

"And Sir Aloysius too. But maybe we'll find them together."

"Maybe they're both with Lord Scott. Maybe we'll arrest them all together tomorrow after I meet with the Home Secretary. But I'm not counting on it."

"No, sir," Royston said, eyeing Carmichael with respect.

25

Dodo was claimed by Heinie for a dance. He offered to come back and dance with me next, which I found rather a daunting prospect. Unlike his Fuhrer, I didn't find him attractive at all. I couldn't imagine what Pip saw in him, unless his aura of authority lent him glamour in her eyes, or was a power grab pure and simple. I stood and watched the room for a moment. The lines of the architecture were softened by the evening clothes of the guests, except for those, mostly German, in uniform. The women's clothes, the soft beiges, the layers of pastels and lace, seemed like a floating symbol of civilization against the stark brutality of the room. I wondered how anyone could have done such violence to a perfectly nice pair of Georgian houses. The music was ghastly, too. At any other bash of that sort, the band would have been playing old-fashioned jazz or just plain dance tunes. This band were playing Strauss waltzes, very correct I suppose, and horrible German dance tunes with a female singer whose voice made my head hurt.

"Isn't that the Duchess of Kent?" a girl with a neck too long for her hairstyle asked me.

"I haven't seen her," I said, looking, but the girl had gone on without a word.

I danced with Captain Keiler, who was very polite and attentive, and seemed genuinely sorry to leave me and go on to his next obligation. He danced well, but I was glad to be alone again. I took a glass of white wine from a tray skillfully wielded by a waiter as he moved through the throng. I watched him move away from me. He was more graceful than the dancers, I thought, not to mention better looking, and wondered how to do that on stage. It could be jolly effective. Dignity of labor didn't seem likely to be fashionable for a while, though.

"Isn't Daphne knocking back a little more than she should be?" a voice brayed over my shoulder. I turned, but the bitch wasn't addressing me but a companion, who replied in lower tones. The braying one was Lady Eversley, a political wife who liked to think she ran the country through her husband. I knew her because she had a son at Oxford at the time of my come-out—he was killed in the war, like all the nicest of our generation—and because she was an incorrigible manager she'd been buzzing around the edges of the debutante scene. Even then she'd never bothered to lower her voice, no matter how unkind she was being about anyone. I looked away from her before she noticed me.

There were plenty of girls called Daphne, but I thought she must mean Daphne Normanby, who had been Daphne Dittany when she was a deb the same year I was. There had been some frightful scandal about her then, which nobody would ever tell me. I don't suppose it was truly any more shocking than half the things I did find out about. It wasn't that she was having a baby, or if she was she must have lost it, poor thing, because although she did get married in rather a hurry she'd never had any children. She'd never been an especial chum of mine, but we had been to each other's parties and once shared a taxi home in the rain and giggled all the way. I looked for her now in the crowd. She was the Prime

Minister's wife now, which must be enough to drive anyone to drink.

She was standing by the buffet table, with a glass of wine in her hand. "Daphne," I said. "You're looking lovely. It's been simply yonks." The bit about looking lovely wasn't much of an exaggeration. She had always been a pretty girl, and good at grooming, and now she had the money to buy clothes to really suit her. Her hair was perfect too, which made me a little self-conscious about my Mollie-matching cut.

Daphne took a moment to focus on me. "Viola Larkin," she said. It was true that she was drunk, I saw, or at least not sober. "What an unusual dress."

"It's my act one costume, from *Hamlet*," I said, wearily. "I thought—"

"Yes, I see, how frightfully clever of you," she interrupted. "I'll be very glad myself when the fashion changes. I do prefer definite colors. But are you sure about that bodice?"

I glanced down at it. "I don't see high necks coming into fashion, no, but it's for the play, it's supposed to suggest purity."

"Purity? Is the play absolutely deadly?" she asked, lowering her voice confidentially. "Shakespeare simply slays me. I'm supposed to be there, flying the flag beside Mark, but if it is, I might contrive to have a headache and miss it."

"Miss it, you'd hate it," I said, with perhaps more urgency than I should have. She stared at me. "If you don't like Shakespeare anyway, you're bound to hate *Hamlet*," I added.

"I prefer comedy, or something with music. I saw you in that funny thing last year, what was it called?"

"*Crotchets*?" I asked.

"You were ever so funny anyway. You even made Mark laugh, and that, my dear, is an achievement."

I laughed. "Are you finding the whole Prime Minister's wife thing a bore?"

"Oh you don't know how deadly, my dear, and it's not been a month yet. You were so right to get away from the whole business and do something you wanted to."

I wondered what Daphne would have wanted to do. "At least you must have the fun of going into a lot of rooms first," I ventured.

Daphne looked over to where Lady Eversley was still casting a disapproving eye on her. "The rules of precedence do have some compensations," she said.

I found Mark Normanby himself at my elbow. "Viola, lovely to see you," he said, though I had never known him well, even when we had moved in the same world. He took Daphne's elbow in a way that seemed affectionate, but which looked too tight.

"I was just telling Viola how much we liked her in *Crotchets* last year," Daphne said. Her voice had closed up and become tense, as if she had the most awful stage fright.

"And we're looking forward to seeing you in *Hamlet* on Friday," Mark said, smiling and affable.

Close up, he did not seem any more than Hitler did, like a dangerous dictator whose removal would ensure the freedom of Europe for a generation.

"I hope you both enjoy it," I said, and saw Daphne relax a little because I didn't give her away.

"Is that a costume from the play you're wearing?" Mark asked.

"You're the first person to work that out for himself," I said.

"Mark's always been exceedingly clever," Daphne said.

"I'm afraid I must drag you away from your chum to do your duty now, darling," he said.

"Lovely to have spoken to you, Viola," Daphne said, as her husband steered her away.

I stared after them. That elbow grip worried me.

"How are you, Viola?" an old man's voice asked over my shoulder. I turned and saw Lord Ullapool. I hadn't seen him since the terrible weekend I'd spent staying with them up in the wilds of Scotland. He had been old then, white-haired at least, but active, taking a leading part in the deer stalking. Now he seemed elderly. His hawk's profile seemed a little fallen in on itself, and he was leaning on a cane.

"Thriving," I said. "I heard about Lady Ullapool and I'm so sorry." I had heard from Mrs. Tring's leisure reading.

"We appreciated your card," he said, which was very kind of him and made me feel glad I'd bothered. He always had been kind, I remembered, even though he was old and dull. After I'd turned down Edward's proposal and was expecting dinner to be rather a minefield, I found myself sitting next to him. He had talked to me soothingly about Gothic arches, which was rather restfully boring in the circumstances. Lady Ullapool had spent the whole meal looking one step away from tears. She kept giving me reproachful glances. Edward on the other hand hadn't looked at me once. I'd been very glad of Lord Ullapool's Gothic arches.

"This doesn't seem like your usual sort of party," I said.

"I was in town to see my doctor, and now Edward's in office he wanted to trot me out." He smiled. "He thinks I don't have enough social life. I can't tell him I don't envy him one if it means standing about eating canapes with a lot of Germans."

"I'm only here myself to see my sisters," I confided.

"But didn't I just see you talking to the Prime Minister?"

He took a glass of wine from a passing waiter. I swallowed what was left in my own glass and took another. "I was talking to Daphne, who is an old friend, and he came up and claimed her. He's frightfully arrogant, isn't he?"

"Well, it's a powerful position." He lowered his voice. "Although Edward is of his party and I shouldn't say this, I don't altogether approve of Mr. Normanby myself. This proposal to have fixed terms and electoral districts arranged by occupation instead of geography goes against the grain with me."

"What do you think would happen if he was killed?" I asked. I know I shouldn't have said it, but the words were out before I knew it.

Lord Ullapool raised his eyebrows in astonishment. "Killed?"

"If he'd been killed instead of Sir James," I said, catching myself. "Would we still have to have the new identity cards, do you think?"

"Oh, the Great Man theory of history, eh?" He smiled at me indulgently, as if I were about six years old and had said something precocious. "No, nothing would be different. Sir James would be Prime Minister no doubt, and taking the same precautions. The loss of liberties is necessary in the circumstances, but regrettable. Some of the laws are left from when we needed to round people up in the war, of course. But Normanby's just doing his job there. Whoever else had his job would have to do exactly what he's doing. This is what the people want, and we can't have communists and Jews going around murdering people left, right, and center. But I don't think Normanby will get his occupational franchise through the Lords, even if we did pass the fixed terms, by a hair."

"Not everyone wants Normanby, surely," I said. "One reads about protests."

"For every protester, there are half a dozen blackshirts, or Ironsides or whatever they call themselves these days, counter-protesting. If you're thinking of that, my advice is to stay away. The Ironsides can get quite violent, and my understanding of the matter is that the police sweep everyone up and let the Ironsides go. A ghillie of mine got caught up in some nonsense of that nature. I had to pay quite a considerable fine to get him out, and he said it seemed hard that he was being fined for being involved in violence when he was the victim.

First-class fellow, Hamish, I daresay he gave as good as he got. But it wouldn't be the place for a young lady."

"No," I agreed, drinking my wine. "I wasn't planning to go."

"Of course not. Just a word to the wise, eh?" He nodded benignly.

"Lord Scott says lots of people agree with the protesters," I said.

Lord Ullapool looked troubled and glanced around to see if anyone was listening to us. Seeing that no one was, he leaned towards me and lowered his voice, so that I had to lean closer to hear him. As I did so, I realized, horrifyingly, that he was afraid. "Scotty says a lot of things he probably shouldn't. But I think he's wrong there. Three Ironsides for every protester, Hamish said. Scotty was right enough about Germany though, so maybe he's on to something."

"What about Germany?" I asked. "That they wanted the war? But they didn't, did they, no more than we did, that's what the Farthing Peace was all about?"

"No, about the camps." Lord Ullapool drained his wineglass and stared off at the dancers, but I don't think he was seeing them. "Anything you've heard about the work camps on the Continent, about enslaving the workers and confiscating their property, about working them to death, about gassing those who can't work, it's all true."

I'd never believed it before, not when Siddy mentioned it in the Lyons, not even when Malcolm was giving me facts and figures, but hearing it now in this gentle old man's quiet voice I couldn't doubt it. "And the stone soap?" I asked, my voice cracking. It was a detail that had always stuck with me, even when I thought it was just a horror story. It was the stuff of nightmare, being given soap and going into a shower but the soap is a stone and the showerheads vent poison gas.

"Yes, the stone soap and the melting down of the gold teeth. I didn't believe it myself until your brother-in-law was kind enough to give me a tour. I had to grit my teeth and apologize to Winston and Scotty when I came back."

"Not even the Jews deserve that," I said.

"No," he agreed. "And they're not all Jews, from what I was told. Gypsies, dissidents, even some sexual deviants. I saw a handful of negroes, heaven only knows how they ended up there."

"That's just foul. Seeing it must have been terrible."

"Oh yes. Like skeletons some of them were, just skin over bone. But I wouldn't talk to Celia about this, if I were you. It puts them into an impossible position, defending the indefensible, and they naturally tend to resent it."

"Celia knows?" I asked. Oh Pip, I thought, how could you?

"Celia certainly knows. And Celia contrives to live with it, somehow, to live next to it. It must be rather like the ancient world, you know, living side by side with slaves and the treatment they received and thinking somehow that they deserved it. But it must be difficult for Celia, as she wasn't brought up to it."

"The Germans weren't brought up to it either. They were the most civilized people in Europe," I protested.

"They say they still are. And there are young men nearly old enough for their National Service who were born the year Hitler came to power. The younger generation must think it natural. They're still fighting the Russians. That unifies them. Everyone can agree on the need to oppose communism, especially when communism's coming at you in a tank."

I felt sick. For the first time in all of this I actually wanted to kill Hitler, and Pip and Heinie too for that matter.

Then Pip was bearing down on me like Nelson's *Victory* on the back of a ha'penny, and there was nothing to do but give the performance of my life and act glad to see her.

26

Wednesday morning Carmichael welcomed the singing birds outside his window and the strip of sunshine that came through the badly drawn curtains to wake him. Jack groaned when Carmichael rose singing, and Carmichael laughed at him. "This case is nearly over," Carmichael said, as Jack dragged himself out of bed.

"Well nobody will be more glad than me," Jack said, pulling on a dressing gown. "Tell me why you have to see the Home Secretary?"

"To get a warrant," Carmichael said.

"I don't understand all this fuss. I'm sure you've arrested hundreds of people without one." Jack padded towards the kitchen.

Carmichael followed. "We either need a warrant in advance or we have to take them to a magistrate afterwards and prove there's a case to answer. Otherwise we could just lock up whoever we like."

"I thought you already did lock up whoever you liked?" Jack said, grumpily, filling the kettle.

"They're trying to change the law so we can," Carmichael said. "That's one of the reasons why I want to get out."

"I hear New Zealand's very nice," Jack said, yawning.

After breakfast Carmichael walked briskly through the June sunlight to the ominous darkness of Scotland Yard. Stebbings had no enlightenment for him. There was no news of Nash, no identification of "Siddy," and worst of all, Mrs. Green had not been located. Stebbings shook his head over the report. "She was sent from Hampstead to Bethnal Green, but they were full up too. From there she was sent to the women's prison at Islington, where a lot of the overflow protesters are, but she was never checked in there. They must have sent her on somewhere else."

"It isn't possible she's escaped, is it sergeant?" Carmichael tapped his reports with his pencil impatiently.

"I can't see how she can have, sir. She was in custody all the time. It's just that she's slipped through the cracks. She might be at Islington but not properly checked in. Or they might have sent her on out of London somewhere."

"Could she have been sent out of the country?"

Stebbings hesitated. "Well, she is a Jew," he said. "I have heard that the general policy with Jewish criminals now, especially those who came from abroad in the first place, is to send them back abroad where they know how to deal with them. And there was a shipload of them sent off on Saturday, protesters mostly but also some old lags, clearing out the cells. But I did check the names, and she wasn't on the manifest."

"That's a relief, sergeant. Thank you." Even apart from the half-promises he had made to Green, Carmichael hated the thought of the bureaucratic nightmare it would be to get a Jew back from the Reich.

"Sorry I couldn't find her for you. We're still working

on it. We'll turn her up. Inspector Jacobson from Hampstead is going round to Islington with a couple of constables to make sure everyone there is properly identified. Are you going to be in this morning, sir?"

"No. I have an appointment with the Home Secretary at ten. I'll check back after that though, but I'll probably be going off into the country, in which case I'll want a car." Carmichael hoped very much that he would be allowed to arrest the conspirators himself.

Stebbings made a note on his pad. "Better be off, sir, if you're walking down to Whitehall."

Carmichael went to his office and picked up the typed transcript of Royston's notes on Green's confession. He had typed it himself the evening before, slowly, on one of the huge black typewriters the Yard provided. He hadn't wanted to trust anyone else with it. He searched for a briefcase and eventually unearthed one under a large pile of papers in the corner. He dusted it before he tucked the transcript inside.

The sun was shining from a clear untroubled sky as Carmichael set off with a jaunty step. He walked down the Kingsway and increased his pace as he wondered if Penn-Barkis might be watching him from his eyrie. He walked the half-circle of the Aldwych, and passed the Siddons Theater as he turned onto the Strand. VIOLA LARK IN HAMLET, the lights said, already, though they were not yet lit. They would be rehearsing in there now, he thought, what a silly idea having a girl play Hamlet. He had played Ophelia himself once, at school, but the whole cast had been boys, naturally. He'd been embarrassed by the ridiculous overwrought lines he'd had to speak. He had been in love with Wroxton Minor, who was playing Claudius, and had trembled when, in character, he had patted him on the shoulder. He hadn't known he was queer then, despite the trembling and although all his experience had been with boys. That was the same for everyone at school, nobody thought it meant anything.

The walk did nothing to dim his good cheer. Nearly

over, he kept thinking, and Jack reconciled to the thought of his resignation. New Zealand had geysers and Maoris, that was all he knew about it, but it was bound to have a police force and would probably be glad to have him. At Charing Cross he turned down Whitehall, and there into the newly reorganized Home Office. The clerk was dubious of his appointment and telephoned twice before sending him in.

When he was eventually ushered in to the Home Secretary's office, Carmichael was not entirely surprised to see the dapper form of Mark Normanby perched on the side of Lord Timothy Cheriton's desk.

"Tea, Inspector?" Normanby asked blandly, and before Carmichael had time to shake hands Normanby handed him a cup of pale China tea in which a slice of lemon floated. Carmichael stared down at the circle of delicate porcelain, then up at the Prime Minister. "I remember how you like it," Normanby said, and Carmichael looked up to meet Normanby's sardonic eyes. This was a threat, and it chilled Carmichael far more than Penn-Barkis's more explicit threats. "They called that the girls' way at Eton," Normanby had said to him at Farthing. He was using the tea to remind Carmichael of the hold they had on him. Not for very much longer now, Carmichael thought.

"Thank you, that's just right," he said.

"Do sit down," Lord Timothy said, sounding a little impatient.

The room had eighteenth-century paneling and windows, and a red and gold Turkish carpet. The desk and chairs were modern, deco; they would have fitted well into the neo-Assyrian style of the Yard but looked out of place here. One wall was lined with steel filing cabinets. A pastoral painting in a gilt frame—could it be an actual Constable rather than a reproduction?—was on the floor propped up against one of the cabinets, and a sturdy steel safe just a little smaller than the picture was open on the wall behind the desk. Carmichael, still holding his tea, took one of the chairs.

"There are certain problems involved with arresting Lord Scott," Lord Timothy began.

"How sure are you?" Normanby interrupted, directly to Carmichael.

"I've brought a typed transcript of Green's interrogation," he said. He put the tea down by his feet and drew out the report. "You can make your own decision from this."

Normanby frowned at the offered report and did not reach for it. "Green is a Jew, and a servant. His accusations alone against a peer of the realm might not be enough."

"These are real terrorists, sir," Carmichael said.

"They're precisely what we've been afraid of and enacted all these measures to prevent, Mark," Lord Timothy added, as if this wasn't the first time he had made this point.

"Yes, Tibs, but does a prominent opposition peer seem like the kind of person you'd expect to be involved in a terrorist plot?" Normanby asked. "We do still have an opposition, and we don't want them to be able to say that we're using these laws to shut people up, especially when we are. Lord Scott has spoken out against us vehemently, and recently. It's much better for us to let him keep criticizing us, harmlessly."

"Not if he's trying to kill us," Lord Timothy pointed out.

Carmichael dropped the report and picked up his tea again. He tried to hide his satisfaction at Normanby's dilemma. He had done so well with pretended terrorists for his own purposes, and now he had to deal with real ones. Of course his extreme measures didn't help, since they were never truly intended for terrorists but to keep the country under control. He clearly didn't know what to do. Normanby had organized all that mummery down at Farthing, wasted Carmichael's time with it, and then when he had discovered the truth, forced him to agree to a lie. Now here was terrorism Normanby hadn't orchestrated and couldn't control, and it served him right. Carmichael decided to make the situation as plain as possible. "The essence of what Green said is that Gilmore heard that you and Mr. Hitler would be attending the first night of *Hamlet*. She then got in touch with everyone she knew who might want to help her blow you up. They came to dinner. Green was in her confidence, the other servants were not. Lord Scott's attendance at that dinner is no doubt a matter of record."

"Can the other servants confirm it?" Lord Timothy asked, leaning forward a little.

"She only had the Greens and a Spanish lady's maid. Miss Carl, the maid, had already left the house before the guests arrived. Probably Lord Scott's servants could confirm it, and no doubt Mrs. Green can."

"You haven't spoken to Mrs. Green?" Normanby pounced on this as if catching Carmichael out.

"She's lost in administrative limbo," Carmichael confessed. "She was arrested on Friday and charged at Hampstead. They didn't have room to keep her in their cells, and she was sent off somewhere we haven't yet been able to trace."

"She's no use as a credible witness anyway; whatever she says she's another Jewish servant with a grudge. Probably in the plot too, whatever her husband says." Lord Timothy leaned back with a sigh.

"Whether other sources confirm it or not, Green says Sir Aloysius Farrell was at the dinner too. Farrell has an IRA past, and bombing convictions."

"I've certainly no objection to giving you a warrant to pull him in," Normanby said.

"If I can find him," Carmichael said. "It seems he's a professional. The only address he's ever given anyone is his house in Ireland."

"Have you tried his club?" Lord Timothy asked. "I think I've seen him around at White's. And he's definitely a member of the Jockey Club. He used to race."

"Thank you, sir," Carmichael said. He took out a

notebook and scribbled rapidly, "Whites, Jockey Club, these people all know each other," and put it back in his inside pocket. "Also present were Lord Scott's secretary Malcolm Nesbitt, a girl called Siddy who we know nothing about, and the two naval lieutenants, Marshall and Nash. According to Green, they talked about bombs and revolution. The next day, Gilmore and Marshall killed themselves making a bomb. If Lord Scott isn't to be apprehended, I think you should cancel your attendance at the play."

"Without Gilmore?" Normanby asked. "They might try something else, but they're unlikely to try that. We'll tighten security at the theater, and at Covent Garden and Wimbledon too."

"Wimbledon?" Carmichael echoed, astonished.

Normanby's lips tightened. "We're taking the Fuhrer to see the tennis on Saturday afternoon."

"I wouldn't have thought it was his sort of thing," Carmichael said.

"That's what I said!" Lord Timothy exclaimed. "It doesn't seem like his style, tennis, I said."

"Combined with the private dinner with the king and queen, these three public appearances, at a German opera, an English play, and to see a German and an Englishman compete at tennis, are the perfect set of events to demonstrate our friendship with the Reich," Normanby said, to Lord Timothy. He turned back to Carmichael. "If we cancel any of them it is tantamount to admitting that we can't handle security and our own terrorists. It wouldn't necessarily be a public admission, but it would be an admission of weakness in front of the Fuhrer, which I don't want to make."

"I understand," Carmichael said, feeling a little dizzy. "You asked how sure I was about Lord Scott's involvement. I think we have quite enough evidence to arrest him on suspicion of involvement, certainly under the new Defence of the Realm Act. I don't know if that's sufficient to hold up under intensive political scrutiny."

"Frankly, arresting him and letting him go again if we couldn't pin it on him would be a disaster," Normanby said, with a disarming smile. "Nor can he disappear. If we arrest him, he has to be tried in public—would that mean in the Lords, Tibs? And he has to hang."

"I think it does mean the Lords," Lord Timothy said. He was frowning. "But he might well admit it if it comes to that. He's just the kind who would, you know, if it's true. He'd stand up and call you a tyrant and admit he was going to blow you to bits and it would be a good thing if he did."

"That wouldn't do us any harm at all," Normanby said, jovially. "It might even be a help, played right. Pity there isn't more of a Jewish communist connection though. Only the Greens. What did you have to offer Green to get him to talk, Inspector?"

"That we'd hang him here and not send him back to the Reich, and not to send Mrs. Green there either."

"I think we can manage that," Normanby said. "I think you're right, Tibs, Scotty would admit it on the stand. Well then. Sign the warrants, and give them to Inspector Carmichael."

Lord Timothy took up his pen and signed. "You'd better take some backup," he said. "Confronting a lord in his manor and all that. I've arranged it."

"Thank you, sir." Carmichael put down his untouched tea and started to rise.

"No, wait, Inspector, there's something else I wanted to discuss with you." Normanby pulled the safe door fully open, took out a file, then pushed it mostly closed again and sat down.

Carmichael settled himself again, nervously. "Yes, sir?"

"It seems to me that all this business of terrorists and anarchists is rather overloading our traditional police forces. Look at your Mrs. Green getting lost in the shuffle. We're building new prisons, of course, and trying to get rid of some of our worst cases to the Continent, but it seems to me we could also do with a special police force to work on this kind of thing. You're a man we know, a man we have reason to trust, a man with experience in these areas, the man who solved the Farthing case, and now you've done so well at investigating this one. You'd be our first choice as head of the new agency."

"A Gestapo?" Carmichael asked. His stomach clenched. He understood what Normanby was saying. He was a man they knew they had a hold over if they needed one, a man they knew would do what he was told if necessary. He wondered if it was his own file Normanby was holding. He wanted to resign, to get away from all of this, not to be drawn further in. Too late, he thought.

"No. Well, yes. We wouldn't call it that of course," Lord Timothy said. "We thought of calling you the Watch. It's a good solid old-fashioned name. It's what they used to call the police in Nelson's day. We thought it had the right ring to it."

"What do you think, Inspector? Or should I say, Chief Inspector?" Normanby asked.

Carmichael looked at Normanby and saw that the Prime Minister saw his torment and was pleased by it. "About the name?" he asked. "I think it seems a good choice."

"About taking the job," Normanby said, impatiently. "Do you think you could handle it?"

"I don't know if I have the qualifications," Carmichael said, woodenly. He knew he had no choice, that if he didn't take it, if he tried to retire now or emigrate he would end up in some hellhole of a camp, and so would Jack. If he took it at least he would have enough power to protect himself from everyone except Normanby, and perhaps in time from Normanby too. He could turn a blind eye sometimes, perhaps avoid the worst injustices. But whatever they called it, his would be the responsibility for the boots on the stair at midnight, the deliberate blurring of lines between guilt and innocence in the service of expediency. He had known it could come to this, or something like this, when he had agreed to Penn-Barkis's deal. He was a fool to have any scruples left. He had already sold his soul, after all.

"Let us be the best judge of that," Lord Timothy said. "I'm sure you'll do a splendid job."

27

The next day, Wednesday, was all rehearsal. We had the Players there, and I must say Antony had done a very good job with their masque. He'd decided to keep the Player King as a king, to echo Claudius. He was dressed in black, head to toe, and there was one other man, Hamlet's father, echoing his outfit but in white. The really clever thing was that he was dark-skinned—he was an Indian law student actually who Antony knew from somewhere. He didn't have to speak at all, so he could get away with it. He was the same height as the Player King, and it really did give the effect of a negative. All the rest of the Players were women, a kind of dancing chorus all in blood red from their tights to the scarves in their hair. It was rather striking.

Antony had arranged it so that the court audience for the play sat at the back on a raised dais. It was a sort of step that for most of the play had a curtain in front of it and was used for exits and entrances, but for this the curtain went up and we sat there exchanging our few words of dialogue and looking down at the masque and beyond it to the audience. Mollie leaned forward too much at one point and her chair fell off the edge, and we went back to the beginning. So I was sitting staring out into the auditorium as the security people went up to the Royal Box and practically took it apart. They examined it inside and out, they banged on things, they measured, they compared the number of struts, loudly, with the other boxes. I was ever so glad we hadn't hidden a bomb in there the week before, because they'd certainly have found it. What worried me was that they were clearly looking for one, and I couldn't think how they knew.

I told Devlin when I got out that evening. He was still picking me up at the theater after rehearsals, despite the armed guard at the stage door. He said changing the pattern would be worse than being recognized, and he was burned anyway when this job was over. "Taking it apart?" he echoed me, putting the car into gear and pulling away between two black taxis. "But they didn't pay any special attention to you, darling?"

"None at all," I said. "Not to any of us. They wouldn't even stop banging when Antony asked them."

"Then it's a question of what they know," he said, frowning. "I'd better make a call."

He parked at the gates of Green Park, where there were two telephone boxes together, looking very red and solid in the dusk. He went into the first one and I could see him dialing and waiting, his pennies ready. After a moment he tried another number, listened, and hung up without putting his coins in. Then he came out of that box and went into the other, and I could only see his back, hunched a little over the receiver. I could see that he was talking.

He looked grim when he came back. "Get out," he said. "We're going to take a little walk."

"They'll be locking the park soon," I objected.

"Come on, love," he said, holding my door open. I got out. He put an arm around me and walked me into the park. "Parliament is that way, and Buckingham Palace is that way," he said, like a tour guide. London rose all around us, but all I could see in the directions he indicated was trees and grass, and one man walking a dog in the distance.

"Are we burned?" I asked, quietly.

He looked down at me, then gave my shoulders a squeeze. "I don't think so. I couldn't spot anybody following us. But there's no reply on the private line at Coltham and the person answering the public line sounded to me like a ploddie. So it looks as if they're on to Lord Scott. But it doesn't quite make sense, because if they have Lord Scott and he's told them about the box, they'd have come for you first thing, you were right there."

"Uncle Phil would never tell them!"

He looked skeptical. "You can't say that about anyone," he said, quite gently. "Enough pain and a little time and you start telling them everything you know, and everything you think they want to know, making it up if you don't know it because you're so desperate to tell. Your uncle Phil didn't think they'd go so far as to use ways like that on a lord, and Loy thought he was right. I wouldn't trust it."

I hated to think of Uncle Phil being tortured, and at the same time I couldn't quite believe it. I suppose it was like the stone soap that I'd known about but not accepted for all that time. There are things one can't take in. I didn't want to think of our police—who I'd always thought of as a special kind of servants, protection, unquestionably on my side—doing terrible things to anyone. I suppose I knew they might do them to terrorists, but I'd classed terrorists as people who deserved it. That emphatically didn't include Uncle Phil.

We walked up and down. "What are we doing?" I asked. It had been a hot day, but now the sun was down and I was wishing for a coat.

"We're waiting for Loy," he said.

"Loy's all right then?"

"Loy wasn't at Coltham," was all he said. Then, after another few turns on the grass, in view of the gates and the car and the telephone boxes, "If we make it through this still alive, darling, if they die and we don't, then run. Take a train to Holyhead, they shouldn't be looking so hard in that direction. In Dublin go to—"

"They wouldn't take me, and anyway that would be no kind of life for me," I interrupted, crossly.

"They could fix you up with papers and get you into America, love," Devlin said. "My people have got contacts across the water. You could go to Hollywood maybe."

"They're hand in glove with Hitler."

"If Hitler was dead they wouldn't be." But he didn't offer again to give me the address in Dublin, and I didn't ask.

The man with the dog walked past us and gave us one incurious look. I suppose lovers cuddling are as common a sight in London parks as men with dogs, and I suppose Devlin knew that. It was a lovely dog, a golden Labrador in beautiful condition. I wished I could have a dog, or better yet two, but it simply wasn't fair in London.

"Are we still going to go through with it?" I asked, after another cold while.

"Don't you just wish we'd cancel? It depends what Loy finds out."

I hadn't told Devlin about changing my mind at the reception, partly because he was supposed to think I'd agreed already, and partly because it was so difficult to say. "I don't want to cancel," I said, feebly. "I want to go through with it now."

It was getting too dark to see Devlin's expression. "I haven't told you the new plan," he said. "It all depends on you, my dear."

"You don't want me to set it off from the stage?" I asked.

"No, you're all right on that one," he said. "Loy's going to be in the ha'pennies and I'm going to be in the front row, as backup. We have our tickets already. The bomb will be hidden in a floral arrangement. It'll be in the base. The flowers will be for the Royal Box, but they'll be delivered to you by mistake, and you'll take them round through the pass door and up to the box."

It was completely mad, of course, but I could see that it could actually work. The security on the stage door would give far less scrutiny to flowers for me than the security at the front-of-house would give to flowers for the box, and if I took the flowers around they'd probably just accept them, especially if they fit in a gap. It made much more sense than any of the other suggestions. "Have you made the bomb?"

"This afternoon. And it's in the base, we just need to have the flowers put in on Friday morning and have it sent round. Everything was moving smoothly until now."

Devlin shifted his grip on my arm, and that reminded me of Daphne and Mark at the reception. "Put your hand on my elbow," I said. He did. I arranged it so it was the way Mark's had been. It wasn't at all comfortable, even with his hand quite loose. "Now squeeze just the tiniest bit." It was excruciating.

"What was that in aid of?" he asked. "Something for the play?"

"No, it's how beastly Mark Normanby was holding his wife's arm at the reception last night. I knew it had to hurt, I just wanted to be sure of it. I think he must be some kind of sadist."

"From what I hear he doesn't have much use for women at all."

I was starting to feel seriously worried about where Loy was. A park keeper came past us, strolling towards the gates. "About to lock up now, mate," he said.

We walked out of the gates and towards the car. "I don't know—," Devlin started, when we both caught sight of Siddy, her camel hair coat swinging around her, walking fast down Piccadilly towards us.

"Let's get into the car and go somewhere," she said.

"Where's Loy?" Devlin asked.

"Keeping a low profile," Siddy said, opening the car door. She sat in the front next to Devlin and I sat in the back and leaned forward, so I could hear them talk. "Nobody's following me."

"Nobody's following us either; hanging around in the park for all that time waiting for you pretty much confirmed that," Devlin said. "Now what's happened?"

"Uncle Phil has been arrested, and they've taken in practically everyone who was at Coltham, servants included," she said, as Devlin started up. "It was very hard for my sources to find out, it was done quite secretly and on orders directly from the Home Secretary. Usually anything like this someone would have warned me, or warned Uncle Phil directly, but they must have guessed that. There was some kind of trouble down there, that's the only reason I know anything at all."

"So how did they get onto him? They knew about him and they knew about the box, but they didn't come after Viola," Devlin said. Siddy was lighting a cigarette, and I saw the side of his face clearly in the flare of the match; he looked fierce and intent, the way he did when he was making love.

Siddy blew out smoke. "We think it must have been through Lauria's servants. The Greens knew. They were in hiding, such good hiding we couldn't find them either, but they were caught last Friday. We managed to get Mrs. Green away, she's safely in, well, safety, but Mr. Green must have talked."

"What did they know?" Devlin asked.

"They knew about the original plan. Nothing about the later developments. Nothing about you, or Viola. And they'd have heard Loy's name, probably only as Loy, but maybe as Sir Aloysius."

"That's as distinctive as a bloody fingerprint," Devlin muttered, stopping at red lights.

"They won't find Loy, you can trust him for that. That's

why I'm here now and not him. I'm quite sure they only heard my name as Siddy, which doesn't mean anything to anyone official."

"It does to people who know you. Policemen might not know you, but you danced with the Prime Minister yesterday!" I said.

"I danced with Heinrich Himmler too, and I didn't vomit and I wasn't arrested, therefore they don't know about me," Siddy said, turning to look at me. "And if they don't know about me they don't know about you and we can go ahead. Besides, Mark Normanby calls me Lady Russell, which is still my name, although Geoff and I are divorced."

"Whether or not we go ahead is my decision," Devlin said. The lights changed. "Where am I supposed to be going, Siddy?"

"I don't see why you can't just go home to the flat," she said. "Loy and I are moving, to be on the safe side, but the flat ought to be fine. No breaking pattern. And the bomb's there, anyway."

"The bomb's there?" I asked, alarmed. I didn't like the thought of sleeping so close to it.

They ignored me. "Lord Scott, and Malcolm, and Bob, all know about Viola and the current plan," Devlin said. "That ought to mean that we all up sticks immediately."

"In an ordinary sort of operation," Siddy agreed. "But this one is so important, and such an opportunity. They know that. They know the timing. They'll hold out that long. I think we should risk it."

"You think?" Devlin was looking hard at her. "Or Moscow thinks?"

"I haven't spoken to Moscow since I heard," she said. "But I assure you, Moscow would think it was quite reasonable to lose all of us to take out Hitler. Loy thinks we should go ahead."

"Loy is addicted to taking risks, you know that," Devlin said. "It's my decision."

We drove in silence for a while. "I know it isn't up to me at all," I said, after a while. "But I think we should try it. We've got a good plan now, one that should work. And this is a chance to get rid of some people who really are evil."

"This is a change. I thought you thought they were only doing their jobs and would be replaced by people just like them?" Siddy asked.

"That was before I met them," I said, firmly. Lord Ullapool had been afraid. I kept thinking of that.

"We'll see how it goes tomorrow before I make up my mind," Devlin said. "Tell Loy to keep his head down, and you keep yours down too just in case. If all goes well, you and I have the Friday morning rendezvous at the florist. Be careful, but be there. If I'm not there, it's off, and I'll probably already be out of the country."

Devlin slowed the car as he was saying this, and drew to a halt outside Notting Hill Gate Underground station.

"Can I call you tomorrow?" Siddy asked, her hand on the handle of the door.

"Don't call the flat at all, from anywhere. Give me your new number. If I need you, I'll call from a box," Devlin said, firmly.

"All right," Siddy said, getting out. "Friday morning then." There were people going in and out of the Underground. She waved jauntily and went in through the doors.

"Those two," Devlin said, talking more to himself than to me. "Come on then," he said, looking at me in the mirror. "Is there anything you absolutely need from the flat for tomorrow morning, love? Because if not, as I swear nobody's following us now, I think we're going to stay on the safe side and spend the night in a little hotel I know near Victoria."

"Won't a hotel need an identity card?" I asked.

"A passport will do, for an Irishman, and I have any number of Irish passports," Devlin said, smiling. "If you can try hard to look as if you're not my wife, I don't expect they'll want to see anything from you at all. Do you need anything?"

"I think I can manage," I said.

"Can't have you going to your dress rehearsal in dirty knickers," Devlin said, teasingly.

"I can buy some in the morning, or we could call Mrs. Tring and ask her to bring me some from home," I said.

"Don't worry," Devlin said. "There's a pack in the boot with a change of clothes for both of us. It's been there since the day you first stayed with me. Just in case."

He drove on through the backstreets of London, and it struck me again how wonderful it was that he knew exactly what he was doing, not at all like me, who when it came to anything that wasn't acting generally just muddled through as best I could.

28

The Home Secretary's idea of the backup necessary to beard a peer of the realm in his den consisted of a Black Maria and another van full of eager constables under a sergeant. Carmichael and Royston led them in the Bentley. The sun beat down on the little procession as it left London and headed for Coltham.

"Kent, Inspector," Royston said, glancing away from the road towards Carmichael. "Remember you said you'd never suspected me of having a Kentish aunt?"

It seemed like something at the other end of a dark tunnel. "On the way down to Farthing," Carmichael said, as he might have said "When I was a boy," or "Before the War," or even "Before the War of the Austrian Succession."

The sunlit countryside was quite unlike the Hampshire countryside that had oppressed Carmichael on that occasion. Here everything was much more open. Villages could be seen from a distance across the rolling Downs. Crows circled above fields of standing corn. Occasional white oasthouses stood up, their towers giving the landscape an almost Dutch feel. "Do you think it's any prettier, sir?" Royston ventured.

"A bit, perhaps. But give me a good Lancashire moorland any day," Carmichael said, making an effort. He wished suddenly that they could get out of the car and walk in the clean country air until he was exhausted.

"No stopping at a pub with this lot behind us, neither, even if it is lunchtime," Royston said, encouraged.

"I think any pub would find that a bit intimidating," Carmichael said.

Royston laughed. "Just a bit," he said. "Do you really think we need them, sir?"

"No," Carmichael said. "The two of us and perhaps a stout bobby to hold the handcuffs would have been quite sufficient, and probably a good deal less alarming. But I couldn't argue with the Home Secretary."

"Of course not, sir," Royston said. "But at least we're getting one of them this time."

"One of who, sergeant?" Carmichael inquired.

"One of the nobs, the bigwigs. He's a lord, isn't he, that we're going to arrest. *Lord* Scott, Green said, and *Sir* Aloysius. It isn't always a protection. They don't always get away with it."

Carmichael digested that thought quietly. It didn't give him as much comfort as he would have liked.

Royston broke the silence. "Nearly there now, just over this hill and up the drive. You can't see the house from the road, but there's a pair of big gates, like the ones at Farthing, and I remember seeing them when I was a nipper coming down here to my auntie's. Always did wonder what was inside them."

"Would you like a new job, Royston?" Carmichael asked as the car began to take the ascent.

"What do you mean?" Royston kept his eyes on the road. "Aren't I giving satisfaction?"

"I mean that Lord Timothy Cheriton and Mr. Mark Normanby, both of whom you remember well enough, have offered me a new job, heading a new branch of special police to deal with terrorists and that sort of thing. I wondered if you'd like to transfer with me. It would mean a pay rise, maybe even a promotion."

Royston was silent as the car swept over the crest of the hill.

"Going to be called the Watch," Carmichael added.

"No offense, but I'm not sure that's the kind of job I'd like," Royston said at last as the road took them down.

"Me neither, sergeant, but I don't have much choice in the matter," Carmichael said. "Well, it would have been nice to have you on board, but I do understand."

They turned in at a pair of magnificent wrought iron gates, which stood open in the sunshine. The procession followed them. They crawled up the gravel driveway and drew to a halt in front of the massed mullioned windows of the house. There were rosebushes everywhere, and a profusion of roses in pink and yellow and red-streaked white. "Not as grand as I expected, somehow," Royston said. "With it being called a Court. Smaller than Farthing. And yellow. Nice roses though."

"I'd better have a word with the escort and make sure they understand they're to wait until called for," Carmichael said.

"Yes, sir, much better not to look as if we're expecting trouble," Royston agreed. "We've always got them there if we do need to manhandle anybody."

Carmichael got out of the car and walked back towards the Maria. He wondered if it would have been more dignified to have sent Royston back to speak to them and waited in the car. Too late now. He'd have plenty of time to get used to dignity in his new appointment. They'd probably keep him stuck in an office like Penn-Barkis. He had taken only a few crunching steps on the gravel when he felt something hard hit him in the shin. It immediately took him back to summer afternoons at school and the blow of a cricket ball. It was the blast that came with it that brought back those nightmare days in France, culminating with Dunkirk, that had been Carmichael's experience of war. He flung himself flat. There was another blast, farther away, and this time he recognized it properly. He wasn't being shelled from a tank or machine-gunned from a plane; someone was shooting at him with a shotgun. That second blast would have been the second barrel, so he should be safe for the time being while they reloaded, assuming there was only one gunman, which was a bad assumption. Lord Scott, Sir Aloysius, Nash, Nesbitt; four men at least, and heaven knows who else. Without raising his head Carmichael drew back behind the Bentley. The gravel would ruin his suit, he thought, and wanted to laugh at the incongruity of it.

A car door banged, and then another. There was another shotgun blast. Then there came the crack of rifle fire. Utterly unarmed, as was the custom of the British police, Carmichael stayed down between the back of the Bentley and the front of the Maria. Judging by the angle of the rifle fire, the Home Secretary's backup were violating police tradition. Carmichael was in general all for tradition, but in this particular case he couldn't feel anything but relief.

After a small eternity, the firing stopped. Then he heard a firm young London voice shouting, "This is the police. Come out with your hands up, all of you."

He raised himself to a crouch and then, attracting no fire, to his feet. He could see a number of bodies on the gravel. The golden stone of the house was streaked by creamy bullet marks, and some of the mullioned windows were broken. At the side of the house an old man with a shock of white hair was leading out a file of servants and retainers, hands in the air.

"Sir," someone said at Carmichael's elbow. He jumped, then turned. It was the flat-faced Deputy Inspector of the Home Secretary's forces. He had lost his uniform cap and looked older than he had when they had set off from the Yard. "Ogilvie, Inspector. Glad to see you're alive."

"I think they winged me," Carmichael said, remembering the blow to his shin. Looking down he was surprised to see his trouser leg soaked with blood. "A pellet I think?"

"That's what they were using, sir, shotguns and quite heavy pellets, like you'd use for hare, maybe, not light birdshot. I saw you go down and thought they'd got a direct hit."

"No, I was lucky," Carmichael said, automatically. "How many of them were there?"

"Four," Ogilvie said. "My marksmen shot two of them, and then the other two surrendered. I've sent an armed search party into the house to check we have absolutely everyone."

"That's right, good," Carmichael said. He felt quite distant from the whole affair. He couldn't even feel any pain from his wound.

"I think you should sit down in the van, sir," Ogilvie said.

Carmichael nodded. Ogilvie supported his elbow and guided him around the side of the vehicles. The bobbies were putting handcuffs on everyone who had left the house and herding them into the Maria.

"Make sure you get their names and papers," Carmichael said as they passed them.

"Yes, sir, they're doing that, sir, as a matter of procedure. But I don't think there's going to be any problem putting this one under the Defence of the Realm Act, considering they shot at us."

They walked down the far side of the van. The back doors were open. Carmichael did not want to climb inside, but he settled himself there on the high floor. It was a relief to get the weight off his leg. Ogilvie stood beside him, looking worried.

"There might be a bomb," Carmichael remembered.

"Yes, sir, I have apprised the men of that possibility," Ogilvie said. "I think you need a doctor sir, to dig the pellet out of your leg. I can carry on here if—"

"You've done very well, Deputy Inspector, and I entirely endorse all the decisions you made when you thought you were in charge," Carmichael said. "But I need to know who has been arrested and if there's any more resistance in the house. I'll stay here."

"Yes, sir," Ogilvie said. One of the bobbies came up with a list, which Ogilvie took and handed to Carmichael. "This is the list of detainees, all matched to identity papers."

Carmichael looked at it. Lord Philip John Scott headed the list. None of his other names were on it, nor were any of the women's names anything like Siddy. "Do we know who we shot?" he asked.

"Just give me a minute," Ogilvie said.

Carmichael sat back, out of the sunshine. He could smell blood, and over that the scent of the roses in front of the house. The lazy peace of a June afternoon was stealing back over what had been the scene of a battle. Somewhere out of sight, high above, a skylark started to sing. Royston must have gone with the inside party, Carmichael thought, because he couldn't see him anywhere. He hoped they didn't run into more trouble. He was glad Royston was with them. These men were all very keen, but Royston had common sense.

Ogilvie came back. "Malcolm Nesbitt and Robert Nash, according to their papers," he said.

"Damn," Carmichael said. He had wanted to speak to Nash for so long now that it seemed a terrible disappointment to know he never would. Death was the end of all possible answers.

"The other man with a shotgun, besides Lord Scott, was his butler, Goldfarb."

"No women arrested, apart from servants?"

"None, sir."

Well, it would be easy enough to get Green to identify the mysterious Siddy if she were hidden among them. The same went for Sir Aloysius, if he were disguising himself as a Jewish butler or anything else.

They had them all. He was disappointed that Nash was beyond questioning, but they would probably get all they needed from Lord Scott.

"We mustn't lose any of them in processing," Carmichael said. "Make sure they're all taken to the same place and kept together. I know there's a lot of overcrowding at present, but this is really important. Probably most of the servants will be released soon, but I need to question them all."

"Most of them seem terrified," Ogilvie said. "All the shooting coming out of nowhere. As best I can tell from what they've said so far, Mr. Nesbitt saw us coming up the drive and came downstairs in a panic, at which Lieutenant Nash and Lord Scott snatched up shotguns from the gun room and prepared a defense."

"I can't think what they hoped to gain from it. It was impossible odds for them. They weren't covering the escape of anyone else by the back?"

"I suppose it's possible, but not from anything anyone has said. Shall I send out a patrol under a sergeant, sir? Or lead one myself?"

"How many men do you have in your command now?" Carmichael asked.

"Twenty-one active, sir. One was shot dead, and another three are wounded."

"Then a patrol isn't worth it. This country looks flat, but it rolls, and there are spinneys, so someone who knows it could easily hide from twenty men, especially with the start he'd have had, even if we could spare them all. We'll find out from the servants who was here and when."

"Yes, sir," Ogilvie said.

A red-faced young constable with a snub nose came up to them. "House secured, sir," he said to Ogilvie, in a manner much more military than Carmichael was used to.

"No bombs, no armed hideouts, nothing of note?" Carmichael asked.

"No, sir. One dead body, a woman, papers identify her as Muriel Nest, Jewish, parlor maid." He hesitated, then added, "Shot through the window by a rifle, sir, pure bad luck."

"These things happen, and they certainly started the shooting, knowing they had innocents on their side," Carmichael said. "We may have killed her, but we were undoubtedly acting in self-defense."

"Yes, sir. And they killed two of us, not to mention the wounded," the red-faced constable said.

"Two?" Carmichael asked. "I thought you said you'd only lost one man, Ogilvie?"

"That's right, sir," Ogilvie said, looking embarrassed. "I thought you knew, sir. The other one was your driver. They took him out early on, quite close range, in the chest, just as he was getting out of the car. Made a mess of the car too, dinged it up badly. Sorry about that, sir."

29

Devlin's idea of a hotel near Victoria was a beastly hole in Pimlico. Our room was actually underground, with a window at street level. It must have been a servant's room when the so-called hotel was a proper house. The bathroom, which was down the hall, had a big old-fashioned bath with claw feet and a free-standing pipe that provided first warm and then lukewarm water. After checking us in, Devlin went off to hide the car. I had a good soak in the bath. When I came back to the room, wishing for talcum powder and face cream, not to mention my Dutch Cap, Devlin was fast asleep right in the middle of the bed. I had to poke him to make him move over.

I lay awake listening to the sound of people's feet on the pavement above my head, afraid one of them would be a policeman come to get us. It was late, but people kept clattering by. It was much too hot to close the window. I kept thinking about Uncle Phil being arrested and maybe tortured, and Malcolm too, and nice thoughtful Bob Nash. How could Siddy be sure they wouldn't tell everything about us right away? Devlin had said they

have ways of making everyone talk. Why did I only believe people when they said things in a tone of breaking
things to me gently? Did I really believe that Pip, my
own sister Pip, was a monster? The terrible thing, lying
awake in the dark, was that I did, and that I recognized
the callous places in myself that could have made me
like her. I don't suppose Pip particularly wanted to be
horrid to the Jews, but she was having a lovely time on
the Continent and she just didn't care.

I would take the bomb and hope that it blew her up,
and her horrible Heinie with his sweaty hands, and sadis-
tic Mark Normanby, and even old Hitler, who seemed
nice enough but must have been as bad as any of them. I
briefly entertained a fantasy that all the horrid details had
been kept from him and he would stop the whole thing if
I explained it to him. He was the only one of them I had
liked. But no, I had heard him raving on the radio at the
huge torchlit rallies at Nuremberg—splendid theater—
and his way of blaming the Jews for whatever had gone
wrong.

I slept eventually, and dreamed of childhood, of Pip
pushing me into the duckpond and the weed catching
and tugging at me and trying to pull me under, while
Pip, transformed somehow into the adult Pip while I
was still a child, stood on the bank and laughed.

The dress rehearsal went wonderfully. Everything that
had been awkward before went smoothly. Mollie didn't
fall off the dais once. Everything came together as it
should. It helped a very great deal that Antony was staying in character as Claudius and not leaping out of it to
berate someone every two minutes. He was a terrific
Claudius now that he had the feel of it, always certain he
knew what was right for everyone. I threw myself into
character, glad to be Hamlet and not myself for a few
hours. Afterwards, he congratulated us all, told us to sleep
well, and to make sure to be at the theater early for the
first night.

Mollie and Pat and some of the others were going to

Mimi's, and I'd have liked to go with them, but Devlin was waiting in the car. "How are things?" I asked.

He didn't answer until he'd driven away from the theater. "Nobody's been near the flat, nobody's following me, we'll see now if anybody's following you," he said. "How did the dress rehearsal go?"

"Almost too well," I said. "Mrs. Tring was practically in tears."

"Too well? They say a bad dress rehearsal means a good first night, but I never heard it the other way around." Devlin was smiling as he drove, but looking in the mirror.

"I have," I said. "Is anyone following?"

"I don't think so." He wasn't doing anything to shake them off if they were, just driving a little slowly so that he'd see anything unusual.

"If we're going ahead, when are you going to do it?" I asked.

"The flowers will arrive in the afternoon, and be taken to your dressing room, then about an hour before curtain you'll spot them and take them around to plug the hole in the box." Devlin's eyes were still on the road. He signaled and waited to turn right, across traffic, onto Regent Street.

"That's not what I meant," I said. "I mean when in the play will you set it off."

"Why?" Devlin asked.

"Because I was wondering after that stupendous dress rehearsal how much of it the audience were going to get to see. If you could wait until my duel with Laertes—"

"I'm not going to tell you, love," he said. "I don't want you to know, you might do something on stage to give us all away. I want you to be as natural as possible when it happens. You passed up the chance to do it yourself, which gives me control of the timing. I'll pick a moment when they're all in the box. But let it surprise you."

"I thought Loy was going to do it," I said.

"No. I am. I told you I couldn't trust him for it," he

said. "And we're clear, nobody following, we can go home. No reason not to go back to the flat, and I take it you'd prefer that to the hotel?"

"Emphatically," I said. "But Loy—"

"Loy will be up in the ha'pennies and he'll try it from there, sitting down. I don't think that will work, but if it does, good. If not, I'll stand up in the front row, just for an instant. That's line of sight, it will work."

"If they get you they get me too, right away," I said.

"True enough, darling. But you don't want me to tell you how to get away. There's a pub on O'Connell Street—"

"There won't be any getting away," I said, impatiently.

"They might not connect us up for a few hours. If you went straight to Paddington you'd have a chance."

I let him tell me about the pub in O'Connell Street, Dublin, and what I was to say. Just in case it isn't burned, I won't say any more about it.

"What are you going to do tomorrow, before going to the theater?" he asked, as we got out of the car at his flat.

"I don't know. I suppose you'll be busy?"

He nodded. "I have my appointment with Siddy. I could meet you afterwards, for lunch if you like, love?"

"Oh, let's go to Benetto's by Camden Lock and eat ice cream!" I said. It was a treat Mollie had introduced me to, and one I often indulged in before first nights. Benetto's is a real Italian ice-cream parlor and they make their own ice cream and often have as many as five or six flavors. I have to watch what I eat, of course, but as Mollie had said long ago, one ice cream per play can't do any harm. "And if you're going to the florist, can you send roses from me to the cast?"

"If you give me money and a list of what you want," he agreed warily.

So Devlin agreed to come back after going with Siddy to the florist and meet me to take me to Benetto's. Before that we had the evening, and the night. Devlin didn't fall asleep like a lump that night, but instead we made love, and it was better than ever. He paid attention, that was what made him so different, he caught my rhythms instead of expecting me to catch on to his the way most men do. I slept much better that night. I didn't even think about being near the bomb until the next morning when he took it out from under the kitchen sink and went off with it.

He was late coming back to pick me up. I'd had breakfast and I wasn't starving—ice cream is hardly something you eat when you're starving anyway—but I was impatient and ready to go. Then I stopped feeling impatient and started to worry. They had arrested Uncle Phil. They could have got Siddy, and she could have led them to Devlin. It might be police cars that came for me. I had an unpleasant half hour before I saw Devlin's little car drawing up outside.

He was sitting very still. He was always very controlled in his movements, very graceful, but there was something about this that was different. He looked really shaken.

"Everything all right?" I asked, getting in.

"Well, the florist was Siddy's boy, or rather Moscow's boy, all right, but not all of the assistants were, so we had to do the work while nobody was looking. But it's done and sent off, so you don't need to worry." He turned the car and set off.

"Siddy's all right?" I asked.

"Siddy is always all right. Siddy is off, she said to tell you good-bye. She'll be in Moscow, or anyway in Lisbon, before you go on stage." He sounded quite savage.

"I didn't know," I said, stupidly.

"No more did we, but it's not unexpected. It might be a shock to Loy, but he'll get over it. What's surprised me is what she's found out since Wednesday night about the arrests at Coltham. Lord Scott's in custody, and so are his servants, but Malcolm and Bob were shot dead by the police. Lord Scott's charged with murdering a policeman with a double-barreled shotgun. Seems as if the silly buggers saw the police were coming and snatched up their hunting weapons to make a desperate last stand."

"Poor Malcolm! Uncle Phil will be gutted," I said. "And poor Bob too. I didn't know him well, but he always seemed so very nice."

"Very nice," Devlin echoed, savagely, mocking me. Then he relented. "They were both good men, none better. I'd have liked to have thought they'd be here making the world a better place. And if they're arming the police that's a bad sign."

"I'd quite understand if you don't want to go and have ice cream in the circumstances," I said.

"I'd like to raise a glass to them," Devlin said.

So we stopped at the next pub, which was called the Queen's Head. It was a horrible place with brass spittoons and drunks, even though it was lunchtime. There were no other women except the barmaid, who gave me an old-fashioned look. Devlin went up to the bar and ordered two whiskies. He brought them over to me in the corner. I took a sip from one of them as a toast to Bob and Malcolm, then Devlin looked at my face and downed mine straight after his and we went out again. He didn't normally drink very much, wine sometimes and beer sometimes, but that time and the time Loy brought whiskey to the flat were the only times I ever saw him drink spirits, despite what they say about the Irish.

"Ice cream," Devlin said when we were back in the air.

"It's still on?" I asked, getting back in the car.

"Makes no difference whether they're dead or imprisoned, does it?" he asked. "Except to them."

I couldn't think of anything to say to that.

"Will you mourn for me, Viola?" he asked after a little while. He must have seen the shock and distress on my unguarded face, because he laughed. "Oh you will, won't you, darling? Not with whiskey, but you'll miss me?"

"Are you expecting to die?" I asked.

"Of course I am, you silly bitch," he said. It was the drink talking. He caught himself a moment later. "I'm sorry, love, but you'd have known that if you thought about it. I'm not about to give them the chance, but I could die tonight if any of the bodyguards are quick enough to pop a shot off after I've pressed the button. Or if not, then they'll hang me after. There's not much chance of me getting out from the front of the stalls, and people will have seen me. We talked about this before."

"Did you think Siddy would help?" I asked, ignoring the name he had called me as best I could. Anyone could see that he was upset.

"Loy may have. I didn't think she'd bugger off quite so quickly, but I didn't expect much out of her. Like we said before, Stalin's no better, only further away."

Perhaps I had two sisters who could bear to support terrible things. "Do you really think it's worth it?" I asked.

"Yes, I do really think it's worth it," he said, imitating my tones exactly. "Jesus! If this wasn't the kind of opportunity that comes along only once don't you think I'd have called it off a hundred times already?"

We were at Benetto's. The whole place is tiled inside and out in ice-cream white with the name set in green tiles. Devlin parked the car and we went in. Mollie and Pat were sitting at one of the tables in the middle of the floor. Mollie spotted us immediately and waved. "They have banana!" she called. "Can you imagine, banana ice cream?"

"Don't have it," Pat advised. "The mint is much nicer."

There was nothing for it but to sit with them and eat ice cream. Devlin was surprisingly good at being casual and friendly to them, though I think Mollie guessed that he was preoccupied. He had the banana ice cream in a banana split and I had a chocolate nut sundae, which wasn't very adventurous but it is my absolute favorite and was wonderfully comforting. There was a certain Twilight of the Gods atmosphere about everything and I thought that perhaps this might be my last ice cream ever. At the same time, everything seemed so real and undramatic that I couldn't quite believe it. I kept on eating ice cream and laughing at Pat's gossip and inside I was thinking that if this had been a play this would have been the time for passionate speeches.

As it was, I didn't even get to have time for passionate farewells. It would have seemed awfully strange for Devlin not to have offered Mollie and Pat a lift to the theater, so of course he did. They crowded into the back and enthused about how much more comfortable it was than the Underground. It occurred to me then that I had hardly been on the Tube for ages, with Devlin running me around everywhere, and normally I used it every day and took it for granted that I would.

"Are you going to be watching tonight, Devlin?" Mollie asked.

"I wouldn't miss it," Devlin said. "I've been looking forward to it."

I kissed him when I got out. "Break a leg," he said. They were still there and could hear. "You're a good girl, Viola. Break both legs, eh love?"

"You too," was all I could think of to reply. He laughed and shook his head. He had such a versatile face. He'd have made a great actor. He could go from looking like thunder to soft as butter in two seconds.

"Break a leg!" he called to Mollie and Pat and then we all went up the alley to the stage door and he went off to park the car.

Mollie let Pat go a bit ahead. "Had the two of you had a fight?" she asked.

"Something like that, but it's all right now," I said.

She looked at me severely. "I hope so. You shouldn't let it upset you and disturb the play."

"No, mother," I said.

We had to show our cards and be searched going in through the stage door. I was glad I didn't have the radio detonator on me, because they even opened my little compact. The man who spoke to me was English, but there were Germans there too, in uniform. I tried to imitate Mollie's impatience with them. "At least this will be back to normal tomorrow," she said, over her shoulder as they were going through my bag.

Unless the bomb had been stopped at the stage door, it ought to be in my dressing room. I had one last cowardly thought then that I could leave it there, where Devlin's detonator wouldn't reach it through the walls, and we could all walk away safely, at least unless Uncle Phil incriminated us. I thought about Lord Ullapool's quiet voice, his fear, although he was who he was, and Devlin saying "Jesus!"

Mrs. Tring was in my dressing room. The place was full of flowers, so many there was almost nowhere to walk. It was quite natural to remark on them. "More flowers than ever," I said, blinking.

"There's a whole tree from your young man," Mrs. Tring said, indicating a huge flowering jasmine in a pot.

"That's really sweet of Devlin," I said, and it was. I knew it was part of a bluff with Siddy's florist, but even so, it was a lovely thing, covered in flowers and very fragrant.

"That'll last the run, if we don't forget to water it," Mrs. Tring said.

"Maybe even longer," I said. "I wonder if we have anywhere to put it at home?"

"Oh, so you're planning on coming home after? I was wondering."

I looked at her, completely at sea.

"Well, you seem so taken up with this Devlin, and he

with you, I wondered if he was thinking of this tree as something he'd be getting back in your bottom drawer."

I wanted to laugh, and I wanted to cry too. Marriage with Devlin was so far from anything we'd been able to think about I couldn't even begin to guess if it was something I wanted—would have wanted, in other circumstances—or whether he would. He had called me "love" there at the last, but he was always calling me love or dear or darling, I had no idea what, if anything, it meant to him. "I don't know," I said, helplessly. "He hasn't said anything about that."

"I didn't mean to speak out of turn," Mrs. Tring said, and put her arm around me.

"Well, what else do we have in the way of flowers?" I asked, hoping she'd think I just wanted to change the subject, but really to get hold of the bomb as fast as possible.

"Huge bunch of roses from Her Hitler." She always pronounced it that way, and it always made me smile. "Big bouquet from Mr. Normanby, orchids and carnations and everything. Irises from your sister Dodo, very pretty, more roses from your sister Celia, and all this lilac from your sister Siddy—your family are very well represented today, I must say! Then these pink roses are from Antony, the spring bouquet is from the management of the theater, the apple blossom is from the cast, this white bud in the vase is from Mollie, and I hope you remembered to send her something."

"A bunch of roses," I said, confident, though I hadn't checked that Devlin had remembered. "I sent buds to everyone else."

"These carnations are from a Captain Keiler," she went on, reading the label. "Then this African violet doesn't have a tag. The purple lilac is from Andrew." Andrew was an old boyfriend.

"How about that big thing in the corner?" I asked, having spotted what I thought was it. It was a red and white box, like a window box, full of red and white azaleas.

"It's from Mrs. Normanby," she said.

I went over and looked, and saw how clever they had been. The top label said it was for me, from Daphne Normanby, which would encourage the guards not to check it too closely, but underneath was another tag, saying it was for the Royal Box. I half-pulled off the top tag, tutting.

"This isn't for me at all. This tag must have come off whatever Daphne really sent me, probably that violet, and got attached to this somehow. This is part of the display for the Royal Box. I should take it round to them at once."

"Get a porter to do it," Mrs. Tring advised. "Not that they'll probably miss it."

"I don't know, they might have a hole this size," I said. I bent and picked up the flower-topped bomb. It wasn't as heavy as I had expected. Devlin had sworn it couldn't go off by anything I could do to it carrying it, but even so I felt quite light-headed holding it and as if I couldn't quite get enough breath. "I'll run round quickly with it, and then when I get back we should start my makeup."

"Plenty of time yet," Mrs. Tring said, but she didn't stop me.

I went out into the corridor. Mollie popped her head out of her dressing room. "Thank you for the roses," she said. "And Devlin sent me some freesia—do thank him for me. That's very kind of him."

"He must like flowers with scent," I said. "He sent me a whole jasmine tree in a pot. Mrs. Tring thinks it means he wants to marry me." I rolled my eyes.

Mollie avoided the issue by changing the subject. "What have you got there? Something misdelivered?"

"Meant for the Royal Box," I said. "I'm taking it through now."

"Right," she said, entirely uninterested.

30

Carmichael limped around the car to see Royston's body on the gravel, his arms flung out away from the red ruin of his chest. "He should have stayed in the car," Ogilvie said, sounding very far away. "He got out after the first shot."

Coming to help, Carmichael thought, uselessly. Royston's eyes were open, staring up in blue outrage at the unclouded sky. He must have taken a whole shotgun blast at close range and fallen backwards.

Ogilvie was saying something about the damage to the car. "They'll be able to beat the dents out and it will be good as new," he said.

"You have no idea what you're talking about," Carmichael said.

"You really should get to the doctor, sir," Ogilvie said. "You're very pale. I'll clear up here."

Carmichael supposed the numb state he was in must be shock. He nodded and let efficient flat-faced Ogilvie manage him and the other wounded into the van and have them driven to the hospital at Maidstone. There he almost welcomed the pain as the doctor dug the pellet out of his calf. He kept his eyes open. Whenever he closed them he saw Royston splayed out on the driveway. He had lost friends in the war and got over it. He wished he could remember the trick of it.

His leg felt much worse with the pellet removed, though it looked much better neatly bandaged. They had cut off his ruined trousers.

The doctor wanted to keep him in hospital for a couple of days for observation. "The wound isn't serious, but you lost a quite a bit of blood," he said. "We'd like to keep an eye on you."

"Just let me telephone the Yard and my man and let them know where I am," Carmichael said.

They pushed him to a corridor phone in a wheelchair. He used his police priority to call the Yard first.

Stebbings took the news calmly, as always. "That's too bad," he said, unemotionally, when Carmichael told him Royston was dead. "So where is Deputy Inspector Ogilvie taking Lord Scott? The Chief will want to know."

"I don't know," Carmichael said. "He didn't say. I told him to keep them all together. No news of Mrs. Green, is there?"

Stebbings remained unruffled. "Nothing has turned up on her yet, sir. Do you know when you'll be fit for duty?"

"They're just keeping me here overnight to keep an eye on me. I daresay I'll be able to limp in tomorrow or Friday."

Jack, who had always been a little jealous of Royston, without any cause at all as far as Carmichael was concerned, was shocked. "Just like that?" he said.

"It's a dangerous job," Carmichael said.

"I suppose you haven't quite taken it in yet," Jack said. "Are you sure you're all right, P. A.?"

"I caught the extreme edge of a blast of bird shot, that's all. I'm fine."

"Where exactly are you? Do you want me to come down?"

The corridor was public, people kept passing. Jack's voice in his ear was like a connection to sanity and warmth. He wished they could speak freely.

"Of course I want you to, I'm not sure it would be wise." A pretty nurse, passing, turned and gave Carmichael a smile. "Why don't you come down tomorrow afternoon and bring me some clothes. They should be ready to let me out by then. It's Maidstone General Hospital. I don't expect it's far from the station, and if it is, take a cab."

"You're not alone, are you?" Jack asked.

"I wish I were," Carmichael said, honestly.

"Good-bye then, P. A. Look after yourself. I'll see you tomorrow." Jack hesitated, and the hesitation came across the line as clearly as if it had been words.

"You know how I feel," Carmichael said. "See you tomorrow."

He was wheeled into a private room and helped into a hospital robe and then into bed. The Yard would pay for him to be patched up, he thought, or if not Normanby's new Watch would. He was glad to be alone. If he had been in a ward, he would not have had any privacy at all. The nurse settled him with a cup of terrible strong tea with milk and what she called a nice book, which meant a trashy American paperback about, judging by its lurid cover, brave Nazi partisans and oppressive Russian commissars in the Ukraine. Carmichael ignored both and, when she left him alone, saying she would be back in an hour with his supper, lay in silence staring at the ceiling, wishing he were a Frenchman or a woman or even a dog, that he might give expression to his grief.

They gave him a sleeping tablet that night, and he did sleep, though his dreams were terrible. Late the next morning the doctor examined him and said he was free to leave, but not to overstress his leg until the wound was healed. Jack arrived soon afterwards with Carmichael's favorite light linen suit and a much brighter tie than

Carmichael preferred. "You're not quite thirty, P. A. You don't have to dress as if you're sixty," Jack said.

"I've always liked the way you call me P. A.," Carmichael said, quietly.

"It's because of all the time in France when I only knew your initials on the company record," Jack said. "I didn't know what they stood for, and I got into the habit of thinking of you that way."

What Carmichael liked about it was that it was something nobody else had ever called him. He smiled at Jack, and straightened his tie. "It should be black, for poor Royston," he said.

"Was he married, do you know?" Jack asked.

"His wife ran off with a docker, three years ago now. He had a little girl, Elvira. He paid his landlady to look after her when he was working. Sometimes she'd be alone in the house and when she opened the door she'd pretend she had a mother who'd just popped out for a moment." Carmichael remembered the last time he had seen Elvira. "We always used to give her something at the end of a case."

"What'll become of her now?" Jack asked, offering his arm to help Carmichael down the steps. "How old is she?"

"She's eight," Carmichael said. "I don't know what'll become of her. Her mother didn't want her and I don't know if there's anyone else. I suppose I ought to go and see her and see if she needs anything."

"You mean she might be left without anybody? And without a ha'penny either?" Jack's voice rose.

They went out into the corridor, in which lingering smells of institutional cooking overlay the scent of disinfectant. "If she's left like that, we should do something for her," Carmichael said. "Send her to school, she's a bright little thing. Adopt her, even."

"What, take her to New Zealand with us?" Jack asked, as they came out into the fresh air. The taxi driver opened the door as soon as he saw them coming.

"We can't go," Carmichael said.

"But you finished the case, P. A.," Jack protested, as they settled into the taxi. "Railway station, please."

"I suppose I did. But—" he stopped. Jack looked at him in some concern. He indicated the driver. "Let's talk about this later."

On the train, alone together in a first-class compartment as it pulled out of Maidstone station, Carmichael went on. "Normanby offered me a job. A promotion. An agency. I— it was the sort of offer with a threat behind it."

"So you can't get out?" Jack asked, his eyes on Carmichael's.

"I can't. It'll mean more money. And maybe the chance to do some good—to turn judicious blind eyes, and to make it better than it might have been." Carmichael looked out of the window and saw the Kentish countryside blur together.

"What is this agency?"

"It'll be called the Watch. It's to keep an eye on terrorists and communists and all that kind of thing," Carmichael said, miserably.

"A Gestapo?" Jack asked.

"That's the first thing I said, too. They might as well call it that and have done." Carmichael gritted his teeth.

"And you think you could really do some good doing that?"

"Well, perhaps, or at least prevent some evil."

Jack shook his head. "I know you've just lost a close friend, P. A., but even so that sounds crazy."

"I'm riding a tiger," Carmichael said. "If I let go, it'll savage me, but if I can hold on I might be able to steer it away from innocents."

"You know what happened to the young lady of Riga," Jack said, but he smiled.

That night Carmichael slept in his own bed, and his dreams were better.

The next day, he rang the Yard. "Are you fit for duty, sir?" Stebbings asked.

"I'm out of hospital but limping along well enough," Carmichael said. "Do you need me to come in, sergeant?"

"Nothing urgent, if you need to rest. There's a pile of papers here for you, shall I send them round?"

"That would be very kind," Carmichael said.

It was midmorning before the pile of papers arrived, brought by Ogilvie. Carmichael winced involuntarily at the sight of him when Jack showed him in. It wasn't Ogilvie's fault, he knew that, but he'd never be able to see him without thinking of Royston's death.

"Are you still in a lot of pain, sir?" Ogilvie asked. "I must say I admire how you carried on with the bullet in you."

"It was one shotgun pellet, at quite long range, nothing really," Carmichael said, regretting now that he had given in to Jack's urging and put his foot up on a footstool.

"Well some light reading might do you good," Ogilvie said, sitting, uninvited, on the sofa. "I also wanted to say, sir, that when you take up your new duties I'm to be one of your officers. It'll be a pleasure to work with you."

"Likewise, likewise," Carmichael said. "You did very well at Coltham, Ogilvie. Any progress on that?"

"I expect it's all in your reports, sir. Shall I leave you to them? If you need anything done, call the Yard. I don't expect I'll be their errand-boy again, I just wanted to come and say hello and see how you were doing, and let you know that even though you lost your driver you'll still have friends about you."

Jack, who had been hovering invisibly doing his butler act, opened the door to show Ogilvie out.

"That man has no cheekbones," Carmichael said, grumpily, as Jack came back alone.

"You can't blame him for that, P. A.," Jack said. "It's the surgical removal of tact that seems to be more the problem."

"He really was very efficient at Coltham," Carmichael said gloomily. "I won't ever be able to find a pretext to sack him."

"Perhaps he writes the worst reports in the world," Jack said, brightly.

"We can only hope," Carmichael said. "Oh Jack, bless you, you do me so much good."

"And tomorrow when you're walking better, we can see if we can find poor Royston's little girl and do some good to her," Jack said.

The reports were terribly dull. Mrs. Green was still missing. Lord Scott categorically refused to speak. He had been charged with murder of Royston and the dead constable, in addition to treason. He refused even to say that the murders were self-defense. Carmichael wondered why on earth he was being quiet. Could he possibly still be hiding something? Sir Aloysius was still at large. He went on, uncomfortably.

The servants made up for Lord Scott's taciturnity with their loquacity. There were detailed reports of the day of the arrests, differing only by point of view. The butler, Goldfarb, who was charged for attempted murder, claimed Lord Scott had ordered him to take up a shotgun. Carmichael wondered if he might get away with that in court. He was the one who had shot at Carmichael, and clearly hadn't been very good with the weapon.

He stopped to eat the light lunch Jack prepared, a pleasant omelette aux fine herbes with fresh brown bread and butter. He lingered over a pot of tea afterwards, then took up the reports again. He was still plodding through them at mid-afternoon, and was about to pick up the eminently tedious lists of people who had been at Coltham for lunch or dinner in the past month, when the doorbell rang. Jack answered it, then came in to Carmichael.

"It's an Inspector Jacobson, from Hampstead."

"I've no idea what he wants, but I'm glad enough to

be interrupted. Send him in," Carmichael said, tossing down the reports. "And bring some tea."

Jacobson came in and hovered uncertainly in the doorway. "How are you?" he asked.

"Bored," Carmichael said. "Do me a favor and have a cup of tea with me if you have time and take my mind off all this."

"I don't know if you'll want to when you hear my news, but I'll be glad to." Jacobson sat down. "First, let me say how sorry I was to hear about Sergeant Royston. He was one of the best. The Force can't afford to lose a man like that."

"I don't know how I'll manage without him," Carmichael said.

"Quite the best type," Jacobson said, and they sat a moment in companionable silence, broken when Jack came in with the tea tray. Carmichael saw he had brought milk and sugar, and used the silver teapot. "Will you pour, please, Jack?" he asked. "You know how I like mine— how about you, Inspector Jacobson? Milk? Sugar?"

"Milk, two sugars," Jacobson said, and took the cup Jack handed him with every appearance of enjoyment. "Not often I get time to stop in the afternoon for tea," he said, taking a sip. "Ah. Better than strong drink that is."

"So what's your bad news?" Carmichael asked, when Jack had gone back to the kitchen, closing the door behind him.

"We've lost Mrs. Green, and I mean really lost, not mislaid." Jacobson looked guilty when Carmichael hissed a breath. "Sorry. But it's plain now she's got away. We might find her again, but she's on the loose."

"You needn't look so confounded guilty, it isn't your fault," Carmichael said.

"I know, but I feel bad about it because I was there when Sergeant Royston pulled her in. And I can't help feeling that if they can find a way to blame me for it they will."

Jacobson might as well have had "scapegoat" tattooed

on his forehead, Carmichael thought. He must be an extremely good officer to have avoided it all his career so far. "Go on," he said.

"Well, I spent all day Wednesday while you were being a hero, and yesterday too, looking at every single woman in Islington Women's Prison, and talking to all the staff, in case they remembered anything. Eventually someone remembered one of the others taking a woman off somewhere, but the other warder, whose name is Jones, denied ever having done such a thing. So I looked into Jones, and what do you know but she's a communist, a red from way back. When I confronted her on that she admitted that she had helped Green escape, but she didn't know where she was now."

"A communist connection," Carmichael said. "I take it Jones is somewhere safe?"

"In our lockup in Hampstead," Jacobson said. "On a suicide watch, no belt, no metal cutlery, and guarded round the clock by men I trust."

"But there weren't any communists in the plot as far as we had it," Carmichael said. "I was putting this down as a conspiracy between Lord Scott and his old-fashioned Churchill-style patriotism and Lauria Gilmore's naive socialism, with an odd IRA connection."

"Well I suppose it might be an *old* IRA connection," Jacobson said. "Churchill and Scott were the negotiators with Michael Collins when the Free State was set up. Scott might have made some friends then."

"I've never understood the Irish," Carmichael said.

Jacobson laughed. "Did you know the only synagogue the Third Reich have ever built is in Dublin?"

"How's that?" Carmichael asked.

"You know how the Irish stayed neutral in the War? Well, some German pilot got lost and thought he was over Liverpool when he was over Dublin, and dropped his stick of bombs. The Irish government complained to Hitler, and he was very eager not to give offense to them because he didn't want them coming in on our side. It might have made all the difference to the Battle of the Atlantic if we'd had bases on the West of Ireland. Anyway, Hitler paid compensation for the damage done in Dublin. One of the buildings bombed was the synagogue. They rebuilt it with the compensation money, better than before."

Carmichael chuckled. "I expect the Jews all over Europe laughed at that one."

Jacobson stopped laughing. "I hope so," he said. "They could do with a good joke."

"Anyway, well done on finding a communist connection at last. You may have lost Mrs. Green, but that connection is something the Home Secretary will be very glad to have. I expect you'll get a commendation or a promotion out of it," Carmichael said, heartily.

Jacobson frowned, and drank his tea. "I don't expect I will," he said. "I would if not for—but some of them can't ever forget I'm a Jew. Sometimes I think about chucking the whole thing. But what else could I do? I'm forty-five, it's a bit late to start again."

"I'd offer you a job in the new Watch, but I'm not sure that's quite what you'd like," Carmichael said.

"Not quite," Jacobson said.

"Think about it," Carmichael said. "I could certainly find a place for you. I'd like to have you." Jacobson was a good man, an honest man, and a man who knew how to resist being made a scapegoat. That would be a useful skill in the Watch. And it might be a good thing, or possible to represent to the Home Secretary as a good thing, to have a good Jew in a prominent position, to show the bleeding hearts that they weren't persecuting all of them, only the guilty.

"Thank you." Jacobson looked thoughtful.

"Well, I suppose I should get back to these reports," Carmichael said, picking up the lists. The top one showed that Sir Aloysius Farrell and Lady Russell had dined at

Coltham on Monday night. He'd have to get Stebbings to work on Lady Russell, in the hope she might be the mysterious Siddy, or lead them to Sir Aloysius.

"If they're really boring you, and if you're well enough, would you be interested in coming to the play?" Jacobson asked. "*Hamlet,* I mean. The security for the first night is so tight that they've taken all the other boxes, and they're filling them with plainclothes police. If you'd like to come along, I'm sure there's room in the Hampstead box."

"I've heard so much about it, I suppose I would like to see it," Carmichael said.

Jacobson looked at his watch. "Get changed then, and have a bite to eat if you want to, and I'll call for you here in an hour and a half."

Jack sulked because Carmichael was going to the theater without him. He refused to sit down while Carmichael ate his steak. "I'll have my menial dinner alone later," he said.

"You don't even like Shakespeare," Carmichael objected.

"I might have liked to have seen the men doing the girls' parts," Jack said. "I might have liked to have been asked if I wanted to."

"I couldn't possibly ask Jacobson if I could take you!"

"And it's always going to be that way, isn't it?" Jack said, whisking away Carmichael's plate though he hadn't quite finished with it.

It took Carmichael longer to change into evening dress than he expected, because his bandaged leg wouldn't fit in the trousers of the first suit he tried. He was only barely ready when Jacobson returned.

The traffic was light, and they arrived at the theater fifteen minutes before the show was due to start. Security was heavy. Carmichael had to show his papers and his police identification four times between the door and the box. "We're getting everyone seated before the VIPs come in," the last bobby confided as he led them around a curving corridor decorated with two hundred years' worth of playbills from forgotten plays.

Their box had ten chairs, packed together. He sat beside Jacobson and looked over into the Royal Box opposite. It was draped with the Union Jack and the blood-red swastika-inscribed flag of the Reich, and stuffed with flowers. There were five seats, but nobody was there yet but three armed and uniformed German soldiers. Carmichael settled down and looked at the program. *Hamlet, Princess of Denmark,* it said, in flowery script. On the back, he was assured that a Double Diamond Worked Wonders, and that Ridgeway's tea was used in this theater and that there was a Marriage Bureau in New Bond Street, where all inquiries were treated in strict confidence.

There was a rustling that made Carmichael look up. The curtain was still down, but the important people were filing into the Royal Box through the door at the back. Mark Normanby came first, looking revoltingly smug in evening dress that included a red cummerbund, accompanied by his beautiful wife Daphne, in a swirl of beige lace that made her look pale. Carmichael remembered her staring out of the window smoking the first time he had ever seen her. Behind them were another couple, a woman in a pretty dress and a thin German in uniform he recognized from photographs as Himmler. Normanby and Daphne sat down, and so did Himmler, but the woman, who looked English, hovered on her feet, waiting, as the rest of the audience was waiting, for the Fuhrer to make his entrance. He came in, dressed in black with a swastika armband, and settled himself in the center of the box. He was flanked by two bodyguards who stood, alert, on either side of the door.

There was applause from the audience. Hitler acknowledged it politely with a casual wave. A moment after, the house lights dimmed and the play began.

Carmichael had thought *Hamlet* thin stuff when they'd

acted it at school. This interpretation made him realize how much he had missed. He thought Viola Lark did very well at bringing out Hamlet's hesitations and difficulties. When Hamlet reached the famous lines that the play was the thing wherein to catch the conscience of the king, he found himself glancing over at Normanby, who had slain Sir James Thirkie, who was his brother-in-law, if not his brother, in order to have his shot at the kingdom. His conscience did not seem caught; he looked intent but not worried. The play wound on, and when the curtain fell at the interval with Hamlet having failed to kill Claudius at prayer, it almost surprised him to be brought back to the real world.

Jacobson asked Carmichael what he thought of it so far.

"I'm really enjoying it," Carmichael said. "I think she's very good. She makes it make sense."

"Viola Lark? She's variable, but she does seem to have hit her stride with this one. I've never seen her so good," Jacobson said, in the tones of a connoisseur. He went on to discuss other plays he had seen her in.

In the Royal Box, Normanby was sharing a pleasantry with Himmler as they shared a drink. Hitler was staring out at the auditorium, looking bored, ignoring the woman beside him.

"Who is that pretty woman in the Royal Box?" Carmichael asked, staring over. "She looks English, but she's fussing over Hitler as if she's German."

"She's Celia Himmler, who was Celia Larkin," Jacobson said.

"Viola Lark's sister, then," Carmichael said, remembering. "One of them was married to old Thirkie, originally."

"Olivia, Celia, Viola, Cressida, Miranda, and Rosalind," Jacobson said. "Like the six wives of Henry VIII, only more Shakespearean. My wife reads the society papers every single week."

"Cressida," Carmichael said, slowly, as the lights

dipped, to indicate that the play was about to begin again. "Siddy?"

"I don't know if that's what they call her. She's Lady Russell," Jacobson said.

"Siddy," Carmichael repeated, and stood up. His wounded leg shook under him. If Viola was the sister of one of the conspirators, and Siddy had been meeting with the conspiracy as recently as Monday night, then there could be a bomb in the theater now. He remembered the Irishman he had met with Viola, who had been introduced as Connelly. Could that have been Sir Aloysius? His body moved as slowly as treacle towards the back of the box, while his brain raced through everything he knew. Lord Scott was keeping silent to protect something. Sir Aloysius hadn't wanted to build a crude bomb but wanted to wait for a better one. It might be on a timer, or it might be radio controlled. If he shouted out, that might cause someone to set it off.

31

There was a guard at the pass door. I gave him my best
smile. "I'm Viola Lark," I said. "These flowers had
the wrong label, they came to me but they were meant
for the Royal Box. I thought I'd bring them through in
case they have a hole up there these are meant to fill."

"Will you want to come back through this way,
miss?" he asked.

"Oh yes, probably in about five minutes."

"I'll still be here then, so I'll just open up for you, no
problem," he said.

It was as easy as that.

The theater was dark in the literal sense. They hadn't
even let the program sellers in yet. I had to be very careful going down the stairs into the pit. I did trust what
Devlin had said about the bomb, but if I fell and
squashed the azaleas nobody would want them anyway.
I picked my way through and then up the stairs at the
back that go to the passage that runs along behind the
grand circle and has doors into the boxes. There were
two men outside the door to the Royal Box, both Germans

in uniform. They carried guns prominently in their holsters, big scary ones. I took a breath and held the flowers in front of me, though my arms were starting to ache, and smiled.

"These were supposed to be for you, but they came to me," I said.

"Flowers comed," one of the soldiers said.

"We flowers have," the other agreed, in slightly better English. That one did at least have the grace to smile as he shook his head.

I was out of ideas, but fortunately Captain Keiler came down the corridor. "Oh, Captain Keiler, I hope you can help," I said. My smile was almost a simper by now.

"Heil Hitler! What can I do for you, Lady Viola?" he asked, bowing. He looked as if he'd probably have kissed my hand if it hadn't been for the azaleas.

"These are your flowers—yours for the box I mean, not the carnations you so kindly sent me—but the labels were mixed on these and they came to me."

"Give them to me," he said. He took the azaleas, glanced at the labels briefly, then handed them to the soldier who had smiled. He said something to the other in German, clearly an order, and the other man opened the box door. I caught a glimpse of the inside, where there were banked masses of azaleas, all absolutely identical to the ones I'd brought up. Then the soldier took mine in and the other one closed the door so I couldn't see exactly where he put them.

"Oh thank you so much," I said to Captain Keiler. "I was so afraid you'd have a hole where they were supposed to go."

"No, thank *you* for taking the time to bring them," he said, bowing again, and this time he did kiss my hand. "I am so much looking forward to seeing you in the play," he said. "And I am touched that you remembered the flowers I sent you. Perhaps one night before I go back to

Berlin when I am not on duty, I might come to see the play again, and perhaps you and I would do supper and dance afterwards?"

I was about to refuse politely when I remembered that this would never happen in any case, and I might as well keep him sweet. "When do you go back to Berlin?" I asked.

"I go back with the Fuhrer, on next Thursday, after his last dinner with the king and queen on Wednesday night. Perhaps Tuesday night?"

"Come around to the stage door after the performance on Tuesday," I said.

I thought I'd got rid of him with that, but he insisted on walking back with me to the pass door. "Will you be watching the play from in the box with the Fuhrer?" I asked.

"I have that honor, yes," he said.

"It's the best view in the house," I said, thinking that I would have this man's soul on my conscience too, but it wouldn't weigh very heavily.

"But I am on duty and will have to give part of my attention to checking for assassins and murderers," he said.

"Surely you're not expecting to find any here?" I said.

"I must always be alert for my Fuhrer," he said.

Then we were at the pass door and he ordered the policeman there to let me through. "Until Tuesday," he said, and kissed my hand again.

As soon as I was backstage again my legs started to shake. I had to lean on the wall for a moment and take deep breaths. Then I pulled myself together and walked back to my dressing room. The part I had been dreading most was over. At least the bomb was out of my possession. Now I could start worrying about when it would go off and ruin the play. I wished Devlin had told me how long we had. It was such a good play, now it had come together. All I had to go on was the joke about putting the trigger in Yorick's skull, which made me hope we had at least until the graveyard scene.

Mrs. Tring did my face, then fussed with my hair and with a wine spot on the sleeve of my dress. It hardly showed close up, and wouldn't show at all to the audience, but I let her fuss. It was familiar and reassuring. After a while she went off to dress Mollie and I looked into the mirror. Usually when I did this before a performance I was going over my lines and thinking myself into the character, but that day my mind kept drifting away from Hamlet and onto myself. It was my own eyes I looked into, not Hamlet's, my own problems with murder I contemplated, not hers. Claudius was her uncle, her father's brother, she must have known him well all her life, no wonder she found it so hard to believe he was a murderer. Pip was my sister, and the murder and slavery she was condoning was far away. Siddy—I didn't want to think about Siddy, but I could picture her shaking hands with Devlin outside the flower shop and stalking straight off to take the next plane to Lisbon. She was more like Cassius than anyone in *Hamlet*.

"Five minutes!" the boy said. "Orchestra and beginners!" Devlin would be out there in the audience now, and Loy, sitting in their places, with their little radio devices, waiting. It was all out of my control. I had passed "to be or not to be" and could coast. Devlin would have made short work of Claudius.

My nerves had quite passed off by the time I got out onto the stage. It was too late, anyway, everything was out of my hands. All I could do now was give the audience as much of *Hamlet* as they were able to get. I was Hamlet, coming back to Elsinore. By the scenes where Antony, blue-lit, played my father's ghost I had almost forgotten everything but the performance. Charlie missed a cue in his first scene, but the others covered for him and I don't think the audience noticed. Mollie was on top form throughout. I almost slipped getting away from Pat in the nunnery scene, but we made it look deliberate. It fit in quite well as a sidestep after Pat had been walking round and round me, taunting me with the gifts he was supposedly returning. It wasn't until we were all sitting along the dais and Antony and I were exchanging banter that I remembered the bomb. I caught myself praying, "Not now, not yet, please God, Devlin!" Devlin, or God, or somebody, heard me, and we made it all the way past Claudius's prayer and to the interval.

"I thought you were going to fall when Pat was holding those letters and things out of your reach," Mollie said as I came off.

Antony took off his usurped crown and held it in his hands. "I loved that slip, Viola, we'll have to keep that. It looked so natural."

"My shoe just skidded under me," I said.

"Well, fake it just the same tomorrow," he said. He opened a crack in the curtains. "They look quite happy in the Royal Box. They're having drinks brought to them."

"I expect Hitler's bored to tears, he doesn't speak English," Mollie said.

"He said Shakespeare transcends language," I said. They both looked at me. "No, he really did. And then he said, 'Alas Poor Yorick' in English."

"Why didn't you tell me!" Antony said, as if it was the most significant thing that had ever happened. I wanted to laugh. "Transcends language," he murmured.

I left him peeking at Hitler and went down to get changed. Mrs. Tring had been reading the *Tatler* in the dressing room as usual between changes. "How's it going then?" she asked, helping me out of my gold play-watching dress.

"Antony says he liked it that I almost fell and wants to keep it in," I said. "The audience seem to be concentrating, which is a good sign with Shakespeare."

"If you're going up to the Royal Box to see Hitler after the curtain, what are you going to wear? Your doublet and hose, or one of the other costumes, or that cream nonsense you had on when you came in?"

"It's a perfectly good street dress," I said, though I

had chosen it with ice cream in mind and it obviously wouldn't do. I couldn't say to Mrs. Tring that there would be no meeting Hitler afterwards, and possibly no Hitler. I couldn't really imagine there being an afterwards.

"Doublet and hose or which Hamlet dress then?" Mrs. Tring asked.

I laughed and put my arm around her. "What do you think?" I asked.

"Well, he saw the blue dress at the Embassy party. He'll have seen the rest on stage as well, but I think the russet one from the gravedigger scene would be the best, and that way Mollie can wear her gold one. It was all very well for you to match on stage, but it might be a bit odd off."

I was taking off my gold dress and putting on my white nightdress for the next scene as we spoke. "It'll do," I said. "Thanks. My change out of it is a really quick one, but get it ready again for me for after."

"Sit down and let me do your shadows," she said. I was supposed to have shadows under my eyes in the second half. I stared into the mirror as she did it and thought that I might never put on the doublet and hose and I'd certainly never put the russet dress on again later. I was back where I had been at the very beginning, mentally, as if the whole bomb thing was a play and everything with Devlin, everything since I met Siddy outside the Empire, was real but only in its own terms, as Hamlet's tragedy was, as if the bomb could explode and yet everything in the real world and my real life would go on as it had been, the way it did at the end of a play. Mrs. Tring always used to express wonder at how Mollie and I learned our lines, and say our heads must be packed full with all the plays we knew. I don't know how it was for Mollie, but although I lived and breathed the play while it was taking shape and while it was running, I would forget my lines afterwards and it would start to recede into the general shape of what I knew. I could feel this business doing the same thing, taking on a dramatic shape in my mind.

"Five minutes," the boy said.

"I must lace Mollie," Mrs. Tring said, and almost ran out. I made my way up to the wings. Antony was still there, and still looking out. "It seems a very happy house," he said. "A lot depends on the critics, of course, and they may be paying more attention to our distinguished audience than to us, but I think things are going as well as can be expected."

He'd have said he thought we had a hit if he wasn't so superstitious. "Break a leg," I said, and he patted me on the arm. Then Mollie and Tim were exchanging their lines and Mollie got into bed and Tim stepped behind the arras and that was my cue so I went on again.

32

The bobby in the corridor outside the Hampstead box was the unimaginative and anti-Semitic one Carmichael had met outside Gilmore's house. Jacobson had followed Carmichael; now he waved him back and shut the door of the box. He needed to act quickly, and he wanted no visible disturbance in case they were being watched.

Out in the curved corridor, the bobby looked at Carmichael incuriously. "There's a possibility there may be a bomb," Carmichael said. "It's not sure, but it's enough of a risk I need to investigate further. I need to speak to the guards on the Royal Box."

"Yes, sir," he said. "Just go around the curve and keep going."

Carmichael ran around the curve, his bad leg dragging and slowing him. His heart was racing. There were two German soldiers outside the entrance to the Royal Box. They brought their pistols up and trained them on him as he approached. "I am Inspector Carmichael of Scotland Yard," he said. He had never expected to be mistaken for a crazed assassin. He showed them his papers, which they examined minutely without a word.

"Has Viola Lark been up here today?" he asked.

They looked at each other. One of them said something in German. "Yes, she flowers bring-ed," the other said.

Carmichael felt almost calm now his guess had been confirmed, although he knew that the bomb she must have brought could go off at any moment.

"Those flowers were probably a bomb. We need to evacuate the box, get everyone out quietly, do you understand? There could be a timer, or there could be someone in the audience who could set it off if they see trouble."

"*Ja*," the soldier said, and rapped twice on the door of the box. A tall SS captain came out immediately and gave Carmichael an assessing look. The soldier spoke to him in German. His eyebrows raised.

"I suppose you have evidence?" he said. "Let me see your papers."

"I have a chain of circumstantial evidence," Carmichael said. "Miss Lark's sister Siddy is a communist and has been part of a plot to put a bomb in this box, along with an Irishman who is still at large." Carmichael handed over his papers and waited while the SS man examined them, almost beside himself with impatience. He could hear the sudden hush and then the opening words of the play beginning again.

The captain frowned. "I find this very hard to believe, but very well. I will bring the Fuhrer out, and then the others."

"Do it with as little disturbance as possible. If there's someone in the audience watching the box they could set off the bomb as soon as you move."

"Give me some credit," the captain said. "Besides, I think this is all a horse's nest. Lady Viola's other sister is sitting beside the Fuhrer. And why would they wait this long, all the first half of the stupid play? But I will move carefully." He unholstered his pistol and went back into the box.

Carmichael stepped away down the corridor as the captain went back in. The door opened again after a moment, and Hitler came out, closely followed by Celia Himmler. Carmichael saw Normanby behind them, then there was a shot from the box. Hitler came another few steps down the corridor towards Carmichael, and then the whole wall of the box blew out, knocking Normanby forward. Hitler staggered a little, and Carmichael steadied him. Celia Himmler opened her mouth as if she were screaming, but Carmichael didn't hear her. Blast deafness, from the concussion. He remembered it from the war.

He pushed her out of the way and went towards Normanby and the German soldiers who were on the floor. Normanby was unconscious, and had a large chunk of wall on top of him. The gash on his forehead was bleeding sluggishly, so he was probably alive, for now at least. Carmichael couldn't see anything immediate to do for him. One of the German soldiers was as unquestionably dead as Royston. The other, the one who had said that Viola Lark had brought flowers, was staring in horror as blood pulsed out of his arm. He had been on the safe side of the corridor, like Carmichael, but he had been unlucky and hit by a piece of flying shrapnel. It must have nicked an artery. Carmichael remembered that from the war too. Funny that these very men might have been trying to kill him then. He took out the silk handkerchief folded into his jacket pocket and made it into a tourniquet, then twisted his pencil into the knot. "Hold it!" he shouted at the soldier.

Then, suddenly, there were police and German uniformed soldiers everywhere. "Get an ambulance," Carmichael bellowed.

One of them detached the hysterical Celia Himmler from Hitler, whom she had been embracing, and led her off down the corridor. Most of the others then started to fuss over Hitler, who was unharmed, but some of them came over and started to clear the fallen bricks from

Mark Normanby. Another said something he couldn't hear and looked apprehensively at Carmichael. He couldn't understand why until he looked down at himself. He laughed. "It's not my blood," he shouted. "Have you called an ambulance?"

The policeman nodded emphatically, having worked out that Carmichael couldn't hear. He would have a terrible earache later, he remembered, and a whistling noise that might last for weeks.

Hitler was pointing at Carmichael and saying something. One of the SS men, not the captain he had spoken to before, came over and tried to speak to Carmichael. He pointed at his ears and gestured. The German took out a pad and wrote neatly in small letters, "The Fuhrer thanks you for your warning and for the first aid to the guard. He will see you are given a German medal for bravery."

Carmichael stared at it for a moment then waved it away. He looked up and saw Hitler smiling at him. The bricks had been removed from Normanby, and people were lifting him carefully onto a stretcher. Carmichael moved to let someone come past him and found himself looking down at the dead face of Daphne Normanby as she was carried past him. She looked years younger, all the wariness drained out of her with her life.

He swallowed hard and felt the half-forgotten yet familiar sensation of pain in his ears. Jacobson arrived, running. "We have to stop the audience from leaving," Carmichael said, in an ordinary tone of voice. They could hear him even if he couldn't hear them. "And I have to go around to the front and arrest Viola Lark. Don't talk to me, I'm deaf from the blast, but I'm all right. Come on."

Jacobson hesitated for only a moment, then nodded. The SS man helpfully offered him the pad and paper. He wrote neatly, "One man shot dead. Audience fleeing." Carmichael read it then led the way down the corridor to where the bobbies had linked arms to control the crowd.

"Don't let anyone leave," Carmichael said. "Check everyone's papers."

The bobby's lips moved. Jacobson touched his arm, and wrote, "Lots of people left already, crowding out from the ha'pennies and the stalls. Shot, explosion, panic."

Only to be expected really. Carmichael sighed. "And heaven knows what the newspapers will be saying. Too late. All the same, check as many papers as you can. Hold any Irishmen, Jews, foreigners."

The bobby nodded, and Jacobson added something. Then the stretcher bearers came up behind them with Mark Normanby groaning between them, and they moved aside to let them through.

Carmichael and Jacobson followed them downstairs and into the stalls. The two policemen at the doorway saluted and let them through. The stalls had clearly been emptied out in a rush. Some seats had coats lying on them. Empty chocolate boxes and programs caught under Carmichael's feet. The stage was empty of actors, though still dominated by a bed and something that looked like a great fire screen. Carmichael rubbed his ears, which were beginning to ache. He realized he had no idea how long it had been since the explosion.

There was a uniformed bobby standing over the body in the front row. He had fallen with his head towards the stage, so it was clear that he must have been standing. He had something clutched in his hand. "Radio detonator!" the bobby bellowed, pointing.

"German?" Carmichael asked. His ears were ringing now, and his hearing was beginning to come back.

"Probably Russian," Jacobson wrote, then underlined the last word. Germans had developed the radio detonator but the Russians had not been slow in copying them. Another communist connection?

Carmichael put the detonator out of his thoughts and stared at the bomber. He had been shot through the head, and was unquestionably dead. Any questions he could have answered were dead with him. By his build, he was the Irishman who had been introduced to Carmichael as Connelly. "Get Viola Lark, bring her here right away," Carmichael said to the bobby. Then, as he scurried off, Carmichael turned to Jacobson. "Keiler must have got him," he said, "I warned him, and he went in and warned the others, and this fellow must have stood up and pushed the button and Keiler was looking and shot him right away. I'm surprised he had time to push the button, really. It must have been damn near simultaneous."

He looked up at the ruins of the box, where uniformed German soldiers were poking about, then back at the body. Jacobson was saying something he couldn't hear. Then the bobby came back with Viola Lark. He was holding her arm protectively, but she was not struggling. She looked pale and somehow shrunken. Her face had no expression at all. She was wearing a white nightdress, which, with her still face, made her look like a sleepwalker.

"Here she is, sir!" the bobby bawled.

"Arrest her under the Defence of the Realm Act," Carmichael said to Jacobson. He half-heard Jacobson going through the ritual words. She didn't react at all, she was looking past them, to the body.

"I am Inspector Carmichael, of Scotland Yard," he said, making an effort not to shout, and wondering if this was the last time he would introduce himself that way, as he would have his new Watch title soon. "We met once before."

"Just about here," Viola Lark said, not shouting, but pitching her voice to project, so he could hear her more plainly than he could hear the others.

"You introduced this dead man as Devlin Connelly. Is that his name, or is he in fact Sir Aloysius Farrell?"

She looked down at the body, tenderly, averting her eyes from the blown-away face. Then she looked up for an instant at the empty theater, not at the ruined box but farther up, towards the ha'pennies. "Of course he is," she said. "And he'll be buried in the Farrell tomb in Arranish, in Ulster, with gold sovereigns on his eyes, not shoveled into a pauper's grave making do with a pair of ha'pennies."

Carmichael wondered if she were entirely unhinged. "Did he make you do this?" he asked, gently. "He and Siddy, Lady Russell?"

" 'For O, for O, the hobby-horse is forgot,' " she said, and began to cry. Carmichael recognized the words from the play, she had said them about Hamlet's father being remembered, but could not see their relevance.

Just then Celia Himmler, clearly recovered from her hysterics, swept up to them. "Stop bullying my sister!" she demanded.

This took Carmichael's breath away. "Your sister has been part of a conspiracy which killed your husband and Mrs. Normanby and almost killed you, and I was asking her to identify the body of her coconspirator."

"There must be some mistake," Celia Himmler said.

"Oh Pip, Pip, I'm sorry," Viola Lark said. She would have stepped forward towards her sister but for the bobby's protective grip on her arm.

Celia stared at her sister for a moment, then slapped her face. "Pull yourself together," she said, ignoring the rest of them and holding out a hand to Viola, who shrank away. "Now come on."

"Your sister is in custody, and you're not taking her anywhere," Carmichael said, rubbing his ears. "One of your other sisters, Lady Russell, also appears to be even deeper in this conspiracy."

"Siddy has flown to Moscow," Viola said. "I'm sorry, Pip."

"To Moscow?" Jacobson echoed.

"We'll see how your evidence stands up in court, if it ever comes to court," Celia said to Carmichael.

"They don't hang people like me," Viola said, and laughed, then dissolved into tears again. "You see to it, don't you? I'm sorry I tried to kill you, Pip, and even more sorry that I killed poor Daphne who never did anyone any harm. But we were trying to kill Hitler, and Normanby. We could have changed everything. I know it isn't what you want. But it's what we wanted."

As she spoke, for the first time Carmichael realized what he had done. He wanted to laugh, or perhaps cry, himself, but he simply stood there, trying to catch his breath. He had saved Hitler, saved Hitler and Normanby, when if he had simply sat still in his box he could have rid the world of them. He could hardly believe he had been such a fool.

Then, as he stood there staring at the sisters, he realized that it didn't matter in the least that he had saved Hitler. It wouldn't have made any difference. He couldn't say it to poor unstable Viola, but he wished he could have said it to Lauria Gilmore, who might have understood. Hitler and Normanby were evil men, and there was a time when killing them would have changed everything, but that time had gone. If they had been killed tonight, it would only have been more ammunition for their side, would have driven Europe deeper in the direction things were going. When men like Kinnerson and girls like Rachel Grunwald began to turn in their friends and family, fascism wasn't something that could be killed by a bomb. He had learned from the Farthing Set that you couldn't just change things from the outside, you had to change how people felt. If people stopped being afraid, they'd get rid of the dictators for themselves.

He would take the Watch, he thought, as the theater filled up with policemen, and make of it something they didn't expect. He would be a hero with a medal, he might not be able to escape them, but they couldn't lightly get rid of him either. He would stay here with Jack, adopt little Elvira Royston if they could, and do what he could to make people brave again.

He turned to one of the sergeants from Hampstead. "Take Frau Himmler outside, please," he said.

He looked back at Viola, meaning to ask her more about the Moscow connection, but before he could she swept into an elaborate curtsey and began to quote Hamlet again. " 'Beggar that I am, I am even poor in thanks; but I thank you, and sure dear friends, my thanks are too dear a ha'penny.' "

Turn the page for a preview of

HALF A CROWN

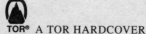

Jo Walton

Available in October 2008

TOR® A TOR HARDCOVER
ISBN-13: 978-0-7653-1621-9   ISBN-10: 0-7653-1621-8

A week before she was due to bring me out, I over-heard Mrs. Maynard saying I was "Not quite . . ." That's just how she said it. "Elvira's not quite . . ."

When she let her voice trail off like that I knew pre-cisely what she meant. I knew it in the pit of my stom-ach. I had been coming down the stairs to join them in the drawing room when I heard her speaking, and stopped dead, clutching the handrail in my left hand and the bunched seersucker of my skirt in the other. It was 1960 and skirts in the spring collections were long enough that they had to be lifted a little to avoid step-ping on them on the stairs.

Mrs. Maynard's friend, Lady Bellingham, made a little sound of inarticulate sympathy. There could be no question what Mrs. Maynard meant, no way that I could think—or that anyone could think—she meant not quite ready, or not quite well, though I knew if I challenged her that's what she would say. "Not quite out of the top drawer" is what she really meant; "not quite a lady." I was still "not quite up to snuff," despite eight years in the best and most expensive girls' schools in England

and a year in Switzerland being "finished." At eighteen I still had two distinct voices: the voice that went with my clothes and my hair, the voice that was indistinguishable in its essentials from Betsy Maynard's, and then the much less acceptable voice of my childhood, the London Cockney voice. My past was never to be forgotten, not quite, however hard I tried.

"Then why ever are you bringing her out with Betsy?" Lady Bellingham asked, her voice positively oozing sympathy the way an eclair oozes cream.

"Well her uncle, you know," Mrs. Maynard said. "He's the head of the Watch. One doesn't like . . ."

Spending time with Mrs. Maynard, you get used to trailing sentences with everything explicit but nothing spelled out. I could have run down the stairs and pushed into the drawing room and shouted that it wasn't anything like so simple. Mrs. Maynard was bringing me out because her daughter Betsy had begged me to go through with it. "I can't face being a deb without you!" she had said. Betsy and I were friends because, in the alphabetically arranged classroom at Arlinghurst, "Elizabeth" and "Elvira" happened to fall next to each other, and Betsy and I had both felt like misfits and clung to each other ever since. I didn't give more than half a damn about coming out and being presented to the Queen. What I wanted was to go to Oxford. You may think it was an odd ambition. Half the people I met did. Going by my born social status rather than my acquired one I couldn't even hope to be admitted. Still, I had been interviewed and accepted at St. Hilda's and had only the summer to wait before I went up. It was April already. Most girls I knew would have hated the idea of grinding away at their books, but I'd always found that side of things easy; it was parties that bored me. But Betsy and Uncle Carmichael had set their hearts on my coming out, so I had agreed I would do that first.

Besides all that, Mrs. Maynard was bringing me out because my uncle, who wasn't really my uncle at all, was paying for me and subsidizing Betsy. However County the Maynards might be, they never had much money to spare, at least by their own standards. By the standards I'd grown up with they were impossibly rich, but by those of the people they moved among, they were struggling to keep up appearances. Anyway, people with money are often horribly mean; that was the first thing I'd learned when I'd started to move among them. But, sickeningly, none of that got a mention. Mrs. Maynard's trailing off made it sound as if she was bringing me out despite my deficiencies because she was afraid of my uncle.

"Might I trouble you for a little more tea, dear?" Lady Bellingham asked.

The banisters were Victorian and rounded, like chair legs, with big round knobs on the newel posts. Between them I could see down into the hall, the faded cream wallpaper, the top of the mahogany side table and a crystal vase of pinky-white carnations. The house was narrow, like all Victorian London houses. I could see the drawing room door, which was open, but I couldn't see in through it, so I didn't know if Betsy was sitting there too. It seemed terribly important to find out if she was listening to all this without protest. I let go of my handful of skirt and slipped off my shoes, feeling absurd, knowing that while I was fairly safe from Mrs. Maynard, the servants could come out of the back part of the house at any time and catch me. They probably wouldn't give me away, but it would still be frightfully embarrassing. I ran one hand lightly down the banister rail and tiptoed gingerly down the strip of carpet in the center of the stairs to the half-landing, where I could see through the drawing room door if I stretched a bit.

I took a good grip, leaned out, and craned my neck. Mrs. Maynard was eating a cream cake with a fork. She was not seen to advantage from above, as she had a squashed-up face like a pug and wore her graying brown hair in a permanent wave so rigid it looked like a helmet. Her afternoon dress was a muslin patterned with roses, that made her stocky figure look as upholstered as the chair she sat in. Lady Bellingham, on the sofa and reaching towards the tea trolley for a sandwich, looked softer, thinner, and altogether more fashionable. I had just determined to my satisfaction that they were alone, when with no warning at all the front door opened.

Of course they saw me at once. They couldn't help it. Mr. Maynard, Betsy's father, took me in with one rapid glance, raised his eyebrows, and looked away. The other man with him was a complete stranger with a dark piratical beard and a perfectly normal bowler hat. I felt myself turn crimson as I pulled myself back onto the half-landing and slipped my shoes back on.

"Ah, Elvira," Mr. Maynard said, with no inflection whatever. I didn't know him well. He did something boring and diplomatic to which I'd never paid much attention and which seemed to take up a great deal of his time. On holidays I'd spent with Betsy he'd never paid much attention to me.

"Sir Alan, this is my daughter's friend Elvira Royston, whom my wife is bringing out with Betsy this summer. Elvira, this is Sir Alan Bellingham."

"Delighted to meet you," I said, coming down the stairs and extending my hand as I had been so painstakingly taught.

Sir Alan ignored my fading blushes and shook hands firmly. He was almost exactly my height, and looked me in the eye. "Charmed," he murmured. "I don't suppose you know if my mother is here?"

"She's taking tea with Mrs. Maynard in the drawing room," I said, blushing again.

"And Betsy?" Mr. Maynard asked.

"I don't know where she is," I said, honestly. "I haven't seen her since lunchtime."

"See if you can rustle her up, there's a good girl. I'm sure she'd be glad to see Sir Alan. You'll take a cup of tea, Sir Alan, while you wait for your mother to be ready?"

Sir Alan smiled at me. Because of the beard, I couldn't tell how old he was. At first I had thought he was Mr. Maynard's age, but when he smiled I thought he was much younger, maybe no more than thirty.

"I'll find her if she's at home," I said, and turned and went back upstairs to look for Betsy.

I tapped on her door.

"Who is it?" she called.

"Me," I said, opening the door. Betsy was lying on the bed in a green check dress that looked distinctly rumpled. "Your father wants you to come down and drink tea, but you'd better tidy yourself up first."

She sighed and sat up. "Who's here?"

"That bitch Lady Bellingham, and a mysterious stranger called Sir Alan who seems to be her son."

Betsy lay down again and put her pillow on her head. "He's not a mysterious stranger, he's my father's idea of a suitable son-in-law," she said, her voice rather muffled. "Do go down and tell them I'm mortally wounded and not likely to make it."

"Don't be a ninny," I said, pulling off the pillow. "They can't make you marry a man with a beard."

"Ghastly Lady B. is Mummy's best friend, and her son's frightfully rich and doing things with the government that seem likely to make him even more frightfully rich, and powerful as well. And he's very polite, which makes him perfect in Mummy's eyes. You don't know how lucky you are being an orphan, Elvira."

In fact, my mother was alive and well and running a pub in Leytonstone, but I thought it better never to mention her in my daily life. She certainly wasn't going to interfere. She hadn't wanted me when she ran off with her fancy man when I was six, and she hadn't wanted me when my father died when I was eight, so she wasn't likely to want me now. I hardly remembered her, but my aunt Ciss, my real aunt, my father's sister, kept me up-to-date with gossip about her. Aunt Ciss would have taken me in, even though she had five children of her own, but she thought having Uncle Carmichael take an interest in me and offering to send me to Arlinghurst was a great opportunity for me to make something of myself. I'd thought it a funny phrase then, like making stew of a neck of lamb, or a fruit cobbler of two bruised apples and a squashy pear. What they had hoped to make of me was a lady, and I'd been too young to question why anyone thought this would be better than what I would have grown into if let alone. It was only in the last year or so I had wondered about this at all, as I'd grown old enough to consider what they had made of me so far and what I might want to make of myself, given the opportunity.

"Put on a clean dress and come down, do," I said. "I'll do my best to draw the cross fire."

That made her smile. It was, of course, Bogart's famous line from the end of *The Battle of Kursk*. She stood up and pulled her dress off over her head. "I met Sir Alan the other night when you were having dinner with your uncle," she said. "Oh, how I loathe this whole dreary business. Men. Dancing. Coming out. And on Wednesday, fittings for our Court dresses, which cost a fortune and which we'll wear for one night next week, to make our curtsey to the Queen, as if it makes any difference at all to anything." She dropped the green dress heedlessly on the floor and opened her wardrobe. "What should I wear?"

"What do you want to look like?"

"I want to look like Elizabeth instead of Betsy." This was her newest enthusiasm. I found it very hard to comply with, and nobody else tried at all. "And I want to look like someone who doesn't need to have her parents drag home a husband for her. I swear Daddy's expression is just like Tigrath's when she's dragged home a mouse and dropped it proudly on my pillow."

I laughed. "Why not the cream seersucker thing with the gold ribbon we bought in Paris?"

"Because we don't want to look like twins," she said. "It only makes me look worse."

I smoothed the ribbon at my neck self-consciously. I can't help being prettier than Betsy. She never cared before Zurich.

She pulled out a forest green dress patterned with leaves so dark you could hardly see them except when the light was angled just right, another of her Paris purchases. Somebody, probably her mother, had once told Betsy that redheads ought to wear green. In my opinion it did nothing for her. "What about this?" she asked.

"What about the gray one?" I countered. It was the same cut, and almost the same fabric only in gray with the leaf pattern in black.

"I hate the gray one," she said, pulling it out. "All the same, I'll wear it, because I hate Sir Alan too. He's such a fascist."

"We're all fascists now, surely?" I asked. "And anyway, what's wrong with fascism? It's fun!"

"I find fascists just too sick-making," Betsy said, pulling on the gray dress and belting it viciously tight. It fell precisely just above her ankles. She looked all right. Most people are neither beautiful nor ugly, they fall somewhere in the range of the middle. If I tried, and trying was what we'd been taught at our expensive Swiss finishing school, I could get into the top end of that range. All right was about as good as poor Betsy could manage.

I passed her her hairbrush, silver-backed with her initials engraved, a present from her father when she turned eighteen. "You're just saying that to be shocking. It's your mother who makes me sick. She said I was 'not quite.' " I tried to say it lightly, but my voice let me down.

"That's ghastly. To Lady B.?" Betsy asked, dragging the brush through her hair much too hard.

I nodded. "Just now. I'd finished studying for the time being and I was coming down the stairs in search of tea and I overheard them."

"She was probably trying to make sure Sir Alan didn't fall for you instead of me," Betsy said.

"Oh Bets— Elizabeth!" I said. "That's ridiculous. As

if he'd look at me when I'm nobody, and about to be an undergraduette too. And anyway, he has a beard!"

"I believe it doesn't impede one's sex life," Betsy said, and we both giggled. "Do my necklace up?"

She ran her hands through the little silver box on her dressing table and fished out a thin gold chain hung with a half circle of seed pearls. I lifted her hair and fastened the clasp. It sat nicely on her skin above the neckline of the dress. "That's pretty," I said. "Where did you get it?"

"My aunt Patsy gave it to me. It was hers when she came out, and she felt it brought her luck. It's a funny length, but I like it." She straightened it. "Do you want something?"

"I'd better not; I can't trust your mother not to say something if I borrow your jewelry. Besides, there's this ribbon." I smoothed it again.

"I'm sure your uncle will give you something of your own soon now," Betsy said. "I expect that's what he's going to do when he takes you out on Thursday, take you to Cartier and let you choose."

"I don't think he has any idea I ought to have something. He has no wife, no daughters of his own, no sister even. I can't really tell him. He's been so good to me already, paying for all this nonsense, and for Oxford too," I said. "But I'm sure that's not what we'll be doing on Thursday. That's our annual date to go down to Kent to look at the primroses, in memory of my father."

Betsy hugged me. "I'd forgotten," she said. "Well, you're welcome to anything of mine any time, whenever Mummy isn't looking. Come on. We'd better go down, or they'll be sending out search parties."

We went down to the drawing room together. There was a much better than normal selection of tea, several kinds of sandwiches, and a whole plate of cream cakes from Gunter's, as well as the usual fruitcake and digestive biscuits. I took an eclair and a cup of tea and retreated towards the wing chair by the window. Sir Alan was on the sofa by his mother, and Mr. Maynard on the other wing chair. "Cross fire," Betsy mouthed, as she cut me off from the wing chair, leaving me the place that had clearly been left for her, at the other end of the sofa. I sat there and sipped my tea. No matter how hard I tried, I thought, these people would never truly accept me. If they did, if I managed to fool some of them for a little while, someone who knew, like Mrs. Maynard, would be sure to tell them that I wasn't quite. This was why I wanted to go to Oxford. Even in the little glimpse I'd had of it so far, I could tell that standards were different; intellectual attainments still mattered there more than who your parents were.

But "not quite" had stung. I might want to turn my back on this world, I didn't want to be rejected by it as not good enough. I'd made so much effort already, worrying about clothes and hair and jewelry. It was just over a week until we made our debut, and then there would be a round of balls and parties over the summer. April, May, June, July, August, September. Then, in October, I could begin my real life. Six months.

The silence in the drawing room now everyone had settled was a little uncomfortable. I leaned towards Sir Alan. "So, Sir Alan, Betsy tells me you're a fascist?" I said.

"Betsy's too kind," Sir Alan replied. "And you, Miss Royston, are you fond of fascism?"

"Oh yes, I think it's the most terrific fun," I said.

Mrs. Maynard winced a little and exchanged a sympathetic glance with Lady Bellingham. The thing was that fascism, while all very well in its place, was in Mrs. Maynard's eyes something to look down on just the tiniest bit, as being very useful of course, and something that did very well for keeping Them in place, but was actually not quite . . . After all, it was open to everyone, except Jews of course.

My reply seemed to please Sir Alan, who nodded and smiled. "Fun, yes, absolutely. Have you ever been to an Ironsides rally?" he asked.

In fact I had, when I was very young. It had been a march through Camden Town, where I lived then, and my father had taken me. I remembered the uniforms and the bands, the fireworks and the tremendous spirit of fellowship. "No," I said, regretfully. "I never have. Only on television."

"Not the place for a young lady, perhaps, Alan," Lady Bellingham said, carefully, her hands fluttering in her lap.

"Nonsense, Mother," her son corrected her robustly. "Certainly not the thing unescorted, but if Miss Royston and Miss Maynard would like to join me, I could see that they had a good time without being near any trouble. You hear much more about trouble than you see these days; the Jews and communists don't try to break up our marches anymore, the Watch have cracked down on them too hard. It's been years since there was any trouble of that kind. There's a torchlit march to Marble Arch tomorrow night, what do you say, ladies?"

Mrs. Maynard was looking like a pug with a stomachache. "I'm not sure it would be quite . . . ," she said, looking at her husband, who was staring at the faded pattern on the rug as if it interested him extremely.

I hadn't quite made up my mind how far I wanted to push this, but Betsy, for all her saying fascism made her sick, decided for me. "We'd love to, Sir Alan," she said, shooting a burning look at her mother.

"Oh yes," I agreed, following her lead. "We'd love to. I've always wanted to see a torchlit parade close up."

"As long as it's quite safe, of course," Betsy added.

"Quite safe these days," Sir Alan reassured everyone, turning around the drawing room with a smile that made him look more than ever like a pirate.

So that's why we were right there when the riot happened.

TOR

Award-winning authors
Compelling stories

Please join us at the website
below for more information
about this author and other great
Tor selections, and to sign up for
our monthly newsletter!